Night Rider

Southern Classics Series

M. E. Bradford, Editor

Southern Classics Series

M. E. Bradford, Series Editor

Night Rider

ROBERT PENN WARREN

with a foreword by George Core

J. S. Sanders & Company

NASHVILLE

Library of Congress Catalog Card Number:
92-082382

ISBN: 1-879941-14-7

Published in the United States by
J. S. Sanders & Company
P. O. Box 50331
Nashville, Tennessee 37205

Distributed to the trade by
National Book Network
4720-A Boston Way
Lanham, Maryland 20706

1992 printing
Manufactured in the United States of America

TO
DOMENICO BRESCIA
AND
DANIEL JUSTIN DONAHOE
IN GRATITUDE

Although this book was suggested by certain events which took place in Kentucky in the early years of this century, it is not, in any strict sense, a historical novel. And more particularly, the characters in this book are not to be identified with any actual persons, living or dead, who participated in those events.

Foreword

What good fiction gives us, Robert Penn Warren observes, is "a powerful image of human nature trying to fulfill itself." He continues: "Neither the economic man nor the political man is the complete man: other concerns may still be important enough to engage the attention of a writer—such concerns as love, death, courage, the point of honor, and the moral scruple. A man has to live with other men in terms not only of economic and political arrangements; and he has to live with himself, he has to define himself." Although Warren is responding to Hemingway and his fiction in this passage, what he says applies equally well to much of his own fiction, including his brilliant first novel, *Night Rider* (1939).

Percy Munn, the protagonist of the novel, tries to define himself in economic—and, more especially, political—terms; but he is far more engaged by the roil and ruck of human possibility that Warren limns—"love, death, courage, the point of honor, and the moral scruple"—than he is by mere economic considerations or even by political necessity. Of course no one can compartmentalize every urge and pressure, every idea and attitude and emotion, in his or her life; and any person, real or fictive, will be subjected to the pressure of events beyond his or her control and understanding. Mr. Munn finds himself buffeted by events throughout the action.

The opening sequence of the novel dramatizes the blind force of circumstance in a simple yet beautifully dramatic way as Munn, standing in a train pulling into Bardsville, Kentucky, finds himself caught in the press of moving bodies as the train brakes—

feeling "the grinding, heavy momentum." "The gathering force which surged up the long aisle behind him like a wave took him and plunged him hard against the back of the next man." Munn has been unable to brace himself properly against that powerful blind force. Mr. Munn never finds his moral bearings and, unable to brace himself, continues to be buffeted by human circumstance. In that image, caught in the action of the packed lurching train, Warren dramatizes a principal theme in *Night Rider:* "Mr. Munn again resented that pressure that was human because it was made by human beings, but was inhuman, too, because you could not isolate and blame any one of those human beings who made it."

One of the ironies of Munn's situation is that he is not only an attorney but a leader in the movement in which he finds himself enlisted; yet, despite his profession and his position of authority, he is unable to follow a course consistently moral and right. There are many instances of this failing, but the most obvious involves his defense of Bunk Trevelyan, who has been charged for murder. Munn, in defending Trevelyan against what he thinks are groundless charges, subverts the judicial process and causes an innocent man to be hanged. Later he realizes Trevelyan is more nearly a fascist than a representative example of the common man, and Munn recognizes that, despite his good motives, he has acted wrongly. Trevelyan, he perceives, is in some respect the dark side of himself, his brutal alter ego. And in the same manner Mr. Munn reacts strongly against Senator Tolliver because he fears that the opportunistic Tolliver's weakness, his tendency to make accommodations and his inability to remain true to a cause, will infect and undermine Munn himself. On the other hand Munn betrays Mr. Christian, and he in turn is betrayed by Professor Ball. Only Captain Todd remains true to himself and his principles as the Association of Growers of Dark Fired Tobacco reels out of control, moving from a democratic to a revolutionary organization, and finally standing for much the same values as those its makers originally bridled against when they organized themselves to fight the vast power of the tobacco companies that colluded against the growers by holding down the wholesale price of dark tobacco. After the growers march on Bardsville and fire the warehouses there, this world goes mad, with the night riders attacking not only the public enemies of the Association but their own private enemies. One is reminded of the Reconstruction South and of contemporary Ireland, but the larger significance of the novel suggests the beginnings of the Third Reich and the Soviet Union as democratic ideals are set aside for totalitarian ends.

Such were the discontinuities and disruptions occurring in western Kentucky during the tobacco wars that raged when Robert Penn Warren (1905–1989) was a little boy. Warren gives us not only the men and the motives that drive them but presents the whole flavor of this world—its sights and sounds and smells, its texture and tonality. Percy Munn, who comes from farming people, is himself a farmer as well as a lawyer; and he constantly measures the weather of his days despite his knowing that weather has nothing to do with his real expectations. But it is his exact sense of the natural world that enables us to savor the life of the small town and the spacious outlying country punctuated by plantations and small farms, country joined by the railroad and traversed by horse or train.

As Percy Munn retreats farther and farther from the community and becomes more isolated and alienated from the human communion, he loses the ability to love anyone, even himself. First his love for his wife, May, withers; and then his affection for Lucille Christian dies as well. In this process his commitments become more abstract and less human, real, and binding; and finally his only friend is Willie Proudfit, who gives him refuge after he falsely is suspected of murdering a witness—another of the novel's many biting ironies.

Munn stands at the head of a long line of Warren's idealistic protagonists who are undone by their idealism. Their very efforts to achieve their ideals, often by immoral or even illegal means, undermines their goals, shakes their senses of identity and their values, and forces them deeper and deeper into the maelstrom of the self. Willie Stark, the leading figure in *All the King's Men,* is but the most obvious instance. By the end of *Night Rider* Percy Munn has lost everything, but he is still "poised on the brink of revelation," as he has been throughout the course of the unfolding action.

Although *Night Rider* is Warren's first published novel, it was the third that he wrote; and it came out of a considerable period of gestation. His first published work of fiction, a long story entitled "Prime Leaf" (1931), concerns many of the same issues and involves the same setting and situation, an instance of what Abraham Cowley called "troublous times," "the best times to write of but the worst to write in." Warren quotes Cowley and then explains: "A period of cultural and moral shock, short of the final cataclysm, does breed art. . . . When the pieties are shaken, you are forced to reexamine the whole basis of life. A new present has to be brought in line with the past, and the other way around." Such is the situation explored in *Night Rider,* and Warren suggests that the reason this particular story picked on him is that writing about it enabled him to find its essential significance, the meaning that had eluded him when he heard it growing up in Guthrie, Kentucky, and then when he first wrote about it in "Prime Leaf."

This story and its ramifications embodies Warren's essential fictive action and plot. The idealistic hero, searching for his place in the world, is misled by his motives and caught in the coils of his idealism. And, in searching for the meaning of self and trying to achieve selfhood in the uncertain world of action and liability, a world fraught by change, he is undone. Hence his effort often takes on a tragic dimension or cast, as Robert B. Heilman and other critics have argued. We are reminded of Aristotle's definition of tragic action in his *Poetics:* the story of "an intermediate personage, a man not preeminently virtuous and just, whose misfortune, however, is brought upon him not by vice and depravity but by some error of judgement" (Butcher translation). Munn, who is such an "intermediate personage," makes a series of such mistakes in judgment, as do many of his associates, with the result that the Association finally becomes a revolutionary and totalitarian organization.

In contemplating the brilliance of *The Tempest,* Mark Van Doren observes that the play is like an electric field in that it lights up if you touch it at any point. This splendid metaphor applies to any enduring work of literature in that there can never be any final reading or any critical orthodoxy about it (I deliberately echo Brooks and Warren on the critical response)—and that there will always be more than one way of interpreting such a work, whether it be fiction or poetry or drama or still another literary mode. You can read *Night Rider* not only as a tragedy of defeated expectations but as an allegory (with Munn as Everyman), as a mystery (with the subplot involving Bunk Trevelyan signifying the novel's larger action), as a novel embodying archetypal American experience (in which case the Willie Proudfit story is essential), and as a naturalistic novel (with Munn caught in the vise of circumstance and event beyond his control to alter or affect). You can also view it, as is the case with any novel by Warren, as a fiction partaking of both the romance and realism that run through the classic American novel in the ways long ago described and defined by Richard Chase and Daniel Hoffman.

My own view is that the novel's weaknesses derive from its being, on occasion, too allegorical on the one hand or too naturalistic on the other. The only other defect of real magnitude that I find in it is that the author rushes the action toward the end, forcing the conclusion. The novel might have been stronger were Percy Munn to confront Senator Tolliver in the same way that he does and then to flee toward the West. But this is a small point, perhaps even a quibble.

In any event, regardless of how one views the action of this superb novel, he should see it as one of the best first novels written over the history of American fiction from Nathaniel Hawthorne to the present time. There are few first novels that are better—perhaps only *Sister Carrie* and *The Sun Also Rises*. Hawthorne did not do so well in his first novel, nor did Herman Melville, Henry James, and a great number of other important American writers. And *Night Rider* is by any reasonable measure a powerful work of fiction for which no apology need be made. It is obvious that Warren, in writing *Night Rider* in his early thirties, did not think of himself as a young writer whose miscues and mistakes "ought to be forgiven." He knew even then what he would say twenty years later at Vanderbilt University about the young writer: "Nothing will be forgiven. It will stink just as much if you did it as if Hemingway did it." And so he played for keeps, and playing at those high stakes, with everything to win or lose, he wrote what Andrew Lytle has said is his best novel—his most finished and fulfilled.

Night Rider's power and urgency and subtlety continue to move us and to appeal to new generations of readers. It is a novel that bears rereading and that repays our closest scrutiny. To expect more of any literary work would be preposterous.

Sewanee, Tennessee   GEORGE CORE

Night Rider

Chapter one

WHEN the train slowed at the first jarring application of the brakes, the crowd packed in the aisle of the coach swayed crushingly forward, with the grinding, heavy momentum of the start of a landslip. Percy Munn, feeling the first pressure as the man behind him lurched into contact, arched his back and tried to brace himself to receive the full impact which, instinctively, he knew would come. But he was not braced right. The gathering force which surged up the long aisle behind him like a wave took him and plunged him hard against the back of the next man. He felt his face ground against that shoulder, and caught the sour smell of sweat and the smell of the lye soap in which the blue shirt had been washed. He discovered that he had stepped on the man's foot. Then Mr. Munn righted himself.

The man, when he half-turned his head and showed his long, red, bony face, looked even taller than before.

'Excuse me for stepping on your foot that way,' Mr. Munn said.

'Hit ain't yore fault none,' the man answered. He paused ruminatively, and then: 'That feller, he ain't fitten to run no train.'

Mr. Munn shook his head.

'Naw,' the man repeated, 'he ain't fitten.'

We ought to be getting in, Mr. Munn thought; but the crowd was too close-packed for him to lean over and look out the windows. The train, however, was slowing a little. He could see the people in the seats with their heads now craned out the windows and could hear their shouts and exclamations. Their excitement communicated itself to the whole mass so that men pressed to bend and look out, demanding to know if they were getting in and what was out there and could you see the crowd. Over the sound of the wheels on the rails and the noises of the people, Mr. Munn heard some man, far back toward the other end of the coach, shouting, 'We gonna do it! We gonna do it!' Over and over again, like a chant.

Then the brakes jammed on hard again, and as he again braced himself to receive the impact, Mr. Munn felt a momentary irritation and disgust with that dead, hot weight of flesh which would plunge against him and press him, with the shouting and talking, with the smell of sweat and whisky, and with the heat of the day and of the crowded bodies. A crowd, he thought, and no better than any other crowd. I ought to be out home, regretting that he had come.

The tall man in front again turned his head, saying, as though in sadness, 'He went and done hit agin.'

'Yes, he did,' Mr. Munn replied.

'He oughtn't to do hit,' the man was saying. 'That-air jousten and jolten lak that don't do folks's innards no good.'

'No,' Mr. Munn said.

'I said that feller wasn't fitten to run no train,' the man asserted, 'and he ain't fitten.'

'No,' Mr. Munn said.

The train had stopped.

The pressure behind now was not the dead weight of bodies flung forward by the abrupt slowing of the train, but a pressure generated by the wills of all those people behind him, people who wanted to move down the aisle and get off the train and get into the streets of Bardsville, where more people, only God knew how many, would be today. And as the movement of the crowd pushed him toward the door, Mr. Munn again resented that pressure that was human because it was made by human beings, but was inhuman, too, because you could not isolate and blame any one of those human beings who made it. Anyway, he was glad May hadn't come into all this, and fleetingly thought of her as he had seen her last that morning, in a white dress, standing on the porch, at the other end of the row of sugar trees, and waving to him as he got into the buggy that was to take him down to the crossing where he could flag the local.

The crowd pushed him through the door. He was aware, as the glare of the morning sun struck his eyes, half-blinding him after the dim interior of the coach, of the solid mass of faces that filled the little platform of the station and the space of the street beyond. The tall man ahead of him half-turned on the steps of the coach, saying, 'Gre't God!' loudly and solemnly, 'I never, I never in all my days seen so many people.' Mr. Munn thought that he, too, had never seen so many people, never before, and as he looked out over the faces — so many of them, it seemed, upturned toward him, as though in greeting or expectation — he felt a sudden surge of excitement, almost of exaltation. 'Great God!' he said, echoing the tall man; but the tall man had stepped down.

Mr. Munn followed him, the exaltation gone.

Carrying his little valise, which was continually being jammed against his knees, he moved painfully with the drift of people that was now going away from the station apparently in the direction of the main street. In the middle of the street were people in wagons and buggies that scarcely seemed to progress at all, the crush was so great. They were like people marooned in the midst of rising flood waters. Here and there a horseman stood out above the crowd, surveying it arrogantly and detachedly like an officer. These people all seemed strangers to him here on the street of Bardsville.

At the corner of the street near the hotel he heard someone calling his name, and stopped, letting the movement of the crowd divide around him. A big, chunky man wearing a black coat was standing up in a buggy and gesticulating toward him. 'Come here!' the man was shouting while he beckoned. Mr. Munn waved, and began to force his way into the street toward the buggy, which held a young woman and the chunky man.

'Get up here,' the chunky man ordered, still standing. 'And you, Sukie, you move over,' he said to the young woman, 'and let Perse get up here.'

'Well, I can't say it looks like you're going anywhere,' Mr. Munn said, and took off his hat.

The chunky man, still standing, swept his arm ferociously over the heads of the crowd. 'Hell, no!' he half-shouted, 'not with all this mob. I been forty minutes getting from the fair ground to here. But you get up here like I say.'

Mr. Munn looked inquiringly at the young woman, who, he discovered, was smiling at him. 'Sukie,' the chunky man announced, 'this is Percy Munn, and this is my girl Sukie. She just got in last week from St. Louis.'

'I'm very glad to know you, Mr. Munn,' she said.

'I'm glad to know you, Miss Christian,' Mr. Munn answered.

'Call her Sukie,' the man interposed, 'and get on up here. Move on over some, Sukie, you're hogging the seat.'

Mr. Munn put his foot on the step and swung up to the seat. He held the valise on his lap. It made him feel awkward, and cramped.

'You needn't call me Sukie,' the girl said. 'My name is Lucille.'

The man sat down heavily, crowding the girl's body against Mr. Munn. 'You call her Sukie like I said,' he ordered.

'Now, Mr. Munn,' the girl asked, leaning back so that she could look up at him from under the brim of her large straw hat with its blue ribbons, 'do you see how he can make Sukie out of a name like Lucille?'

'I've made Sukie out of more kinds of names than you ever

heard,' the man declared grimly. 'I can make Sukie out of any name once I set my mind on it.'

'I remembered your name was Lucille,' Mr. Munn said.

'You did?'

'I did,' he replied. He did remember that it was Lucille, though certainly he had never heard Mr. Christian ever refer by any other name than Sukie to his daughter, who had been away in St. Louis all the seven years since he himself had been back in Bardsville. Perhaps, he thought, he remembered it from the time before he went off to school and used to go out to the Christian place to see little Bill Christian. Bill had had a little sister, not much more than a baby then. He must remember the name from that time, somehow, having forgotten it all the fifteen years in between. He could not remember anything about the child, though, not even what she looked like. 'And I remember you, too,' he said.

'I don't remember you,' she returned blandly, almost as though with pleasure in the fact.

'We ain't got ten feet,' Mr. Christian said. He took off his black felt hat and mopped a handkerchief over his sunburned, heavy-jowled face and red mustaches, and over his bald, enormous skull, that shone in the light like a piece of some stone, like onyx veined with tiny red lines, carved to that shape and polished to a glitter. 'God knows I'm glad these folks are here. I been working two months to get 'em here, but can't they move just a little faster?' he demanded, and glared at his daughter and Mr. Munn as though they were responsible for the confused and dilatory pack of people and the crowded vehicles. 'All I want to do is get this nag in the livery stable and get to my meeting.' Mr. Christian pushed the soaked wad of his handkerchief into the breast pocket of his black coat and pulled the black felt hat over the glittering, red-veined dome of his skull.

'Mr. Bill,' Mr. Munn said, 'I can get a boy from the hotel

stable to take the buggy. He can put the horse in my stall. I got a stall there now, and I rode out home the other day and came back on the train this morning.'

'That's fine,' Mr. Christian replied.

Mr. Munn stepped to the ground, took off his hat to the girl, and began to force his way toward the hotel. The wide doorway was almost blocked by loiterers who took advantage of the shade there and of the height to peer out over the heads of the crowd. Mr. Munn got past them. After the brightness of the sun in the street, the interior of the hotel was, for the moment, like a great dark cavern full of shadowy moving forms and the insistent rise and hum of voices, a sound like an autumn flock of roosting grackles disturbed and quarreling in the branches of a darkened tree.

He found a negro boy at last and took him out to get Mr. Christian's buggy. The buggy by now was another twenty-five yards down the street. 'Mr. Munn,' the girl said, as he reached to take her hand and help her down, 'since you left, the pace has been breath-taking. The mare's in a lather.'

'So I see,' Mr. Munn answered shortly.

'Like hell,' Mr. Christian said, and heaved his bulk into the street. 'Don't pay her no mind, Perse,' he added, and shook himself like a dog and beat the dust out of his black coat with his red, hairy hands, 'she just talks that way. Besides, I didn't tell her you're married.' He seized the girl's arm and shook her playfully, as one shakes a child. 'I fooled you, huh, Sukie; I just told you he was a coming young lawyer, but I didn't tell you he was married.' He laughed, short, hearty bursts from under the red mustaches, and beat more dust out of the black coat. 'I fooled you, huh, Sukie?'

As they pushed through the crowd, the girl turned to Mr. Munn and inquired in a tone in which he detected, he thought, a mincing parody of politeness, 'And how long have you been married, Mr. Munn?'

'Over a year.'

'How nice!' she exclaimed.

He did not like her, he suddenly decided, and did not answer, pretending, for the moment, to be absorbed in the difficulty of clearing a way toward the hotel through the mob. She talked to him like a grown person talking to a child, asking a child his age, for instance, or what grade he was in.

'And what is your wife's name, Mr. Munn?' she was asking.

He'd be damned if he'd tell her, not when she asked the question that way, but he knew he'd have to for the sake of politeness. But Mr. Christian was saying in his big voice: 'Oh, her name's May, May Cox before she married Perse here — which was a mistake, God knows — and she's pretty as a picture, even if she is a little on the skinny side. Say, Perse, why don't you fatten her up a little, huh?'

Mr. Munn did not answer, but made a way for them through the loiterers in the hotel doorway.

'Mr. Bill,' Mr. Munn told him, 'I've got a room here, been having it for the last month, I have to stay over so much lately. I wish you all would use it today if you want. I thought you might want to wash up before your meeting and all. And maybe you' — he turned to the girl — 'might want to wait there for your father and —— '

'That's fine,' Mr. Christian declared.

Mr. Munn got his key from the sick-looking old man at the desk, who said to him that there was a big crowd in town, wasn't there, and led the way up the staircase from the lobby. At the top he turned, and said that he was sorry but Miss Christian would have to climb up another flight, because the room was on the top floor. They followed him up again, and down the dim hall, along which a narrow strip of red carpet was laid on the painted floor.

The room itself was almost dark, with the curtains drawn together and the shade down so that only a narrow pencil line of sunlight lay across the rug. The air was motionless and cool. The window being closed, the clamor and excitement of the packed street seemed suddenly far away, filtering in only dimly and irrelevantly. Mr. Munn set his valise on the floor, and turned to them: 'I'll leave the key with you, Mr. Bill. I can get it at the desk when I come in tonight.' He proffered the key.

'Hell, no,' said Mr. Christian. 'You wait here while I go wash the big road off the back of my neck. I want to talk to you soon as we get shet of her,' and he pointed at his daughter.

'All right,' Mr. Munn responded somewhat grudgingly. He did not want to do it, but he usually found that he, like other people, did what Mr. Christian said. Mr. Christian would bellow at you, standing in front of you with his short, heavy, always booted legs spread wide apart, waving his thick arms in the air, or grabbing your shoulder with his great red, hairy hand. Mr. Bill was all right, it wasn't that. He just wanted — why, he didn't know — to be by himself.

'That's fine,' Mr. Christian had said.

Mr. Munn went to the window, parted the curtains, raised the shade, letting the sun blaze directly in, and raised the sash. The noise of the street was on them at the instant, full and immediate, and Mr. Christian, as though at a signal, took three quick, heavy steps to the window to peer out over the heads of the people. Dispassionately, Mr. Munn looked out too. There they were, as far as you could see from the window, the slow streams of bodies milling and dividing on the pavements and in the street, and the retarded movement of the wagons and buggies and carriages between. On Mr. Christian's face grew a rapt and distant expression, that vanished suddenly into an excitement as he straightened up and slapped Mr. Munn on the back and exclaimed: 'By God, boy, we gonna do it, we gonna do it! They're here for it, and they'll do it. We'll show those bastards now, by God!'

'I hope so,' Mr. Munn rejoined.

'Hope!' Mr. Christian exclaimed, waving his arms. 'Hope, hell! It ain't hope, it's here and now, by God!'

He turned again to the window, and again that rapt and impersonal expression touched his features fleetingly so that, for the instant before it faded, the face almost lost the resemblance to itself, like the face of someone sleeping or praying. He pulled himself, as though by an effort, from the sight, and asked in a matter-of-fact tone, 'You got any towels, Perse?'

Mr. Munn got a towel from the bureau, and remarked, 'The washroom is just down to your right.'

'You wait,' Mr. Christian ordered, and strode from the room, slamming the door behind him.

Mr. Munn returned to the window. The girl, he had observed, was standing the whole time in the middle of the room, perfectly still, the blue ribbons of her hat, her blue linen skirt, and her white waist creating a focus of brightness that made the room seem small and worn. He had not guessed that she was the kind of person who could be still like that. Then, while he looked out the window, he was aware of her steps coming toward him. When he heard no other sound, he knew that she had stopped behind him. He continued to gaze into the street, taking some pleasure in the fact that he had not turned.

'Mr. Munn,' she said.

'Yes, Miss Christian,' he answered, and did turn, with a pretense of being startled to recollect himself and his obligations. 'I'm sorry.'

'You see how it is with papa,' she began, and fixed him directly with her glance.

'Yes,' he answered.

'You see how it is with him. He's absolutely wrapped up in it. It's not just that he wants to get more money for his crop, you can see that. It's something else, Mr. Munn.'

'I reckon he just wants his rights,' Mr. Munn said. 'People do.'

'That,' she admitted, 'and something else.'

He made a sweeping gesture toward the street, where the clamor was unceasing. 'There's a lot more folks with your father,' he remarked.

She took a step toward the window and looked down at the moving mass. Then she shook her head, very slightly, as though meditating, and said, 'No, they're different.'

'Maybe,' he replied, and shrugged a little. He disengaged his glance from hers, and gave his attention again to the street. He did not want to be rude, but he couldn't help it; and because he was rude he was irritated with himself, and with her. It was their bringing May into it, he supposed; that, and the way she had talked to him. My God, just because she had lived in St. Louis, she didn't have to behave like that. He had been in Philadelphia four years studying law, and he hadn't forgotten how people acted.

'Mr. Munn,' she said.

'Yes?'

'How is it going to come out?'

'I can't say' — and he pointed to the crowd below — 'but if they get the Association and they sign up even half the people for the counties round here, tobacco'll go up three hundred per cent in two seasons. Right here, in this section of Tennessee and Kentucky, is the center of the world market. They'll sew up the market.' He noticed the excitement beginning to appear in her face and how a glitter came into her dark blue, too large eyes. 'But' — and he shook his head — 'that's the catch. Germany and France and Italy and the big tobacco companies here aren't going to take it lying down, you can bet.'

'No, I guess not,' she replied. The momentary excitement and pleasure had left her face. Which was fine, he thought, for she was the kind of woman who was too easy in the world, thinking the world would bow down to her or something. She had been pleased just because the price going up would give her more money to spend on herself, up in St. Louis or some place. Well — and it gave him a moment of righteous satisfaction — the German and French and English buyers and the big companies wouldn't bow down to her. Or to God Almighty, for that matter.

'Anyway,' she went on, now looking out the window, 'I'll be here to see it all happen. I'm going to stay now and run the house for papa.'

'Oh,' he said.

Mr. Christian came in, shoving the door shut behind him with the heel of his boot. He carried his coat, tie, and collar in one hand, and in the other the dirty towel. 'Well,' he remarked, 'I'll be with you soon as I get my collar on.' He flung the coat and towel to the bed, and went to the bureau, where, with legs wide apart, as though for a strenuous endeavor, he braced himself before the mirror. Between grunts, as he tightened the collar around the big shaft of his neck, he demanded, 'What she been telling you?'

Mr. Munn thought that he detected in the daughter's eyes a warning. Perhaps, even, she shook her head ever so slightly. 'That she's come home to keep house for you,' he replied.

'And that's a fact!' Mr. Christian exclaimed, wheeling from the mirror, the ends of his collar popping up, his big face glowing with sudden pleasure at the thought. 'Ain't it a fact, Sukie?'

She nodded at him.

He's certainly crazy about her, Mr. Munn remarked to himself, making the discovery with surprise. But, then, she was all human he had, his wife dead all these years and little Bill shot with a shotgun out hunting. Not that he had ever thought of Mr. Bill as needing anything human, not with his six hundred acres of land and his horses and tobacco and the eternal bird dogs and coon dogs.

Struggling before the mirror, Mr. Christian kept repeating, as though to himself, but loudly, 'And that's a fact.' He got the collar and tie adjusted at last, and swung around, saying, 'Ain't it, Sukie, huh?'

'Yes,' she said.

He tugged the coat, its seams apparently ready to burst with the bulk it contained, and picked up his hat. 'We better get on now,' he announced. 'I'll come get you, Sukie, when it's time to eat.' And to Mr. Munn, 'Come on, Perse.'

Mr. Munn turned to the girl, telling her: 'My wife keeps a few things here. You might find a comb and brush in the top drawer.' Then he laid the key to the room on the bureau, said good-bye quite formally, and followed Mr. Christian down the hall. In the lobby, at the foot of the stairs, he told Mr. Christian that he hoped it would all turn out all right and he would see him later. But Mr. Christian laid his heavy, compelling hand on his shoulder, and brought his red face, from which stared the flat, china-blue eyes, closer to Mr. Munn's face, and said, 'No, boy, you come with me.'

'I better not.'

'You come on with me, now,' and Mr. Christian's hand bore down on his shoulder. 'I want you to go with me.'

'I better not,' Mr. Munn answered. At the moment the words passed his lips, he knew that he would go, regretting the fact that he had ever come to town, and almost hating this man, who was a good friend. And all the while he felt, as though he were a culprit, the bearing-down weight of the hand. 'I'm not in on it, Mr. Bill, I don't belong at the meeting with you all.'

'Hell, it's not official or anything,' Mr. Christian said. He had the other man by the arm now, leading him across the lobby while he spoke in a strident, rasping undertone. 'We're just gonna talk over things a little, Mr. Peacham and Jim Sills and some of us. And I want you in on it; you're a smart man, Perse, and I want you to hear what they say, and I want to hear you say what you think about things.'

'I'd be intruding,' Mr. Munn remonstrated. But he was already in the street, moving, with Mr. Christian's hand gripping his arm, through the crowd toward the bank building, where he knew the meeting was to be.

'And it won't do you no harm, Perse. You're a smart man, and a man like you is bound to be getting into politics some of these days, and — well, this thing won't do you no harm.'

'I'm not planning to go into politics,' Mr. Munn replied. Not planning to, no, not exactly, he told himself, even though it had sometimes presented itself to his mind as a possibility for the future. 'No,' he went on, shaking his head, 'I've got enough to do already with my farm and my law practice.' But, as he spoke, he was almost aware of the discomfort of a lie, for what had, in the past, never seemed more than a daydream, a remote possibility out of many possibilities, now rose like a certainty before his mind, solid and beckoning.

But by the time they turned in at the side door of the bank building, the certainty had disappeared before the logical, skeptical scrutiny of his mind, which was his natural attitude, and before the satisfaction he took in his life as it now was. Politicians were slaves, he had sometimes told himself, dispelling the casual speculations in the past; and if he desired anything of life, that thing was to be free, and himself.

When he entered the long, shabby room above the bank, shoved in by Mr. Christian, he was aware of the surprise that touched the faces of the men already there about the baize-covered table, a surprise that did not disappear, but was only mitigated, when Mr. Christian promptly followed, and shut the door.

'I just ran into Mr. Munn here,' Mr. Christian said, 'and I brought him along. Now, Perse, he's a smart man, gentlemen, and he might tell you all something.' Mr. Christian strode to the table, laid his black hat on the green baize, and swept his eyes over the group, but with a glance that seemed to linger infinitesimally on the face of each man.

Good Lord, Mr. Munn thought, he's bullying the lot; he just brought me to show he could do it if he wanted without asking. Then he heard Mr. Christian saying, 'I know you all'd be glad I brought him.'

'That's fine,' one of the men rejoined, but, Mr. Munn observed, without much enthusiasm.

'Come here, Perse,' Mr. Christian ordered. 'I want to introduce you to some of these fellows. You know Mr. Peacham and Mr. Sills, but here's Mr. Burden from over near Princeton.'

Mr. Munn did know Mr. Peacham and Mr. Sills, and had known them all of his life, both farmers from the same county, Mr. Peacham, tall, spare, gray, and preacherish, with a hooked, paper-thin nose, and Mr. Sills, an aimless-looking, nondescript, small man, who had, in twenty years, built up a fine place from eroded fields bought for taxes, and who had a sharp, mean tongue and a great piety. Mr. Munn greeted them, and shook hands. He shook hands with Mr. Burden, a dark man of middle age, well set up, with a quiet way of speaking. He had never heard of Mr. Burden.

He knew some of the other men well. There was Mr. Morse, who ran a newspaper in Millsborough; Captain Todd, a kindly, bearded man, a veteran of the Civil War, and Mr. Dicey Short, both tobacco farmers and good ones, men whom he had seen on the streets of Bardsville from the time of his earliest recollections. He shook hands with them, detecting in them, he felt, some nervousness of constraint, and shook hands with Senator Tolliver. Senator Tolliver was affable, smiling from his long, aquiline face and saying that he knew Mr. Munn would have something valuable to say.

'I'm afraid not,' Mr. Munn answered, 'and I'm afraid I'm intruding.'

'Not at all, not at all,' Senator Tolliver insisted, 'and I personally am very glad to see you again.'

Mr. Munn thanked him, shook hands with two more men,

who were strangers to him and whose names he missed, and took a chair at the lower end of the table from Mr. Morse, who was apparently acting as a kind of chairman. It was a bad seat, facing the glare of the windows, but it was the only seat left, for Mr. Christian, with a grunt of animal satisfaction, had dropped his bulk into the one beside the Senator, and now sat there blowing through his powerful-looking yellow teeth and fanning himself with his hat.

The meeting was what he could have predicted, Mr. Munn decided, if he had taken the trouble to speculate about it before-hand. Mr. Sills, in his colorless voice and with the manner he must use in his missionary societies and meetings of stewards in his church, read a long list of names. It was a list of men who, according to Mr. Sills, might be depended upon to support the purposes and ideals of the Association of Growers of Dark Fired Tobacco. 'Which purposes and ideals,' Mr. Christian had interrupted Mr. Sills before the list began, 'is to make those son-a-bitching buyers pay me what my tobacco's worth.'

At that, someone had laughed, and Mr. Munn, in the midst of his own smile, had suddenly seen again in his mind the rapt and distant expression Mr. Christian's face had worn when he first looked from the window of the hotel room over the heads of the crowd in the street.

But after the laughter stopped, Mr. Sills, clearing his throat slightly, repeated with his colorless equanimity, '... to support the purposes and ideals of the Association of Growers of Dark Fired Tobacco,' and began to read the list.

The names proceeded. Mr. Munn listened idly to them. There were a great many names, and many of them now already were checked off as promised supporters. He had not thought that matters had gone quite so far. The Association might, after all, come to something at this rate. He tried to study the faces of the men at the table between him and the light, ordinary faces and ordinary men, on the whole, men whom he had known all his life, or like men he had known. Then it occurred to him that behind all the names he was hearing without attention were other men, scattered over the section, in other countries, perfectly real men, all different from each other in their own ways, but drawn together by the fact that their names were on the pieces of paper which Mr. Sills held. From that paper invisible threads, as it were, stretched off to Hunter County and Caldwell County and into Tennessee to those men. They were all webbed together by those strands, parts of their beings, which were their own, different each from each, coming together here, and becoming one thing. An idea — that was it — an idea seized parts of their individual beings and held them together and made them coalesce. And something was made that had not existed before. He looked around him again at those faces at the table. Perhaps Mr. Bill and these other men here at the table, who seemed so ordinary, were not so ordinary after all; for they had done it. Whatever it was. The thing which they had created, which they were, at this moment, in the act of creating, had no meaning as yet, no form. You couldn't tell — you couldn't ever tell what a thing was until it was dead, until the time for action was past.

'All very satisfactory, very satisfactory,' the Senator was saying as soon as the last name had been read. 'With these commitments to go on, and the crowd we've got here today, we may go far. It may be the biggest thing this section has ever seen.'

'You're damned tooting,' Mr. Christian put in, 'and you tell 'em today. You get up there and r'ar back and tell 'em.'

'I'll do my best,' the Senator promised.

'You better,' Mr. Christian said.

Then Mr. Morse, who was acting as chairman, interrupted and asked Mr. Burden, the dark man from over near Princeton, if he had any further information about warehouses. There was, Mr. Burden said, a little to add to previous reports. Warehouses would have to be built at Millsborough and Gill's Crossing, it seemed. There was nothing available for lease at Millsborough, for the tobacco companies had every likely building already tied up in one way or another — he had found that out quick enough. They would have to build. That was too bad. But the one at Gill's Crossing would be a good thing, more convenient to all the farmers up the Rose Creek section than anything the buyers could offer. It would save the farmers hauling and would give the Association a good name in that section where there weren't too many sympathizers now.

'We'll get those babies, too,' Mr. Christian said, and whistled through his yellow teeth.

With gravity, Captain Todd shook his head. 'Maybe,' he replied, 'and maybe not. A lot of 'em up there are a mite ornery. Half those folks went with the Yankees in the war.'

'I don't care if they went with the Turks,' Mr. Christian declared. 'A hand of tobacco is a hand of tobacco, and I like any Yankee I ever saw a hell of a sight better'n I like a buyer.'

The meeting was soon over. The men shoved back their chairs gratingly, and rose. Mr. Christian came and stood beside Mr. Munn. The Senator and Captain Todd remained by the windows, talking. The other men began to go from the room, the footsteps resounding hollowly on the wooden stairs beyond. When all except the two men by the window had gone, Mr. Christian said: 'Perse, the Senator and Captain Todd and me are going to eat over at Wilson's, we got a room reserved in the back. We want you to come with us.'

Mr. Munn, hesitating, said that it was mighty nice, and Mr. Christian put his hand on Mr. Munn's shoulder and urged, 'You better; it's the only chance you got to get a bite with this mob in town.'

Mr. Munn answered that he appreciated the invitation and would go. And at that Mr. Christian called to the men by the window that Perse was going with them to eat and that he

himself would meet them at Wilson's, for he had to go get
Sukie. Mr. Christian went down the stairs with a great clatter,
and Mr. Munn was left alone by the door. Captain Todd,
apparently, cut short his conversation, and came toward Mr.
Munn, moving with his easy gait that gave no hint of impending
age. That always struck Mr. Munn, how the man carried his
years, and it struck him now; and now it struck him that of all
the people present Captain Todd was the only man who had
seemed fully himself, not nervous or constrained.

'Come along, Perse,' Captain Todd called. 'We better get
on over, I reckon.'

Mr. Munn stood aside to permit the Senator and Captain
Todd to precede him. Bowing slightly, they did so. Captain
Todd, with the air of impersonal gravity that characterized him,
closed the door, shutting off the light that came from the room.

Conversation was impossible as they fought their way through
the crowd toward the corner where Wilson's restaurant and
saloon were situated. At that corner the crowd was thickest.
People were packed solid before the door to the restaurant side
of the building, apparently in some sort of line waiting turn to
get in.

'I guess I'm lucky you all picked me up,' Mr. Munn said.

'It's fortunate for us,' the Senator answered.

They made their way to the side door of the restaurant,
entered a short passage, and found the room that had been
reserved. It was a smallish room, not too well lighted by the
single window, which opened on an alley. They had scarcely
seated themselves before a skinny negro boy entered, his stained
white coat sticking to him with sweat.

'You better lay another place, boy,' Captain Todd ordered.

'Yassuh,' the boy replied, with a quick, secretive gesture
lifting a little wad of towel to wipe the sweat from one cheek.

'And boy,' the Senator added, 'you better bring us a bowl of
ice and a pitcher of water and a pint of whatever good rye you've

got. For I' — and he turned to the others — 'need some refreshment and trust you will join me.'

'I've had the pleasure of voting for you on occasion,' Captain Todd said, 'and so I don't reckon I'll pass up the privilege of drinking with you one more time, Edmund.'

The slightest cloud, as Mr. Munn noticed, touched the Senator's handsome face, and then was instantly dispelled by his smile. 'I was grateful to my friends,' he remarked, 'and when I didn't hold my seat last election, I almost felt I had let them down.'

'There's another one coming up,' Captain Todd pointed out, 'not fifteen months off.'

'Not for me,' and the Senator, still smiling, shook his head. 'I hope I can do more good here than in Washington, here with the Association. Here's where the fight is.' But the smile, though not fading from his face, no longer seemed, at least to Mr. Munn, who regarded him closely, the true token of ease and geniality. And then the smile itself faded, while the Senator raised his glance, which was cold and abstract now, to the blank brick wall visible beyond the single window. Captain Todd did not seem to notice, Mr. Munn thought; but then you could never tell what Captain Todd noticed, for he was always the same behind his neat beard, always with the same poise and amiable gravity. No, you couldn't tell about Captain Todd, or for that matter about anybody, about the Senator. There was no telling what made his smile fade that way and his eyes withdraw and fix upon that blank, sunlit wall across the alley.

But the negro boy had come back with the ice and the pitcher and the whisky, and the Senator, now smiling again, and again one of them, was pouring the liquor. He added ice and a little water to each glass, and with a slightly ceremonious air offered drinks to the Captain and to Mr. Munn. Then he raised his own glass and called, 'To the Association and our prosperity!'

The others raised their glasses, and then drank. Then they sat without speaking for a little, as though to relish the first flush of the liquor. The Senator drained his glass, and replenished it. 'It's hot in here,' he said.

'Pretty hot,' Captain Todd agreed, 'but it's better than most folks got today. At least we'll eat. A lot of empty bellies will growl this afternoon.'

'There must be twenty thousand people in town,' the Senator said. 'Nobody expected that many. The town hasn't made preparation.'

'More'n that,' Captain Todd declared. 'They were moving in all day yesterday, they say. All yesterday afternoon I could see wagons and buggies coming down the pike past my place. The dust never got settled before somebody stirred it up again coming toward town. They've come from all over, all these counties round here. They say people slept in their wagons or on the ground or sat up all night talking and singing.' He took a slow sip from his glass, and shook his head. 'It's been forty years since I've seen this many folks together — not since the war.'

'It is a kind of war,' the Senator remarked.

Captain Todd shook his head, smiling a little. 'Well, just a kind of one, I hope. I had four years of another kind, and I reckon that's enough to hold a man the rest of his life.'

At that moment there was the sound of Mr. Christian's boots on the boards of the passage and his voice calling for Captain Todd. Then he entered the room, flushed and perspiring, with his daughter behind him. He turned and pointed accusingly at her, saying: 'She had to primp, she took ten minutes primping and kept me standing there! We gonna be late at this rate.'

'I don't think so,' the Senator said.

'Come here, Sukie,' Mr. Christian commanded, then turning to the men, announced: 'This is my girl Sukie. She's come home to run my house for me, like I told you.'

'This is a great pleasure,' the Senator declared, and bowed as he took her hand.

'I used to know you,' Captain Todd said, 'when you were a little girl.'

Somewhat embarrassed, as though he were alone in front of the thousands of eyes, and not knowing precisely how he came to be there, Mr. Munn sat in a chair on the high platform under the awning, which was hung with red, white, and blue bunting. But the eyes, he knew, were not fixed upon him. The Senator was speaking, his full, rich voice, which could, at need, ring out like a trumpet, dominating the hot emptiness of the afternoon air. People, men for the most part, crowded up to the very edge of the platform, which was so high that those directly in front had to crane their necks upward to watch the speaker. Their attention never wavered from him, and as they held their faces upward, gazing and immobile, they gave the impression of a slow, animal patience.

The platform had been erected toward one end of the oval area defined by the race track, and that entire space was filled with people. Those toward the front sat on the board benches that had been prepared for the occasion, or on the ground in the wide aisles. But there were not enough seats, far from enough, and people stood beyond the seats, ring after ring of them packed together, all of them staring at the man on the platform, who must appear, at such a distance, as nothing more than a tiny black-garbed marionette that gesticulated in almost soundless pantomime under the brilliant patch of bunting.

Over to the right, Mr. Munn could see the white walls of the stables, and on the roofs the forms of the people who had seized that point of vantage. Beyond the stables was a grove of oaks. The afternoon was peculiarly windless, peculiarly still. The steady sunlight burned down over the heads of the people, over the distant oak trees, and over the wide, brown fields that were visible to the left beyond the fair grounds. At a great height, a single buzzard hung motionless as though sustained in the incandescent blue of the sky.

Mr. Munn could feel the weight of the sun beating upon him through the awning. Perspiration was running down the back of the Senator's neck and his iron-gray hair was streaked darker with dampness, but he seemed oblivious to that discomfort, for, standing very erect at the edge of the platform, he poured forth his full and powerful discourse, never lifting a hand to relieve his streaming forehead. Occasionally, Mr. Munn wiped his own face with his handkerchief, and shifted in his chair. He wished again that he had never come to Bardsville. He could have found out all he wanted to know from the papers. But here he was, and here upon the platform. The Senator had urged it, saying, 'Of course, if your sympathies are not fully with the movement, I shan't insist, but——' And Mr. Bill had seized him by the arm and bellowed at him. They were kind. They were giving him a lift, helping his law practice by putting him up in front of people. And it would help.

He could tell that the rally was going well; better, probably, than the most sanguine had dared to hope. Since they had mounted the platform and the silence had fallen over the people, Mr. Christian's face had burned with a great excitement. He sat leaning forward in his chair, his heavy boots set squarely on the boards, and his wide, pale blue eyes roved constantly over the crowd as though to seize them and compel them, every man. He had not changed that posture since Brother Morgan, the Methodist preacher, had opened the rally with a prayer that this great occasion might serve in the end to glorify the goodness of God as well as to increase the prosperity of His children upon earth. Mr. Munn had speculated a little at the presence of Brother Morgan and at his apparent enthusiasm for the Association of Growers of Dark Fired Tobacco; but shortly he had remembered that Mr. Sills was a rich man and that he was a power in the First Methodist Church of Bardsville.

The two short speeches before the Senator's had gone well, speeches outlining the method of organization of the Association, and the financial relation of members to the Association. But the Senator's speech was the big one.

The Senator was, Mr. Munn decided, a real orator — no ranting and bellowing, but perfect composure or ardent gesture as the moment demanded, and always that flowing, full, compelling voice moving out over the lifted faces. The time was ripe, he had said, for a struggle for the rights of the people of this section. It was against all justice for the price of the staple product of thousands upon thousands of people to be set, not by a competitive process of buying, but by the cold-blooded and malicious agreement of buyers without reference to the commercial worth of the product, to the investment of capital, to the sweat of the brow and the cunning of the hand that had created it, or to the needs of the people.

In absolute silence, under the blazing sun, the crowd had listened, and were listening, to him. Now, mounting to the close, he was saying that the condition was one that no true man would longer endure. That it was his firm faith that God Himself would no longer endure to witness it. Now was the time for the struggle. The men of Kentucky and Tennessee had never showed themselves weaklings. Let them now show fight, and show that they were true sons of their fathers. Let them support the Association and the Association would give them justice.

Upon the word 'justice,' which seemed to hang in the hot air for a long instant, vibrating powerfully like a plucked cord, the Senator slowly raised his right hand in a gesture that suggested the solemnity of benediction and the incitement of salute. As the hand began, slowly, to descend, the first spatter of applause broke sporadically from the people grouped closest to the platform, coming like the first heavy, individual, tumescent drops exploding upon the dry roof before the storm breaks in full volume. Then the sound, mounting, swept back from the platform, over the whole multitude to the outermost fringe by the fence and on the stables, involving those distant spectators who could scarcely have heard the words, swelling outward like fire leaping through dry brush or waves plunging toward a beach very far off.

With dignity, the Senator turned and resumed his seat. Even now he did not show the strain of his effort, or lift a hand to wipe his face, from which the perspiration was streaming. His face was perfectly impassive, except for the sharp and unnatural gleam of his eyes.

Mr. Munn, as the Senator turned to take his seat, saw Doctor Milton, who was chairman, glance covertly at his watch. Then Doctor Milton rose and stood quietly behind the little table while the applause and excitement of the crowd wore itself out. When it was over, Doctor Milton thanked the speaker on behalf of the audience and himself, and said that the Senator had once more appeared as the friend of the people and of their rights. He proceeded to say that he wished to call upon one more speaker for a few words, a man who was well known to many present and who was a representative citizen. Mr. Munn, scarcely attending to what the Doctor said, was suddenly aware that his own name had been spoken. At that sound, so familiar, and, at the moment, so strange, he experienced an enveloping wave of nausea and his bowels seemed to turn coldly within him, as though his body, before his mind could seize the full import of what was being said, had known it all and had, in its own violent language of sensation, interpreted the meaning as best it could for the tardy intelligence.

Doctor Milton was gesturing toward him. He began slowly and painfully to rise, as though by retarding that habitual act he might avoid the ordeal. He had to get up, there was nothing else he could do. He approached the little table, placing himself behind that frail barrier, while **Doctor Milton** sat down. A few people near the platform applauded perfunctorily. He saw the expanse of faces before him stretching back toward the distant fence and the grove of oaks. He opened his lips dryly, but no sound came out. He had intended to say, 'My friends.' He lifted his gaze from the people. The solitary buzzard, he observed impersonally, had gone, leaving nothing but the empty and intense blue of the sky.

'My friends,' he managed to begin, wetting his lips. Then he said that he was unprepared to speak, for he had not been warned, hating himself for the worn and sterile phrases that formed on his tongue. While he uttered the words his glance fell upon a man who stood on the ground directly at the edge of the platform. It was a lanky, stooped man of about fifty, wearing faded blue overalls and a straw hat. The man's red-rimmed, dull eyes were fixed directly upon him. Then, at that instant, he realized with a profound force that that man there was an individual person, not like anybody else in the world. He realized the fact more profoundly than he had ever realized it about his friends or even his wife; and he saw as clearly as in a vision that man sitting with other men before a small blaze of sticks on which something was cooking, in the dark in the open field, just as Captain Todd had said the people had camped the night before.

'My friends,' he said again hesitatingly, 'I know that many of you have come a long way. You left your houses and your families and came here, some of you from a long way off, from other counties. Some of you stayed out in the fields last night because the town was full or because you did not have any money. In my mind I can see you there. You came here through the dust and heat' — and he felt his own voice growing stronger within him and the words coming — 'because you thought you could get something here to help you.' He came from behind the table and went to the edge of the platform, what seemed the tremendous emptiness of the crowd, like the emptiness of the sky when one fixes his steady gaze upon its depth, drawing him as though against his will. 'But there is nothing here to help you. You came here to find hope. But there is no hope here for you. There is nothing here in Bardsville for you. There is no hope in the Association for you.'

He heard the shuffling of feet on the boards behind him, and a short, nervous cough. 'There is nothing here,' he went on, 'except what you have brought with you from your homes, wherever they are. There is no hope except the hope you bring here. There is nothing here but an idea. And that idea is dead unless you have brought it life by your long trip here. It does not exist unless you give it life by your own hope and loyalty.'

He could not tell whether they were listening to him, and found that he did not care, for his own voice filled him and he was completely himself. '— your own hope and loyalty. That idea will not give you quick comfort. Before it gives you comfort it will give you suffering and privation. And it will not give you anything in payment for your suffering, now or later, unless you give your full loyalty to it. The loyalty you have brought with you here today is everything, it is your only hope.' Then he told them what he felt each man owed to the others.

He did not talk long. And afterward he could never remember precisely what he had said, though he remembered in perfect clarity the face of the man in the faded blue overalls who had stood just below the platform and had looked up at him. Though he could not, later, recall the words he had spoken, or even, very certainly, the ideas he had wanted to express, he could remember how the speech had welled up powerfully in him, how still and sharp the distant oak trees had appeared, and how incredibly brilliant and empty had been the sky from which the light poured over the landscape and the innumerable faces.

When he turned to take his seat, he felt like a somnambulist who is gradually recalled to himself, the rising sound of shouts and applause bringing him back to the reality of the hot, bunting-draped platform and his friends beside him. Mr. Christian was standing in front of him, wringing his hand and slapping him on the back and shouting, 'By God, Perse, you got the bastards told!' The Senator and the other men were grouped around him, the Senator smiling and stretching out his hand. Over in front of the little table, Doctor Milton was waving his arms toward the crowd, trying to say something.

The rally was soon over.

When Mr. Munn entered his room at the hotel that night, he was very tired. He switched on the light and unpacked his valise, which he found pushed under the bed. Outside, people were singing in the street. He probably wouldn't be able to get much sleep, for that sort of thing might be going on past midnight. He undressed hurriedly, turned out the light, and got into bed. At least, he could relax.

As soon as he touched the pillow, the sense of despondency which had been growing, almost unawares, within him for the past several hours engrossed him completely. He was simply tired, he told himself. He tried to force himself into his accustomed state of mind, fixing his attention upon the obligations of the next day. He had to see witnesses all morning to get ready for Bunk Trevelyan's trial; and ticking their names off in his mind and trying to remember what he knew about them, he was suddenly struck by the thought that he might be, after all, deceived, that Bunk Trevelyan might be guilty, and that he himself was a fool to put his energies into such a case when he'd never get a penny of return. People would laugh at him for a sucker. He hadn't had to take the case, the court hadn't assigned him to it. The Trevelyan woman had come to his office with her tale, and he was a sucker.

The singing in the street seemed to be louder than ever. He

tried to ignore the disturbance; then he recognized the tune, which began to run in his own head. They were singing something to the tune of 'John Brown's Body.' They were singing, over and over again as they marched up and down the street, that they were going to hang tobacco buyers to a sour apple tree. He supposed that tobacco buyers, who usually ganged around the lobby of the hotel and the saloons, would be pretty scarce tonight. They'd be under cover. Not that anybody would bother them, but they wouldn't feel exactly popular. The singing moved off down the street to the south.

He turned on his right side and tried to compose himself. Then, as he struck an habitual posture, with his right arm stretched out and his knee raised a little, he knew that the present unrest was not due to the excitement of the day or doubt about Bunk Trevelyan or the noise in the street, but to the fact that he was alone. Last night, and most nights for over a year now, he had had May beside him. If she were here now, as she had been here in this very bed, her head would be on his outflung right arm. He had not known what was the matter with him, that he was missing May, until his muscles and nerves told him when he struck the posture that was his accustomed one for sleep.

Now he thought of May, and tried to visualize her alone in the shadowy big bed in his house. She had very blonde hair, and it would be loose on the pillow, on which her head would seem small, like a child's head. She was a smallish woman, smaller than medium, and when she slept she seemed even smaller, as though the spark of her vitality withdrew deeply inward to secret recesses and let her body shrink a little, but perfectly and smoothly to scale. Once or twice, noticing this, he had thought with a despairing presentiment of loss how small she would look after she was dead. Now he tried to see how she must look sleeping alone in the big bed. She always curled up when she slept, her hands lying loosely together at her chin and her knees drawn up. That made her look even smaller, too. She always went to sleep with her head on his right arm. Always, after he himself had slept for a little while, he would wake and cautiously withdraw his arm. She would never even stir.

But now he could not sleep. Men moved down the hall outside his door, talking in vague, drunken voices. One of them lurched heavily against the wall, shaking it, and the others laughed. And the singing had begun again in the street, broken now by shouts. Drunk, too, he reckoned. The men in the hall had now gone into the room adjoining his own. They continued their talk and laughter. His irritation gave way to a kind of disgust as his imagination presented to him that adjoining room, lit by a hanging electric bulb, and the almost-realized smell of sour whisky-breath, and the flushed, loose faces of the men who were there. They, too, were singing now. They would have their arms draped about each other's shoulders with their hot, sweaty faces close together while they sang. They would be like brothers tonight, slapping each other on the back and mixing their stinking breaths in song.

He rolled over again and tried to cut out the sound by jamming the other pillow against his exposed ear. That helped some. It was then that he noticed the faint perfume. The odor came, he discovered, from the second pillow. Mr. Christian's daughter must have lain down to rest on his bed while she waited for her father. He wondered if she had taken off her skirt and shirtwaist before she lay down. She had been wearing a linen skirt, a blue linen skirt, he remembered, and linen wrinkled easily. She must have taken it off, for when she had entered the door of the room at Wilson's restaurant behind her father, her clothes had looked perfectly fresh and unwrinkled. That had made Mr. Christian late. He had said she had to primp. She had had to dress, for she had probably gone to sleep. She had pulled down the shade in the room, cutting out the sunlight, and had taken off her skirt and shirtwaist and had lain down on his bed. She had left that odor on his pillow.

He got up and went to the window. He could look over the roofs of the two-story buildings across the street. The white moonlight falling on those roofs gave them a clean and frosty and lonely look that was somehow comforting to him. Below him, he could see the people still on the street, not a crowd exactly, but a big number for the time of night. They stood on the curb under the arc lamps or wandered idly up and down, even in the middle of the street. Those who were singing were now just south of the hotel in a ragged group of some thirty or forty. Drunk, he thought. They had come here for a serious purpose, to save themselves, to assure their future, and here they were, drunk and roaming the street at midnight. His disgust mounted, disgust not only for them but for himself, for what he had said that afternoon and for the pure poise and exaltation he had felt as his words came. He had been drunk, too, drunk in a different way, but drunk. He felt cheated and betrayed.

For a long time, possessed by that feeling, he watched them in their idle and aimless movements. He thought how small and irrelevant they seemed even at the distance of three stories below him. The singers moved farther off, and some of the people left began to walk away, more firmly now, as though they had some purpose and destination. Then it occurred to him that one man was very much like another man. He recalled that that afternoon he had said something about what one man owed to another. One man was very much like another. He was like those men, one of them. Unbidden, warm and pulsing, that exaltation returned to him, more perfect than under the brilliant sun, as now he looked over the white, moon-frosted roofs. Involuntarily, he raised his arm as though to address a great multitude and tell them what he knew to be the truth.

Chapter two

In late August Mr. Munn became a member of the board which directed the organization and management of the Association. When a Mr. Morphee resigned because of ill health, the members of the board appointed Mr. Munn to fill the unexpired short term for the Bardsville district; and some four months later he was elected by the members of his district for a full term of two years.

He was sitting in his office, one afternoon, when they brought the news of his appointment to him. He had been sorting some papers when they came — the Senator, followed by Mr. Sills and Mr. Christian. They had, they said, smiling, a little news for him. He got up, somehow vaguely disturbed despite their smiles, and asked them to have seats. No, they said, they had just dropped in for a minute to give him a little bit of news that might interest him. The expression on his face must have betrayed his almost painful puzzlement and the confusion of his anticipation, for Mr. Christian said: 'Hell, Senator, go on and tell the boy. Don't leave him standing up there looking like a fool.'

'My boy,' the Senator announced, and approached him with an outstretched hand, 'we have come to tell you that you are a member of the Association board.' He took Mr. Munn's hand, which was automatically extended to him, and shook it with the slightly ceremonious air which marked all of his actions. He added, shaking the hand, 'To complete the unexpired term of Mr. Morphee.'

The puzzlement and confusion which Mr. Munn had first experienced assumed positive form, crystallizing suddenly into the word 'No,' which burst sharply from his lips; and the sound of his own unpremeditated refusal started a surprise in him to match the surprise which he observed on the faces of his friends. Then he added, 'I haven't got any business on the board.' He shook his head doubtfully. 'I appreciate the fact you all want me on the board with you, and all that — I want you to know that, all right — but I'm not the man for it. I'd better just say no.'

The surprise had gone now from the Senator's face, which was again smiling. 'No, my boy' — he was shaking his head reprovingly as though at a child — 'we expected to have to persuade you a little. We expected you would be surprised. But nobody else will be surprised. You may not know it, my boy, but you are a coming man in the community. We need you with us. And a young man. These mossbacks' — and he waved a patronizing hand at his companions — 'and the rest of us, we could use a little fresh blood.'

Mr. Munn still shook his head.

'Now you mustn't let your modesty,' the Senator began again, 'stand in the way of your duty. Your modesty . . .'

In the end Mr. Munn accepted.

It had not been modesty that prompted his first, almost uncivil, blurted-out refusal. When the Senator referred to his modesty, he told him that it wasn't modesty. But he had no language to define for the Senator and Mr. Christian and Mr. Sills what it actually was that made him refuse the place at first. Nor had he been able, standing before them there in the office that day, to define it for himself. If he had been able to give a name to the secret but violent promptings that thrust the 'No' to his lips, he might have obeyed them and stood his ground against the courtesy of the Senator, the bullying of Mr. Christian, and the dry, satirical silence of Mr. Sills. Mr. Munn's common sense, his logic, had conspired with his friends to force his acceptance. Such chances to get along didn't turn up every day to a young man of thirty. He had better grab it.

But for months afterwards, even when he was wrapped up, body and soul, in the business of the Association and knew, without any regrets, that more and more the Association was claiming, not only his energies and interest, but also that inner substance of his being which was peculiarly himself, he still speculated upon the meaning of his impulses that afternoon in his office. He knew that modesty had had nothing to do with the matter, or fear concerning his own capacity. What those men could do, he could do. Even though elusive, it had been something more fundamental to his nature than modesty, he admitted even after he was at ease in his new condition, for it had moved him powerfully that afternoon. He was bound in candor to admit that fact, remembering how, after he had accepted and the men were gone, he had felt unmanned and ashamed, as though an unsuspected weakness had betrayed him. It was as though steel had snapped at the point where the crystal had secretly formed, or the bough at the point of hidden rot. He had felt the impulse to rush down into the street to catch them and tell them he wouldn't do it, tell them he had changed his mind.

He did not follow the men, but almost immediately after he had resisted his impulse to do so, he hurried to the livery stable back of the hotel and told the negro boy to saddle his mare. While waiting, he paced up and down the dusty alley between the stable and the hotel. The boy took forever. When, at last, the boy led the mare out, Mr. Munn, without a word, swung to the saddle and rode off. By the time he reached the edge of town and could see before him the expanse of white, dusty road stretching westward, his impatience was consuming him. It was a hot afternoon, the sun still high enough to have force, and no air in motion. On each side of the white road lay fields of tobacco, still uncut, the rows of plants running perfectly back from the road until they lost themselves in the undifferentiated mass of deep, rich green which was the body of the field. The great tropical-looping leaves of the plants near the road, however, were powdered with the white dust that had been raised by wheels and hoofs to settle there. He rode too fast, and knew he was riding too fast, and cursed himself for a fool even as he leaned forward a little, relishing the supple and powerful thrust of the mare's hoofs upon the dusty road. He wanted to get home. He wanted to see May.

He found her in the side garden. He had not even bothered to go into the house, for without thought he was certain she would be here. He had ridden into the barn lot, where an old negro man, regarding the mare's condition, exclaimed, 'Lord God, Mister Perse, you ain't gone and wind-broke her!'

'No,' Mr. Munn said shortly, and swung down from the saddle and tossed the reins to the negro. 'Take care of her,' he ordered, and started to walk rapidly across the lot toward the wide and heavily shaded lawn. He walked directly across the lawn, and around the house to the side garden.

May, apparently, did not hear his coming when he turned the corner of the house and walked toward her, for grass had long ago crept over and padded the gravel of the path; and so he saw her in the posture and stillness that must belong to her when she was alone. He thought, during the instant or two before she was aware of his presence, that that was the way she looked when she was alone, for it had become a habit of his mind to try to picture her as she must be in solitude, or to seize on such glimpses as this, as though these images could give him a clue to what she truly was in herself, in her essence. For he felt that when he was with her she was not herself, not wholly; his presence, or the presence of anyone, must, like a single drop of some stain, tincture the crystal liquid that was absolutely herself. She is alone, he thought, and moved rapidly toward her, knowing that the instant she turned and raised her eyes she would not be purely herself but would be colored by him.

'Hello,' he said, and approached and kissed her

'You're early, aren't you?' she asked, smiling.

'Yes,' he answered. 'I wanted to come home and tell you something.' He felt convinced, as the words left his mouth, of his own stupidity. He had not come home for that. He had come home, putting his mare in a lather, not because he wanted to tell her that he was a member of the board, but because her words or expression, or even her mere presence, might help explain himself to himself. Obscurely, he felt that he might discover from her something about the meaning of the nameless impulse that had first prompted him to blurt out his refusal to the Senator. The conviction of weakness and shame which he had experienced after the men left was still fresh to him, and she might banish it for good, or, failing that, give him some hint whereby he could realize and master his own nature.

'Senator Tolliver,' he began, 'and Mr. Christian and Mr. Sills came by this afternoon. They came to tell me I'm on the Association board.'

He watched the look of pleasure form on her face. 'Why, Perse,' she exclaimed, 'that's wonderful!'

When, ordinarily, some word or action of his could provoke that look on her face, he experienced his own greatest satisfaction. If he brought her some gift from town, or propped up a vine for her that she would forget in less than half an hour, or unexpectedly leaned over to kiss her, that look would come to her face, as now, the lips very slightly parted and the blue eyes a little wider than usual and shining.

But the look was fading from her face.

'Why, Perse,' she said, 'what's the matter? Did anything else happen, something bad?'

'Nothing's the matter.'

'Aren't you glad?'

'Yes,' he answered, thinking, yes, he supposed he was.

'But you looked at me so funny.'

'Did I?' he asked, having intended his question to be light and jocular, but catching in his own tone a hint of something else, a hardness. He corrected his inflection, repeating, 'Did I?'

'I thought something might be the matter.'

'Nothing is,' he said. And nothing was, perhaps. At least, nothing that he had been able to put into words. He had stood staring at her while the pleasure showed on her face, and had tried to find a way to tell her what had happened to him that afternoon. There was no way. She had been pleased, pleased for him, of course; but that fact in itself meant only that she took the same view of him as the Senator and the others took. That he would be pleased to get on the board. Just that. He shouldn't be disappointed, he told himself, that she could not name for him the impulse which he himself had been unable to name. It was not her fault. Or disappointed that her presence now, and the expression of her face, failed to give him the clue to understanding. Her smile had touched him as clearly and simply, and in fact as impersonally, as the sunlight falling over an entire landscape. If that was not enough, it wasn't her fault.

He told her he had to go back to the stable and see about the mare.

It was not anger at her, or disappointment, that forced him to go. He had felt no anger, and the disappointment had been dissipated even as he stood before her. He simply wanted to be alone. He saw that the mare was rubbed down, and in her stall. He wandered about the stable, inspecting the stalls, here arranging a piece of gear that had been too carelessly hung up, there straightening a coil of line on its peg. The mare began to move restlessly in her stall, but he paid no attention to her. It was getting dark inside the stable. Shortly before supper-time he returned to the house. Whatever fleeting disappointment he had felt in his wife was forgotten that night, for when he took her in his arms the conviction came back to him that here he had found his substantial happiness.

And in the succeeding months, if he did occasionally speculate about the events of that afternoon in his office, he was
moved by a spirit of objective and honest inquiry into his own
nature, and not by distress. For the new activities more and
more engrossed him, and he lived in a state of excitement that
precluded the question of happiness or unhappiness. All fall
he traveled much around the section.

Buying was slowed down, and what tobacco the companies
could pick up from farmers outside the Association was coming
higher. Even most of the farmers outside who could afford to
were holding on, playing safe, waiting to see how the cat would
jump. 'I reckon I'll just hold on a mite longer if I kin git me
something to eat for my folks,' they would tell him. But when
he said that now was the time to sign, that the Association
would see its members through, they would say, 'Naw, I ain't
signing nothing.' And their long, grave faces would stiffen as
they shook their heads. 'You've signed mortgages,' he would
tell them bitterly, 'you've signed away your land all right.'
They would shake their heads, saying: 'I've signed mortgages,
God's plenty of 'em, but I ain't signing this. I never was one
to let any man tell me what I could do. I don't aim to have
any man tell me when I can sell my crop.'

When one of those men with whom he talked face to face at
the small meetings around the section did sign, Mr. Munn
would regard the process with a cold avidity, his eyes never
leaving the red, strong-knuckled fingers that guided the pen
until he saw the last stroke completed. Each name, it always
seemed in retrospect, involved himself peculiarly, representing
something of himself to himself; and almost always, upon wit-
nessing the act of signing, he experienced the grip of an absolute, throbless pleasure in which he seemed poised out of
himself and, as it were, out of time. Then the man who had
signed would slowly lay down the pen, and look up.

He attended dozens of such meetings. People would come

together, on a good afternoon, in front of a country store or in the clearing before some little white church at a crossroads. He would glance restlessly about him, at the calm blue of the sky, the dust-covered growth along the fencerow by the road, the trees hung with the colored leaves. Then, getting up on the steps of the church, he would look at the people who had come together to hear him. Then, when the people grew quiet, he would lean toward them earnestly, and speak.

In late November he attended a meeting in the Rose Creek section. It had been raining for three days before the meeting, and he had to ride a borrowed horse seven miles north of Morris Crossing through mud that sucked about the fetlocks at every step. The meeting was to be in the evening, at a schoolhouse near the creek. The rain left off in the afternoon, but the sky did not clear. While he rode down the muddy road, under the sky that seemed to sag sodden above him, he ate the sandwiches he had put in his pocket. The dry crumbs stuck in his throat. He saw no one on the road.

Just as the last gray twilight went out, he discovered the schoolhouse. Only some eighteen or twenty men were there, huddling about the stove, in which a fire had just been made. The single room was lighted by two oil lamps; the pale yellow flames under smoky glass seemed themselves to be stiffened and faded by the chill. The men silently made a place for Mr. Munn at the stove, and he introduced himself. Each of the men, repeating his name as though it were a lesson to be learned by rote, took his hand and shook it. In silence, then, they stood about the stove while the fire caught and the steam began to ascend from their drying clothes. When the room got warmer, the men scattered among the desks, looking somewhat embarrassed to be seen in those cramped seats that reminded them of the period of childhood and dependence.

Shortly after Mr. Munn had taken his position by the table, where the two lamps sat, and had begun to talk to the men, the rain started again. It beat steadily on the roof, its insistent sound mingling with the sound of his voice, and he had the feeling that it was beating upon his very mind, flattening out the thoughts he would speak as rain flattens out grain, dulling him, conquering him, and those other men, into a kind of immemorial passivity and acceptance. The faces of the men seemed to say that to him, to speak to him louder than his words to them. But the four thin walls and the roof held out the rain. It was almost a mystery, a mystery whose profoundness drew him as he stood there, that he and those men should be together in that little cubicle of comforting warmth and light while the rain and darkness and wind prevailed over the land outside.

After he finished talking, nobody signed. The men gathered again about the stove, in which the fire was dying now, to wait for the rain to stop so that they could go home and go to bed. Mr. Munn ceased to urge them. He sensed that it was useless. He was fighting in himself a conviction of futility, a presentiment of despair. He told himself that he was behaving like a child, that this was nothing, that he only dreaded the long ride back to Morris Crossing through the wet. He tried to fall into ordinary conversation with the men, but his words were forced and came false to his own ears. The men were not talking to each other much. Each one seemed silently engrossed in the process of the life that was hidden deeply within himself, that bore no relation to anything beyond himself, not even, it seemed, to his own feet set solidly on the plank floor or his own heavy hands that hung inert by his sides. Occasionally one of the men would say, 'It ain't letting up none to speak of,' and another would agree. Or one would go to a window to try to peer out, his own black shadow blotting out the reflection of the lamp flames and the faint, silvery glint the water made streaming down the pane.

By ten o'clock the rain had stopped. All the men went out to the shed to get their horses. Most of them started directly off, the hoofs of their horses making a slow, plopping sound in the mud. But one of them asked Mr. Munn to hold his horse while he went back inside to put the fire out and close up the schoolhouse. The others who had lingered said good night and rode away. Through the window Mr. Munn could see the man moving before the stove. He saw him bend over one of the lamps and blow it out. Then the man approached the other lamp and bent over it, his face sharp and intent as though in prayer. Suddenly the light was out, and the window blank blackness, blacker than the night.

The man locked the door and came to take the reins from Mr. Munn's hand. He mounted his horse, then drew alongside Mr. Munn. He thrust out his hand, which Mr. Munn took. He could not make out the man's face.

'I'm glad you come,' the man told him, 'and hit wet and all.'

'Thanks,' Mr. Munn said, 'and good night.'

'Good night,' the man replied, and turned away.

As Mr. Munn rode through the darkness, the constant undertone of the swollen creek filled his consciousness. His eyes were more accustomed to the darkness now, or the overcast of cloud was becoming lighter, for he could make out the line of the road ahead of him for a little way between the tall growths that bordered it. Then, for a while, he could not hear the rushing water any more. The road, he decided, must bend some distance from the creek here. He thought of the men, by this time asleep, alone or with their wives; the walls and roofs of their houses would conceal them and protect them. But the awareness of the fact of their comfort and his own wakeful isolation gave him no envy. Nor did the apparent failure of his effort that night disturb him now. It had gone black out for him, as suddenly and as irrelevantly as the man's face above the lamp the instant the flame was extinguished. He might feel differently tomorrow, as he had felt differently in the past. At what moment could a man trust his feelings, his convictions? At what point define the true and unmoved center of his being, the focus of his obligations? He could not say. And who could say? But for the present the comfort of the night and isolation wrapped him like a blanket.

During the fall the meetings of the board occurred often. And always they were characterized by a half-suppressed spirit of jubilation, of triumph, even when the most serious issues rose for discussion. Captain Todd alone seemed to guard himself from the prevailing temper, sitting quietly with his grave smile, his fingers drumming soundlessly on the green baize of the table, while the excitement moved around him. It infected the Senator, so that his gestures became abrupt and his eyes gleamed unnaturally; and Mr. Christian, sometimes in the middle of a discussion, would rise and tramp the floor with his heavy, booted stride, and wave his arms, and exclaim, 'By God, we got 'em!' And the other men, each in his way, exhibited the same excitement and the same confidence. Mr. Munn could feel it the moment he entered their presence. He wondered once or twice how Captain Todd managed to hold himself aloof from it when it charged the very atmosphere of the dingy room above the bank where they met. Once Mr. Christian, stopping in the middle of his stride with a sentence unfinished and his arm halted in mid-air, turned suddenly on the Captain as though he had just discovered a rebuke in the older man's detachment, and inquired, 'By God, Captain, don't you ever get heated up over anything?'

'I reckon I've been known to,' the Captain said. 'Once or twice.'

'Not by me,' Mr. Christian asserted.

The Captain shook his head a little, smiling. 'We thought we had the Yankees licked in 'sixty-two,' he remarked, 'but it didn't seem to turn out that way. You better take it easy, Bill.'

'This'll be different,' Mr. Christian affirmed. 'We got 'em by the short hairs!'

'Bill,' the Captain said soberly, 'just because they're paying three dollars a hundred more'n they paid last year, it don't mean a thing.'

'They just paid me four dollars and a half a hundred for prime leaf last year' — and Mr. Christian took two plunging strides — 'the bastards!'

'Whatever they pay more'n that now, they're just paying to bust the Association. They figure they're putting that money in the bank, Bill.' The Captain took out his pipe, tamped it, and with an excess of care lighted it. 'Every good price they pay outside the Association they figure will make somebody inside dissatisfied, wondering if maybe he hadn't better be outside grabbing his while the grabbing is good.'

Mr. Christian stood stock-still in the middle of the floor with his thick arms crooked and his hands almost together before his chest, the fingers spread and curved as though grasping an invisible object. 'Just let me get my hands on any two-timing bastard that sells one leaf outside after he's signed,' he said slowly and distinctly, his lips drawing back a little to show the strong, yellow teeth, 'and I'll——' He jerked his hands apart with a quick, twisting motion.

'Take it easy, Bill,' the Captain remarked. 'It's just human nature some of 'em will try to crawl out and sell when they figure the time comes. We've got to expect that. It's in the cards. It's always in the cards, Bill. The Lord Jesus picked out what he figured was twelve good men, you know, and one of 'em sold him out.'

'Just let——' Mr. Christian muttered.

'Why, Bill, the Lord Jesus was a pretty good picker. He just got stung on one out of a round dozen. The only wonder is, somebody didn't beat Judas to it and give a cut price.'

Mr. Christian sat down at the table. His fingers, with their flat, thick nails, began to twist the edge of the black felt hat that lay on the table before him. He was silent and morose for the rest of the afternoon.

At some time or other during the course of almost every meeting of the board, Mr. Munn himself would feel the general confidence and excitement taking hold of him. That feeling made everything seem so easy, every difficulty so superficial, the future so clear. It was like the sustaining and transforming warmth of liquor in a man's stomach. Not even the example of Captain Todd, whom Mr. Munn admired, or his own habit of holding an idea suspended in his mind, turning it and considering it, could readily temper that feeling when it seized him. He would study Captain Todd's face, motionless or smiling behind the clipped gray beard, and wonder about his calmness, what appeared to be his deep, inner certainty of self, his caution and detachment and tolerance in regard to the world outside himself. He was getting old, perhaps. He must be getting on to seventy. But his attitude seemed something different from the tiredness and skepticism of age. Perhaps you could only get to be like Captain Todd if you lived through some firm conviction, some enveloping confidence, some time in your life; that is, if you were stout enough to come out on the other side of it afterward and still be yourself. Mr. Munn remembered that somebody sometime had told him how Captain Todd once down in South Tennessee held a ford on a frozen creek all night and half a day with just forty or fifty men against a couple of companies of Yankee cavalry. That must have been in the last winter of the war when Hood was trying to get what was left of his army out of Tennessee. Anybody ought to have seen then that everything was folding up, going to pieces. But Captain Todd and his men had lain out there in the brush and rocks all night, waiting for the next rush at the ford; and all the next morning, too, when it got light enough to see how many there were on the other side and how many more were coming up. Once or twice Mr. Munn wondered about those other men with Captain Todd, those who weren't killed at the ford or later, and who lived on — had they, when they got old, grown to be like Captain Todd, too? Or had they, that night at the ford, been sustained, not by a conviction and confidence truly their own, but merely by partaking for the time, communally, from the rich and fundamental store owned by somebody else? By Captain Todd?

But now Captain Todd sat among the other men, aware, it seemed, of a ripe, secret security that he could count on, out of the swirl and reach of the general excitement, supported by a confidence different from the confidence in events and circumstances that would be subject to change and accident and the casual appetites and weaknesses of people. He was like a great gray boulder, still unsubmerged, in the course of some violent, flooded stream. You knew that when the flood season was past and the waters had lost their turbulence and had shrunk back into their normal and modest bed, the boulder would be there still, still itself and solid as ever. Captain Todd could be confident because he had no confidence in things and events; he knew things and events were blind. Blind as a bat.

Mr. Munn felt that he knew that much about the old man, but knowing it did him no good. He would be caught up and drawn, in the very face of Captain Todd's example, into the same current that gripped the other men about him. And at the same time he would know that, for himself at least, there was something unreal about those meetings in the long, dingy room above the bank, about the dry voice of Mr. Sills going on and on with his figures and reports, and about the exclamations and the vehement, booted tread of Mr. Christian. Mr. Sills found those figures real and final, and trusted them. Mr. Christian trusted that deep and prodigal surge of energy within himself. But the events that took place in that room did not afford Mr. Munn the true sense of reality. Rather, at moments he found it during those meetings in front of the country stores or in the spaces before the white, weatherboarded churches at the crossroads; or when some man, picking up the pen, said, 'Well, I reckon I'll do it'; or, even, that night when the rain beat on the roof of the schoolhouse at Rose Creek and he looked into the faces of the men, or when, afterwards, he rode alone through the darkness, within earshot of the sounding, swollen creek. Those times were more real to him, and even though they spoke to him in vague, untranslatable, and perhaps contradictory voices, he felt that sometime he might be able to define the truth that certainly they were proclaiming.

And so, while the fall passed and winter came on, he lived, it sometimes seemed to him, as though poised on the brink of revelation. He did not know what was to happen, what the impending revelation might be that made him wake with that expectation. Sometimes, on waking, it sharpened his farmer's sense of the weather, so that he would jump out of bed and, still in his nightshirt, hurry to the window to scan the sky. Then, when he had discovered what the sky promised, bad or good, he would feel a little puzzled, wondering why he had been so concerned; for the weather of that day, or of any day, had no bearing on the expectation that had prompted him to leap up.

Though the expectation never came to focus now, as in the mornings of his childhood when he would remember, suddenly, that it was Saturday or Christmas, it filled him, even during the absorbing activities of the day, with an energy that drove him through the execution of his duties, as though every small obligation fulfilled would bring him that much nearer to the unnamed object of his excitement. And the energy seemed boundless. Even when, sitting with May at home at night, he would lean back in the chair and be silent, it was not because he was tired. He was never tired now. His nerves would be alive, and if he was silent, it was because his mind was, at those moments, like an eye unseeing but straining forward into the dark.

'You look tired, Perse,' his wife would say.

'I'm not tired.'

'Perse, I wish you wouldn't work so hard,' she would urge him. 'You're wearing yourself out.'

'No,' he would answer shortly, but in a tone more patient than irritated.

'I wish you wouldn't, Perse; you look tired.'

'No, May.'

'Other men don't work that hard,' she would insist.

'It'll be over soon.'

She might come to sit in his lap then, and lean her head against his shoulder. He would put his arm around her waist and spread his fingers on her small, rounded hip, his thumb aware of the upper edge of her hip bone beneath the flesh, the bone in its fragility like a valuable bowl, or cup, wrapped to prevent damage.

'Soon?' she would ask.

'Yes.'

'I never see you much, any more,' she would say. 'You're so busy, you're away so much, Perse.'

'I have to be away, honey,' he would reply. Several times he tried to tell her precisely how he felt, carefully choosing some incident that had seemed to speak to him. 'Up at the meeting at New Sharon Church,' he would say, 'there was an old man. I didn't notice him much at first, because he sort of hung around the back of the crowd. It wasn't a very big crowd, just about forty-five or fifty people, including the women there too. He didn't look much different from other people, I reckon, but I got to noticing him ——'

'Yes,' she would put in, the question in her voice.

'He was a sort of broken-down-looking old man, you might say. About sixty, maybe. I got to noticing him while the meet-

ing went on. He had a wen — I reckon you would call it a
wen — or something like that, on his left temple. About the
size of a quarter, and purple-colored. He looked something like
old Mr. Murdock — you know old Mr. Murdock, Bill Casady's
father-in-law? Used to crop over on the Tyler place.'

'I don't believe I remember him,' and she would peer into
the fire as though she were trying to stir her memory.

'Well, anyway, that isn't the point. He looked something
like old Mr. Murdock, though, except for the wen. He had on
overalls and an old black coat and a straw hat. I kept noticing
him back in the crowd. After I got through talking, I called for
people to sign up with the Association. Nobody came. Then I
said I would like to answer any questions they had about how
the Association worked, and then maybe they could see their
way clear to signing up. Nobody said a word, and nobody
budged. Then that old man started coming up toward the
front.' Then, telling that incident or another, he would be
aware that the story was going to pieces in his hands. He had
thought that, if he could tell her the story exactly as it happened,
the meaning would become clear too, and the way he felt.

He would finish somewhat lamely, apologetically: 'Well, he
signed up. After he signed up, three other men signed, too.'

'That makes four who signed that time,' then May had said
ruminatively and politely.

'Every little bit helps,' he replied, suddenly irritated with
his insufficiency. He did not even try to finish the story the
way it had happened, although the scene was sharp in his mind.
The old man had walked through the crowd, apparently
oblivious of the other people. He might have been walking
through an open field. He had said, 'Boy, if you'll please
gimme that pen-staff, I'll sign my name.' But before he signed
he looked up at Mr. Munn, and added: 'I got me a little piece
of ground, nigh onto thirty years back. All that time ain't no
man said me yea nor nay, nor go nor come. I'm gonna put my

name down now, boy, and if you say yea, it's yea, and nay, it's nay. What little crop I got don't amount to nothing. My crop ain't a pea in the dish. But I aim to sign.'

After signing, he had looked up, still holding the pen-staff. 'Hit ain't wrote very fair,' he had said.

At the moment of its occurrence that event, which now was nothing, which now stuck in his throat when he tried to put it into words, had possessed tremendous importance. It had seemed as if that moment was a point of vantage from which he could survey other moments in their true perspective and worth, moments of the past and, perhaps, moments of the future. Perhaps it still was, but, sitting before the fire with the slight and pleasant weight of May on his lap and his hand laid protectively upon her hip, he shook his head with a sudden motion of confusion.

He had failed again in his attempt to explain himself to May, and to himself. The explanation, the thing that made him wake up suddenly in the morning as at the sound of a voice, the imminence of revelation — these things were real to him, certainly, but elusive. He was aware of them as of something seen out of the corner of the eye; when he turned his gaze directly, it was gone. But the expectation, even though it defied his definitions, colored everything, even his love for May. That love had been, for more than a year, a thing in itself, set off from other things by its fullness and completeness and poise. Now that could scarcely be said with truth any longer, for the love seemed now not an end and a reward, but a beginning and, however enchanting and happy, a task, not a whole but a part of a whole which he could not see, not a poise but a motion, blind though sweet, toward some unforetellable target. It was not the answer, as it had once seemed, but the question. Holding May on his lap, as when he told her the story of the old man, he would close his eyes and bend to kiss her neck, burying his face in the curve of flesh where the neck joined the shoulder. Or he would seize her in his arms and press her to him so tightly that he could feel the resilience of her ribs giving, as though by this small cruelty he might extort the satisfaction and the supreme assurance not to be had merely by love.

'Don't, Perse,' she would then gasp out; 'don't, not that way!'

He would not relieve the pressure in the slightest degree, a small germ of hardness sprouting in his mind, so that her words seemed addressed to someone else, not meant for him, impersonally overheard. Then, when she would again say, breathlessly, 'Don't, Perse,' he would slacken his hold, feeling as he did so almost a hint of disappointment behind the fact of his pleasure in her. 'I love you so much,' he would say.

'I love you, Perse,' she would answer.

Or standing with her before the fire at night, or in the yard under the unleafing trees on a Sunday afternoon, he might suddenly grasp her with her shoulders between his two hands and hold her out from him, staring into her eyes, and shake her a little, as one shakes a sullen child to make it speak and tell the truth. But there was nothing for her to tell. He did not even know what he wanted to hear her say. What she actually would say was, 'I love you, Perse.' That was enough, and not enough.

But the same expectation of discovery and fulfillment that came on waking, or forced him to try to tell May some incident or to grasp her shoulders between his hands, made him sometimes stop for a split instant, unconscious of himself, and scrutinize the face of someone with whom he was talking. They said the same things now as they, or other people, had said before in this very same office. They were in trouble. They had quarreled with somebody else over money or land or cattle. They could no longer live with their wives or husbands. They expected death and wanted to make their wills. Listening all the while with professional care to their words, he watched their faces and was aware of something behind the words and faces, something that was unnamed for all their talk.

When, back in the middle of the summer, he had seen Bunk Trevelyan's wife for the first time, he had not noticed her at all as an individual and could not have said whether her face was sadder than another. Sitting in his office, her small, dry-clay-colored fingers clasped together with a painful stillness on the lap of her faded and sun-streaked blue crêpe-de-Chine dress, she had been like other women who had sat there, dressed in their good clothes for the occasion, and told him their troubles in just such a dead, monotonous, and impersonal voice. She had sat there with the look and the manner of all those other wives of croppers and poor farmers; having at that time no meaning except in so far as she had the meaning of those other women, no one of whom had meaning except that meaningless meaning of resemblance to all the others. She was, she had said in that flat, impersonal voice, the wife of Harris Trevelyan; maybe he knew Harris Trevelyan, he had a little place out the Murray Mill road.

'I don't believe I do,' Mr. Munn had said.

'He goes by the name of Bunk a right smart,' she had continued. 'But that ain't his right and given name. Folks just call him that and there ain't no sayen why. But I call him Harris. Which is his right name.'

'I don't reckon I know him by that name.'

'He's a right tall man, taller'n most,' she had said with a flicker of pride in her voice. 'He's got red hair.'

'I think I know him,' Mr. Munn had said, and nodded as though on sudden recollection, not having ever laid eyes, as far as he knew, on the man who was named Harris or Bunk Trevelyan.

'I reckoned you might know him,' she had rejoined. Then, in that flat voice, almost with the tone of an afterthought, as though the real business of her call were already settled, she had remarked, 'They got him in jail.'

'In jail,' Mr. Munn had repeated, not because of surprise but because of absent-mindedness, all the while wishing that the woman would leave so he could go out home and get out of the heat and sit on his porch with May.

'They come and got him this morning.'

'What did they arrest him for?'

'He never done it,' she had said.

'Done what?'

'Killed him.' She must have seen the question in Mr. Munn's eyes, for she had added, with the tone of apology and explanation: 'Old Tad Duffy. They found him layen dead on the big road. He was a mean man, but Harris never killed him.'

'I read about that part in the paper,' Mr. Munn had said.

'He never done it,' the woman had insisted, her small, clay-colored fingers beginning to move aimlessly over the lap of the faded blue crêpe-de-Chine dress.

'Tell me all about it,' he had commanded her, 'from the beginning.'

That had been in early August. The office had been hot, and outside the sun had filled the street with a white incandescence. The heavy awning over the office window, with that glare beyond it, had seemed to be no more than dirty tissue paper. Mr. Munn had known that he would not get out soon to the coolness of his house. He would stay here listening to this woman, who sat very straight on the edge of her chair, a miserable straw hat with a ribbon on it stuck askew on her head, red dust streaking the hem of her blue dress, and who talked to him in that dry and distant voice.

Bunk Trevelyan, his wife said, had quarreled with the man named Tad Duffy about a spring. Water was getting low in the well on the place Trevelyan had and they were using the spring to get drinking water from. The branch on the place was about dried up and they had to get water there at the spring, too, for the stock, because they couldn't let the stock tramp in the spring if it was going to be fit for people to drink out of. Bunk Trevelyan found out Duffy was getting water from the spring, when the spring was on Trevelyan's side. He told Duffy to stay away from the spring, but two days later he caught him there again putting water in a barrel set up in a wagon. The wagon was on Duffy's side of the line, and Duffy had a negro boy helping him carry water to fill the barrel. When Trevelyan saw Duffy filling the barrel, he was so mad he didn't say a word, he told his wife later, but ran to the house to get his rifle. When she saw him get the rifle and start running toward the spring, she followed him so as to stop him, she said, in case there was any trouble. By the time Trevelyan got to the spring, Duffy was in the wagon driving off. Trevelyan pointed his rifle all right — she said she couldn't deny that — and the boy was telling the truth when he told the sheriff that, and she grabbed his arm and made him put the rifle down, but what he said was that he was going to fill that barrel so full of holes you could see daylight through it and that he was going to scare Duffy. He didn't really shoot. And he never was going to shoot Duffy.

'Exactly what did he say when he had the rifle?' Mr. Munn asked.

'He said he was going to fill that barrel so full of holes you could see daylight through it and he was going to scare Duffy.'

'Do you remember the exact words he used, exactly what he said about Duffy?'

She looked at him expressionlessly, her tongue-tip coming out to wet her gray lips.

'Don't you remember?' he demanded a little sharply.

'He said,' she began tonelessly, and wet her lips again, 'he said he was going to scare that son-of-a-bitch so bad he ——' Her voice trailed off.

'Yes?'

She stared at him pleadingly, the blood darkening the yellow-ish cast of her face. She shook her head. 'I can't say it,' she said.

'Is it because he used strong language?' Mr. Munn asked.

'It was right strong, you might say,' she answered.

'That's the reason you don't want to tell me,' he demanded, 'not because he said something you don't want me to know, something incriminating?'

'That's the reason,' she admitted, and wet her lips. 'It was strong language. I can't say it myself. Not in front of nobody.'

'Well, tell me the rest,' he ordered. At that moment he had begun to feel, for some reason, that Bunk Trevelyan was inno-cent.

She told him how her husband went to town in his wagon the day Duffy was killed. When he got back from town she was out hilling up some hills for some late squash. When he got home he got his hoe and came on out to the field with her. The next day somebody told them old Tad Duffy was killed. He was stabbed and left by the road in some buckberry bushes. That was all they knew till the sheriff and two men came out and got Trevel-yan out of the lot where he was milking and took him to jail.

'I'm going down to the jail and talk to him,' Mr. Munn said. 'You better wait here till I get back. I won't be gone very long.' He went down the stairs, knowing that when he got back to his office Bunk Trevelyan's wife would still be sitting, very erect, on the edge of her chair with her hands clasped in painful mo-tionlessness on her lap. But at that time she had been in no true sense real to him. It was not until he saw her in her own house, the day when he went out there to ask her again about the quarrel before Tad Duffy was killed, that he understood her to be complete and individual, the center of a world as real and important as the world he knew concentric to himself. They stood in the two-room shack, the objects of her life around them — the split-bottom chairs, the pine table with the well-scrubbed top, the dresser with the cracked mirror, the stove, the wooden bed — and all those objects insinuated upon him, as with persistent whispers, the new knowledge about her. Because of the scrubbed pine top of the table, the small, dry, cracked hands themselves became in their motionlessness eloquent and, as it were, beckoned him on to a fuller penetration and knowledge. And the rickety bed, covered by the patchwork quilt with colors faded and washed dim, implied to him the secret integrity and purity of her passion — in any case, it must have been that way once, for instance, when Trevelyan brought her here for the first time. He recalled the inflection of pride with which, that day in his office, she had said her husband was taller than most. She set him off from other men. With irritation, the irritation of one who does not want to be disturbed, he suddenly knew how now at night, her skinny body wrapped in the flannel nightgown, she would stir in her dog-tired sleep and thrust out an arm emptily across the lumpy mattress to the place where Trevelyan wasn't now.

'Mrs. Trevelyan,' he said, interrupting her as she told him how the new knife and the other things had been stolen from the kitchen that day after her husband got home and came out to the field, 'Mrs. Trevelyan, do you have any children?'

'No, sir,' she answered, giving him a look of surprise, adjusting herself to the new question after what she had been saying. 'No, sir, but I had two. They're dead.'

'When did they die?'

'Last summer a year ago,' she replied. 'It was the bloody flux.'

'I'm sorry,' Mr. Munn said.

Late that afternoon, when he was back out home taking a walk with May along the edge of a field where the tobacco had been cut, he thought of Bunk Trevelyan's wife again. He wondered what that world she lived in was really like, what she herself was really like. But it was complete and individual and important, as much so as the one of his own or the world of May. He had an overpowering curiosity to know what it was like, to know what she was like. But how was it possible, he thought, when he could not even know about May, and could only guess? May was a small woman with a mass of blonde hair that seemed too heavy for her, as though she carried it courageously, with an effort. She had a gentle way of speaking, and when she was pleased her glance would brighten startlingly. In the spring she always seemed to be interested in gardening and would put seeds in the ground and would exclaim at the first tender shoots, but by the time the warm weather had settled in earnest, she forgot the garden, and the weeds might take it for all she noticed; in the fall she would stand for hours alone in the withered side garden, or walk about, wrapped in a sober, sweet meditation. She loved him, and at night she fell asleep with her head on his arm. And he loved her. Those things, and perhaps a thousand things like them, were what he knew about May. But they were not May. And if he could not penetrate to her world, and could only guess, what could he know about Bunk Trevelyan's wife, whom he had seen only two or three times and whom he had never even touched with a finger?

He reached to take May by the hand. She slipped her arm through the crook of his and walked close beside him.

The tobacco had only recently been cut. The reddish field, marked accurately into the distance by the stobs of stalk where the plants had been, looked peculiarly bare, peculiarly at peace, under the rays of the last, long, level light. On the slight rise of ground at the far end of the field where the barn was, a wagon had been abandoned. It seemed to belong to the field, part of the impression of fulfillment and repose. 'It's a good crop,' he said, as they walked up the lift of ground toward the barn.

She did not answer, but pressed his arm in acknowledgment of the fact that he had spoken.

'We might even get a decent price, too,' he went on, 'for a
change. When I think that last year the best I got was four dollars and a half a hundred, and for prime leaf, I get so mad I
wonder we stood it as long as we did. That damned buyer for
the Alta Company, coming to my own barn door, this one right
here in this field' — and he pointed to the barn, where strands
of blue smoke stood out from the eaves and thinned upward —
'and saying to me, "Mr. Munn, we can give you four-seventy-
five for your prime leaf and three for seconds," and then telling
me when I said no: "Mr. Munn, your place falls in my territory
for buying and you won't get an offer from anybody else; for
your own convenience I'm telling you this so you can take my
price and save yourself trouble, because when I come back again
it's likely the price won't be so good, the price is falling so sharp
the last few days." I told him ——'

May patted his arm and said: 'I know, Perse. Don't get
wrought up about it, it was last year ——'

He gently disengaged his arm from hers, and approached the
door of the barn. 'I just want to take a look,' he said. 'Do you
want to?'

'All right,' she replied.

Inside the barn it was almost dark except for the unwinking
redness of the logs that smouldered on the dirt floor. He stared
into the upper obscurity of the barn where the tobacco plants
hung in solid tier on tier. Scarcely visible in the pall of smoke
that sluggishly shifted in the upper reaches, the inverted plants
looked like great bats sleeping in their clusters.

'It's not cured enough to be very risky yet,' he said.

He continued to stare upward at the suspended leaves. May
came to stand beside him, putting her hand on his arm. 'It's
not just getting more for your tobacco,' he said, 'even if we
haven't had an honest price in five years. It's a little more than
that' — he hesitated a little — 'at least, it might be.'

A great flake of ash scaled off one of the logs, releasing a new

puff of smoke and revealing, beneath, the steady brilliant redness of the heart of the burning wood.

'It's hot,' May complained. 'I feel a little faint.'

'Let's go,' he said.

Before he got to the house he remembered that he had told
the Trevelyan woman he would send some negroes out to cut
her patch of tobacco and get the firing started. It had been
standing too long already.

Chapter three

In the end Mr. Munn was certain that Bunk Trevelyan was telling the truth. 'Shore, I put a gun on him,' Bunk Trevelyan said, sitting on the edge of his cot in the jail, humped forward with his great red hands hanging from off his knees. On his hands the coarse, red hairs looked pale against the redness of the skin. 'But that don't mean to say I stobbed the bastud. I never aimed to shoot him, even. I aimed to fill that-air barr'l so full of holes you could see daylight through hit. And I aimed to scare the bastud so he'd wet his pants leg. And I might a-done hit, too, if'n my wife didn't grab holt of my arm that-a-way. Any man might a-done hit, finden the bastud down tote-en water off yore place and hit a drout and yore well nigh dry. When I seen him tote-en water outer my spring toward that-air barr'l, I didn't say nuthen. I didn't open my mouth. I just come to the house and grabbed my rifle and tore out toward the spring. When I come to the turn in the path whar that big old sweet-gum is and seen him whippen up that old mule of his'n and my water a-sloshen outer his barr'l, I just up and put a bead on that-air barr'l. Any man might a-done sich. But I didn't pull no trigger, even. My wife grabbed holt of my arm. What I done wasn't no crime, and if'n that durn nigger boy didn't go blabben off his durn mouth about what he seen to some other nigger and that nigger didn't go blabben off his mouth to somebody else, I wouldn't be here now. Let me git that nigger, I'll frail him. But Duffy. Shore I put a gun on him, and shore I'm glad the bastud's dead and don't keer who knows hit, but that don't go to say I kilt him. Now does hit?'

'No,' Mr. Munn admitted, 'it doesn't. Not before the law.'
'Naw, hit don't.'

He was sure that Bunk Trevelyan was innocent. If he had intended to kill Tad Duffy he would have done it that day at the
spring. If he had planned, later, to kill Duffy in cold blood, he
would have planned it differently. Not on the road in the middle of the afternoon, with no cover. He would have found Duffy
in the path through the woodlot some evening or down in the
canebrake by the river. Mr. Munn looked at the big man lolling
somnolently on the cot, and for the instant could almost see him
leaning against a tree-trunk in the woods in the gathering dusk,
with a knife appearing small and inconsequential in his great
hand; or crouching in the cane by the path, and suddenly rising
to seize the wrist of the passing man and swing him around
while the knife fell and fell.

He shook his head abruptly. No, that was not the way Bunk
Trevelyan would do it. Not planned and calculated like that,
but all at once in the blaze of fury, not in the woods or in the
canebrake after waiting. He studied the man's face, full-
fleshed, but the flesh not concealing the long, heavy structure of
the bone; and the blood seemed just below the surface of the
sunburned, too-thin skin that was tight over the strong flesh.
Against the redness of the flesh the red, unkempt, sun-streaked
hair, like the hairs on his hands, looked pale. No, Bunk Trevelyan would do it all in a moment, with the sudden leap, or the
rage-blind squeeze of the trigger. He would have done it, if at
all, at the spring.

This conviction was so firm in him that it was scarcely shaken
even when, in the early afternoon of the second day of the trial,
Mr. Little was called to the stand and testified about the knife.
Mr. Little testified that in his hardware store, early in the afternoon of August second, 1904, he sold a butcher knife to the
defendant. He recollected it just as it was without any question,
he said, because the knife he sold to the defendant was the first

knife in a new order that had just come in the day before. He knew that that was the exact day because he had the record in his store of the day the box came in, and he had checked up by the express company, too, before he ever opened his mouth to anybody about it, because, he said, he never was a man to open his mouth about something he couldn't back up. It was a gross of knives, bought from the Dewey Jobbing Company in Nashville, and the stock number of the knives was M-120073. This was how he remembered it so good. The defendant had asked to look at some butcher knives, but he said he didn't like any of the knives he saw and did Mr. Little have any other kind. The defendant said he didn't want any of those tin knives, which, Mr. Little said, was just a way of talking because all the knives were good grade and most were *A-number-1* grade steel. They were all good merchandise. What the defendant said he wanted was a good heavy knife without too long a blade nor too curved, something his wife could use round the kitchen and he could use when hog-killing time came in.

When Mr. Little said 'hog-killing time,' somebody snickered in the courtroom and the judge rapped with his gavel. 'When hog-killing time came in,' Mr. Little repeated with an air of impersonal dignity, and proceeded. The new knives would be just what the defendant wanted, he had told the defendant. Then he went back and opened up the new box and got one out. It would do all right, the defendant said. He took it and paid for it and said, 'Much obliged,' and went on out.

'Could you identify the type of knife which you sold to the defendant?' the prosecuting attorney asked Mr. Little.

Mr. Little said that he would be able to do so. The blade was shorter than ordinary, he said, and a little thicker on the blunt edge, and the brass brads in the handle weren't round, they were square, and they weren't set in a straight line. And the trade-mark was on the blade up near the handle. It read 'Maiden Steel.'

The prosecuting attorney unwrapped a newspaper-covered parcel and held up a knife. 'Was it a knife like this?' he demanded.

Mr. Little examined the knife, and said that it was the same kind.

All the while Mr. Little was giving his testimony, Mr. Munn was covertly watching Bunk Trevelyan. Trevelyan was leaning back in his chair, his size filling it. Part of the time he seemed to be giving attention to what the witness was saying, but only with a kind of strained and uninterested politeness; then his glance would stray to one of the high windows beyond which, against the chilly-looking, impersonal blueness of the sky, the tips of black boughs were visible, bare except for a few rags of leaves. He did not seem disturbed or surprised at the testimony about the knife; he did not even seem interested. Without looking at the jury Mr. Munn could feel the tension there. This was the moment that was bringing the trial to focus for them. There was almost always such a moment, when the men in the jury box would lean forward a little bit, and you just about knew whether you had won or lost.

This was the time, he was almost sure, hopelessly; and was surer when, immediately after Mr. Little got down, the coroner, Doctor Abel, was put on the stand again and, holding the bright, clean knife in his hand and turning it slowly over and over, said that the four stab wounds in the back of the deceased could have been made by this kind of knife. They were wide enough and deep enough, he said, for the first wound entered the back just below the twelfth rib and penetrated the inner half of the right kidney of the deceased, opening the renal artery. 'That's the one,' he said, assuming an air of authority, 'that must have been made first.' And he reached to his own back, clumsily, for he was a fat man, to indicate the point of entry. 'Just like I said,' he added; then continued, 'and that second wound between the eleventh and twelfth ribs, that one was clean in to the liver and penetrated the portal vein, yes, sir. And the one up in the lung — the one that must have been made last, like I said, when the man was sinking down — up between the third and fourth ribs about the middle between the fourth dorsal vertebra and ——' The voice went on and on, but Mr. Munn was not listening.

The coroner was the last witness for the prosecution. While he spoke, Bunk Trevelyan was looking out the window, at the clear sky. When the judge granted Mr. Munn's motion for a postponement until the next morning, Mr. Munn, without a word to his client, walked out of the courtroom, and down the stairs to the dingy main hall of the courthouse and out into the sunlight. He leaned against a tree on one side of the courthouse yard, lighting his pipe and staring down at the faded grass of the late season. The pleasure of the first flavor of the tobacco after the abstinence of the afternoon filled him, and then was forgotten. People who had been at the trial began to cross the yard in scattered groups.

A man stopped in front of him and said, 'Well, Perse, it looks kinda like they might get your boy this time.'

Regarding the man, Mr. Munn puffed the smoke idly from his lips before he spoke. 'Maybe not,' he rejoined, and shook his head.

'It looks like it.'

'Maybe not,' Mr. Munn repeated. 'You can't ever tell.' Meanwhile he was watching the open yard behind the courthouse.

'So long, Perse,' the man said.

'So long,' Mr. Munn replied, and started toward the rear of the courthouse. He had seen Bunk Trevelyan being led across the yard, his red, uncovered, shaggy head well above the heads of the two deputies who escorted him. He followed at a little distance, making no effort to catch up. They were taking Trevelyan back to his cage until tomorrow.

He stood outside the door of the jail until the deputies came back. 'Hello,' he said to them, and nodded.

'You want to see your boy, Mr. Munn?' one of them asked.

'Is anybody back there to let me in?'

'Old man Dickey,' the first deputy answered. Then he spat a stream of tobacco juice into the dust by the curbstone, and with a mild wonderment shook his head. 'Yore boy, now,' he uttered, 'he ain't turned a hair. Just don't look like he gives a damn. Don't look like nothing'll faze him.'

'I reckon a piece of rope'll faze him,' the second deputy said, grinning.

Mr. Munn looked into the face of the second deputy, seeing, as for the first time, the face of this man whom he had met around the town for years: the small, bloodshot eyes set deep in the puckered, pouched, bluish flesh, the heavy, pocked nose, the lips grinning with a malicious and insinuating brotherliness back over the yellow teeth through which the stinking breath secretly hissed. He continued to look, thinking, No, I never really saw this face before.

The man stopped grinning, the grin fading under Mr. Munn's scrutiny.

Mr. Munn slowly turned to the first deputy.

'I didn't mean nothing,' the second deputy was saying.

Mr. Munn ignored him, saying to the other, 'So long.' Abruptly he stepped into the hall of the jail, where it was shadowy and cool. He stood there for a moment, before pushing open the little door that led back into the corridor and calling for Mr. Dickey.

Bunk Trevelyan was lolling on his cot as on that first day, detachedly, but with an appearance of swiftness and great competence despite the indolent posture. Standing in the little space by the cot, Mr. Munn looked down at him, and said, 'Trevelyan, you lied to me.'

'Ain't nobody ever said that to me,' Trevelyan remarked impersonally, then adding, as by way of careful explanation, 'I ain't never let no man.'

'I'm saying it,' Mr. Munn retorted.

'What I told you was the truth.'

'You didn't tell me about that knife.'

'Naw, I reckon I did'n, come to think about it,' Trevelyan said meditatively, 'but what I did tell you was true, all right.'

Mr. Munn took a step closer to the cot and stood directly over the bulk of the man sprawled there. 'Trevelyan, I took this case because I thought you didn't kill Duffy. That's the only reason I took it. Now you sit up here and tell me the truth about that knife. Every damned word of it.'

Trevelyan squinted up at the face of the man above him, as though he were squinting against too much light. Then he rolled over to his side and heaved himself up to lean against the stone wall behind the cot.

'Now, tell me,' Mr. Munn ordered.

'Shore,' Trevelyan said, 'shore, I bought that-air knife. Lak he said. But that don't prove I killed Duffy, the bastud.'

'What became of it?'

'I taken hit on home and put hit on the kitchen table.'

'Is it out to your place now?'

'Naw, I can't say as hit is. Hit was stole.'

'Stolen?'

'That's right,' Trevelyan replied. 'Hit was stole off'n the kitchen table. That afternoon when I come home.'

'My God, man!' — and Mr. Munn stepped back from the cot — 'you mean I've got to stand up there and tell that jury somebody stole that knife that very afternoon?'

'Hit's the God's truth,' Trevelyan asserted, and shrugged his shoulders. 'I can't make hit no diff'rent.'

'All right,' Mr. Munn said. 'Go on.'

'I come home from town and I put that-air knife and a hunk of cheese I bought in town on the kitchen table. Lak I said.

Then I seen my wife wasn't round the house and I knowed she was out to the field hilling up some hills fer some late squash. So I taken me my hoe and went out thar, too. When we come back to the house that cheese and that-air knife was gone.'

'Is that all?' Mr. Munn demanded.

Squinting at him, cocking his head a little to one side, Trevelyan said: 'Naw, hit ain't all. But hit's nigh all.' He was studying Mr. Munn's face, squinting. 'I recollect I seen one of them niggers up thar prowlen nigh the road. One of them niggers lives over on Mr. May's place, or round thar. I seen him round, but I don't rightly know his name. I seen that cheese and that-air knife gone, and I was so mad I figgered I'd go and beat on me some nigger-meat. But my wife, she said, "Naw, Harris, naw, hit ain't nuthen." And I said, "God-a-mighty, nuthen, and money tight lak hit is." But I didn't go. I oughter gone,' he said meditatively. He spat, a tiny, hissing stream that flicked brightly on the stone. 'I oughter broke his black neck,' he declared.

'All right,' Mr. Munn said, 'but why didn't you tell me at first?'

Trevelyan spread his great red hands on his knees and appeared to be studying them. Then he looked up at Mr. Munn and answered: 'I ain't one to be crossen no crick a-fore I come to hit.'

'You should've told me at first,' Mr. Munn said, remembering the wife. 'You should've trusted me.'

'Mebbe,' Trevelyan replied.

When Mr. Munn asked what time he got home that afternoon, Trevelyan said he didn't know exactly, but it was the middle of the afternoon. Duffy's body was found just before dark, lying in the buckberry bushes. He had been dead some little time, but there had been plenty of time, Mr. Munn decided, for somebody to steal the knife off the table and meet Duffy on the road and kill him and rob him.

'You should have told me sooner,' Mr. Munn said, 'and I might have had a chance to do something, find the knife or something. Now I got till nine o'clock in the morning.' He stopped reflectively. 'You sure you don't know that nigger's name? The one you saw,' he demanded.

'Naw,' Trevelyan answered. 'But he's one of them lives on Mr. May's place. Or round thar. Them niggers over thar's all mixed up, kin and all.'

Mr. Munn turned to the door and called for Mr. Dickey to come and let him out. While Mr. Dickey fumbled with his keys, Mr. Munn stepped to the spot directly in front of Trevelyan, and said, 'I'll do what I can.' He put out his hand; and with a slightly bewildered expression, Trevelyan took it. 'So long,' Mr. Munn added, and went out.

He walked directly across the square, which was almost empty now, to the courthouse, and through the side door to the sheriff's office. The lanky, middle-aged man propped up against the desk there said, 'Hello, Perse. What can I do for you?' and gestured toward a chair.

'I want you to do me a favor, Mr. Sam.'

'Tell me about it,' the sheriff replied, and added, 'Why don't you take a chair? You make me tired looking at you.'

'No, thanks, I'll stand.'

'You'll wear yourself out, boy, before your span, standing up all your life.' The sheriff tilted his own chair farther back and began to finger his gray mustache. His silver-rimmed glasses, set loosely on his long nose, gave him an air of great benevolence.

'I want to borrow a couple of your deputies, Mr. Sam.'

'They ain't worth a God-damn,' the sheriff declared, 'but you can have 'em. You don't even have to bring 'em back.'

'I just want a couple. To help me at a little job.'

'What little job, Perse?'

'To be perfectly fair with you, Mr. Sam, I want them to go out and help me break the law. I'm a lawyer, and I know. I want them to help me shake down about twenty-five nigger cabins. I'm hunting something.'

'You can have Monroe and Carson,' the sheriff said.

'I don't want Carson,' Mr. Munn answered.

'What's the matter with Carson?'

'Nothing's the matter with Carson,' Mr. Munn replied. 'I met him a few minutes ago when he came out of the jail. He just makes me want to puke.'

The sheriff put his long yellow forefinger to the silver nose-bar of his spectacles and pushed them into place. 'Carson's all right,' he said deprecatorily. 'He does the best he can according to his lights.'

'He's a son-of-a-bitch,' Mr. Munn announced simply.

'All right, all right, Perse. I'll call up Burke, if I can get him. It's a moonlight night tonight and somebody might see you out with Carson. I don't blame you a mite. I never go out with the son-of-a-bitch myself in the light of the moon. Somebody might see me.' He cocked his chair back farther, reached up and twisted the crank on the telephone box, put the receiver to his ear, and called for a number. Waiting for a response, he looked up at Mr. Munn and said conversationally, 'Burke, now he's a son-of-a-bitch, too.'

'He's not Carson, anyway,' Mr. Munn replied.

Under the uneven light of the moon the three horsemen moved at a brisk trot down the road, the hoofs making a soft, muffled sound on the earth. Just beyond a little wooden bridge, at a bend on the road where the shadows of a clump of cedars made a dark patch on the pale-colored moonlit road, one of the horsemen drew rein and pointed into the underbrush beside the road. 'They found him along here,' he said.

'I know,' Mr. Munn answered.

'He was layen in them buckberry bushes. I come out here when they got him.'

'Do you know this section out here?' Mr. Munn demanded.

'Pretty good,' the man replied. 'I been all over it hunting birds. They's a passel of niggers lives round through here. They lives up and down a little road runs in this-here road 'bout a mile on out. Mr. Sutter, now, he's got 'bout six cabins on his place. And Mr. May, he's——'

'We'll start working down the road,' Mr. Munn said, and lifted his rein. He rode a little ahead of the other men, looking straight down the road, and not speaking again until they came to the place where the little side road joined the main one. 'Is this it?' Mr. Munn asked, and pointed down the little road, scarcely more than a lane, that was shortly lost from sight in the woods there.

'That's right,' the first deputy told him. 'They's a cabin in the far side of these-here woods. Old, yaller, wall-eyed nigger man lives there, used to live on the Burdett place. You remember, Burke'—and he turned to the other deputy—'that old, yaller, wall-eyed nigger's name?'

'It doesn't matter,' Mr. Munn said.

'Naw,' the first deputy agreed, 'it don't matter what he calls hisself. This ain't exactly what you might call a social visit.'

The almost bare boughs of the trees made a web-like pattern of shadow on the road. Overhead, the highest twigs seemed touched with a delicate, pale tinsel. The main trunks against the moonlight were of an inky and unreal blackness. 'I come out here once at night coon-hunting,' the deputy called Burke said. 'I wasn't much more'n a boy, I reckon, and I come out here with some fellers.'

The other men seemed to be paying him no attention, looking down the road.

'They was Ike Summer, I recollect, and George Hicks. I can't name the other fellers right off. I reckon some of 'em ain't round here no more.'

Distantly, off to the right, an owl hooted in the woods. Mr.

Munn looked in that direction, and then gave his attention again to the road.

'It was a long time back,' the deputy called Burke added, and fell silent.

The other deputy sniggered. 'You say you was coon-hunting?' he inquired.

'Yes,' Burke said. 'We come coon-hunting. We got two coons, I recollect.'

'Well' — and the other sniggered again — 'you might say as you're coon-hunting tonight, too.'

For a moment Burke, as though irritated or truculent, did not respond. Then he exclaimed, 'Huh, coon-hunting, that's good, huh!' And laughed. 'Well,' he added, his laughter over, 'I been doing this kind of coon-hunting all over hell for a long time now.'

Mr. Munn stretched out his arm toward a clearing by the road some sixty or seventy yards ahead. 'Is that the place?' he asked.

The first deputy said it was the place.

'You better hitch your horse, Mr. Monroe,' Mr. Munn directed, 'and go around to the back through the woods, in case anybody comes out that way. We'll go in the front.'

The deputy named Monroe swung off his horse and hitched it to a sapling by the road. The other men sat their horses quietly. Monroe moved off through the woods over the carpet of dry leaves, getting over the ground with a long, cautious stride that scarcely made a rustle.

'He sure doesn't make any noise,' Mr. Munn said.

The other man shook his head. 'Naw,' he rejoined, 'he's right light on his feet for a big man.'

They watched the man in the woods out of sight, and then could see him again when he crossed patches of open moonlight.

'We better get on,' Mr. Munn said, aware, as he spoke, of

breaking a compulsion that would draw his gaze up into the woods after that man who was treading so softly the dead leaves in the moonlit spaces and in the shadows.

He and the man named Burke stopped at the corner of the clearing and hitched their horses. They approached the cabin. In the bright light that flooded the little clearing, the separate logs of which the cabin was built, and even the individual, small roughnesses of the chinking, seemed, somehow, more clear and emphatic than in the full day. In that light the limestone chimney was licked bone-white.

The deputy knocked on the door.

A noise of stirring preceded the question, muffled by sleep and the walls, that came from someone within the cabin: 'Who's dare?'

'Open up,' the deputy said.

There was no answer. There was more stirring and a sound like low voices.

'We just want to ask you a question,' Mr. Munn called out.

The voice from within said, 'I'se come-en, boss.' Then the door swung open grudgingly and with a rasp of the hinges that seemed, suddenly, loud. A man stuck his head out, a negro man, Mr. Munn remembered with surprise, seeing how palish that face looked in the moonlight.

The deputy put his hand firmly against the door, and leaned forward with his shoulder against it, but almost casually. 'Open up,' he commanded, 'and, Uncle, maybe you better light a lamp.'

Mr. Munn followed the deputy through the door into the interior of the cabin, where the dark seemed, on the instant, close and inimical and suffocating, like a depth.

The match flared in the hand of the man and touched the wick of the lamp to a smoky flame. The man turned his gaze on Mr. Munn. His face, Mr. Munn now observed, was yellowish, and the eyeballs were yellow, too, and too large.

'Whut you want, boss?' he asked Mr. Munn.

'Well——' and Mr. Munn hesitated, and looked toward the deputy's impassive face. He felt like a coward, a sneak, when the rest of the sentence wouldn't come out and he looked toward the deputy; and he was sure the deputy, noticing his hesitation and his appealing glance, had put him down as a coward, too, or a fool.

'Well, Uncle,' the deputy said matter-of-factly, 'where do you do you all's cooking? You got a kitchen?'

Even as the deputy spoke, Mr. Munn was aware of the woman who lay huddled under the quilt in the bed just outside the direct rays of the lamp. He was aware of her because of her eyes, which in the shadow were glinting and dark and steady and not quite human, like the eyes of a nesting bird staring at the intruder from the interior shadow of a tree, or the eyes of a rabbit in its form.

'We cooks in the other room,' the negro man was saying; and the deputy stepped to the closed door and pushed it back with a familiar gesture. 'Bring the light,' he directed. Mr. Munn followed the negro man, who carried the lamp, into the other room, aware all the while of those eyes fixed on him.

'Where do you keep your knives and forks and such?' the deputy demanded.

'In that-air drawer in the safe,' the negro said, and pointed toward the dark, leaning cabinet, which was propped up on bricks.

The deputy opened the drawers and rattled the implements about with a forefinger. He looked up at the man, asking, 'This all you got?' The man nodded and said, 'Yassuh.' The deputy turned to Mr. Munn, inquiring with an inflection of patience, 'Reckon we better shake it down?'

Mr. Munn nodded.

'You better call Monroe in, then,' the deputy said.

Mr. Munn went to the back door of the room, opened it, and

spoke the man's name loudly. He watched the tall figure detach itself from the ring of shadow under the trees and approach across the clearing, its own dark shadow swimming before it in the pure light.

When Monroe entered, Burke looked up from a box of nails and scrap-iron and wire and twine which he was examining, and said, 'Just start in anywhere.' Monroe went to a trunk that stood in the corner across from the stove and lifted the lid. In it, Mr. Munn could see, was nothing but a small heap of clothes on the bottom. Monroe seized them with both hands and shook them. There was nothing else in the trunk.

'It ain't in here,' Burke announced shortly; 'we better go in the other room.' He turned to the negro. 'Bring the lamp.' They all followed Burke into the other room, where the woman gazed at them from the bed without a sound.

'It's gonna be a long night of it at this rate,' Burke said, as they moved off down the road.

'We might git in luck at the next one,' Monroe ventured.

But they did not. As before, Monroe went to the rear of the cabin and the other two approached the front door. Here a dog rushed at them, barking, and circled beyond their reach. They searched the cabin systematically, while the negro man, holding a lamp, stood in the middle of the floor, with an expression of strain and puzzlement conquering the sleep on his features, and the woman and the children stared at them with a fixed and uncommunicating gaze. And at each cabin the scene was the same: the spurt of a match and then the wavering and inadequate lamplight scarcely defining the objects of the room, the deputies leaning over to rummage in boxes or to pull open drawers that would rasp with sudden sharpness in the night stillness, and always, just beyond the direct ring of the lamp's rays, it seemed, the fixed and intent eyes watching from the tumbled bed or pallet. In two cabins babies began to cry as soon as the lamp was lighted, falling quickly into rhythmical, gasping sobs that gave no promise of stopping. At the second, when the child began crying, Mr. Munn turned to the woman and exclaimed, 'My God, can't you stop it!' Without taking her gaze from his face, the woman in a blind, groping motion gathered the baby to her and thrust the nipple of her breast into its mouth.

At the eleventh cabin they found it. Burke straightened up suddenly from a box in which he had been fumbling, and exclaimed, 'By Jesus!' very softly, and, 'By Jesus!' He turned about, and laid the knife on the table in the full light of the lamp. Monroe, seeing it, glanced sharply at the negro man standing there by the table, and then took a couple of steps toward the door, to block it. The negro looked down at the object, for the moment dispassionately and without more than casual interest.

Mr. Munn picked up the knife, and, bending toward the flame of the lamp, turned it in his hands. 'That looks like it,' he observed; and then Burke seemed, lounging, to be closer to the negro man than before.

'Mr. Monroe,' Mr. Munn said, 'I'll be obliged if you'll get that other knife. It's in my saddlebags.'

Monroe slipped out the door.

Mr. Munn continued to turn the knife slowly over and over in his hands, handling it gingerly and contemplatively. 'Is this yours?' he asked the negro man, but without looking at him, his eyes fixed, instead, on the knife.

'I been having it round here,' the man admitted.

'You been having it round?' Mr. Munn echoed.

'Yassuh.'

'Long?' Mr. Munn still did not look at the man, looking at the knife, which he turned over and over in his hand.

'I reckin as you might say so,' the negro said.

Monroe re-entered the room, in his hand a knife that shone bright and new in the light. He gave the knife to Mr. Munn. Mr. Munn held the two knives side by side, comparing their shapes.

'They got them same little square-headed brass brads and I figgered we done had it.'

'It's got the trade-mark,' Mr. Munn pointed out. 'You can see that.'

Burke reached over and picked up the knife which he had found, and inspected it. 'Yes,' he said, 'that's right.' He tossed it onto the table.

Mr. Munn raised his eyes and looked directly at the negro. 'Where did you get this knife?' he demanded.

The negro looked down at the knife, which lay where Burke had dropped it, and then at his questioner. 'Boss,' he began — and his tongue licked out tentatively to wet his lips, a sudden childish and innocent pink against the black skin and the parched-looking grayness of the lips — 'boss, a great-big ole bullfrog done found me that-air knife. Hit wuz——'

'Sweet Jesus!' Burke breathed softly.

'— hit wuz this-a-way. I wuz goen down to slop me some shoats I got me, one day last summer long 'bout sun. I seen a great-big ole bullfrog a-hoppen along this side that-air branch whar my shoats does they walleren, and I figgered I'd ketch him and I set that-air bucket down and I started towards him and he kept on a-hoppen and a-hoppen, and I thowed my hat at him and I tried to ketch him, but he kept on a-hoppen. 'Fore I knowed hit he hopped right up under that-air cawn-crib, right up under whar the log wuz a-setten on the hunk of limerock, and I retched up under and grabbed holt of his laig and pulled him out, and 'fore-God-a-mighty, he drug out that-air knife, and I say, now, I never, but I seen hit wuz a good knife, so I taken hit and cut off his laigs and put 'em in my pocket and thowed that ole frog in the dirt, then I say, naw, I'll give him to my shoats, so I picked him up and put him in the slop. He kept on a-sloshen round in the slop, but he could'n swim none to speak of, and I thowed him to them shoats. Hit wuz that big ole red shoat got him, I seen him when she done hit. She done taken him——'

The negro man hesitated, looking at Mr. Munn's face. Mr. Munn was nodding slightly at Burke.

"'Fore God,' the negro declared, his voice rising now, "'fore God, I done found hit lak I say. Ast my wife thar,' and he pointed toward the bed.

'Lak he say,' the woman said, nodding. 'He come to the house, and he say, look, a great-big ole bullfrog ——'

'Yassuh,' the man broke in, 'that big ole bullfrog. Shore, boss, I never knowed that knife wuz yore'n. If'n I knowed that knife wuz yore'n, I' — Burke laid his hand on the man's arm, but the man did not seem to notice — 'shore would a-brung hit back. I'd a-found whar yore place wuz, and brung hit back and give hit to you. I never wants nuthen not rightful and truly mine in God's sight, and I'd a-brung hit back. If'n I knowed ——'

'For God's sake!' Mr. Munn interrupted petulantly and resentfully.

It was almost dawn when they got outside. A cold pallor was on the sky in the east over the far woods. They made the negro man, handcuffed, ride behind Burke. The men rode without talking, their faces now slack and heavy with sleep. The negro ceased his protestations and did not speak to them again after they put him on the horse, but sometimes he seemed to be mumbling to himself.

The case against Bunk Trevelyan was dismissed at noon the next day. The knife found in the cabin of the negro was identified by Mr. Little as one of the order from which Trevelyan had made his purchase. It was further established that the type of knife in question had been sold only by the A. C. Little Hardware Company; and a telegram from the jobbers in Nashville established the fact that the type had only been manufactured since early summer. By eleven-thirty the sheriff had come back from the cabin of the negro, where further investigations were being made. He and his men had, earlier, taken the negro out to the cabin and had made him indicate the precise place where, according to his story, the frog found the knife. Then one of the deputies had taken the negro back to town, handcuffed to the buggy seat. The sheriff and his men had searched the cabin and the shed and the crib. On the north side of the crib, diagonally across from the place indicated by the negro, they had found a large silver watch on a plaited thong, stuck in a crevice between two pieces of limestone on which the crib was set. The watch was identified as Duffy's, by Duffy's son. After the defendant had told on the stand of the theft of the knife from the table in his kitchen, and after the knife and the watch had been produced and identified, Mr. Munn moved that the case against Harris Trevelyan be dismissed. The motion was granted.

Mr. Munn walked toward the chair where Trevelyan sat. He forced himself to smile as he put his hand out to Trevelyan, saying,

'Well, and that's that, and I hope it'll be the end of your troubles.'

Trevelyan rose slowly from his chair, looked for an instant at Mr. Munn's outstretched hand as though he did not comprehend the gesture, and then offered his own hand. 'Kin I go now?' he asked.

Mr. Munn nodded, and moved toward the aisle. Trevelyan's wife was standing there with a hand on the railing, looking toward her husband. But when Mr. Munn approached her, she turned to him and seemed to be about to speak. She was wearing that blue crêpe-de-Chine dress, he noticed, and an old brown coat which hung loosely from her shoulders. 'I'm much obliged,' she said, her voice flat.

'That's all right,' Mr. Munn replied, feeling suddenly embarrassed and, somehow, unworthy.

'I'm much obliged,' she repeated.

'That's all right. We just had luck,' Mr. Munn told her, and then realized that the woman was not looking at him but at Trevelyan, who was approaching them. When he was close enough, she reached out and laid her hand on his arm, fleetingly, and then withdrew it. Mr. Munn noticed how the sleeve of the too-big, old brown coat came down almost to the knuckles of her hand.

'Le's git goen,' Trevelyan said to her.

Mr. Munn moved down the aisle, and they followed him. He forced his way through the crowd at the door, and then went down the corridor and out into the yard. He turned to them and called, 'Well, good-bye.'

'Good-bye,' Trevelyan replied. The woman said nothing, staring at him.

He had not taken five steps before he heard the man's voice calling, 'Kin you wait a minute, please?' Trevelyan approached him slowly, and Mr. Munn, watching that meaty, impassive face, and the small blue eyes that squinted now a little against the light, was struck with a sudden irritation at the man. He did not want to see him again. And he was tired, for he had had only two hours' sleep.

'Well?' he asked.

Trevelyan looked at him a moment, and then said, 'You're calcerlaten to come out and git my crop.' There was no inflection of question in the words; they were a statement rendered impartially, judicially, flatly, almost casually.

Mr. Munn studied his face and the slightly squinting eyes, but there was nothing there. Then he replied, 'No, I wasn't figuring on taking your crop.'

'You sent yore niggers out to cut hit and fire hit. That's whut my wife said.'

'Your wife couldn't do it herself.'

'You ain't aimen to take hit.'

'No, I'm not going to take it,' Mr. Munn said. 'I sent those niggers out there because I didn't want to see that tobacco go to waste. I didn't want to get anything out of this case, or expect to. I took it because I didn't think you killed Duffy.'

'You ain't aimen to take hit.' The expression of Trevelyan's face had not changed, and he spoke in that same flat and judicial tone of statement.

'No, I said I wasn't.'

Trevelyan seemed about to turn away; then he said, 'Much obliged.'

'There's just one thing,' Mr. Munn added. He hesitated, making up his mind, for the idea had just that instant come to him. '. . . if you can see your way clear to it, I'd like to see you put your crop in the Association. If you can see your way clear to it.'

Trevelyan raised his eyes ruminatively toward the almost-bare branches of the maples in the yard. 'Hit ain't fer my likes, I reckin. I ain't got nuthen but a little pissy-ant crop,' he said. 'Hit ain't nuthen to speak of.'

'That's not the point.' Mr. Munn took a step toward him. 'It's not the size of a man's crop that matters. We want the man in. The Association is for everybody, everybody that raises any tobacco. And the Association will see you through the winter till the price is right and we can sell. It's not how much to-bacco——' Mr. Munn broke off suddenly. The man was not looking at him, but toward the sky beyond the bare boughs. He felt embarrassed and angry at himself. 'Of course,' he said, 'I don't want you to join unless you see your way to it.'

Trevelyan lowered his gaze until his eyes met the eyes of Mr. Munn. 'Since I got too big fer my pappy to beat, ain't no man ever named to me whut I could do and whut I couldn't do. But,' he said, 'I reckin I'll join.'

'You won't regret it,' Mr. Munn said.

'Mebbe not,' Trevelyan replied.

'I hope you'll use your influence for the Association. Talk about it to people. Let them know you came in.'

'Hit ain't no secret,' Trevelyan remarked.

'Good-bye,' Mr. Munn said. 'Somebody'll come and sign you up.'

'Good-bye,' the man answered, and Mr. Munn watched him move off to join his wife, who had been standing there waiting, with her hands clasped together at the level of her breast.

Mr. Munn approached the group of men who clustered about the foot of the courthouse steps, and nodded to them. Two men detached themselves from the group and fell into step beside Mr. Munn. 'Le's get a drink, Perse,' one of the men said. 'We're just going to have a quick one before we get back to work.'

'No, thanks,' Mr. Munn replied.

'You oughter celebrate,' the other man said, 'getting your boy off and all.'

'It's the other feller ought to celebrate,' the first man put in. 'He's got something to celebrate about, not going to Eddyville, where they don't come back. I'll bet he's tighter'n a tick on a rich widder-woman right now, laying up one of these alleys here in town.'

'No,' Mr. Munn said, 'he's gone home with his wife.' He took pleasure, he discovered, in being able to say that.

'Well, you ought to celebrate, then,' the first man rejoined. 'Just one quick one. Somebody ought to celebrate.'

'I was thinking about going out home. I'm tired.'

'One quick one won't take long, Perse. Then you can go home. It won't take but fifteen minutes. We're just going to have one and then get on back to work. You know how it is.'

Mr. Munn found himself walking across the street with them. He was tired, after all. A drink would pick him up. And maybe a sandwich. They entered the saloon together. The first man ordered the drinks.

Two other men were leaning against the bar and talking to the bartender. One of the men Mr. Munn didn't know, though he recalled seeing him now and then on the street and in the

lobby of the hotel. He knew the other one all right — Joe
Means, a loud-mouthed fellow who claimed to sell insurance
and real estate and who walked up and down the street all day,
calling out, 'Hi, there, Tom!' to somebody passing, or 'Hi, there,
Baldy!' and slapping men on the shoulder while his big, slack
lips parted to say, 'I sure God got one to tell you now, that's a
fact!'

'Hi, there,' Means called, and lounged down the bar toward
them.

The two men with Mr. Munn said hello, but Mr. Munn
merely nodded. The man whose name Mr. Munn did not know
approached them, and thrust his way into the group, hanging
his arm across Joe Means's shoulder. 'Hello, Alec,' he said to
one of the men with Mr. Munn, and 'Hello, Morris.'

'Do you all know each other?' the man named Alec asked,
turning from Mr. Munn to the newcomer. 'This is Mr.
Holt —— '

Holt set his drink on the bar and thrust out his hand, saying:
'Sure I know Munn. I been seeing him around town. I seen
him this morning over to the courthouse. Joe and me was over
there, wasn't we, Joe?' All the while he was gripping Mr.
Munn's hand and pumping it up and down with an absent-
minded, mechanical motion.

'I'm glad to know you,' Mr. Munn said, and with a slight
effort disengaged his hand. He was sorry he had come.

'And pour another one here,' Alec was demanding, indicating
the empty glass in front of Mr. Munn.

'No, no more for me,' Mr. Munn insisted, but the whisky
was already in the glass.

'It'll do you good,' Alec told him.

'What I always say,' Holt said, 'is there ain't nothing better'n
a good slug of whisky for putting a man on his feet except two
good slugs of whisky. Now ain't that what I always say, eh,
Joe? That's what I always —— '

'Besides, you ought to celebrate,' Alec asserted, 'getting your man off and all.'

'You sure got him off, now. Joe and me was over there, wasn't we, Joe?'

'Yeah, now,' Joe Means said, 'we saw you hang it on the nigger, all right.'

'You sure hung it on him now, I'll say that.'

'It looks like he did it,' Mr. Munn replied.

'It sure looks that way now,' Joe Means said, and laughed.

'One less nigger, that's what I always say. What I say is, just get you a good lawyer and he'll find you a good nigger to hang it on, all right. That's what I say,' and Holt reached out to prod Mr. Munn in the ribs with a blunt, brotherly motion, inviting him to join the laughter.

Mr. Munn did not laugh. He looked at the man's round, loose face and the open, gold-tooth-studded mouth, from which the snorts of laughter came, and thought, My God, he looks exactly like Joe Means, he might be Joe Means's brother; the town's full of them. Then he realized that his own face was set stiffly in an expression of amiability and merriment. He glanced quickly at the mirror back of the bar, and saw there his face grinning, a long, swarthy face, with dark eyes, and with the grinning lips drawn back over the long teeth.

'He had the knife,' Mr. Munn said coldly, swinging away from the image in the mirror toward the men. 'And the watch.'

'You bet,' Joe Means exclaimed. 'You sure hung it on him.'

'And you didn't have to, either,' Holt said, 'but I always say it never hurts nobody to take pains.' He prodded Mr. Munn in the side again. 'And you didn't have to, to get your man off, not with all them Association men on the jury. My God, they'd hang a jury all week to get your man off. That's what I was saying, that feller was a gone gosling, but hell, I said, not with all them Association men on the jury —— '

Mr. Munn set his empty glass down on the bar, again caught

a glimpse in the mirror of his own face with its smile, and with a full sweep of his arm smacked the man solidly across the mouth. Taken entirely off his balance, the man staggered back one step, and fell to the floor in a sitting position.

At the very instant when the blow landed, Mr. Munn was filled with surprise. He had not contemplated the act. The thought of it had scarcely grazed his mind, as it were, and had in that instant become action. He saw his hand still in the air before him, feeling that it was detached from him and responsible, and even as the man fell, he took a step forward, on his lips the words, 'I'm sorry, I —— ' Then he saw the man's face, and stopped. It only showed an expression of blank surprise, the mouth hanging open. A little blood was gathering at the corners of the mouth. He stopped because of that expression of surprise; and anger began to mount in him, as he realized that that surprise was not merely physical shock from the blow, but a surprise, profound and fundamental, that a blow on that provocation should have been struck at all.

The man on the floor clambered to his feet and lunged toward Mr. Munn, but Alec grabbed him and shoved him back.

'Jesus!' Joe Means cried, in a voice filled with a kind of peevish reproach, 'what do you go and do that for?'

Holt was struggling, but without much force, in the arms of Alec and the other man. Blood was running down his chin now, and a few splotches had fallen on his shirt front.

'He says I framed a nigger and fixed a jury, then he wonders why I hit him,' Mr. Munn said, not as though in answer to the question from Joe Means, but half absent-mindedly. Then he added, without fervor, 'My God!'

Alec had released Holt and stepped aside, but the other man still clung to him. 'Ain't nobody gonna do that to me,' Holt kept on saying, 'not and get away with it, ain't nobody.'

'Let him loose,' Alec ordered.

The other man stepped back.

'Ain't nobody,' Holt repeated.

'You can have me arrested and fined,' Mr. Munn said, 'if you think that'll do you any good.' He laid a half-dollar on the bar and turned to the bartender: 'Or you can, if you want to.'

'For all of me' — the bartender detachedly picked up the coin — 'you can slap the pee outer him every day next week. But I'd a little rather you did it out in the street.'

Mr. Munn pushed his way through the swinging doors and stood in the street. He felt a slight nausea mounting. I ought never gone in there, he thought.

Chapter four

Two days after Christmas, Senator Tolliver gave a party at his place for the board of directors of the Association. The members were to arrive early in the morning so that a meeting could be held before dinner. 'We should discuss those matters,' the Senator pointed out, 'before our heads are impaired by the fumes.' Mr. Munn was to bring his wife and stay the night. 'You must bring your wife,' the Senator urged, 'who, I hear, is charming. There will be a few other ladies there, and so she will not be entirely cut off from human companionship while we men are ruining our digestions with our weighty concerns. I trust that you can prevail upon her to come.' They were to come by train, arriving at nine in the morning on the local that would stop at the crossroads below Monclair, the Senator's place.

When they got off the train that morning the sky was an undifferentiated gray from horizon to horizon. It seemed, almost, to be suspended from the low, wooded hills that circled the valley, a slack canopy, not a bold, deep dome. One could not even distinguish, as sometimes on such lowering days, the formless splotch of lighter gray, scarcely luminous, that marks the position of the sun. The cedar woods on the distant ridges looked dead black, like smudges of soot. There was no wind.

'It's going to snow,' May said as soon as her husband had swung her clear of the step of the coach and she could raise her glance to the sky.

'It'll snow, I reckon,' he agreed.

The train pulled off between the dun-colored fields, the steam that trailed above the locomotive looking unbelievably white and delicate against the dullness of the sky. For a moment, standing on the hard-trodden red clay beside the tracks, they watched the receding train. Then Mr. Munn turned to look at the negro man who was approaching from the direction of the little dilapidated yellow shed that bore the sign 'Monclair Crossing.' The negro man took off his hat, and said, 'I'se come atter you all.'

'That's fine,' Mr. Munn replied.

The negro picked up the valise, and led them toward the carriage, which stood beyond the yellow shed.

'Hit's gonna snow,' the negro said; 'yassuh, 'fore Gawd.'

The train whistled for the cut, far away now to the east. Mr. Munn turned toward the east, toward that almost inaudible sound, but the train was out of sight now; and the track, curving into the distance to find a gap in the low ridges, made those broad, empty fields seem more empty still.

'I wish it had snowed for Christmas,' May said, as the carriage pulled into the lane. 'Christmas isn't really Christmas without snow, and it never seems to snow on Christmas any more.'

Mr. Munn said nothing, but watched her face as she lifted it pensively again toward the sky.

'Not like when I was little. When it snows now — and it snowed a little bit two Christmases ago — I like to sit by the window with nobody else in the room and look at it coming down outside. It makes me feel the way I did when I was little, when it snowed on Christmas. Everything ought to be different on Christmas — and when I was little I used to wake up long before day and before anybody else woke up, and lie in my bed and wait for the window to get a little light, maybe, and for somebody to get up, and I would be sure that when day did come and I got up, everything, the whole world, would be different. And if there was snow on the ground, everything would be different.'

Mr. Munn looked at the stooped back of the negro man on

the front seat. Then he leaned and put his mouth close to his wife's ear. 'I love you,' he whispered.

She nodded. Then, as though recollecting, she said, 'You weren't paying any attention, you're making fun of me.'

'No,' he denied.

They were silent for a while as the carriage moved over the hard ruts of the lane. On each side was a grove of bare trees, with dry underbrush choking the space between the trunks and coming almost up to the first branches. When the lane turned sharply and came out of the grove, so that the view gave again on the open country, they saw the house sitting at the head of a long rise, an enormous house of red brick, with symmetrical wings and white columns, flanked by masses of tall, black cedars. White fences bordered the lane that led up to the house. On the long rise toward the house the few black, leafless trees seemed arbitrary and unnatural, their holes sticking up from the colorless earth. At that distance the house, set against the background of the ridges that defined the horizon, and dominating the slope of the lane and the wide fields and pastures, was blank and lonely and severe.

'There it is,' Mr. Munn said.

'Yassuh,' the negro put in, 'dar hit.'

The house was not old. The Senator had built it fifteen years before on the site of the old house, which had burned. He always said that he had built it as much like the old one as possible; and he usually added, 'Only, of course, somewhat larger.' It was much larger than the old one had been. The central section, though much deeper, did resemble the old house, which had been a ten-room brick farmhouse with a high, white portico. But few people now could remember what the old place had looked like; and people by now had forgotten to say, when remarking on the new house, that Senator Tolliver had built it with his wife's money, and that she had a lot but it wouldn't last forever.

Senator Tolliver did build the house with his wife's money, for he had little of his own. He came of a good, moderately wealthy family, which had been ruined in the Civil War by the father's almost fanatical devotion to the Southern cause. Old Mr. Tolliver had outfitted half a company of cavalry, and had strained all of his resources to buy Confederate bonds. He was reported missing after the battle of Franklin. One year after the end of the war, the Tolliver property was·lost by foreclosure, and four months later Mrs. Tolliver died of a galloping consumption. For four months she lay on a great tester bed, in a shack that would scarcely shed water, and spat blood daintily into handkerchiefs made out of old clothes or sacking. Toward the end of her illness she would rouse herself from her stupor and, in a careful and monotonous voice, curse her husband, whose selfish madness and willful pride had brought ruin on those nearest and dearest to him. He was dead and rotten somewhere down in Tennessee, and she was glad of it, she said, and she hoped his soul was in eternal hell. She would dwell with orderly and precise detail on the corruption of his body, which she maintained she could see before her — how the flesh had fallen away from his left cheek to expose the place where he had lost three teeth, a place which he in his unholy and ungodly vanity had tried to hide when he smiled; how he lay in a ditch, covered shallowly with a little muck and dead leaves, food for worms; how there was no top to his hollow head, for the ball had taken it off. Just after dark she would prop herself up in the bed and describe the picture, night by night adding in her monotonous and careful voice new details to the familiar horror. She was obscene and eloquent, and the very restraint and monotony of her voice gave a magical, a hypnotic conviction to all she said. Her two children, Edmund, sixteen years old, and Matilda, four years older, would stand beside her bed, rigid and stony-eyed, and listen to her until she fell silent from exhaustion.

When she had fallen silent, Edmund would look at her and then at the hard and masklike face of his sister, which seemed hacked down to the very bone. Then he would dash from the shack and run aimlessly down the road and across the fields. On nights when the moon was bright and the ground was frozen like iron, or when the steady winter rains beat down and he plunged blindly through mud and slush, he would range the country like a starving wolf. His breath would come in dry gasps, and he would long to be able to weep. As he ran he would think of the sweet, the divine, deliverance and fulfillment of weeping. But he could not weep. Some time before morning, exhausted and sick, he would creep into the shack and fling himself upon his pallet. One night he returned to find the grease-wick lamp burning, and his sister standing in the middle of the floor. Her tall, bony frame cast a shadow toward the tester bed.

'She is dead,' the sister said, quite evenly.

'Dead,' he repeated, and was filled at the moment with an immeasurable relief and bliss.

'Yes, and you were not here.' Then she added quietly, almost as an afterthought, 'And I shall never forgive you.'

The day his mother was buried, Edmund Tolliver started to walk the hundred and forty miles to Louisville. He knew that Louisville was the biggest city in the state. He had no money. On his way he worked at odd jobs on the farms and in the towns in order to live. It took him over a month to reach Louisville. His first job was in a slaughter pen, where the stench of blood and the sight of flies swarming on the soaked earth sickened him. At night he would spend hours scrubbing his hands, but a faint pinkish tinge would linger at the base of his nails and under them, and in the very flesh of his palms. At night, after he got into bed, he would usually remember the horrible and hypnotic monologues of his mother. He began to understand the true nature and depth of her hatred.

By the time Edmund Tolliver was nineteen he was reading law in the office of a Mr. Watson, who had a very good practice and who was an attorney for the Louisville and Nashville Railway. 'Son,' Mr. Watson sometimes said to him, 'there are only two things for a lawyer to do nowadays, get in right with the railroads or get into politics.' At twenty-four Edmund Tolliver began his independent practice. At twenty-six he married Joan Palmer, the only child of a man named Morton Palmer, who had made a fortune in the war by selling beef and hides to the Federal Government and by speculating in grain. By this time he was, however, a banker. Edmund Tolliver hated him for his success, just as he hated the memory of his own father for his failure. But the hatred was secret, and Edmund Tolliver flattered him, took what business the old man threw his way, and waited for him to die. He died suddenly, of apoplexy, some years before Tolliver had dared to hope for the event.

Joan Palmer was a frail and sickly woman several years older than her husband. She was not pretty, for chronic ill health had marked her, and a dull, mottled complexion obscured the precise chiseling of her features, but at moments of happiness and excitement she could exhibit a delicate and transparent beauty that hovered insubstantially and then faded, as it were, under the steadiness of the onlooker's profaning gaze. When Edmund Tolliver asked her to marry him, she was thus transfigured; and at that moment, seeing that unexpected beauty, he forgot what calculations had inspired his suit, and was so deeply moved, as by a revelation, that his sight swam with tears. He was overcome with humility and purifying joy at this gift which a gracious fate had so unexpectedly extended to him. He told Joan Palmer, and told himself, believingly, that no service for her would ever be too great, no care too tender, and that he would do everything in the world to make her happy. Saying nothing, she drew his head down to her bosom and held it there, with her small fingers pressed into the strong, crisp,

thick hair of his head, while she stared unseeingly at the pro-
fusion of gilt and brocade and white marble and plush over
which the crystal chandelier of her father's parlor spilled its
gleams.

The promises which Edmund Tolliver made that night to
her and to himself were truly meant. But her strength was not
like his. She was never well. For days at a time she would lie
in a darkened room, motionless, staring at the ceiling, or pressing her fingers to her eyes and brow. And as time passed, that
gesture became habitual, even when the pain was not present,
a small gesture of desperation in the face of all the nameless
forces of sorrow and destruction that circled her silently like
wolves. Despairingly, sitting alone or when people talked among
themselves and did not look at her, she would press her fingers
to her eyes, and her vision would become a velvety and bottom-
less inward well of blackness on the sweet verge of which she
seemed to be poised.

Her strength was not like Edmund Tolliver's strength and
appetite, and her beauty was insubstantial. For several years,
whenever he caught, and more rarely as the years went by, that
moment of beauty, he would experience again that sense of
gratitude and dedication, and sometimes would lay his head on
her bosom. But later, when such moments occurred, they would
stab him as with a knife; first remorse and pity for her, then
pity for himself and an indefinable sense of betrayal and frustra-
tion. He would rush out of her presence, without a word. The
sharp and full remembrance of the night when he had asked her
to marry him and she had drawn down his head, even the clean
smell of the cloth of her dress and of her flesh, would possess
him. Beneath the cloth of her dress her breast was so small,
he had thought, scarcely womanly at all, so suggestive of innocence and frailty, that he had seemed that night to discover a
perfect and final truth; and his very soul had stood still within
him. Pausing in the hall outside her door, he would remember

these things, and strike his right fist heavily into the palm of his left hand, time and time again, with the retarded and mechanical regularity of a pendulum. His anguish was like that of a damned man who has once been granted the clear, cool vision of paradise, or that of a drowning man who sees how clearly, how lovingly the bright sunshine defines all familiar and comfortable objects on the bank where once he has walked.

After the death of old Morton Palmer, Edmund Tolliver sold his rather modest house and moved from Louisville to the southern part of the state. He did not return to the exact locality where his father had lived. The painful recollections of his early youth forbade that. He did not want to hear every day the names he had heard in his youth, or to see the same cross-roads and houses. So he bought a farm in an adjoining county, six hundred acres of good land, well watered and gently rolling, with the blue haze of knobs in the background. His wife's health was getting steadily worse, and so he brought to keep house for him his older sister Matilda, who, unmarried, had been teaching in the smaller country schools of her section.

Tolliver put white fences around the pastures of his farm, and built new barns and stables, the barns high and red and the stables low and white like the long fences. He bred blooded cattle and kept blooded horses, and he grew tobacco. He always asked advice of old residents in the section and listened attentively while they gave it. He rode much about the country, talking to the farmers and fishing and hunting with them. Then he went into politics, and was elected to the state senate. When his house burned, he built the new one, and soon afterward, strangers from Louisville and Frankfort and Lexington and Nashville began to come to the new house and drink whisky in the high-ceilinged rooms and walk out to the stables to look at the horses. After Tolliver went to Congress the first time, people from Washington and Baltimore began to come, now and then important people whose names were in the papers. And then Tolliver was elected to the Senate. But he still rode around the country and went fishing and hunting with the farmers and occasionally went to church at the little white weatherboarded Methodist church at Hope Springs. He did not put on airs, and often in his campaign speaking he would say, 'I tell you I have known the pinch of poverty and the gnawing of the belly, and I have known what it is to get up in the cold dark before sun and go with bare feet out on the frozen ground.' Gradually people forgot that the new house had been built with his wife's money. And they forgot about her. She had died very shortly after the house was finished.

As the carriage drew up the slope toward the house, a few flakes of snow drifted down from the gray sky. They were visible clinging to the stalks of dead weed by the lane.

'Oh, it's really going to snow!' May exclaimed.

Now they could see the wreaths of holly and red ribbons in the windows of the house, and the big one hung on the white door. Smoke stood up from the big chimneys. The house, which from a distance had appeared blank and severe, now seemed to promise, in contrast with the slowly descending snow and the empty fields and the gray sky, and to promise abundantly, everything that could make for happiness and peace — steaming and delicately odorous food, the gleam of firelight on silver, the soft sinking of the foot into the deep-piled rug, the musical clink of glasses.

'How good of you to come,' Senator Tolliver said, when he took May's hand and leaned slightly over it as though he might kiss it, if he dared. 'Mr. Christian has brought his daughter, they're going to stay all night too, and we'll try to liven up this dull old house a little tonight with some youth and beauty. And I must say this house gets dull enough some days. But now I'll turn you over to my sister.' And indicating the tall, black-clothed woman who came from the room behind him, he went on, 'Matilda, this is May, the wife of my good friend Percy Munn, I've told you so much about.' He stretched out his hand paternally and laid it on Mr. Munn's shoulder. 'The coming boy,' he declared, and patted Mr. Munn's shoulder. 'We'll have him in Congress yet.'

'I don't know about that,' Mr. Munn said, a little embarrassed, but pleased by the words and by the hand on his shoulder. Here in the white-paneled hall, after the sullen sky and the empty land, were warmth and kindliness, the glitter of mirrors, and the sound of fire crackling in a farther room. Even the face of Matilda seemed, as Mr. Munn took her hand, to be less distant and rigid than he had at first believed.

May went up the wide stairs beside the older woman, appearing smaller than ever beside her bony height. At the turn in the stairs, May looked backward fleetingly over her shoulder and gave a quick, almost shy smile, which Mr. Munn took for a good-bye. Then with the Senator he walked across the hall and the length of a long room, where a fire was burning but no one was present. 'I thought we'd have the meeting in the library,' the Senator was saying. 'All the men are here now but Captain Todd. He ought to come driving up any minute. He's going to bring his boy over. You know his boy, he's off at college in Virginia. I think it's Virginia.'

When they entered the library, the men there were standing around the wide fireplace, in which a log was blazing and sputtering. Mr. Munn shook hands with each of them. Then he took out his pipe and began to pack it.

'I reckon the Captain'll be here any minute,' Senator Tolliver said, and walked over to look from one of the windows that gave on the long slope at the front. It was definitely snowing now, not heavily but steadily. A few flakes clung to the base of the window-panes. 'He's not in sight yet,' the Senator added, and then returned to the group of men at the hearth. He stood there among them, smiling easily, his hands thrust into the pockets of his coat and his head thrown back a little. Over across the room Mr. Sills and Mr. Burden stood, cut off from the rest of the group. Mr. Burden leaned his heavy, dark, unkempt head down toward Mr. Sills, who was talking earnestly and tapping a pencil on a pad of paper which he held in his left hand. Mr. Munn packed his pipe and lit it, and then looked at the shelves of books around the room — lawbooks mostly, he guessed, and history, for the Senator had the name of an inveterate reader of history and could quote pages of Macaulay and Gibbon when he wanted to — and at the big table and the desk, and the great engravings on the wall. Then, idly, he looked at the faces of the men around him. Good men, he thought, even old Sills; good men. He rocked a little on his heels, feeling the comfortable glow of the fire on his back. He took long, deep pulls on his pipe. It was a sweet pipe.

No one had noticed Captain Todd driving up the long lane, and no one had heard the bell. A negro man opened the library door, and there Captain Todd stood, nodding his head slightly and wearing his grave smile. 'I'm sorry I'm late,' he said, 'but I ain't been on time since General Buell beat me and General Bragg to Louisville and saved our glorious Commonwealth of Kentucky for Mr. Lincoln.' The Senator, with outstretched hand, moved quickly toward him, saying: 'Why, that's all right, plenty of time. Come up to the fire and warm up.'

'Thank you,' and Captain Todd moved around the group, shaking hands with each man. Then he stood on the hearth and spread his long, brown fingers to the vigorous blaze. 'Right sharp outside,' he said.

'Where's your boy?' the Senator asked.

'I put him in the other room,' Captain Todd replied. 'He's reading a book he found out there, or' — and he paused, smiling — 'I reckon he's reading. He claims he knows how.'

'I'll go speak to him,' the Senator said. He turned at the door. 'I'll be back in a minute; then we can start.'

Mr. Munn looked at Captain Todd, who was still leaning toward the blaze with his fine, strong-looking hands spread out for the warmth. The brown skin was splotched a little, he noticed, and the veins across the back looked too big. He wondered if Captain Todd's boy would be like the Captain. He did favor the Captain, he remembered, or rather he had favored him three or four years before. He hadn't seen the boy now for some time, not since he went off to college. In Virginia, the Senator had said. That was right, he remembered, the boy had gone to Virginia to college, to Washington and Lee. Before he left, the boy had favored the Captain, tallish and cleanly put together, with blue-green eyes, like the Captain's and a good nose. That was nice of the Senator to take the trouble to go out and speak to the boy. He was a good man, the Senator, but Captain Todd was a better. The best of the lot. But the Senator was a good man.

Before four o'clock everybody who was not going to spend the night had left. They had driven off down the hill in the steadily falling snow, the flakes settling on their shoulders and on the lap-robes and the backs of the horses. The snow had begun to obliterate the tracks of the wheels and the hoofprints of the horses, and the gray light began to fade from the sky. As they parted in the hallway of the house, the men had been full of good temper and laughter, all except Mr. Sills, who rarely if ever took more than one drink of anything. The cold and snow and the early twilight had seemed like nothing to them then.

Lounging in the library, where the fire leaped and flickered up at the deep, black throat of the chimney and the bottles sat solidly on the big silver tray on the table, they had drunk glass after glass. They had thrust their legs out before them and held their glasses in their hands and comfortably digested the turkey and ham and pudding, their conversation grave and slow at first, and then, with the warmth of the liquor, more brisk, and punctuated by bursts of deep laughter. But behind the pleasure of the hour there had been a more substantial cause for satisfaction. The secretary had reported that the Alta Company was prepared to open negotiations at the rate of nine-fifty for prime leaf, and that a private buyer was offering ten for Australian, grade A, and seven for snuff leaf, fine. The board had voted against consideration of the offers. 'By God!' Mr. Christian had exclaimed, slapping the top of the table with the weight of his red hand, 'we've got the bastards by the short hairs! Make 'em say papa, make 'em wish they never heard about tobacco. Make 'em wish they was in the ribbon business. They're up that old creek and ain't got no paddle. By God' — and he had paused to take a deep breath, like a thirsty man who has been drinking deep — 'nine-fifty, they say! After we've published our price schedule, Australian, grade A, sixteen dollars; Italian, grade A, fifteen-twenty-five; spinners, fine, twelve' — and he paused again, his breath sucking through his teeth — 'they ain't a thing on the schedule I don't know in my sleep. I read it every night like old maids read the Bible, to keep their feet warm. Nine-fifty, they say! Pretty Jesus, they can't read. But we got 'em, and we gonna give 'em hell, and you, Mr. Secretary, you write the bastards and tell 'em I said so!'

'We're not trying to break the tobacco companies,' the Senator had said; and then quickly added: 'Not that I'm trying to talk you gentlemen into accepting this offer. But we aren't trying to break them. What we want is a fair price. Just a fair price. When they offer us that I'm in favor of doing business with them. We just want to be fair, we don't want to gouge them —— '

'The hell I don't!' Mr. Christian shouted. 'Who says I don't? I'd like to gouge their God-damned eyes out and feed 'em to 'em for oysters. By God, I would, and I'd pay money to do it. I'd like to cut their guts out and tie 'em in bow knots around their necks and hang the bastards on Christmas trees, for orphan children in hell' — he had slapped the table again — 'and if anybody here still has a hog's eyebrow of doubt in his mind as to how I'm gonna vote on this proposition, I'll break down and tell him. I won't let him languish for information. I'm gonna vote no.'

'I suppose,' Mr. Sills had said, 'it won't be necessary to enter these remarks in full in the minutes.'

'You can frame 'em, for all of me, and hang 'em over your bed,' Mr. Christian had replied. 'You can teach 'em to nursing mothers and small children.'

Even the knowledge that some eight hundred thousand pounds of tobacco outside the Association had moved within the past ten days did not do much to impair the confidence and pleasure of the day; nor the clipping from the paper which Mr. Sills had brought. He bought a paper when he came through the settlement above Monclair Crossing, he had said. He had carefully removed the clipping from his long slick leather wallet, which he always kept bound with three big rubber bands, and had read the item to the board. The item was to the effect that Mr. Ben Sullins, a respected tobacco farmer of the Allen Settlement section and a strong anti-Association man, had found a bundle of switches and an anonymous letter in his mailbox the morning after Christmas. 'Attached to a bundle of willow switches,' the clipping said, 'was a note in childish or illiterate penmanship which read as follows: "This is whut Santy Claws brings bad littul boys whut aint got sense to keep frum running off at the mouth and holes there terbacco but dont join the Assoc." Mr. Sullins has stated that he attaches no importance to the message and is not one to be intimidated, and the *Edgerton Messenger* must strongly endorse and applaud the attitude of Mr. Sullins and condemn the cowardice of those who send unsigned communications. However, Mr. Sullins has also stated that he believes the incident to be some childish prank committed by boys who have heard their parents comment on his attitude toward the Association of Growers of Dark Fired Tobacco. The *Edgerton Messenger* hopes that this is the true case.'

'A childish prank,' Mr. Burden had said meditatively, lifting his dark, untidy-looking head.

'Now it looks to me,' Mr. Christian had observed, 'folks in the Allen Settlement section have got some right forward and thriving children. Bet they was born feet-first and grinding their teeth.'

'No,' Mr. Burden had said in his slow voice, 'no, it wasn't children did it. Some poor farmer had a bad Christmas. The Association is seeing folks through the best it can, but the best ain't a whoop and a holler better'n sowbelly for most. Not for some poor man with a few thousand pounds with us. What kind of an advance can he get? Not Christmas fixings.'

'He must think of the future,' Mr. Sills had answered.

'But he has a bad Christmas and there ain't much for the kids and he catches his wife off in the kitchen crying a little and one of his kids tells him what the Sullins children got for Christmas — how the Sullins boy came down the road with a new rifle, maybe — and he figures Sullins has been selling off some tobacco to run on, and at the price made because the Association was holding out. Then he stomps off down to the barn and gets to figuring about Sullins. He gets madder and madder, and then being a complete damn fool he goes to the house and gets him some paper outer one of the children's writing tablets and a pencil and fixes up the letter. Then he gets him a piece of binder twine outer the barn and goes down by the creek and cuts him some willow switches and after it gets dark he walks down the road toward the Sullins place and sticks 'em in the mailbox. Then,' Mr. Burden had lamely finished, 'he goes on back home.'

There had been a moment of silence in which the men seemed to be turning Mr. Burden's words over and over in their minds. Then Captain Todd had broken the silence. 'Mr.

Chairman,' he had said quietly, 'it seems to me it don't exactly matter who wrote the letter or why, really. It seems to me, being the board, we'll just have to take it as done with malice aforethought and act accordingly. Mr. Chairman' — and he had hesitated while the other men all looked at him — 'I move that the board of directors of the Association of Growers of Dark Fired Tobacco make a statement condemning the author of the anonymous communication received by Mr. Ben Sullins and that the statement be given to all the papers of this section for publication.'

'I second the motion,' Mr. Munn had said.

The motion had been unanimously carried.

'And that's a good thing, gentlemen, in my opinion,' the Senator had observed while the secretary was writing out the statement. 'What the Association wants is justice, but we must have it in an orderly fashion. We do not want to see the passions inflamed.'

'I just hate to think how easy it is to inflame my passions,' Mr. Christian had said to no one in particular, showing his big yellow teeth in an amiable grin.

Within fifteen minutes the whole matter had been forgotten, apparently, and no one referred to it again after the reading of the board's statement by Mr. Sills. It did not recur to Mr. Munn's mind until late that evening when Mr. Christian, after the ladies had gone to bed, began to tell what he knew about Ben Sullins. For after Mr. Sills and Mr. Burden and the rest had left, there was no further talk of business. The Senator's sister, Lucille Christian, and May came down, and they all sat around the fire in the long room which opened to the library. The Senator told jokes, jokes that kept everyone laughing, and yet he seemed to be doing it naturally and effortlessly, without attempting to dominate the party. But, Mr. Munn noticed, his sister never laughed, never even smiled.

She sat very upright in a small wing chair, somewhat withdrawn on one side of the fireplace. While the light died at the windows and the voices went on around her, her gaze would wander to the center of the flames. Her hands were laid palms-down on her knees, the size and boniness of the knees being somehow apparent under the folds of the black silk. She did not seem discourteous, or cold in her remoteness, her lack of attention. Rather, Mr. Munn thought, she was like a grown person who sits in the midst of children while they play. Once when May, who sat near her, spoke to her, she leaned toward her, apparently not catching the words, and said, 'Yes, child?' May seemed to get along with her.

But when they sat at the table that night, and the light fell more directly on her face, the hardness and the bitterness there were more obvious. Her brows were square, the cheekbones high, the mouth large-lipped but drawn into a fixed pattern of will, and the chin bony and prominent. The nose had a kind of rough aquilinity. The eyes were deep-set and slaty-blue. Her whole face was like a sculpture in some grayish stone left unfinished. He noticed her earth-colored, bony hands holding the silver or picking up a glass, and remembered how her hand had felt in his own that morning.

After the meal was over they sat again in the long room. A negro man came to put more wood on the fire. The men held glasses of whisky in their hands and took slow, careful sips. Lucille Christian, drinking a glass of port, was amiably shaking her head at her father, who had just said he couldn't figure out why she didn't like to be called Sukie.

'I don't mind the name,' she said, 'if you'd just save it for me.'

'Now you see, Senator, the girl is downright selfish,' and Mr. Christian nodded his head toward Senator Tolliver.

The girl took a sip of the wine, and explained: 'No, it's just that you call half the animals on the place Sukie, then you call me Sukie too. Bird dogs, cows, mares. After all, I'm your daughter, you know.'

'It's a good name. When you come right down to it, now, I can't say as I know a better, not for a she-critter. And I always wanted my daughter to have the best. Yes, sir, I took one look at her when she was born and I said to my wife: "You name her Lucille if you want, but she's a likely-looking passel and she'll be Sukie to me. If she keeps on improving." '

'Along with fifty bird dogs at one time and another,' the girl said, 'and the Lord knows how many hounds.'

'Selfish,' Mr. Christian observed, and shook his head despondently. 'Selfish and self-centered.'

The son of Captain Todd was sitting beside Mr. Munn on a sofa. Leaning forward with his elbows on his knees, he watched Lucille Christian, whose profile was toward him, or now and then turned to glance at Mr. Munn as though he were about to say something. Mr. Munn decided that he was a good boy. He did look like Captain Todd, still did. Probably would look more like as time passed. But he didn't have any hint of the Captain's quality of control, of certainty. But what boy could?

'You finish this year, don't you?' Mr. Munn asked the boy.

The boy straightened up suddenly, and turned to Mr. Munn, a hint of pleasure and of anxiety to please showing in his face. 'Yes, sir, next June. Barring accidents.' He seemed about to say more, then stopped, flushing a little.

'Going to practice in this section?'

'Well, you see, not until lately I didn't think so. You see' — the boy hesitated — 'I was thinking about going into a man's office in Cincinnati. A Mr. Lightfoot; he used to know Father a long time ago. He's got a lot of railroad business and some big companies in Ohio get him to do work for them, him and his partners.'

'Lightfoot,' Mr. Munn said ruminatively, 'Lightfoot.'

'Yes, sir, Lightfoot; and the firm's name is Hayden, Hughes, and Lightfoot. Father used to know him in Tennessee.'

'In Tennessee?'

'Yes, sir, in the war, I believe it was. He went up North after the war. He came down to see Father once a long time ago when I was a kid. I just barely remember him there. They still write letters off and on, or used to. Then I met him again. His boy went to Washington and Lee, too, but he didn't take law. He's working on a newspaper in Baltimore. I met his father again when he came down to school one time to see Mose. Mose didn't want to be a lawyer.'

'Getting in a firm like that, that's got a big practice, and working up,' Mr. Munn said, nodding, 'that's a good way to get a start in the law. I reckon it's the best way, these days. But I reckon I was homesick, being away from home so long going to school and all, and then my mother died and left me the place, so I just hung my shingle out in Bardsville. Made a mistake, maybe.'

'No, no, I didn't mean that,' the boy asserted vehemently, and then hesitated in obvious embarrassment. 'That isn't what I meant. I'm changing my mind, I guess. I don't believe I'm going to Cincinnati like I thought. Being back this Christmas and all —— ' The sentence hung unfinished in the air.

'You might be passing something up,' Mr. Munn pointed out, sucking his pipe. 'That's where they tell me the money is. Up yonder across the river. God knows there's not much around here.'

'That's not the point. Exactly —— '

'It's a pretty big point, a right smart of the time.'

The boy looked across the room, and Mr. Munn followed his glance. Mr. Christian was telling some tale, leaning forward with his hands on his spread knees and his arms bowed out like a bulldog's legs. His glass was on the floor beside him. Lucille Christian was regarding her father with an air of affectionate amusement, which made Mr. Munn, for the first time, become aware of a real liking for her. The boy, he noticed, was looking at her too. Then he turned back to Mr. Munn. 'Lucille told me — Miss Christian, that is — she told me about the first big rally when they organized the Association. I wish I'd been here last summer and heard your speech. She told me about your speech. It was wonderful, she said. She said everybody thought it was wonderful. Her father and Senator Tolliver. Everybody.'

'It was an accident,' Mr. Munn said. An accident, he thought. And the substance of that moment when he had stood speechless on the platform that day before all those people was powerfully and immediately in his mind: the enormous emptiness of the swinging, incandescent blue depth of the sky, the emptiness, tugging like an abyss, of all these faces lifted under the beating light, the dryness of his own throat. And the old man whose face he had seen below the platform. Yes, an accident. And an accident that I'm here now, he decided. And looking across the big, pleasant room with its soft carpet and fine furnishings and at the leaping firelight and the known faces, he was aware how strong accident was — how here he was, warmed and fed and surrounded by these people who, if he spoke a single word, would turn pleasantly to him, and how cold it was snowing outside, all the countryside filling up with snow that would blind all familiar contours, and how but for the accidents which were his history he might be out there, or elsewhere, miserable, lost, unbefriended. How anyone might be. That thought made the room, and all in it seem suddenly insubstantial, like a dream. The bottom might drop out; it was dropping out even while you looked, maybe. He shook his head, as though in a dismissal, and turning to the boy, repeated, 'It was an accident.'

'That's not what people say. They've heard you make speeches since —— '

Mr. Munn looked sharply at the boy. 'There was an old man there,' he began, 'standing just at the edge of the platform.

When I got up I saw him. I just saw him there. He was just an ordinary sort of old fellow, straw hat and overalls, nothing out of the way.' Mr. Munn realized that he did not remember what he had actually said that day at the rally. Instead, he only remembered the face of that old man. That was what seemed important now, but it was hard to find words for the importance. He discovered that the boy was not really attending to him, that he was following his own thought, and so, somewhat embarrassedly, he said, 'Well, you see, it was just sort of an accident.'

'Yes, sir, I see,' the boy replied, leaping on with his own idea; 'but you know, about not going into Mr. Lightfoot's office in Cincinnati and all. If I went up there, there'd just be a lot of desk work, making up briefs and so on. There wouldn't be any chance for what you're doing. Things like the rally. What you're doing.'

'If we win, it'll be worth it,' Mr. Munn said. 'It'll be something. If we don't, it'll be something else.'

'You'll win, all right,' the boy rejoined, leaning forward with his elbows on his knees and his hands clasped before him. They were long, brown, sinewy hands, and they sprang strongly from the brown wrists. 'You're bound to win. Everybody down round here'll be better off. Everybody'll see that.'

'Maybe,' Mr. Munn replied. It was all so simple to the boy. People just saw what was good for them, and did it. And he was all fired up about making speeches. Telling people what was good for them. Then Mr. Munn saw the boy watching Lucille Christian again, and added to himself: And he talks to that Christian girl a couple of hours and decides he'll settle down here. It's all surface to him yet. Everything. He's not much better than a child. Getting older is breaking through the surfaces. Layer after layer. Peeling them off to find what's inside. What's inside. Mighty few seemed to know, and they never told. Captain Todd seemed to know. Then, with a flash of discovery as he remembered Matilda's face, he decided that she knew, too. But there were few Captains and Matildas. The chances were you never knew. Just kept on peeling. Like skin off an onion. And if you stopped you died, or rather, you were dead already. 'We may not win,' he said meditatively, and sucked at his pipe, 'but win or lose, we're in up to our necks now.'

The boy wasn't listening now. He was looking across the room. The other women were standing, and Lucille Christian was getting to her feet. The boy got up and moved quickly across to her, and waited at her side while she told everyone good night. Then, when she went out with May and Matilda, he walked with her as far as the foot of the stairs. The Senator, who had escorted them all that far, returned immediately to the room, rubbing his hands together and saying, 'Well, gentlemen, I propose another sample of the most glorious product of our glorious commonwealth.' He poured the drinks, heavier this time, and turned to his guests.

'I'll have mine straight,' Captain Todd said, 'if you please. You know,' he added, picking up a glass, 'it's the man who puts water in his whisky they say gets to be a chronic drunkard. A man drinks whisky straight and he knows what he's doing. But whisky and water now, that's downright insidious. I never allow myself but so much whisky and water, then I take me a straight one so I can get a grip on the facts of the case. To that, gentlemen, I attribute my success in not becoming a chronic drunkard in a world so liberally strewn, you might say, with temptation.'

Mr. Christian squared off before the hearth, his legs spread apart and his feet dug solidly into the thick rug, and took a gulp from his glass. 'Naw,' he declared, 'naw, I say ride it saddle or bareback. No matter if it's a horse or a dog or whisky or a woman, I say a man's got to wear the pants. All alike, they'll all break over if they can. But I say, crow where you roost. A man's got to do the riding. It's me riding the whisky. Not the whisky riding me.' Throwing his head back, he took another gulp, and his Adam's apple bobbed up and down like a great red cork.

'You're right,' the Senator said, 'in a way. Whisky is like a woman. You get the best results if you handle it right. You build it up, you might say. Don't just plunge in. You have to treat it like you loved it. A little coaxing and courting, that gives the best results, every time.' He turned his glass gently in his hand, as though to illustrate his words, and his gaze seemed to draw deeply inward. For a moment he appeared to be oblivious to the men about him.

Mr. Munn observed him. They say he's hell with the women, he thought, when he's off away from home. Not much chance for carrying on in this section, not for a prominent man. But Louisville and Washington, he made up for lost time when he got up there, they said.

' — whisky,' Mr. Christian was saying, 'a great democratic institution. Next to the Declaration of Independence and Bunker Hill, damned if it ain't the greatest. Why, whisky, it makes a rich man pore, like they say, and a pore man rich.'

Mr. Munn was watching the Todd boy. He heard Mr. Christian's voice pronounce the name 'Sullins,' and turned again toward him.

' — and the Sullinses, I've known 'em all my life,' Mr. Christian was saying, still standing on the rug before the hearth with his heels dug in. 'I've known my bellyful of Sullinses. And this Ben Sullins, he's like all the rest. Anything for money, and butter wouldn't melt in their mouth. Why, old Ben Sullins — that's Ben's father, dead now and in hell sure as the good God put tail feathers on jaybirds to hide their ragged asses — for two dimes and a shinplaster he'd have sold his gray-haired mother to be boiled down for lye soap. And I'm not saying I'd blame him too much, for any woman in the

Sullins family gets to be mighty nigh like an egg-sucking bitch 'fore she's done. You just let a good, ordinary, God-fearing girl marry into them Sullinses, and in five years she'll be just like 'em. I've seen it happen too often. Look at Ben Sullins's wife. Come of good honest folks and looked human. But you let a woman get married with a Sullins and in five years you can't tell 'em apart. The woman gets that sharp, gray look, like a she-rat with lard on her whiskers. That's a way to tell a Sullins, male or female. Except when the wind's right, and then you don't have to look —— '

'Now, now, Bill,' Captain Todd said, 'not bad as all that.'

'You don't know. You never made a study of Sullinses, like me. Years now, and I lay up in the bed some nights just studying about Sullinses. Somebody told me one time about a Sullins I never heard of. Lived down in Tennessee in Cheatham County, and I just took me a trip down to look at him. I just wanted to be sure he was like all the rest, and he was. I didn't see him, but it didn't turn out to be necessary. I saw his woman. I went up to the house where they lived and I said as polite as I could, "I'll be mighty grateful, mam, to have a drink of water." I'd rented me a rig just to ride out to their place, and I said, "I'm just traveling through and it's a right warm day." She got me the water all right. Not fresh, though, and a well right there in the side yard in plain sight. And when I got me a second dipperful, she got that Sullins look on and said, "You know, they say it promises a drouth in this section, and our well never does so good in a drouth." So I just poured what was left in the dipper back in the bucket, and said, "Madam, I believe your name must be Sullins." And she said it was, and asked me how I knew, did I read it on the mailbox? And I said no, it hadn't been necessary somehow, and of course it was none of my business, but was she and her husband professing Christians? She said yes, professing Christians and Baptists. And I said I was glad to hear it, and did she know Saint Matthew, 10:42. And she said no, she didn't know offhand. So I just said it to her: "Whoever gives to drink unto one of these little ones a cup of cold water in the name of a disciple, verily I say unto you, he shall in no wise lose his reward." And she looked sort of funny, so I said: "Madam, I know I ain't so little, but then your water ain't so cold either. And please pay my respects to Mr. Sullins." She was like all the Sullins women. They marry a Sullins, and it's like a disease. It's catching. A woman marries a Sullins and she's ruined for life. It's a disease, like the clap. And by God, it's hereditary, too, and all the children get it, because they're all Sullinses. Now, I tell you —— '

Mr. Munn found that his mind was not following. And the room was close and hot. Too much likker, he thought, and then wondered how many drinks he had had that evening. Or not enough. He drained his glass, feeling the drink revive him a little. Then the Senator poured another for him, smiling at him, and Mr. Munn lifted it to his lips. Captain Todd was talking now. He saw the Captain sitting very erect in his chair and talking gravely to Mr. Christian. Mr. Christian still stood on the rug in front of the hearth, and his face and the great dome of his bald skull were a single, deep, unvariegated crimson.

Much later they all went upstairs. Senator Tolliver showed Mr. Munn to his room, wished him a pleasant rest, and went off down the hall. When Mr. Munn entered, and closed the door as softly as possible behind him, the darkness leaped suddenly at him, like a live thing, and clutched him. In the total blackness he was aware only of a motion and a drumming in his head: a motion like the lift and swing of the horizon when one is at sea in a small boat, but all was blackness, both sea and sky. What I hear is my own blood beating in my head, he thought. He began to undress in the dark room so as not to disturb May, letting the garments fall to the floor at his feet. It was cold in the room, and he was aware of the cold, but as knowledge, as it were, not as sensation; and he thought of the snow, which must be falling outside, as falling on naked flesh, coldly and with loving gentleness. And then it came to him that all he knew was the blackness into which he stared and the swinging motion and the beat of the blood. But was he staring into blackness, a blackness external to him and circumambient, or was he the blackness, his own head of terrific circumference embracing, enclosing, defining the blackness, and the effort of staring into the blackness a staring inward into himself, into his own head which enclosed the blackness and everything? And enclosed the snow that gently fell in darkness.

When he leaned over to untie and remove his shoes, the beating in his head grew more powerful, and accelerated until the separate beats merged into a pervasive, pulsing roar. He was aware of his hands doing their work, but aware as one is of a thought, not as of a fact of the body. Finishing, he straightened up, and the roaring ceased. Suddenly, as though by contrast, there was silence. Then he knew again the beating of the blood, but gently now, and more retarded. And then he was aware of another sound, scarcely audible, another rhythm. It was the breathing of May. He thought that he must be standing near the bed, and tried to recall its position in the room. Yes, near the door.

He concentrated on that sound, straining in the darkness, and it seemed to become more pronounced. He tried to imagine her lying there, her posture, the expression on her face, remote and rapt, but could not. The image would not stick in his mind. It would flicker and be gone. But the almost inaudible breathing, that was steady, was real, was everything. Anonymous, nameless in the dark, it was the focus of the dark. There was nothing else.

There was a stirring from the bed. 'Perse?' May's voice said, questioningly, heavy with sleep.

For a moment he did not answer. He felt cheated, angry,

despairing, as one from whom revelation has been snatched away. 'Yes,' he managed to say. His desire had left him.

When morning came, the snow lay evenly over the fields. The morning was unusually cold, and unusually bright. The very air seemed to exist as pure, icy brilliance, and the whole countryside, under the sun, returned that brilliance. Wrapped in that brilliance, the Senator, Captain Todd, Mr. Christian, Mr. Munn, and May walked slowly across the pasture. Ahead of them some twenty-five yards, their forms very precise in the pure light and their shadows sharp on the snow, walked Lucille Christian and Captain Todd's son. The Senator nodded toward them, and said: 'Well, it seems they're getting along right well. Isn't that right, Bill?'

'It looks like she's managing to put up with him,' Mr. Christian admitted.

'You can't blame him,' May said. 'She is awfully pretty, Mr. Christian.'

'Now ain't it a wonder, looking at me,' Mr. Christian rejoined. He was obviously pleased. He struck his gloved hands together in front of him, as though to stimulate the circulation, and then thrust them hard into the side pockets of his coat. 'It's sure a fine day!' he exclaimed.

'Beautiful,' May said, 'so beautiful! Only, why didn't it snow in time for Christmas? It never does any more.' She swept her glance around the gleaming horizon, and took a deep breath as though that act gave her a fuller possession of the distant scene.

Mr. Munn recalled that those were the precise words she had used that morning on first looking out the window to see the snow over everything and the bright sun. And that, looking at her pleasure then, and thinking of standing in the dark the night before and listening to her breathing, he had been swept by shame and remorse, as though at an infidelity. Now, in the brilliant light, while she stood there delicately and swept her gaze over the pure and glittering fields, the incident of the night, even the shame of the morning, did not seem credible. He thrust the matter from his consciousness; but by an act of will. As she walked on ahead with Captain Todd and Mr. Christian, he continued to stare somberly after her.

The Senator began to talk about the meeting of the day before, speaking fluently, confidentially, with his head bowed a little and his hands clasped behind his back. He was glad, he said, to see that Mr. Munn had backed Captain Todd's motion to draw up a public statement condemning the anonymous letter to Mr. Sullins. He was glad that he felt so keenly the danger of engendering ill feeling and thoughtless passion in any controversial movement such as the Association was. 'We must be reasonable,' he asserted, 'and must try to keep the extreme sentiment of the Association under control.'

' I haven't observed anything very extreme,' Mr. Munn said almost diffidently. 'That letter, now, I wonder how much that really means. Just a sort of accident, not a sentiment.'

'Oh, not that kind of extremism, even. I don't necessarily mean that. Though in any popular movement there is a tendency toward extreme action that you don't see. That only needs a leader. They say a ship can burn for days and not much harm done until somebody opens a hatch and the air strikes. A leader is like that, he just opens a hatch. We must guard against the development of any such sentiment. We must keep the hatches down, so to speak. Now take Bill, for instance. I never knew a finer man than Bill Christian. Great sincerity and great strength of character. But he is sometimes given to violent speech. A kind of noble rage, you might say. But he speaks now, not as an individual but as a representative of something bigger than any individual, bigger than he is, or you, or I. He speaks with more than personal authority. And there is no telling what a chance word of random violence or exaggerated feeling might start, what train of thought that might in the end mean action to be regretted by all. And by him most of all, perhaps.'

The Senator lifted his eyes and looked off across the slope toward the little group of figures. Mr. Christian and the rest were near the house now. 'Of course, what I am saying is confidential,' the Senator went on, 'and I say it in all loyalty. I simply say it to you, my boy, because you are one of those who can best help to promote the successful growth of the Association along sound and reasonable lines. We must keep our main objective in view — not to make a fortune in tobacco this year, perhaps, but to be stronger next year and the next. Wars are won, history teaches, not by winning battles, but by winning the right battle. And that is something one must learn in the rough and tumble of politics. Which compromises to make, for all life is a compromise with the ideal, but at the same time to move always toward the ideal and never to lose sight of it or lose the grasp of it in one's thoughts. God knows, I've made mistakes, I've made the wrong compromises sometimes and gone right down the line with the boys, but I've tried not to lose sight of the final objective' — he lifted his head again and looked across the gleaming fields — 'to be of some service to the people of my section. And you,' he said, turning suddenly, as though, engaged in his own musings, he had become oblivious of Mr. Munn's presence and but now recollected himself, 'you have a great future before you. Your prestige is increasing every day. If the Association survives and prospers, there is no way to say how far you may go. You have youth. Energy. Intelligence. Sound legal training. There is no telling, my boy.'

He reached out and laid his hand paternally on Mr. Munn's shoulder. Then, as though embarrassed at betraying his own feelings, he removed it.

Chapter five

ALL the elements that were to combine in a more violent chemistry had been present, it later seemed upon looking back, that Christmas at the Senator's house. None was lacking, but their combination at that time appeared so natural, so calm, so innocent, so stable, that only the slow attrition of time might be believed to threaten it. If Mr. Munn, remembering the occasion of his speech at the first rally and looking about the pleasant, firelit room, had been struck for a moment with the force of accident and change and the thought of the solitariness of the snowy night outside, it had been only for a moment. Later, he was to curse his blindness, his stupidity, and his vanity. The signs of the future had been there in all his experiences of that time, but he had lacked the key, the clue to the code, and had seen only the ignorant surface. Or those events of the future had appeared at that time like icebergs which are seen riding on the blue and placid horizon, patches of white cloud no bigger than a man's hand, which, with seven eighths of their enormous, steel-hard, ram-like bulk submerged, may be moving unpredictably toward a fatal conjunction. And more than once or twice, in a moment of self-accusation or in the grip of an impersonal fatalism, such as the loser feels when the cards of the last hand begin to fall under the glaring, green-shaded light, he was to demand of himself: If I couldn't know myself, how could I know any of the rest of them? Or anything? Certainly he had not known himself, he would decide; if indeed the self of that time could claim any continuator in the self that was to look backward and speculate, and torture the question. Then, thinking that the self he remembered, and perhaps remembered but imperfectly, and the later self were nothing more than superimposed exposures on the same film of a camera, he felt that all of his actions had been as unaimed and meaningless as the blows of a blind man who strikes out at the undefined sounds which penetrate his private darkness.

Certainly, he was to decide, he had not known Senator Tolliver. He had not sensed for a moment the desperation that lurked beneath his urbanity, his gestures of consideration and kindness, the assured and commanding glance of his gray eyes. And, not knowing, he had been the dupe in the game which the Senator was playing with the cunning of his long experience of men and their weaknesses and with the desperation of his own immediate need. When the game had been begun, Mr. Munn could never guess. Perhaps the Senator had started in the fullest sincerity; or had started one game only to find himself involved in another, not the will then but the hand, not the hand but the instrument. That did not matter, Mr. Munn was to tell himself bitterly — the question of intention — for the Senator was one of those men whose day-to-day behavior, whose most casual gesture or familiar word, was like the campaign of a good general in that it made him able to strike in this direction or that, at need. But, in any case, he himself had been the Senator's dupe, his lackey-boy. He had been taken in. When the Senator said jump, he had jumped. And he had not been alone.

In early spring the Alta Company, Dismukes and Brothers Tobacco Company, two smaller companies, the Morton and the Regal, and a group of independent buyers made offers within one week. The offers exhibited some variations, a fraction of a cent more for prime leaf in one than in another, a fraction less for seconds, but the more closely the offers were investigated, especially in the light of the poundages on which they were based, the more superficial the variations appeared. 'I feel inclined to believe,' Mr. Sills said when he presented the offers to the board, 'that these offers represent an agreement among the concerns and individuals in question. I believe they got together on it and figured it out so the prices would work out about the same. Of course, that by itself doesn't mean the offers oughtn't to be accepted. That just occurred to me.'

'It occurred to me a long time before you even started reading any offers,' Mr. Christian muttered, as though to himself. He was lounging back in his chair, his booted legs stuck straight out under the table and his black felt on the green baize before him. Red-clay mud clung to his boots, for he had just ridden in from his place; and the hat made a dark ring of spreading moisture on the faded color of the baize. It was still raining, the water sluicing oilily down the gray panes of the windows that overlooked the alley back of the bank building.

'Ten dollars a hundred,' Mr. Peacham remarked meditatively. 'I've sure God seen the time I wished I could get that for my leaf. Last year, now.'

'Me, too,' Mr. Christian said, 'but this ain't last year.'

'Before the discussion starts —— ' Mr. Sills began.

'What!' Mr. Christian exclaimed with a ponderous sarcasm, 'you mean there's gonna be some discussion of that figure?'

'Before the discussion starts, I might remind the gentlemen here that what would have been an advantageous price to a private grower in the past is not necessarily an advantageous price under the present circumstances. We've got a considerable investment in warehousing right now. There's the interest on that investment to be considered. And the interest on sums outstanding as advances to growers whose condition made financial assistance imperative. And the costs of handling the tobacco. In calculating what would be a fair return to the individual grower we must take into consideration the Association demand to defray these necessary expenses. I can give you the precise amount' — he began to shuffle through the stacks of papers before him, his colorless eyes peering through his spectacles — 'that should be called for per thousand pounds.

And as you gentlemen know, you have to add to that amount the percentage on the gross price for the Association sinking fund.' He continued to shuffle the papers, very deliberately and with his lips moving as though he were reading to himself, and his eyes blinking slowly behind his spectacles.

'We've got those figures down to rock bottom,' Mr. Peacham said. 'I know that all right. But I wish we could shave off a little more, some way. The antis are always saying the whole principle just isn't economic. Now take that editorial last week in the *Messenger*. They say we run the price of tobacco up by tacking on a lot of items and the farmer never sees that money. And that we hurt business and hurt the community.'

'All those arguments have been satisfactorily answered, I believe.' It was Senator Tolliver talking. He was holding an unlit cigar in his hand, rolling it delicately between his fingers. 'In the papers and on the platforms. We know it is an economically justifiable method. And all reasonable men whose interest hasn't blinded them —— '

'Such a calf ain't been dropped yet,' Mr. Christian said.

' — they all see that. Even the companies themselves will probably come to accept the situation with good grace. They will save a good deal of money by being able to deal directly with a responsible organization such as the Association. It will no longer be necessary for them to run from one individual grower to another. In the end they will save more than the Association expense and per cent. They will come to see the advantages, I am sure.' He kept rolling the cigar, slowly and delicately, between the forefinger and thumb of his right hand. Now and then as he spoke — and he spoke with a slight air of constraint, of abstraction — he would glance at the pile of documents in front of Mr. Sills. Mr. Sills had, apparently, found his paper now, for he coughed sharply and catarrhally.

'And I am sure,' the Senator continued, 'they will bow to the inevitable and accept the position of the Association. I interpret these offers as a token of a new, a more reasonable attitude toward our organization.'

'I've located the figures on Association costs,' Mr. Sills said, and coughed again, dryly, matter-of-factly, this time. 'Based on the thousand pounds. Of course, next year, if we increase the poundage in the Association warehouses, we automatically reduce the costs per thousand pounds. But they are not exorbitant now. I just thought I'd go over these figures another time before we discussed the new offers.' Mr. Sills coughed once more, now apologetically.

In his dry, monotonous voice, Mr. Sills was reading his list of figures.

Even after the offers had been read, and the chairman had asked for an expression of sentiment, Mr. Munn did not sense a fundamental difference between this meeting and meetings of the past; or even when the Senator, after Mr. Christian had slammed the table and said 'Hell, no,' and the others had indecisively dropped into silence, began to speak in a calm, restrained voice, the very falling cadences of which carried an impression of tolerance and finality. He had, he said, foreseen this moment, and had tried to prepare his mind for it, the moment when they would discover a division of policy in the board. But that would not impair their harmony of purpose, he was sure. He said that the time had come to sell, that now was the time to forget the past and to think of the future. They had won a victory. No one could deny that. And next year a greater victory. And to reach an agreement with the companies would do much to relieve the tension which had resulted in those irresponsible acts of violence in Hunter County which had so embarrassed the Association. He felt it his duty, as a citizen and as a member of the Association board, to vote for an immediate acceptance of the several offers.

'There is one more thing,' Mr. Peacham said, breaking in almost before Senator Tolliver had ceased, 'and that's the fact that we've got to sell soon, anyway. If we are left with any substantial amount of this season's crop in the warehouses, we're ruined, and no doubt about that. We know we're close to the edge now. We can't borrow much more for carrying. We've got to get money for our people. That means selling. I've been thinking about this —— '

'Wait!' Mr. Christian pushed his chair back a little with a rasping sound. 'I'll sink five thousand personally in a holding fund. Till we get every God-damned penny on our published price schedule. I can raise that much, and I'll turn that in on a note of hand to the treasurer, and not a note for ninety days, either, but till the tobacco's sold. I reckon there's others can do the same thing, all right. Here in this room, and other members of the Association. And on these pissy-ant offers' — he lowered his head a little, his neck reddening and thickened with the motion, and swung his glance around the table — 'I'll vote no.'

Then the clamor of voices broke out suddenly, and the voice of Mr. Morse, the chairman, saying, 'Gentlemen, gentlemen!'

In the end it was voted to reject the offers. Mr. Munn voted for acceptance, with the Senator, Mr. Peacham, Mr. Burden, and Mr. Dicey Short. The chairman broke the tie, going to rejection. In the gray light from the rain-sluicing windows, the Senator's face appeared gray, too, and when Mr. Morse cast his deciding vote, the face seemed suddenly loose, as though the inner structure had failed that kept the lips so firmly together and maintained the fine arch of the cheek. He stopped rolling the long, pale cigar between his fingers and laid it on the green baize before him. His motion was very deliberate. The covering leaf of the cigar was frayed and cracked now. It wouldn't be any good.

Just as the meeting was breaking up, when some of the men were already moving toward the door, Mr. Christian said: 'Hey! wait a minute. I just want to say, any time you start raising subscription money to tide the Association over, that five thousand is still good. At least,' he added, grinning heavily, and pointing toward the floor, 'if those bastards downstairs there in the bank will give me another mortgage on my place.'

No one made any answer to Mr. Christian's words.

Standing near the door, Mr. Munn watched the Senator detach himself from the group of men who remained and start to leave. The Senator looked more like himself now, but still grayish and strained, as though from loss of sleep. As he turned to go, Mr. Christian barred his way. With the back of his hand, Mr. Christian tapped him solidly on the chest, and said, 'Well, Ed, no hard feelings, huh?'

'No, Bill,' the Senator answered.

Mr. Christian took a sharp look at his face. 'Fine,' he said, and stepped aside.

The Senator walked slowly to the door. He hesitated a moment beside Mr. Munn, and then reached out to touch him on the shoulder. 'Well, boy,' he said in a low voice, 'we did the best we could.' Without waiting for a reply, he passed quickly out of the door and down the dark stairs.

At the next meeting Senator Tolliver did not appear. The last members to enter the long, dingy room looked inquiringly at the Senator's accustomed chair, empty now, and then at the faces of the men already assembled. 'I reckon he's late this morning,' Mr. Dicey Short remarked.

Mr. Sills had been staring at a long beam of sunlight that fell athwart the floor beside the table. The motes that flickered brightly in it had held all his attention, apparently; but at Mr. Dicey Short's remark he turned slowly to the group, readjusted his spectacles, through which his colorless eyes peered distantly, and said: 'No, not late. Not coming is my guess.'

'Not coming?' Captain Todd demanded with a sudden and unaccustomed sharpness.

'Not now, and not later,' Mr. Sills replied, and fumbled in his coat pocket to produce a long envelope, 'if this is what I think it is.' He turned it carefully in his hands, while every man there leaned forward a little, except Captain Todd, and fixed his eyes upon the object. 'I got it this morning,' Mr. Sills said. 'Not in the mail. A nigger man was standing down here at the door of the bank, and he gave it to me when I came in. The envelope says it's to be opened at the meeting this morning.' The small sound of the tearing of the paper began, and was finished; then Mr. Sills coughed once, lightly and inwardly, while he glanced at the enclosed sheet.

'Yes,' he said, 'that's it.' And he began to read in his flat, toneless voice, stopping once or twice to clear his throat and to press his spectacles more precisely into place on the bridge of his thin, putty-colored nose:

Members of the Board of Directors, The Association of Growers of Dark Fired Tobacco — and he coughed.

Gentlemen: The conviction has been forcibly borne in upon me that my views concerning the policy of the Association are not in harmony with those of the majority of the members of the Board of Directors, even though it is my firm belief that the policy I have supported is the one of reason and peace and would be endorsed by an overwhelming majority of the actual members of the Association itself. Therefore, under these circumstances, I feel that it is my sad duty to resign from the Board of Directors of the Association of Growers of Dark Fired Tobacco, although it is with the deepest regret that I sever my connection with the esteemed gentlemen with whom it has been my privilege and honor to serve.

Very respectfully,

EDMUND TOLLIVER

Mr. Sills finished the reading, folded the sheet with a precise motion of his fingers, laid it on the table before him, and, as though to abjure responsibility, turned his head to resume his inspection of the drifting motes in the ray of sunlight. There was absolute silence in the room for some fifteen seconds. Then Mr. Christian, half-rising from his chair, leaned forward across the table and thrust out his hand toward Mr. Sills and commanded, 'Lemme see that letter.'

Mr. Sills swung his expressionless face toward Mr. Christian, then handed him the letter. Mr. Christian spread out the sheet, crackling the paper. He stared at it, and his lips moved slowly as though he could read only with difficulty. The others watched him intently. Then he flung it on the table and remarked, with an abstracted and deliberate air, 'Well, I'll be God-damned.'

The voices at the table rose clamorously.

'What I can't see is' — and Mr. Christian swung about on his heel and glared at them all — 'is why he got out. Unless it's a rule or ruin proposition with him. But you can't tell me' — and he shook his great red fist indiscriminately at the table — 'he just got his little feelings hurt. Not in harmony, my Blessed Redeemer! Don't try to tell me they used to wash behind his ears and blow his little nose for him and give him his sugar-tit every morning up there in the Senate. Harmony, my God! And he never resigned from the Senate, nor anything else before — not him!'

Captain Todd approached Mr. Christian, saying, 'Now, man, be fair to the Senator. You can't be sure —— '

'Sure? Sure! My God!'

'A man's got to go his own gait, Bill. You know that. Let Tolliver. His lights ain't your lights, nor my lights, but let him act according to his lights.'

Mr. Christian was standing before him, his head still thrust out, the blood still beating in his neck, and his stare fixed on the

Captain's face. Slowly he nodded his head, saying: 'All right, all right. His own gait.' He walked back to his chair and sat down. While the others talked, he read the letter again, that same laborious intentness again on his face.

'But it's bad, and no doubt about it,' the Captain was declaring, 'coming at this time. The loss of his prestige will hurt. No doubt about it. And to select a new man to finish out his term. It's a bad time. But it's up to us.'

Mr. Christian raised his eyes from the paper, and said somewhat restrainedly: 'Listen to this, what he says: "... even though it is my firm belief that the policy I have supported is the one of reason and peace and would be endorsed by an overwhelming majority of the actual members of the Association itself." ' He let his glance move down the table, face by face, and come to rest at last upon Captain Todd. 'Do you believe he's right?' he demanded.

'If I did, I'd have supported him,' the Captain replied quietly.

'Do you think he thinks that is right?'

'I don't know,' the Captain said. 'He's written it.'

'What made him write that down?' And Mr. Christian tapped the very sentence with his thick forefinger.

'Every man has to go his own gait,' the Captain answered.

As Mr. Christian read that sentence aloud, it struck Mr. Munn's mind, as it had not before, with a force that seemed to graze off tangentially, and lead to a confused darkness of speculations. Mr. Christian was right, it was the key of the letter. It was not like the rest of the letter. It really didn't belong in the letter, at least not when stated that way. Especially that about the overwhelming majority. It didn't belong. Not in this letter to them. Then the thought slipped from his mind, to return, but only casually, just before he fell asleep that night, and then again, sharply and fully, the next morning when he sat at breakfast in the hotel dining-room and saw that very sentence in the newspaper.

There was a big story about the resignation, and the letter was printed in full in the body of the story. It was a Nashville paper. He rose hurriedly from his chair and went into the lobby to get the local paper and the *Edgerton Messenger*. In both the letter was reprinted in full. The *Bardsville Ledger* carried, in addition, an editorial under the heading 'Does Association Betray Farmers' Interest?' It began: 'When a man who has served the people of his section so long and ably as has Senator Edmund Tolliver feels it necessary to resign from the organization he has helped to create, because he feels it is betraying its trust and is leading the community into paths of disorder against the will of the majority, then it is time for all thinking men to stop and reconsider the whole situation.' It was the same sentence, the very same, transparently re-dressed. All right, Mr. Munn thought, out in the open, the belly-dragging dog. He crushed the paper between his hands, gulped the last of his coffee, which was cold now, and went back into the lobby.

He telephoned Mr. Sills. When Mr. Sills answered the call, he said: 'I want to talk to you bad, Mr. Sills, but I don't want every old woman out your pike hanging on the line listening. Are you going to be in town today? It may be important.'

Mr. Sills was coming to town. 'Right away,' he replied.

He hurried up to his office, and tried to work until Mr. Sills appeared. But it was little use. The page of the book would blur before his eyes. He thought of the Senator's words, 'Well, boy, we did the best we could,' and of his back as he had seen it that day disappearing down the dark stairs. He slammed his book shut and began to pace about his office. He sent the girl who did his letters and typing out to buy him some matches, even though he had a dozen in his pocket. While she was gone he got the bottle out of his desk and took two moderate drinks. Then, incongruously, while he tried to penetrate to the nature of the Senator's motives, he thought of May, how sometimes when he looked at her most intently, into the very depth of her eyes, she seemed to be withdrawing from him, fading, almost imperceptibly but surely, into an impersonal and ambiguous distance.

When he heard steps in the outer room, he rushed to the door, and flung it open. At the sight of Mr. Sills, the impatience and curiosity that had been consuming him suddenly were chilled.

'Well, sir?' Mr. Sills demanded in his flat voice.

'Did you' — and Mr. Munn hesitated that last second as one who poises on the brink, not because of failure in decision but because the mechanism of the body registered, as it were, a last blind protest — 'did you provide any newspaper, or individual, with a copy of Senator Tolliver's letter of resignation?'

He knew what the answer would be; he had known all the time. It came like an echo of his knowledge. 'No, I didn't,' Mr. Sills said.

Mr. Munn handed the papers to him and indicated the reports and the editorial. Mr. Sills read them slowly, and with no show of emotion. When he had finished, he raised his eyes to Mr. Munn, and remarked, 'Well?'

'My God!' Mr. Munn exclaimed. 'In every one. The Louisville paper isn't here yet, but I bet it's in there too. He sent copies out, to every paper. That's why he wrote that letter that way. He wrote it to do the most harm to us all.'

'Well,' Mr. Sills said.

'But why? What's he up to?' Mr. Munn swung on his heel and strode across the office, then swung back toward Mr. Sills with his bony, dark face thrust forward. 'I don't see; I don't know what to think.'

'It'll all come out soon enough. Time. Time will bring it out.' Mr. Sills' eyes blinked unhurriedly behind his spectacles.

It was almost a month before Mr. Munn was to know even the next step in the process. More than once during that period he had the impulse to go to Monclair and see Senator Tolliver

and ask him what his motives were. How could a man behave
as he had done? But he had no right, he would conclude. In
the end, he scarcely knew Senator Tolliver. The illusion of old
intimacy and trust was something which the Senator had created
with the touch of his hand on the shoulder and the modulation
of his voice. There was no reason to feel, as he did nevertheless
feel, that the Senator had betrayed him, personally. But
despite his reasoning, that sense of a personal betrayal was his
first reaction when, late one afternoon, Mr. Sills telephoned to
say that Senator Tolliver and the Dismukes and Brothers Tobacco Company were jointly suing the Association to recover
the crop which the Senator had committed to the Association.
That night the Nashville papers carried news of the filing of
the suit; and the next day in the *Bardsville Ledger* Senator Tolliver
gave out the statement that his conscience would no longer
permit him to be party, even passively, to the policies of an
organization that had become an enemy of law and order and
individual integrity.

'There hasn't been any trouble lately, not at all,' Mr. Munn
asserted when Mr. Christian thrust the paper with the statement under his eyes; 'not in over a month. Not since Sullins'
crop was burned. And they'll probably catch whoever did
that.'

'No,' Mr. Christian said shortly, 'there ain't been much
trouble, but Edmund Tolliver is shore God getting ready to
cause a whole lot of trouble. Bad trouble,' and he stared
probingly into Mr. Munn's face.

'Trouble,' Mr. Munn repeated. 'What do you mean?'

'I mean there's a lot of men don't take things lying down.
You can't blame 'em. Fire with fire.'

Mr. Munn looked somberly away, out the window toward the
sidewalk, which was empty of all life except for an old negro
man sitting on the curb. 'It'll wreck us,' he declared. 'That's
what we've tried to stop. The companies want trouble. I'll

bet half the trouble over in Hunter County was started by blackguards who got paid to start it. You never can tell. It's the best way to kill the Association. The companies want trouble.'

'And by God!' Mr. Christian said, 'they may get their bellyful.'

As he rode home that afternoon he turned the question over and over in his mind. Did the Senator want power? He assumed that that was the objective. Power. But if Senator Tolliver, who had helped to create the Association, had remained on the board, and the Association had succeeded, then he would have been in a position of power. The Association people would have been behind him, and a good solid farm vote in the section went a long way toward electing a man to anything. But now he was out to break what he had made. To destroy what you create — that was power, the fullest manifestation. Maybe that was it, he thought. The last vanity.

May was in the side garden, as she had been that afternoon months before, when he had ridden his mare to a lather to get home to tell May that he was to be on the board. But the season was different now. It had been almost fall then, the zinnias dry and rusty, the maple leaves pocked and faded and hanging motionless on the boughs or lying sparsely on the overgrown gravel of the walk, one here, one there. She had been standing there, as she was accustomed to do in the fall, among the ruins of the garden which she had forgotten all summer. He had moved swiftly toward her then, the grass over the gravel carpeting his tread, and had tried to seize on and understand the very essence of her aloneness as she stood there unaware of his approach.

Now, as then, he moved swiftly toward her, his steps muffled, and his attention poised for the moment when she would turn to discover him. She was kneeling beside the walk. She wore no hat, and her hair was disheveled and slipping from its heavy coils. The pale light that washed through the budding trees accented delicately the yellow of her hair.

He was almost upon her before she lifted her head.

'Hello,' he said, and stretched out his hand to help her to her feet. She dropped the trowel with which she had been digging in the flower bed, and stood up to kiss him. 'Oh, Perse,' she told him, 'I'm getting ready to plant some nasturtiums. Along the walk here. Don't you think that would be nice?'

'Yes,' he answered. Her gaze went back to the little patch of black earth and mold which she had turned up from under the cover of last year's leaves.

'You know,' he said, 'Tolliver is suing the Association. For his tobacco.'

'Oh, Perse, can he do that?'

'He's doing it,' he commented. He noticed that she was still looking at the patch of ground. 'If he wins, it's all up with us. That's all.'

At that she looked at him, and her face assumed an expression of concern. 'But he won't,' she predicted. 'You all will win, won't you, Perse?'

'Maybe not. You can't ever tell, and the Dismukes people are suing jointly. You see, he's trying to sell his crop to them. Probably we won't win.' He had not previously considered the possibility that the Association would lose such a suit. He had not been worried about that particular thing. The damage, the worst damage, was being done in other ways. And even now he had not settled the probabilities in his own mind. But he was saying it, saying that the Association would probably lose. And saying it because he wanted, as he discovered at that moment with a cold sense of satisfaction, to deepen that look of concern on her face, to frighten her, to make her aware of the evil and the instability in the world, to make her suffer. Then, with that discovery, he took a stronger relish even as he ended:

'Yes, it's very likely we'll lose. Then you'll feel the pinch.' He enjoyed the moment, postponing consideration of the event, and of the judgment which, he knew, he would later bring to bear bitterly against himself.

'I'm sorry, Perse,' she said, and laid her hand on his arm. 'But don't worry, Perse, don't worry so much.'

He stared at her face for an instant, as though he drew a nourishment from the distress which was so obvious upon it. Then he asked: 'And why shouldn't I worry? Tell me that.'

'Oh, Perse, don't be that way,' she pleaded, and clung to his arm, drawing it against her side. He made no reply, looking away from her, at the young grass over the gravel of the walk.

'I never did like him,' she said after a minute meditatively. 'Not a bit. I tried, but I never could.'

'You never said anything,' he observed.

'No' — and she hesitated — 'I didn't. I didn't know anything. And you liked him so much and thought so much of him, and looked up to him the way you did. I didn't want to say anything, when you felt that way. But I never liked him, I don't know why.'

'It's easy for you to say that now,' he said bitterly, still not looking at her.

'No, it's been for a long time. Maybe it was something that day at his house. The way his sister always acted when he was around, the way she never took her eyes off him in a way that made you creepy.'

'You imagined it,' he said. He was irritated with her story. He did not want to hear it.

'No, and that night when she took me upstairs, I happened to glance at that little picture at the head of the stairs — maybe you saw it, a picture of a woman — and she stopped and held the light close up, and said, "That was his wife." Then she turned around and looked at him — he was standing in the hall down there, just getting ready to go back to the living-room.

She looked at him that way, then she said, "She was an angel." It made you believe that old story about them, about her.'

'About him driving her to being a dope fiend?' he demanded. 'Killing herself with morphine? That's scandalmongering. She was rich and he got her money, when she died. That made the gossip.'

'I never liked him from the moment I laid eyes on him,' she declared.

He drew his arm from her clasp. 'He'll ruin us all,' he said. He looked directly into her face. 'You and me, too,' he added, 'he'll ruin us.'

'Don't worry so, Perse,' she begged, reaching for his arm again. 'It'll all be all right. It's bound to —— '

'Nothing's bound to,' he said.

'You mustn't worry; just try to forget it now.' She drew him, trying to lead him a step or two down the path, pulling his arm, and reluctantly he followed. 'I'm going to make another bed here,' she announced, 'for some nasturtiums. And cosmos over there.' She gestured toward the open space beyond which stood the weathered, soft-toned brick wall of the house. 'And marigolds, they'll be nice against the house. And around that old stump there' — she pointed to a thick stump, black with rot, which stood in the middle of a patch of pale, newly springing grass — 'there is a good place for pansies. The ground ought to be rich there.' She took a step toward the old stump, and quickly knelt and dug her fingers into the soft, crumbly earth. Then, with her face lighted by pleasure, she looked upward, over her shoulder, at him.

She rose and came back to him, holding her stained hands toward him and still smiling. They began to move toward the house. 'But I'll need somebody to help me,' she was saying, 'a man to spade up and all. You'll let a man come up soon, won't you, Perse? The next day or two, before —— '

He stopped still in the middle of the walk, and looked her in the face. 'No,' he answered, and heard his own words coming with that impersonal and measured decision, 'you know every hand on the place is busy right now. It's a rush season, and I can't spare one. Not one. You've lived on a farm all your life, you ought to know that much.' He watched the expression of her face change from pleasure to surprise, then from pain to bewilderment; and then he continued: 'Besides, you don't really want to have a garden. After a few weeks you never look at it. I've noticed that, as long as I've known you. It's just something you do, and then you don't even take the trouble to direct somebody about keeping it in condition in the summer. Why do you want to start a garden? It's very unreasonable, you know, under the circumstances. You being the way you are. About things.'

She had taken a step away from him, but with her face still toward him. She turned, very suddenly, and began to walk away, down the path. Impersonally, he noticed the light falling palely over her and the way her shoulders moved and hunched together a little. She was trying to suppress a sob, he knew.

His first impulse was to rush after her. But he did not. He stood in the middle of the path, staring after her. Then he looked down at the spot where, before his arrival, she had been digging. There lay the old, rusty trowel, which she had grasped with her small and inadequate fingers. Not four square feet of the soil was turned up, and that had merely been pecked at with the useless instrument. As he looked, a sadness overcame him, more than sadness, a despair that seemed to well from some profound truth that he had never before suspected, and that even now was veiled from his view.

Mr. Munn had gone down with Captain Todd to the Association warehouse in Bardsville one afternoon a couple of weeks later to inspect an extension that was almost completed, when

Mr. Christian came to tell him the whole truth about Senator Tolliver.

'There's some chance those sheds'll never be filled,' the Captain had commented gravely as they left the new section and went back into the pungent gloom of the main warehouse. 'But even if we could have broken the contract for the new building, to do it would've just been a way of saying we were half-licked already.'

'It's hard,' Mr. Munn had said, standing there in the middle of the floor under the high, shadowy rafters and beams. 'It's hard to know what to do. Where to strike.'

'Win the suit. That's first.'

'That's just one thing. If everything could just be brought together at one time, one place, just so you could fight it and have it over' — he had raised his right fist slowly — 'so you could get at it, all at once.' He had brought his fist hard into the palm of his left hand with a solid, smacking sound: 'Like that.'

Captain Todd had peered at him in the dim light, and answered: 'No, Perse. No way in the world. Never a time in a man's life when everything is like that, so you can just lift up your hand, and win or lose and settle everything. Almost that way, maybe once or twice in a man's life. But never so you can settle everything. It's too much to ask.'

Mr. Munn had thought of Captain Todd lying out that night with his men at the ford, waiting for the next rush; and then, looking at the Captain's quiet face, he had wondered how much had seemed to come together that night, how much had seemed to be settling itself there for good and all, with almost a single blow. 'Maybe not,' Mr. Munn had slowly replied.

Mr. Christian found them there. As he approached, they could guess, even in the gloom, the rigidity of controlled fury in his stiff-legged stride and in the heavy hunch of his shoulders. He came directly to them and stopped directly in front of them.

His jaws were clamped shut as though by an effort of will he kept himself from speech. When he did allow himself to speak, his voice was harsh and measured.

'Well,' he said, 'they got at Tolliver.'

'Sure, they did,' Mr. Munn replied. 'Dismukes.'

'Naw, naw' — Mr. Christian spoke as though with impatience at stupidity. 'Long before that. They got at him, because he's broke. Broke, and owes money.'

Captain Todd whistled softly through his teeth, and lifted his hand to touch his beard.

'Yeah, broke! The bank in Morgansville holds a mortgage for fifteen thousand and something, and God knows how much he owes to the Mercantile National in Louisville. The mortgage in Morgansville was coming due, and they began putting the screws on him. The tobacco people are thick as thieves with the Mercantile National, and the big boys up at the Mercantile just pass on the word to Morgansville.' He spoke with a sharp expulsion of breath at every word, as though he would spit the words out of his great yellow teeth, from which the lips drew back; but he spoke with a strained and artificial deliberation. 'And he was to see that the Association sold out, took up all those offers. That was the first thing. No telling what was next on the ticket. But we didn't sell, and so they decided to play it the other way. The way they are.'

'How do you know?' the Captain demanded. 'Do you know for a fact?'

'For a fact! By God, a fact! There's a man over in Morgansville named Pottle, works in the bank. And he married a cousin of Sills and he owes Sills money and favors, and he's been picking up stuff. So Sills got to putting the screws on him, and now he's scared to death he'll lose his job, and he will if he don't keep on playing ball. The egg-sucking dog!' Mr. Christian spat viciously, then put his booted foot over the spot and ground his heel.

'Can you believe this fellow?' the Captain asked.

'Hell, I wouldn't trust the bastard as far as I can fling a Jersey bull by the tail. Not if he's playing it his way. But, by God, he's so yellow you can scare the pee outer him with a couple of unkind words. And we worked on him last night, Sills and me' — he leered with a deep satisfaction — 'and by God, I mean to say we worked on him. When he got in his buggy long about one o'clock this morning to drive back to town from Sills' place, he was pale as a man with a three-weeks spell of summer complaint. By God, he was cleaned out.'

'You never can tell,' the Captain said slowly, 'what's in a man's mind. You never can.'

'Hell, no, and him coming to my house all this winter, and sitting there talking to me and looking me in the eye, and talking pretty, and saying, "Now, Bill, now, Bill" — and knowing all the time how it was with him. Knowing how it was. How he was gonna sell us out, one way or another. Knowing it and just feeling it grow inside him. Sitting there and feeling it grow inside him like a tumor or something. And looking a man straight in the eye. By God —— ' He stopped breathlessly, the quality of his accustomed violence coming back to him and his face reddening, while he waved his arms. Then he swung toward Mr. Munn, and said, 'And you, Perse, you swallowing him hook, line, and sinker, by God, he was taking you in, you voting right along with him.'

'I know,' Mr. Munn said gloomily.

'Trying to take us all in,' Mr. Christian continued, 'giving a party up there in that big house a dope fiend's money built, and patting us on the back and pouring out the likker. By God, it makes a man want to puke. What does he think I am? Is a man a hog to come to his holler because he slopped him? I ask you now, am I a whore to unbutton just because I see a five-dollar bill? Hell, no! and it's all the same whether it's in a feather bed or behind the barn. Whether he's rich or poor, it don't matter to me. And there's hams in my smokehouse better'n the bastard ever put on his table, and flour in the flour barrel, and whisky on the shelf, and no woman I drove dope-crazy built my house. Hell, no, my folks built it, and ain't a joist slipped yet, nor a rafter sagged.'

'Good-bye,' the Captain said, and put out his hand. 'I think I'll go out home.'

They shook hands with him. His face, Mr. Munn noticed, even in the dim light, was pale and drawn. As he walked away toward the bright square of the doorway, his figure seemed to have lost some of its erectness, and his step seemed less firm. Mr. Munn nodded after him, saying, 'This'll hurt him. He thought something of Tolliver.'

'Yeah,' Mr. Christian grunted. He was studying Mr. Munn's face. Then he asked, 'Well, what are you gonna do now?'

'I don't know,' Mr. Munn said. 'I don't know what to do.'

'I know what to do.'

'What?' Mr. Munn demanded.

'Naw,' Mr. Christian said, 'naw. Not today.' He suddenly stepped directly in front of Mr. Munn, and seized him by the shoulder, and stared into his face. 'You come out to my house tomorrow night. And I'll tell you. You come and spend the night.'

Mr. Munn nodded slowly, abstractedly.

Chapter six

LUCILLE CHRISTIAN admitted Mr. Munn into the hall when he arrived at the Christian place just after dark.

'I'm sorry I couldn't get out for supper,' he told her. 'It was nice of you all to ask me. But I had more work than I could get through this afternoon.'

'We were sorry,' she said. She pushed the door closed, and though it was heavy it swung soundlessly on the hinges. Then she stood there with her hand on the knob, not as though waiting for him to speak or move, but as though he were not there at all, as though she could sink at will into the deep and complete satisfaction of her own being. The light from the lamp on the marble-topped table gave her dark blue, too-large eyes a velvety appearance, and gave the flesh of her face a faint gold tinge, as though an almost infinitesimal amount of light had been captured by the flesh itself and was now released. Mr. Munn glanced at the flesh of her arm under the lace insertion of the sleeve, trying to determine if that golden tinge was caught there too, but he could not tell.

Actually, she stood there for only an instant, balancing herself at the end of the gesture that had closed the door; but it was long enough to give him that impression of complete stillness, of absorbed repose, which he had discovered, with surprise, that day of the rally when she had stood in the middle of the floor of the shadowy, dull room at the hotel.

'The others are already here,' she said. 'In the parlor.'

The others, he thought wonderingly.

She moved across the hall briskly and laid her hand on the knob of a closed door. Her waist was small and straight, where the lawn was gathered at the wide, embroidered belt, and her neck rose very straight from the banded lace collar of the guimpe. She pushed open the door with a firm motion. 'Just go in,' she told him.

'Thank you,' he replied, and bowed slightly.

She made no reply.

He saw Mr. Christian rising to meet him, and then the two other men. 'Well, you got here,' Mr. Christian was saying. 'Wish you'd had supper with us. We had some right good vittles, if I do say it. Sukie, now, she sets a good table; she keeps the niggers humping round that kitchen.' He thrust out his big hand at Mr. Munn, and said, 'Sorry you couldn't come.'

'I know I missed something,' Mr. Munn rejoined.

'Maybe he did, didn't he, Mac?' Mr. Christian nodded in the direction of one of the two other men, a stranger, a lanky man with coarse, reddish hair.

'He sure did,' the red-haired man said in a gentle, drawling voice, 'and I'm a judge.'

Mr. Christian led Mr. Munn across the room to the other man, who was tall too, and so gauntly rawboned that his long, square-cut black coat hung from his shoulders in apparently empty folds. 'Well, Professor,' Mr. Christian said, 'this is Percy Munn.' And turning to Mr. Munn: 'And this is Professor Ball. But I bet you know him. Everybody knows the Professor.'

'I know Mr. Munn,' the rawboned man responded, and thrust out his hand, 'but I haven't seen him in a long time, years, in fact. Tonight is a privilege.'

'Thank you, sir,' Mr. Munn said, and was about to grasp the offered hand when he saw that it was completely swathed in bandages. Involuntarily he stopped, his glance resting on the carefully wound cloths. Each finger was wrapped separately to make a great, clumsy, club-like glove. Then he remembered.

'It will cause me no pain,' the Professor assured him, and seized Mr. Munn's hand. 'A trifling affliction which time and the ministrations of my learned son-in-law over there' — and he nodded toward the red-haired man — 'may serve to remedy. And ——'

'A case of impetigo,' the red-haired man added, 'and peculiarly stubborn.'

'Vulgarly known,' the Professor continued, 'as the country leprosy. But not Biblical, I rejoice to state —— But, as I was about to say, it is a privilege to shake your hand, if I may say so. A young man who does credit to his community. A privilege for an old man who is about to go from the stage of action to greet the rising Roscius.'

'Thank you, sir,' Mr. Munn said. 'It is my privilege.' The Professor couldn't be very old, he noticed, not much more than sixty. His hair was not gray, and there was scarcely any gray in his scraggly, red-brown beard which sprang in tangled tufts from the bony chin and cheeks, like vegetation that hardily finds a foothold on an arid and rocky hillside.

Mr. Christian introduced him to the lanky, red-haired man. That was Doctor MacDonald, the son-in-law of Professor Ball, and, he added, a native of Louisiana but by way of being an adopted Kentuckian.

'Yes, sir, an adopted Kentuckian,' the Professor repeated. 'A good woman will do a lot for a man, now. They've saved some from the curse of the bottle. They've led some to the light of salvation. And my daughter Cordelia — as I may remark with pardonable paternal pride — has almost made a Kentuckian out of Doctor MacDonald.'

'Now that's a fact,' Doctor MacDonald agreed, laughing. He laughed easily and softly, easily like a man who finds the world hung together right and himself at home in it, and softly like a man who finds part of his pleasure always in the privacy of himself. 'A fact, now,' he repeated, letting his lanky frame fold back in the big rocking chair, and laying his long, sinewy hands on his knees.

I wonder what they're doing here, Mr. Munn thought. They hadn't just happened in, apparently, for Lucille Christian's words, 'The others are already here,' had implied that they were expected, and presumably that they were expecting him. He knew Professor Ball, all right, even if not much more than by sight. But he hadn't seen him in years. Had a farm over in Hunter County and wrote letters to the papers about the preservation of fertility and all. Letters full of quotations from Thomas Jefferson and old John Taylor, and from the Latin — Virgil mostly, he remembered. And he ran an academy for boys. But Mr. Munn had never heard of Doctor Mac-Donald.

'I knew your uncle,' Professor Ball was saying, 'over in our section.'

'Uncle Mord?' Mr. Munn asked.

'Mordecai Munn, and a fine Christian gentleman he was, I can assure you. The happy warrior, for a fact now,

> Who, doomed to go in company with Pain,
> And Fear, and Bloodshed, miserable train!
> Turns his necessity to glorious gain.

Mordecai Munn, his spitten-image.'

'I'm glad to hear you say that,' Mr. Munn said.

'You might say we led forth our flock together, as the poet puts it, for we were in Professor Bowie's old academy together. Yes, sir, side by side, and I knew him well. Smart as a whip he was, and a spirited boy, but not an apt scholar, I regret to state. Many's the time he said to me, "Now, Beany" — for they called me by that name, having begun by calling me Beanpole, I always being spare-made, boy as well as man — "Now, Beany, you do my Cicero for me, and I'll lend you my cap-and-ball when you go squirrel hunting next time." And I would do it all right, and I like as not never took the loan of his cap-and-ball, never till this day being much of a sporting man, and even then having a love of the beautiful and eloquent word. But

Mordecai, you might say he scarce took a sup of the Pierian spring, so to speak. He couldn't sit still, it seemed like. I'd speak with him and remonstrate sometimes, but he'd say, "You know, Beany, if I just sit still I go to sleep." And he did, for a fact — sound asleep like a man with that jewel above price, an easy conscience. Yes, sir.' Professor Ball suddenly leaned forward in his chair and thrust his long neck out, with a quick, viper-like motion, and spat accurately into the dead, gray wood ashes that filled the cold fireplace.

My God, Mr. Munn thought, is he going to talk all night? Mr. Christian, he observed, was staring gloomily into the empty fireplace, with his head bowed a little so that the lamp-light shone on the slick, pink surface of his bald skull; and Doctor MacDonald lay comfortably sprawled in the rocking chair, his legs thrust out before him, and his unlit pipe stuck be-tween his teeth, which were revealed in a kind of secret half smile.

'Yes, sir,' Professor Ball continued, 'sound asleep, and never a subjunctive to disturb his slumber. But then the war came on, and he said, "Beany, my boy, off I go." And he did, not nineteen years of age. He bore a charmed life, they all said. And when it was over, he came back, after what you might denominate as feats of superhuman endurance and heroic valor. Then' — and Professor Ball spat again, with that quick, viper-like forward thrust of the long neck — 'that man who had been, you might say miraculously, preserved through storms of shot and shell, just stops to light his pipe one morning when he comes out on the front porch to look at the state of the weather, and he stumbles and falls down the front steps and breaks his neck. Before the prime of life, and the porch not very high. Truly, man knoweth not the hour of his going forth.' Professor Ball slowly raised one of his big, clumsy, club-like bandaged hands in an oracular gesture, then let it subside.

'He died a long time ago,' Mr. Munn said. 'I just barely remember him when he'd come to see us sometimes.'

'It was in 'seventy-eight he fell down the steps. Thirty-five years old, I recollect, and just three years older than me. But when we were boys we were together in Professor Bowie's Academy, because I was forward with my books, if I may be permitted without immodesty to say so. And Mordecai not having the name of an apt scholar.' He shook his head gravely, then added, 'But he was a God-fearing gentleman.'

Mr. Christian got heavily to his feet, and stood by the table where the lamp was. Professor Ball glanced at him, then said: 'But you must condone my rambling recollections. The vice of approaching age, my boy.' He stopped a moment, then spoke again. 'I know we are gathered here for a serious purpose.' He looked inquiringly at Mr. Christian.

'You're damned tooting, Professor,' Mr. Christian returned. 'You r'ar back and tell him. I believe the boy's ripe and honing for gospel.'

'It's a simple proposition,' Professor Ball said. 'Very simple.' He lifted his hands and put the tips of his bandaged fingers together and meditatively tapped them, while his voice assumed an impersonal tone. Just like in his school, Mr. Munn thought.

'Very simple. It unfolded from a few family conversations between my son-in-law here, Doctor MacDonald, and me. Just two things determine the price of any commodity. Supply and demand.' He gently tapped the bandaged fingers together. 'Yes, sir. Now, the demand for tobacco, you might say, is constant from one year to the next. *Ergo*, the supply of tobacco is what determines the price. It is on that principle that the Association is founded.'

'That's right,' Mr. Munn said.

'But the Association is being attacked by fair means and foul. In the public press and in the courts of justice, by the moneyed interests. These interests walk in darkness and strike the unwary man and rob him of the fruit of his toil. What the Association needs is a means of controlling the supply of tobacco.'

'You can't do that,' Mr. Munn pointed out, 'except by getting everybody in the Association. God knows, we've tried hard enough.'

Professor Ball lifted one commanding hand, as though for silence in a schoolroom, and smiled. 'Let us suppose that there were another Association with the sole aim of controlling supply. But let me digress, if you please, sir. When, I ask, is the tobacco plant most vulnerable? When it is young and tender. In the plant bed before it is set in the field. Then a few strokes of a hoe, and a thousand pounds of leaf have disappeared. Very simple.'

'You mean ——' Mr. Munn hesitated. He looked at Professor Ball's palish, preacherish face, with its high, narrow forehead and scraggly beard. 'You mean, scrape a man's plant bed?'

'You might go so far as to say it was his own fault,' Professor Ball said. 'He'd have a free option. He could join the Association and abide by its rules and regulations, or' — he looked away from Mr. Munn and fixed his mild gaze on some imaginary spot across the room in the shadow — 'it would be his own responsibility.'

Mr. Munn shook his head and rose slowly to his feet. 'It just isn't in me, I reckon,' he admitted. Mr. Christian came quickly to him and put a heavy hand on his shoulder, as though to force him back into his seat, and said, 'Now, Perse, don't be going off half-cocked!' Doctor MacDonald, who had not changed his position, was watching with that same secret half smile on his face and the dead pipe stuck between his bared teeth.

'You'd be surprised what's in you,' Professor Ball said quietly, 'sometimes. Now take me, for instance.'

Mr. Munn sank slowly into his chair.

'I'm a peaceful man. My hand has never been raised in anger against a fellow creature. When I was young, my weak constitution kept me from following the path of patriotic valor, like your uncle Mordecai. And I often meditated going into the ministry and preaching the gospel of Jesus Christ, and many's the night I wrestled with the angel in sweat and prayer to know if I had a clear and certain call. Yes, sir, I'm a man of peace. But it's surprising to a man what he'll find in himself sometimes.'

Mr. Munn shook his head meditatively. 'No,' he said.

But Professor Ball seemed to be paying him no attention. He was not even looking at him. 'Now what's the right thing one time, that thing the next time is wrong. It's in the Bible that way, and the Stagirite. If I peruse him aright. Yes, sir, there is a time. For one thing and another. And a man never knows what he'll find in himself when the time comes.' Suddenly he jerked himself forward, toward Mr. Munn, with that same viper-like thrust as when he had spat, but now his whole attenuated body partook of the motion, and he pointed his arm at Mr. Munn, shaking the long, knobby bandage of his forefinger. 'And now's the time. Now. Before that case ever gets to a jury. Now.' The long, bandaged finger flickered and came to rest pointed at Mr. Munn's chest, like a loaded pistol. 'There's trouble in the air and in the hearts of men now, this minute. You won't be making the trouble. There's been trouble in Hunter County, and there'll be worse. You won't be making it, but you'll be making it mean something. You can't stop it. It's coming. You can't stop the mountain torrent, but you can make it feed the fruitful plain and not waste itself.'

'Hell, no, you didn't make the trouble' — Mr. Christian lunged to his feet again. 'That bastard Tolliver made it, and all those bastards behind him, whose names I don't know, but, by God! I wish I did so I could say 'em over every night. Tolliver and Tolliver's kind. And don't tell me you're gonna sit there right now and suck right along with him. Like you did. My God!'

Before he went to bed that night, Mr. Munn agreed to join

the Free Farmers' Brotherhood of Protection and Control. Before he finally said, 'Yes, I'm with you, I reckon,' he knew that he would do it. He resisted their arguments, and resisted the impulse that grew within himself, clinging to the present with that blind instinct that opposes even desired and expected change and makes a man linger even at the moment when he escapes from an unhappy, though accustomed, scene; or clinging to it that the delay might make all the sweeter his acquiescence, all the greater his relief when he should make the final plunge into certainty. He said, 'Yes, I'm with you, I reckon,' and saw Doctor MacDonald, who had never said a word the whole time, looking at him with that same half smile, an expression that seemed to say he had foreknown the entire matter.

'The Free Farmers' Brotherhood of Protection and Control,' Mr. Christian commented; 'now ain't that something? Protection and control. Professor, you're a mighty smart man. Now ain't he, Perse?'

Mr. Munn replied, 'Yes, sir.'

'I always said good learning's a fine thing. It never hurt nobody. And just look'— and he gestured toward the erect and emaciated figure of Professor Ball—'that's what it'll do for a man!'

'Thank you, sir,' Professor Ball said, and turned and spat into the fireplace. 'I have a little motto which came into my head for the Brotherhood. In the French tongue,' he added, clearing his throat slightly. '*Le bras pour le droit.*'

'That's fine,' Mr. Christian declared. 'That sounds mighty fine.'

'Thank you, sir,' Professor Ball answered.

'What does it go on to say?'

'It says'— and Professor Ball laid the tips of his bandaged fingers together—'"The arm for the right."'

'By God!' Mr. Christian exclaimed, 'the arm for the right! Professor, you're a smart man, sure as a dog's got fleas. Now ain't he, Perse?' He turned and slapped Mr. Munn on the shoulder and shook him.

'Yes, sir,' Mr. Munn agreed. 'That's true.'

'And the doc there, too,' Mr. Christian said, and waved his arm toward Doctor MacDonald's chair. 'The doc, too. He's a smart man.' Then he turned directly to him, and urged, 'Mac, you tell him about the start you made over in your section.'

The doctor unclenched his pipestem from his teeth, and said in his gentle, drawling voice: 'Now, it's nothing much to talk about. We've just got three little bands of Free Farmers together and organized already. We call them bands; ten men to a band, and a captain. We calculated that ten men was a good round number. And ten bands would make a company with a commander at the head. Professor Ball here' — and with his pipestem he indicated his father-in-law — 'he wanted to call the commander a centurion, but we figured——'

'In their great days, the Romans,' Professor Ball interrupted, 'were a people of sturdy farmers. History teaches us that. Remember Cincinnatus, plowing his four jugera of land. A simple farmer. And what does Cicero say in a similar connection?'

'Durned if I know,' Mr. Christian said.

'He says' — and he fixed his gaze severely upon Mr. Christian, and then, in turn, upon the other two men, 'he says, "a villa in senatum arcessebatur et Curius et ceteri senes, exquo qui eos arcessebant viatores nominati sunt."'

'Is that a fact?' demanded Mr. Christian.

'It is,' Professor Ball affirmed. 'And the word "centurion," to come back——'

'Yes,' Doctor MacDonald interrupted, 'we figured "centurion" might confuse a lot of people over in Hunter County, sounding sort of foreign the way it does, and there being so many foreign tobacco buyers around here.'

'It's in the Bible,' Professor Ball said; '"And Jesus said unto the centurion, Go thy way, and as thou hast believed, so be it done unto thee." It's in the Bible.'

'Sure, sure,' Doctor MacDonald granted amiably, 'yes, sir. But, now, not every man over in Hunter County is as good a Bible scholar as you, Professor, and it might just get a lot of them twisted up. So "commander" looks like it might be better.'

'Maybe so,' Professor Ball said grudgingly.

'And over all the companies there would be a chief. The men in every band would elect their captain, and the captains would elect their commanders, and the chief and his council would direct the policy. That's the way it would be. And fast, if it's gonna do any good.'

'But careful,' Professor Ball warned. 'Only men of good name. No blackguards and riffraff, only worthy and respectable men with a good name in their community. That's the kind of men we've got joined up over in Hunter County.'

'That's right,' Doctor MacDonald said. 'Only men of good name. And what we want you to do, Mr. Munn, is to give us a few names. And to speak to a few men yourself — sort of sound them out, you know. You might get a few to come in when you do, and take the oath at the same time.'

'The oath?' Mr. Munn asked. 'You take an oath?'

Professor Ball nodded gravely. 'It would stick in the throat of no honorable man,' he said. And he added, 'A sacred oath.'

'We just want you to use your influence a little, now,' Doctor MacDonald said. 'And give us a list to be working on.'

'I'll give you a list,' Mr. Munn promised, 'but I won't speak to anybody until after I've joined myself. Until after. I don't know why, but that's just the way I feel about it.'

'That's what you might call a pretty scruple,' Professor Ball said, nodding. 'I always respect a man's scruples, whatsoe'er they be, when he names them and abides by them.'

'But I'll give you some names. If you'll let me have something to write with, Mr. Bill.'

Mr. Christian got a piece of paper, a bottle of ink, and a pen out of the tall, scroll-worked rosewood secretary in the corner, the door of which creaked when he opened it. He uncorked the bottle with fingers that seemed too thick and impatient for the task, and set it down near Mr. Munn's elbow, under the yellow rays of the lamp. The marble of the table-top had faint, yellowish graining, and stains as of a delicate golden rust, which the light emphasized. As Mr. Munn picked up the pen, he noticed the fact, and idly recollected how, when he first entered the house, the light in the hall had given the flesh of Lucille Christian's face a golden tinge. Like the light on this marble now.

The ink bottle was almost dry, and was crusted about the neck. Mr. Munn had to tilt it to wet the point of the pen.

'I'll be damned,' Mr. Christian remarked, 'it's aggravating now. There ain't much writing goes on around here. I never was much of a hand to be writing letters and such, but, by God, when the time comes when a man does want to do a little writing, looks like there'd be some ink in the bottle.'

'It'll do all right,' Mr. Munn said.

'It's aggravating,' Mr. Christian reiterated.

Mr. Munn wrote down two names; Joseph Foster, Murray Mill Pike, Bardsville; and Kimball G. Snider, Strawberry Creek Ford, Morganstown Pike, Bardsville.

'I think they'll come in,' Mr. Munn reflected. Then he wrote down another name, Aaron Smythe, and held the pen meditatively poised.

'That boy of yours,' Mr. Christian asked, 'now, you know — what's-his-name — the one whose neck you pulled outer the rope?'

'Trevelyan — Bunk Trevelyan.'

'He's a likely-looking specimen. If he's got any gratitude and you said a word to him sometime, I bet he'd come in.'

Mr. Munn shook his head, holding the pen poised over the paper. 'No, I reckon I won't say anything to him. Now, or later. He might think he had to join just because I got him off, that I had some sort of hold on him. But you haven't got any right to force a man into something like this just out of gratitude or because you've got a hold on him.' He wrote the name down, Harris Trevelyan, and looked around at the other men. 'But you all can speak to him and maybe he'd come in. Only don't mention my name.'

'We'll respect your wish, Mr. Munn,' Professor Ball said.

'I don't think of any more right off. I'll think of some more in the next day or two. Some I can recommend all right.'

'We've got a lot to go on right now,' Doctor MacDonald said. 'Men we've talked to have been making recommendations. We've got enough names to make up more than twenty bands, right in this section. And we've talked to some.'

'Right around here?' Mr. Munn demanded.

'Yes, sir, and we've got names in seven different counties. We've got a line on a good many, too.'

'It looks like you're looking forward to something pretty big,' Mr. Munn said.

Doctor MacDonald swung his lanky body up from the rocking chair and leaned toward Mr. Munn, pointing the stem of the unlit pipe at him. 'Man,' he said, and his lips drew back from the teeth in that secret half smile, 'man, you don't know how big it might be.' He dropped his arm to his side, slowly. The sleeve was too short for him, and the long, sinewy hand, with its knobby knuckles and clean-looking fingers, hung far out.

Before he went to sleep that night, Mr. Munn decided that he liked Doctor MacDonald. He liked his good nature, and the hardness that lay just beneath it, you could tell, just as the potentiality of speed and strength seemed to reside, upon second glance, in the slow motions of his lanky frame. Mr. Munn was not excited by the events of the evening. He was not sleepy, but calm and detached, as he lay on his back in the strange bed and stared up at the black ceiling and let the words and faces drift through his mind. He was at peace with himself, he told himself. His decision, his action, seemed so inevitable, like a thing done long before and remembered, like a part of the old, accustomed furniture of memory and being. Then it occurred to him that Senator Tolliver, not Christian and Mac-Donald and Ball, was really responsible for his decision, if anybody was. If the Senator had never laid a hand on his shoulder, had never leaned confidentially toward him, had not used him and betrayed him, he might never have taken this step. But that seemed part of the pattern, a sure and inevitable part. And the Senator's face, which, smiling and dignified, flickered across his inward vision, was replaced by another and another, faces of people he knew, faces he had merely seen for a moment and had wondered about, the face of the old man with the purplish wen on his temple, the old man he had tried to tell May about that time, the old man who had been the only one to sign up that time at one of the meetings way out in the sticks, who had walked up to the front, oblivious of the other people as if he had been in an open field, and had said, 'Boy, if you'll gimme that-air pen-staff I'll sign my name,' and then: 'I got me a little piece of ground nigh onto thirty years back. All that time ain't no man said me yea nor nay, nor go nor come. I'm gonna put my name down now, boy, and if you say yea it's yea, and nay it's nay. What little crop I got don't amount to nothing. My crop ain't a pea in the dish. But I aim to sign.' The words of the old man with the purplish wen on his temple were as clear to him as if he heard the voice saying them out loud to him that minute. He tried to phrase for himself the effect the recollection of the man always had on him, but he could not. He had never been able to do so. And he had not been able to do so for May, who had sat on his lap listening, or trying to listen, to his insufficient speech. What held him to the old man?

He could not say. But what had held him to the Senator, he knew that. His vanity. He had been flattered. The Senator had touched his vanity. What spring of action, more obscure, more profound, had the old man touched? A deeper vanity. A vanity below another surface, which had been peeled away. It did not matter what name a man gave it.

He rose from the bed, not restlessly as a nervous man does at night when he cannot sleep, but deliberately and comfortably as if the night were the new day. He walked across the room and leaned on the wide ledge of the window and looked over the lawn. There was no moon, but in the swimming starlight the newly springing grass looked pale, except where the shadows of the cedars lay. Those shadows were of inky blackness. He looked across the yard and toward the fields beyond, and thought how night changed everything, even the most accustomed landscape, your own fields. Or the face of somebody you knew and loved.

As he rode down the narrow gravel road that dipped from the pike toward the creek bottoms, the spring twilight was fading softly out. He tried to remember if he had ever been down this road before. When a boy, perhaps. In those days he had ranged pretty widely over the countryside. He had thrown a line at one time or another into almost every creek in the section — Strawberry, Cold Spring, Elk Horn, Dorris — and at almost every bend for many miles in Black Water River. And he had clambered up brushy hills at night, scratching his face and tearing his clothes in his haste to reach the spot where the dogs had treed. There had been the blood-stirring, hollow sound of the dogs barking for the tree, a sound in the frosty woods that reverberated as in a long cavern, and the hollering of another boy somewhere in the woods. He himself had run like a dog, not caring for the whipping brush, straight toward that tree, where the eyes would shine down from the darkness of the boughs. He had camped on a good many of these creeks, on Strawberry Creek itself, but farther down, he remembered. With boys like little Bill Christian, who was dead now a long time, shot with his own shotgun. Maybe sometimes he had camped at Murray Mill itself with the boys. It would be like all the other old mills, anyhow: the stone dam, hung with moss, across the creek bed; the disintegrating structure of the mill; the two-story dwelling-house beyond in a grove of cedars, or the chimneys where one had burned. At night the motionless water above the dam would look like slick, black metal.

Anyway, he knew what the country was like up here, for he had been up the main Murray Mill road, many times. The good soil gave out along here. Here the hillsides rose sharply from the creek bottom, nothing but the red clay sticking to bunks of limestone, and cedars with their stringy roots grappling at the fissures in the rock.

Mr. Munn could hear the sound of the flowing water, and thought of the night in the fall when he had gone to the meeting in the schoolhouse, up Rose Creek section, and how they had waited silently in the schoolhouse for the rain to let up, and how he had ridden back alone through the sodden countryside with the drumming of the rushing stream in his ears. It was much the same kind of place here. The valley was quite dark now, even though when he looked above the undifferentiated mass of the hills, he saw that a little light lingered in the upper air.

A horseman separated himself from the impenetrable shadow of the cedars by the side of the road, and moved slowly toward Mr. Munn. Mr. Munn drew rein, and waited while the rider slowly approached. The sound of the hoofs of the other horse made a casual, crunching sound on the loose gravel. Mr. Munn's own mount stood perfectly still, and he listened to the sound of its breathing. He could not tell anything about the appearance of the man, it was so dark, except that he seemed to sit his horse with a natural grace.

'Fair weather,' the man said in an everyday tone.

'Fairer tomorrow,' Mr. Munn said.

'Pass on,' the man said. He moved back into the darkness of the overhanging cedar boughs.

Two hundred yards farther, the road made a bend. There the mill was, an irregular, indefinable bulk on the other side of an open space, which was a little lighter than the road had been. Where the road debouched on that open space, he stopped. He could make out the fallen rail fence that bordered what must be an overgrown pasture, and how one fork of the road went down to a ford below the dam. The other fork was quickly lost in the dark shadow that enveloped the mill. The scene was as he had guessed: there the bulk of the mill, and the black, still water above the dam, and over the whole place the calmness of night and long disuse which he had known when he used to go camping at such localities when he was a boy.

But he felt an almost overmastering impulse to stop in the shadow where he was, not to cross that open space. It was different from what he had expected. He had expected, in so far as he had consciously expected any definite thing, to find people here, men lounging about waiting, their pipes in their mouths, perhaps, talking in low voices as on some country occasion, such as evening services at a crossroad church. But there was nothing here. Absolute stillness, except for the sound of water on the stones, and no movement in the lighter space, where the fallen rail fence was. Then he heard the short whinny of a horse. Well, he said to himself, and lifted his rein, and his mount moved slowly forward into the open, up the road beside the old fence, and then up the fork toward the mill. Some men were standing in the shadow by the loading platform, he discovered when he was almost upon them. He could only make out the whitish blur of their faces.

'Good evening, gentlemen,' he said.

The men replied nothing.

He rode on past them, and tethered his mare to a sapling. They were looking at me all the time I rode across that light place, he thought. He walked back toward them, and took his place, leaning against the loading platform. The men were not in a group, he found, and they were not talking to each other. They were cut off from each other, as it were, each one drawn in upon himself; and yet they were so close that each man could have reached out to touch a neighbor.

'Good evening,' the man nearest him said in a low voice.

'Good evening,' Mr. Munn replied.

Not another word was spoken, until someone came out on the loading platform from the interior of the mill and in a low voice pronounced the name Jim Talbot. Then the man on the platform asked, more sharply now, 'Is Jim Talbot here?'

One of the men on the ground vaulted clumsily onto the platform, and said, 'I'm Jim Talbot.'

'Come on in,' the other man directed, and disappeared into the interior of the mill. No light could be seen from the inside. The man named Talbot took a step forward, paused as though to hitch up his belt, and remarked, to no one in particular, 'Well, here goes.' Then he followed, gropingly, through the door where the other man had gone.

After a short while, that other man came out on the platform again, and pronounced another name, Fuqua G. Morris. It was the same man, Mr. Munn decided, for he could tell by the voice.

The man who answered to the name of Morris vaulted onto the platform, and entered the mill.

There was no conversation among the men left at the loading platform. Now and then one of them would shift his feet restlessly, scraping the gravel. Once a man asked another for a chew, and the other, without a word, passed it to him; and once a man struck a match for a pipe. The two men nearest him seemed to withdraw from the little sphere of light. Then the man's hand cupped around the flame, and he touched it to the pipe. It illuminated only his upper face, the heavy curve of the nose, which was bronze-colored in that small light, and the staring, faintly glittering orbs of the eyes under the low hat-brim. Then the man dropped the burning match to the gravel and ground it with his heel. Now and then a man would be summoned, and would enter the mill.

Once a horseman emerged from the shadow of the trees across the open space, and began to move toward the mill. Mr. Munn knew that that stranger could not see them there, and that the eyes of every man were fixed on that exposed and approaching figure. The stranger rode slowly past, tethered his horse, and came to lounge against the platform. 'Good evening,' he said, just as Mr. Munn had done.

'Good evening,' some man answered. But no one else replied.

When Mr. Munn heard his own name pronounced from the platform behind him, it came with as much surprise as though he had thought himself entirely alone. And yet, the first several times that man had appeared, Mr. Munn had been sure the summons would be for him. Then, somehow, he had assumed each time that the call would not be. As on the day of the rally when he had uncomprehendingly heard himself introduced to the crowd, now his body stiffened in response to the sound of the name before his mind had accepted the full fact. Then he said, 'All right,' and swung himself onto the platform, and followed the man in.

In the blacker, interior darkness, he followed close to his guide for a few paces. Under his tread he felt the unevenness of the worn boards, which creaked startlingly. Then they must have come to a corner, Mr. Munn thought, for to his left he could see narrow streaks of light apparently outlining a door.

'Just walk through that door there,' the guide commanded, 'and stand in the middle of the floor.'

'All right,' Mr. Munn said, and walked to the door, fumbled at the wooden latch, and entered.

A beam of light lay widening toward him, and he stood in its center. It came from some kind of lantern with a reflector and a screen that threw the other half of the big room into darkness — to his eyes, pitch darkness. They are over there, he thought. He stood just inside the door, blinking against the light.

'Come closer,' a voice commanded.

Mr. Munn tried to identify the voice, but could not. He took three slow steps forward, lifting his head a little so that the light would not fall directly in his eyes. The ceiling of the room was very high. He could make out the rafters above the lighted section. The room had probably been a granary.

'Go to the table,' the voice said.

Mr. Munn went to the table, which stood some ten feet away from the lantern and directly in front of it. He touched his fingers to the table-top, and waited. On the table a book lay, a Bible, an ordinary kind of Bible with worn, imitation leather covers. He had seen many a Bible like that, many a one, lying on the table in the family room of a farmhouse, or on the mantelpiece beside a carved wood clock, probably, and a glass vase full of paper spills, and a spectacle case.

'Percy Munn,' the voice said, 'you are about to take a most serious step. It is not necessary to impress upon you the gravity of that step. And about to take a most sacred oath. If you are to turn back, now is the time to turn back.'

Someone coughed twice in the darkness. Mr. Munn turned his head slightly toward that direction.

'You can turn your back now and go out of this room and mount your horse and ride away and never speak one word of your coming here tonight, and no single soul will think the less of your manhood. But now is the time. Look in your heart and mind, and consider.'

Mr. Munn waited with his eyes raised above the direct rays of the light. There was silence for some thirty or forty seconds.

'Percy Munn,' the voice then said, 'are you clear in your mind, and determined?'

'I am,' Mr. Munn said.

'You are about to take the oath of membership in the Free Farmers' Brotherhood for Protection and Control. The sole purpose of this organization is to see that a fair price is paid for dark fired tobacco, and it will adopt such means as seem advisable to further that purpose. Are you, Percy Munn, prepared to take the oath?'

'I am,' Mr. Munn said.

'Place your left hand upon that book.'

Mr. Munn did so.

'That book, Percy Munn, is the Holy Bible. An oath taken upon it and in God's name is sacred for all time and eternity. Will you swear upon it?'

'I will,' Mr. Munn said.

'Raise your right hand and repeat these words,' and the voice proceeded: 'I, Percy Munn, knowing the injustice under which our people groan ——' and it paused for Mr. Munn to repeat the words.

'I, Percy Munn, knowing the injustice under which our people groan ——' Mr. Munn said slowly and distinctly.

'—— and being willing to abide it no longer ——'

Mr. Munn repeated: '—— and being willing to abide it no longer ——'

The voice resumed: '—— do swear on this holy book and on the name of God our Creator . . . that I will steadfastly support the purpose of the Free Farmers' Brotherhood for Protection and Control —— and whatever measures may be deemed advisable for the accomplishment of that purpose —— and that I will loyally obey the commands of the truly elected officers superior to me in this organization —— and that never, under any circumstances, will I speak one word of this organization or its affairs — to any man or woman not of this organization — not excepting the wife of my bosom. — This I solemnly swear.'

'— This I solemnly swear,' Mr. Munn concluded. He removed his hand from the book.

'Come forward,' the voice said, and he walked across the intervening ten feet or so of floor toward the lantern and the voice. He passed beyond the range of the lantern's rays, was completely blind for an instant before his eyes could accustom themselves to the dark, and then saw the man standing behind the table that supported the lantern, and the other men sitting on benches and boxes beyond. The man behind the lantern shook Mr. Munn's hand, and said, 'Well, sir, we're happy to welcome you in.'

'Thank you,' Mr. Munn said. He peered at the man's face, thinking he had seen it somewhere before, but in that light he couldn't be sure.

'If you'll just have a seat, we'll be proceeding,' the man said.

One of the men on the bench just behind the table moved over, and Mr. Munn sat down beside him.

He watched the other men, one after another, come through the door over there across the wide floor, and stand motionless just inside it until the voice gave the command, and then move slowly forward, blinking at the light. Some of them peered hard at a spot just by the light, straining, apparently, to penetrate the depth of darkness where people were; and others, as Mr. Munn himself had done, lifted their eyes toward the obscurity of the ceiling. The first kind were nervous, and they would wet the lips with the tongue before they began to repeat the words of the oath. Mr. Munn tried to recall whether or not he himself had wet his lips that way. He had not been nervous, he decided. He had really felt nothing, nothing at all, when he stood out there in the middle of the floor in the full beam of the light. That was what surprised him. A man was due to feel something out there, taking the oath. Then he began to think how the taking of the oath changed the relation of all those men to each other there beside him in the dark. The oath had said, God our Creator. He wondered how many of those men believed in God. And then if he himself did. It had been a long time since he had thought of that, he remembered. The man who was, at that moment, taking the oath finished, and at the command, advanced to join the group in the shadow.

A minute later the door opened, and a man entered, a tall man, and stood there in the full beam of light. The man was Bunk Trevelyan.

Chapter seven

IT WAS hard to believe, he would think, sitting at his desk in the office over the drugstore, with his papers spread out on the desk, or a client sitting there before him, and with the comforting and irregular ticking of the girl's typewriter coming to his ears from the outer room. Many afternoons that spring, when the windows were open to let in the warming air, or when the pavements glistened in the quick sunlight that had followed a flurry of rain and people came out again to walk up and down, idling and calling to each other, he would find it hard to believe that such afternoons did not belong to the spring before, or to the spring before that.

And once or twice, Mr. Munn got up from his desk and looked at himself in the mirror of the old walnut hatrack by the door. He had not changed since last spring, or the spring before. Or at least, he could tell no difference. When he shaved in the mornings he would regard his face in the mirror, the long, slightly hooked nose, his dark, deep-set eyes, the close-growing, dark hair, and sometimes he would think, well, it doesn't show a mark of change, not a mark. He himself was the same, and everything was the same, May's glance and gesture, the way the fields lay outside the window, the very food on the table for breakfast and the smell of coffee. Presently, he would mount his mare and ride off toward town, as before.

'What's the matter, Perse?' May had asked him two or three times.

'Matter? Nothing's the matter,' he had answered. The first time he answered with an effort at a jocose and affectionate tone. He set his pipe on the mantelshelf, for he was standing there just after dinner with an unlit match in his fingers, and drew her to him with one hand while with the other he touched the mass of hair above her small face. 'Nothing,' he said. 'You're just crazy as a little hoot owl. Don't you know that? A little hoot owl?' At the very moment of utterance he had been aware that his voice sounded exactly as always when he spoke teasingly to her. Hell, he thought, I sound like a fool.

'But there is, Perse. You know there is. Are you sick?'

'No,' he said shortly, feeling his nerves stiffen.

'I know there is, Perse.'

'No.'

'But you've changed, Perse, you know you have. You aren't like you used to be. To me, or in any way. What's the matter, Perse?'

By that time he had released her and moved from her a pace or two. With those words she stretched out her hand to him, not strongly, as though to grasp him or command him to her, but with a motion that from the start confessed its own ineffectuality.

'Nothing,' he said, watching her gesture and feeling an unnamable and deep dissatisfaction at it. He turned suddenly and walked across the room and through the hall and out to the porch, permitting the screen door to slam behind him with a flat sound. He walked away across the yard and down the lane leading to the big road. After a while he came back and stood, with his cold pipe between his teeth, in the yard under the leafing sugar trees. He was able to see May seated on the sofa in the living-room, her face averted and the lamplight falling on her hair. Once, long before, at night like this, he had stood under one of the blasted cedars on the Burnham place, where May lived then with her aunt, Miss Lucy Burnham, and he had looked back toward the house. Like tonight, May sat alone then, beyond the window, with the lamplight falling upon her hair. How bravely, it had always seemed to him, her head supported those massy-looking coils, which appeared too heavy for her smallness, too grown-up, almost, for the delicate clarity of the face beneath them. Ordinarily, she carried her head high; as though by a consistent act of will, but an act not quite comprehending its own meaning and purpose, she supported the glowing and weighty coils. But that night at the Burnham place, like tonight, her head drooped, the weight seeming too great and unrelenting.

What had she promised him, he asked himself tonight, looking across the darkness to the lighted interior of the room where she sat? Happiness, that was it. He had found in her the promise of happiness, happiness as a thing in itself, an entity separate from the past activities of his life. Or rather, he had thought of that happiness, in so far as he had thought at all of its relation to other things, as something concealed, preciously, at the center of his life, like the fruit within the rind, the meat of the nut within the gross and useless outer shell. What was the center of his life, he demanded of himself. He could not say.

Then he remembered that she had not promised him happiness. That was what he had promised himself, generously, looking at her, walking beside her across the eroded and failing fields of the Burnham place, or sitting in the musty parlor out there, with the clutter of knick-knacks and mirrors around him and the smell of horsehair in his nostrils. She had promised him nothing, or, at least, only herself. He had her, now. But what was she? She was a certain form, certain words to which he was accustomed and which pretended to tell him of some reality within herself. What that was, what she truly was, he did not know.

Now, looking at her sitting there in the room, framed in the lighted square of the window, he felt as he had felt when, as a child, he had removed a picture-card from the stereopticon apparatus to look at it as it was without the aid of the lenses. Sometimes on Sunday afternoons, in winter, when he was a child, he had lain on the floor with the glasses and the stack of picture-cards, each with its duplicate scene. Through the lenses, the card would show a rich, three-dimensional little world, the figures of persons there seeming to stand up, solid and vital in their own right, about to move about their own mysterious businesses. It was a little world with light falling over the objects there and casting shadows, as in the real world, with distances and depths like the real world, and recesses more secret and fascinating. Sometimes, pressing his forehead into the wooden frame until it ached, he had felt that if he could just break through into that little world where everything was motionless but seemed about to move, where everything was living, it seemed, but at the same time frozen in its tiny perfections, he would know the most unutterable bliss. Then, slowly, he would take the frame from his eyes and remove the card from the clamps. He would inspect it: the flat, dull, fading picture printed in duplicate, the frayed, yellow edges of the cardboard. No life would be there, no depth. That card which he held in his hand, then, would be a part of the ordinary world in which he was living. He would look about him at the familiar furniture of the room; at the fire failing now in the grate, perhaps; at the pattern of the carpet on which he lay. There would be the slow, somnolent, saddening sound of water murmuring and chinking in the gutters, or the sound of wind finding the corners of the house and the recesses of the eaves. Soon, they would come and get him and make him eat his supper, even if he wasn't hungry, and then they would put him to bed. The stereopticon cards would be left stacked in a neat pile on the table in the deserted living-room. That was the way it had been. He had taken the card from behind the lenses, and there was only the flat card which he held in his hand. He looked toward the lighted window, where May was now, and thought of that, and how he had felt when he was a child.

But she had not changed. She was as she had always been.

Whatever change there was — and there was a change, she was right when she accused him — was in him. He knew that. He had known it first that day when he had refused to promise to send a negro up to prepare the flower beds for her. He thought of how she had moved away from him down the path, how her small shoulders had drawn together in the contortion of a silent sob, and how he had stared down at the rusty old trowel beside the patch of inadequately turned loam. He had stared down at the trowel, and had felt that he was suddenly staring at a darkly coiling depth within himself. That moment had been like the moment in there, tonight. He had, in the end, sent a negro up to fix the flower beds on the morning of the day before the night of the taking of the oath, as though the act might have been a kind of atonement offered to her for the step he was about to take, a gesture toward her across a widening distance. She had never mentioned the matter of the garden to him again, not even to thank him.

She went upstairs very early that night when he watched her from the shadow of the sugar trees, but he waited for the light to go out in the bedroom, and then for a considerable time after.

A few days later she again asked him, 'Perse, what's the matter?' And feeling his nerves stiffen and the food just swallowed turn to a cold mass in his stomach, he carefully laid down his fork and said in a voice which, despite its control, betrayed the vibration of an inner tension, 'Nothing.' She continued to study his face while she pretended to eat and while the negro cook padded in and out of the room. She said nothing else the entire meal. The next morning, after he had told her good-bye at the front door and had taken a couple of steps across the porch, he turned abruptly and came back to her and pressed her to him. She clung to him while the pressure of his grip increased and while he bent over her to hold his lips hard against the mass of hair on top of her head. 'Oh, Perse, Perse,' she breathed.

Her eyes, he noticed when he had released her and stepped away from her, were swimming with unshed tears.

'Do you love me, Perse?' she demanded.

'Sure,' he said, 'sure, I love you.'

'Love me, Perse. Love me always,' she pleaded.

'Always,' he promised, and turned away down the over-grown, mossy brick walk, beside which unkempt jonquils were in full bloom. His mare, saddled and ready, was hitched at the gate, and the clear sunshine flooded over the green meadows and the vigorous-looking plowed fields.

But the night before, as once or twice earlier and on several nights to come, he had waked up in the middle of the night and raised himself on his elbow and stared at her sleeping face. It is hard to know anybody, he had thought, really know them. Now, riding along the lane in the morning freshness, he recalled that incident.

And then he puzzled over the fact that he, who was now riding off down the lane toward town, had stood at the edge of a patch of woods five nights before, his ears sharpened to catch any warning whistle from the posted watchers, and had waited while three men dragged the plant bed there before him. That did not disturb him.

He felt no sense of guilt because he could not tell May, even if there had been no oath of secrecy he would not have told her. He knew that. There was no reason to tell her. She lived in another kind of world, but on the occasions when he was to meet with the men of his band, Band Number 17, he told her that he had to stay in town late for work and would sleep at the hotel. If he should come in too late, it would disturb her. But, then, he did not want to go to the hotel at such an hour. The old man who kept the desk at night, and slept the fitful sleep of the aged on a cot in a cubbyhole just behind it, might wake up and notice him; or some late sitter in the lobby, one of those men who sat there alone some nights, hour after hour, smoking and spitting into the brass cuspidors, and staring at the opposite wall. Several times he spent the night with Mr. Wyngard, a member of Band 17 who was a bachelor and had a place near town. On other occasions, although Mr. Christian did not belong to his band, he stayed at the Christian place. Once they left the lamp burning in the hall for him, and he took his shoes off on the front porch, and carrying the lamp in one hand and the shoes in the other, crept up the stairs to the room which he had occupied that night when Mr. Ball had been there. But Mr. Christian heard him on the stairs and came out in his nightshirt to ask about the night's business. He made Mr. Munn, who was dog-tired and rocking on his heels with sleep, stand there, holding the lamp, and go over every detail, point by point.

'Yeah, yeah?' Mr. Christian kept saying in a harsh, demanding half whisper every time Mr. Munn hesitated. Then, while Mr. Munn went on with the account, Mr. Christian would nod his head and in gentle, meditative strokes scratch his chest, which was covered with reddish hairs. Occasionally, he tugged at the hairs, rolling them between his big fingers.

'That makes five you all took care of tonight, huh?' Mr. Christian asked.

'Yes, five.'

'All of 'em had warning?'

'Yes, and two had second warnings, Giles and Wagner. All their plants were scraped. The others, just half a bed.'

'Wagner,' Mr. Christian said, 'now I'd thought he'd come in long ago, ain't no starch to him. Yellow-bellied as a sapsucker. I reckon something was keeping him out. But Giles' — and he shook his head — 'now Giles, he's a tough one, he's a man, he is. I just hate to see him on the wrong side this-away. I hate to see his bed scraped.'

'Yes,' Mr. Munn answered, the fog of sleep coming heavily over him so that he could scarcely keep his eyes open, and the lamp wobbling in his grasp.

'Good night,' Mr. Christian said.

'Good night,' Mr. Munn replied, and went off to his room, leaving Mr. Christian standing there barefooted, in his nightshirt, in the dark hall.

Two of the other times when he stayed at the Christian place were nights when there were meetings of the band captains, but two of the times were nights when Mr. Christian's band had also operated. Every time, after they had stabled their horses and gone up to the house, they found Lucille Christian waiting up. Once, she rose from the swing in the yard, her white dress wavering in the shadow, and came toward them soundlessly over the dew-drenched grass. It had been warm inside, she said, and she was just sitting out in the air. The other time, coming out of the dark parlor, her eyes deep and calm with sleep as though she had just been awakened, she met them in the hall. The lamp in the hall was turned half down.

Both times she led them down the back hall, past a cot, where an old negro woman slept with her head thrown back and slow snores fluttering her lips in the uncertain lamplight.

'Old Aunt Cassie,' Mr. Christian explained the first time; 'she stays up here to keep the bugaboos off Sukie when I ain't here.'

'Just for company,' Lucille Christian said casually, 'just company. I can keep the bugaboos off myself.' She walked on into the kitchen, with the lamp held high in her right hand.

'By God!' Mr. Christian exclaimed, 'by God, I believe that for a fact. I believe Sukie could. She ain't scared of a thing. Not a thing. Are you now, Sukie?'

'Not bugaboos, anyway,' she said, and dropped a lighted match to the ready-laid wood and paper in the range, and shook the coffee-pot.

'No, Sukie ain't. And you oughter seen her handle General Smuts. Ain't ten men in the county would hone to ride him, and Sukie here, she just marches out one morning and climbs on him. And stays on him. What she mounts, I bet she rides. She's got as pretty a way on a horse, now, as ever you laid eyes on. For a fact. Now, ain't you, Sukie?'

'I rode him,' she said.

'For a fact,' he agreed, and whacked her lightly across the buttocks.

When she turned around, Mr. Munn expected a blush, or some slight expression of embarrassment on her face, or a word of remonstrance. But there was none of these things. 'I rode him,' she repeated, 'now didn't I?'

'For a fact,' Mr. Christian agreed.

Then, stepping past him on her way to the safe, she paused to strike him solidly on the seat with the flat of her hand. He grunted with surprise, and swung around toward her. She was getting a covered dish out of the safe, beyond his reach. He wagged his head at her, saying: 'You see that? I told you now, Perse, she'll take care of herself all right. She'd dust off a bugaboo.'

She set the covered dish on the table, laid two plates and forks, and went to the stove to see about the coffee.

'None for me, thanks,' Mr. Munn told her.

'Just go on and pour his out, and I'll drink it,' Mr. Christian directed.

She poured two cups of coffee, and uncovered the dish to expose half of an apple pie. Mr. Christian divided that into two equal portions, slid one piece onto a plate, and set the plate before Mr. Munn.

'I couldn't eat anything like that much,' Mr. Munn said.

'Like you say, Perse,' Mr. Christian replied, and put a smaller slice on another plate. Then he put three spoons of sugar into the cup of coffee before him, stirred it briskly, and took a long draught. He began to eat the large piece of pie, cutting it into slabs and thrusting those into his mouth. When he chewed, the muscles at the jawbone knotted and rippled under the red skin.

Lucille Christian sat across the table from the two men, but she kept her eyes on her father. She sugared the second cup of coffee for him, just as he drained the first.

'Looks like all that coffee'd keep you awake,' Mr. Munn observed.

'Not me,' Mr. Christian said. 'I ain't any nervous wreck, and I got a clean conscience. I can sleep any time I want to. And the funny part is' — he paused to put another piece of piecrust into his mouth and to chew it — 'is how any little thing, anything outer the way, that is, will wake me up right off. Now you let a rat or a mouse come in my room and he can just raise hell, and it'll never faze me. Or a thunderstorm, now, that'll never faze me, unless I know I oughter pull a window down, maybe. But you just let somebody move round downstairs, even on tiptoe, or turn a doorknob, and, by God, I'm wide awake. And it just seems like I know what it was waked me up. Just like a voice told me ——'

'Papa's like a cat,' Lucille Christian interrupted, 'a big, red, old tomcat. With one ear bitten off,' she added.

'Now you take that other night when you spent the night here, and I came out in the hall and talked to you. I bet I knew you was coming before a dog ever got wind of you. I woke up, and I knew, just like a voice said, Somebody's riding over that little plank bridge on the pike. And I said to myself, There's Perse coming now. Then, pretty quick, old Miss Belle Cunningham — now she's got as good a nose as any dog I ever took off after ——'

'It's a touching habit,' Lucille Christian interrupted, 'papa has of naming dogs after young ladies he used to admire when he was young. He keeps their memory green.'

'Get me some coffee, Sukie,' he said, and shoved the cup toward her. She rose to obey him. 'And Miss Belle Cunningham, now,' he resumed, 'she started to barking, and the others took it up. But I knew it long before that. Just like a voice spoke in the dark when your mare set a hoof on that bridge.'

Lucille Christian placed the cup before her father. 'I was awake, too, before all of papa's old loves started to give tongue,' she said, while she leaned over to sugar his coffee for him. 'But I didn't hear the bridge, or didn't notice. Then I heard papa's door screak when he went out in the hall, and I saw the light from the hall under my door.'

Mr. Munn wondered which room was hers, the one directly before which they had stood that night?

'You all certainly found a lot to talk about that time of night,' she remarked. She returned to her chair.

'Sure,' Mr. Christian agreed, and lifted his cup.

After he was in bed, it occurred to Mr. Munn that the real reason Lucille Christian stayed up was not to make coffee for her father. She wouldn't sit up to all hours for that, and he could do it perfectly well himself. She sat up because she knew about everything. She had said she was out in the yard, in the swing, because it was warm. But it wasn't a warm night, certainly not a particularly warm one. She had sat up because she knew, and wanted to see her father come in. Not worried, exactly. That was the wrong word, for he recalled the calmness of her face that night. She would not worry like most women, probably. But she had sat up, he was sure, to see her father come home.

Twice in early June, when Mr. Munn rode up with Mr. Christian, Lucille Christian was not waiting alone. Captain Todd's son, Benton, was there with her, sitting out in the yard in the swing. He was back from Virginia, and, he said, glad to be home. He shook hands firmly with Mr. Munn on both occasions, and shortly afterward said good-bye all around and got on his horse and rode off. It once crossed Mr. Munn's mind that the boy was keeping mighty late hours with a young lady, and all. But then it occurred to him that Mr. Christian didn't seem to mind, and if he had minded, he would have expressed himself in all likelihood so you couldn't mistake him. And Lucille Christian could probably run her own business well enough.

By the middle of June everybody knew that Benton Todd was courting Lucille Christian, hot and heavy. That was some time after Captain Todd had resigned from the board of directors of the Association of Growers of Dark Fired Tobacco.

Toward the middle of the spring all of the tobacco held by the Association was sold, except for a small amount of nubbins and snuff leaf common. The price had ranged from ten-ninety down in a usual proportion. Some of the sales during the winter outside the Association had brought more than some of the final sales in the Association. Ten days after the last Association sale, the first plant-bed raids occurred.

By that time the new plants were well up — small, pale green, narrow-leafed plants growing closely together in beds that had been covered with canvas while the infinitesimal seeds sprouted and took root. The beds lay on slopes exposed to the south, or in places protected by woods. In them the earth was new, and burned-over, and black. Those beds, bounded by old boards and logs, contained the entire crop for the coming season. A long stroke of the hoe could destroy a thousand pounds.

On one night forty-seven plant beds in three counties were raided. The beds belonging to six men who had been particularly active in opposing the Association were completely destroyed. Half of each of the remaining forty-one beds was scraped. No warning notes had been sent, and no notes were left. No notes were necessary. The implications were plain enough. Within two weeks, eighteen of the forty-one men whose plant beds had been only half-scraped joined the Association. They did this quietly, without much comment to their neighbors, although some of them had at first given out public statements of defiance.

A sheriff and his deputies would go to the spot where the plant bed had been. The scene was always the same, the dug-up earth in the frame, the boards that had been jerked apart with the shreds of canvas still clinging to them, the patch of trodden ground with the marks of boot heels, and somewhere in the vicinity the pawed spot where the horses had been held. Once they found a dead dog lying in the bushes just beyond the plant bed. It had been killed by a crushing blow over the skull, probably when it had attacked one of the raiders. The stick which had killed it lay there too, in the bushes. A few coarse, yellow hairs from the dog's head were stuck in the dried blood on the stick. 'Took a right stout man to do that,' one of the deputies said, looking down at the dog. 'One lick.' That was all they could find.

A band would get its orders to go to a certain point at a certain time, a crossroads, a church, an abandoned store, and there it would pick up a guide, probably a man who was unknown to the members of the band. He would give them the words agreed on, and the band captain would reply, and the guide would say, 'Well, let's get going,' and would lead them away. The men did not have to scrape the beds of their own immediate neighbors. Sometimes they might not even know the names of the owners of the beds. Only the guide and the band captain were sure to know. That was Doctor Mac-Donald's idea. He was chief, elected unanimously by the thirty-four captains and four commanders at their first general meeting. Nobody knew much about him, but they elected him. Afterward, he had stood up and said in his gentle, offhand voice, 'Well, gentlemen, I appreciate this, and I'll try not to get you into any more trouble than necessary.' That was all he had said then, by way of acceptance.

At that same meeting, in planning the first raids he proposed his idea that a band should not operate in its own immediate neighborhood. Before the meeting, while the men were gathering, he had explained it to Mr. Munn.

'Don't you think that's a good idea?' he had asked Mr. Munn.

'Yes,' Mr. Munn had said, 'I reckon so.'

'At first, anyway,' Doctor MacDonald had said.

'At first?' Mr. Munn had echoed, looking up at the other man's face. Doctor MacDonald had worn that half smile, and his dead pipe had been stuck between his teeth, as was his habit.

'Just to break them in, Mr. Munn, you might say,' he had observed. Then he had turned away to enter the door of the schoolhouse where the meeting was to be held. But he had stopped, removed the pipe from between his teeth, and said, 'You don't know, it might turn out to be a long winter.'

Mr. Munn had stood there, wondering how he would feel to go down the road and scrape the plant bed belonging to old Mr. Goodwood, whose place lay next to his. But old Mr. Goodwood was a strong Association man. Now and then, later, Mr. Munn thought how he would feel if he had to do that. He had known Mr. Goodwood all his life. He would do it, he decided, if he had to, but he would hate it. He would do it, because the idea of the Association was more important than how he felt about Mr. Goodwood. The idea bound a lot of men together and would get justice for all of them. And even for men who were not in the Association; even, in the end, for men whose beds were scraped now. It was win or lose now, he decided, and no turning back. And that was what Mr. Christian said to him that night when the council decided to take some men out and make them scrape their own beds, for the sake of example. 'By God, Perse!' Mr. Christian exclaimed, 'we're shooting our wad now. If we don't win now, we never will.'

'I know, I know,' Mr. Munn replied. 'I voted against that business of taking a man out, and all, but I'll do what's voted. It just doesn't look like the best way, that's all. To me, anyway.'

'It'll do the trick, don't you worry. And we gotta do that fast. If we don't win, every man that plants tobacco is gonna be eating stinkweed and dog meat instead of greens and sowbelly this time next year. And that means damned near everybody in ten counties. By God, there won't be nothing left if those tobacco buyers win out. It'll be worse'n Indians. I'd rather fight Indians like my folks did when they come over the mountains, durned if I hadn't.'

'That's the whole trouble,' Mr. Munn said; 'those fellows aren't Indians.'

'Now look here, Perse. I'll fight fair long as any man, and I'll let any man call the tune, but if he says it's stomp and gouge, then, by God, it's stomp and gouge. And that's what they called, stomp and gouge. Nobody ever thought this'd be a Baptist Sunday-School picnic with chess pie all round and wading in the creek. Hell, Perse, you're a grown man.' He slapped Mr. Munn on the back so hard that the flesh stung under the impact. 'Buck up,' he said.

Then Doctor MacDonald came out and stood beside them under the oak trees by the hitching-rack.

'Well, doc,' Mr. Christian remarked conversationally, 'I was just saying to Perse here how it looks like the boys took to it all right.'

Doctor MacDonald nodded. 'Yes, sir,' he then said, 'yes, sir. And it'll sorter break the men in. By degrees.' He turned to Mr. Munn, looked directly into his face for an instant, and added, 'Won't it, Mr. Munn?'

'I reckon so,' Mr. Munn answered. He was not really paying attention to Doctor MacDonald's words.

Some fifteen men on the same night, but in widely separated localities, were to be taken out and made to scrape their own plant beds. For the purpose the bands were to operate in pairs. 'Then they'll multiply that twenty men a few times when they tell about it,' Mr. Christian had said, 'if they do tell.' Band 17 was to join with Band 18. The men were to gather at an old camp-meeting ground a little way beyond the place owned by Mr. Thomas Sorrell, who was the captain of Band 18, and then move up the Murray Mill road, which ran northeast, until they came to a covered wooden bridge over a creek. The guide would be waiting for them there.

It rained a little in the early evening, a soft spring rain that let up not long after dark. The clouds broke up and drifted off the sky, and the starry sky, except around the horizon, where low mists hung, had a clean, washed look. Here and there along the road, the wet leaves glistened dully, catching a little of that distant light.

'Hit's gitten right seasonable,' one of the men said.

'Yeah,' another responded. 'Not long now till setten-out time. Come a good rain about ten days from now, an' I'd be setten a crop out.'

'I reckon they's some as ain't,' the first man returned.

But there was little talking as the men rode along toward the covered bridge. They did not travel in a body, but strung out in groups of two and three for almost a mile. Mr. Sorrell rode with the first group, and Mr. Munn with the last. They met no one on the road.

When Mr. Munn read in the newspapers about the very actions in which he had participated, he felt, almost always, as if he were reading of something in which he had had no part, of something that had happened a very long time before. The event, in the print there on the page, was meaningless and ghostly, for he would recall, for instance, how one man had said, riding along, 'Hit's gitten right seasonable.' That made it all very different from what was on the page, deeds done by men for reasons that involved their flesh and blood, their hunger, pride, and hopes, their whole beings. The definition of things on a page was different. Or when he read the statement made by a victim he felt the same unreality, the same lack of conviction.

About two in the morning, or maybe it was half-past two, I woke up because I heard a noise. Then my wife said to me somebody was at the door. So I put on some clothes and went to the door and asked who was there. They said they had to use the telephone, it was important, and so I opened the door. There were two men standing there on the porch, and one of them said, 'Sir, it won't do you any good to resist.' Or something like that. Then I could see some other men coming out in the open from the shadow. They had white masks on, as good as I could tell.

It was different, for Mr. Munn could remember the pale, strained face of the man standing in the doorway of the house, the sleepy call of the woman's voice from back inside, asking who it was there, her husband's answer that nothing was wrong, and then her shrill voice calling, 'Tom, Tom, don't you go off with those men, don't you do it.' She must have looked out a window and seen the men in the yard.

Even a man telling with his own lips what had happened to him seemed to be talking about something that had no immediate importance. 'Yeah, yeah,' the man said, 'they roused me out, and said they wanted to talk to me. And seeing how many they was I 'lowed as how it'd be a pleasure, sure, polite as I could. And they was mighty polite too, and said they had heard as how I was a fine man, could do as good a day's work as any man, stout and handy with my hands. I said, "Now, gentlemen ——"'

'Now, I wonder who'd ever told 'em that, now,' another man there in the barber shop said, and winked around at the group. 'I'd call that rumor pretty grossly exaggerated, like they say.'

The first man paid him no attention, continuing: ' "Now, gentlemen," I said, "I shore am mighty proud to be having a name like that with my neighbors, and proud to have them taking an interest that-away, even if it was sorter late at night." They said yeah, they'd heard a lot about me, and how I was specially good handling a hoe. I said that was mighty kind of whoever said it. And they said, did I have a hoe, and I 'lowed I did. They said, "Well, now, we been hearing so much and all we just thought we'd drop by and see if all the bragging people did about you was firmly grounded in fact." That's what that fellow said, "firmly grounded in fact." Then he said, "If you'll just take a hoe, Mr. McCarthy, and step down to yore plant bed, we'll just be seeing, and we don't mean no pissy-ass garden hoe, neither." And I just said, "Yes, sir," and went down to the toolshed and got the biggest hoe you ever laid eyes on, a great, big, old clod-busten field hoe. Then we all went down to the plant bed, down near the branch, and one man said, "Well, I reckon you know what to do," and I said I reckon I did. And I done it.'

'Be durned,' another man said, 'if I'd ever let anybody make me scrape my plant bed. They might scrape it, all right, but be durned if they'd make me.'

'Sure, you can talk big, Suggs,' another man told him, 'not having any plant bed.'

'And no place to put one on,' McCarthy said.

'Well, if I did have one.'

'Naw, naw,' the man named McCarthy insisted, 'you'd do it, like I done it. They was mighty polite and all, but you could just figger they meant what they said, being up so late and gal-livanten round over the country that-away, losing their rest. So I scraped. Yeah, and, by God, I mean to say I worked fast. All I was sorry for was I didn't have me a hoe in both hands. Then, when I got through, they said they was glad to see I was such a stout man and a willen worker and they wanted to com-pliment me, they said. Then they all said "Good night, Mr. McCarthy," and went off, and left me standing down there by the plant bed. Then I come on back up to the house.'

He was a slow, angular fellow. He wore freshly washed over-alls, and a blue shirt and an old black coat. When he finished a sentence, he would stop and lean forward and spit between his teeth with a small, hissing sound. Mr. Munn had never seen him before. He tried to imagine the events the man described, but they seemed unreal, remote, and fantastic. He thought, I might just as well have been one of those men, and here I am sitting here, listening to him. He looked covertly about at the other men on the benches and in the chairs, and thought that some of those very men might be night riders, you couldn't tell, and might even have been in the band that called on McCarthy.

One of the barbers called, 'You're next, Mr. Munn.' And Mr. Munn rose, and went to the chair. As he lay there in the chair, with his eyes closed and the steaming towels on his face and the muffled and confused sound of voices coming to him, he thought how little you could really tell about another man, even a man you saw every day. 'You're next, Mr. Munn,' the barber had said, calling him by his name. He knew his name, and spoke it, but what did he know? Or anybody else? A man might be to another man only the sound of a voice muffled and incoherent like the voices he now heard. Lying there in the chair, he recalled the moment of sickness, almost nausea, that first night when they had called a man out. 'What do you all aim to do to me?' the man had asked. He had been very calm. And the same sickness had recurred later when another man — Mr. Trice had been his name — had refused to get a hoe, and Bunk Trevelyan had, without warning, struck him across the mouth and nose, from which the blood gushed suddenly, unexpectedly bright and clean-looking in the inadequate starlight. Then Trevelyan had twisted the man's arm back, saying, 'You will, you bastard, will you?'

'Take your hands off,' Mr. Munn had ordered.

Trevelyan had hesitated, still twisting the arm.

'Take your hands off that man, or I'll kill you where you stand,' Mr. Munn had said to Trevelyan in a perfectly matter-of-fact tone. His stomach had felt like ice.

Trevelyan had released the man, mumbling something under the strip of cloth that covered his face.

Mr. Munn had turned to the man and said, 'Now get your hoe, Mr. Trice, and let's get this thing over with.' The man had obeyed him.

That had happened, and now it happened again in his mind as he lay there in the chair with his eyes closed and the towels on his face and the sweetish taste of steam on his lips. That was inside his mind, was part of him, as he lay there locked inside the darkness that was himself when he closed his eyes. He could see himself standing there by the stile, surrounded by men with the white cloth masks on their faces, and Mr. Trice standing there. He could see himself clearly, as if he were another person, a spectator. Another person. The passage of time had made him another person, a week's time. He himself, Percy Munn, lay there in the barber's chair and another man was speaking those words and performing those actions there by the stile, rehearsing them all. A man in his head. Then he thought how the night may be, in truth, mirror to the day, returning the reflection of a man's self to him twisted and confused and almost unrecognizable like the reflection in a flawed, pocked, and dirty glass, or in those contorting mirrors you see in tent shows, or in disturbed water.

At the last meeting of the board in May, Captain Todd resigned. He waited until the routine business had been finished, and then rose slowly to his feet.

'Mr. Chairman,' he began, addressing Mr. Morse, who looked up at him with some surprise on his features, 'with your kind indulgence there's something I'd like to say to the board.'

'Certainly,' Mr. Morse said, glanced quickly about at the other men, and then returned his gaze to the speaker. They, too, were fixing their eyes on the erect figure of Captain Todd. It was not customary to stand while speaking. Captain Todd's expression betrayed nothing as he looked around the group. In his curiosity, Mr. Munn leaned forward a little, and then, with certainty as though the immediate future were perfectly clear to him even before the Captain began to speak, he knew what was about to happen. He's getting out, he thought. He leaned back in his chair, waiting.

'I am going to resign from the board of the Association,' the Captain announced. His tone was even, almost casual. 'I want my resignation to take effect now.'

Somebody said, 'For God's sake!'

'Now, now, Captain,' Mr. Morse remonstrated. 'Now, Captain——'

'Now,' Captain Todd said, lifting one hand a little in a gesture for silence. 'I'm getting off the board. I'm getting off the board because the board isn't running the Association any more. The night riders are running it——'

Mr. Sills leaned forward as though about to rise, then stopped rigidly as the Captain turned toward him.

'I beg your pardon, I beg your pardon, Captain,' Mr. Morse was saying.

'It's a fact,' the Captain insisted. 'A fact, and you all know it. We just meet up here and talk, but it's the night riders run things. It's a false position.' He looked around the table, his glance seeming to pause for the flicker of an instant on each face. 'I'm not saying it's wrong. I'm not saying I know what another man has to do. I'm just saying I know what I've got to do.'

'Captain,' Mr. Sills said, and coughed dryly.

'Yes?' Captain Todd answered.

'Captain, I believe it's common knowledge you were in the Klan. Down in Tennessee.'

'Yes.'

'And you were in the war.'

'Four years,' the Captain answered, nodding.

'And, Captain'— Mr. Sills coughed again— 'I've heard it

said that right after the war, before the Klan got started, you and some other men just out of the war took care of a gang of bushwhackers and guerrillas in East Tennessee. Is that a fact?'

'We hanged them,' the Captain admitted. 'Nobody else would, so we did it. Blackguards and desperadoes.'

'Well,' Mr. Sills said, and leaned back in his chair.

Mr. Morse struck the table with his pipe as though with a gavel. 'All that has no bearing, no bearing at all. Captain Todd is not talking about resigning from the night riders. Whoever they are. He's talking about resigning from the board ——'

'Well,' Mr. Sills repeated, still looking at Captain Todd.

'Well, what?' Captain Todd demanded.

'Well, I was just thinking ——' Mr. Sills began.

Mr. Morse rapped with his pipe.

'Begging your pardon, Mr. Chairman,' the Captain said. Then to Mr. Sills: 'You mean I haven't got the stomach I used to have. Is that it?'

'Well ——'

'I was in the war and in the Klan, all right. And I helped hang those men. I acted according to my lights, Mr. Sills. And I'm acting according to them now. I thought I knew who my people were then. I still think I know. I didn't think a man had much choice when it came to taking sides, and all. Mr. Sills — I just don't know as I can say who my people are now. Or your people. And I mean no disrespect — but I don't believe any of you gentlemen do.'

'It's all off the point,' Mr. Morse said sharply.

'Maybe I'm just getting old. I'm not criticizing what a man does when he thinks he sees his way to it. But I'm resigning.'

Mr. Peacham stood up suddenly and stepped to Captain Todd's side. 'You can't do it,' he declared. Then Mr. Dicey Short interposed: 'Remember Tolliver. He made matters worse.' And he got to his feet and approached Captain Todd.

There was a quick scraping of chairs and then the sound of

five or six voices talking at once. The men crowded around Captain Todd. Mr. Munn rose, too, and moved toward the group.

'Remember Tolliver!' another voice was saying, louder now.

Captain Todd, in the middle of the group, kept holding up one hand as though he wished to speak or as though, perhaps, to ward off a blow. They crowded more closely around him. Then Mr. Munn, out of the corner of his eye, saw with astonishment that Mr. Christian was still seated at the table, alone. He seemed scarcely to be paying attention to the movements and voices before him. On the instant, as though Mr. Munn's glance were a signal, Mr. Christian stood up, shoved his chair raspingly aside with his foot, and took two heavy strides toward the group. 'Great God!' he exclaimed. 'Great God!' Then, as the voices ceased, and the men turned to look at him, 'Great God, can't you all see when a man's got his mind made up?'

He looked at the group for a moment, then crammed his black felt hat onto his skull, jerked down the brim, and went out the door into the dark hall. His boot heels hit the stairs heavily as he went down.

Captain Todd had stood in the midst of the group, his hand raised slightly as though for silence, but the other men had been silent at that moment, their eyes turned toward the door through which Mr. Christian had disappeared. Mr. Munn was to remember that scene — the Captain standing there with his hand raised a little — was to remember it very sharply, almost with the distinctness of reality, when he saw, some six weeks later, Benton Todd advance, with eyes blinking against the strongly focused rays of lantern light, and lift his hand for the oath. With his hand raised that way, he looked, somehow, more like the old man than ever.

Chapter eight

It was hot in the little back room of Wilson's restaurant. The sweat gathered in the edges of Mr. Munn's hair, and now and then a drop would slide down his forehead or down his cheek. He would be conscious of its tickling motion, but he would not lift his hand to wipe his face. He would, in fact, cherish, though peevishly, that small sensation of discomfort, for it distracted him from the immediate world around him. He could feel, too, the sweat gathering at his armpits. He felt the matted hair there, and then a minute movement down the flesh under his left arm, for a drop had detached itself and was sliding down. He shuddered with a sudden wave of cold that was within him, that grew out of his own body, and had no relation to the hot, motionless air of the room and the glaring light pouring in from the alley window. He lifted his glass and took a full drink, not savoring the taste, but letting the ice-cold liquid flow down his throat all at once. Then he waited for the shudder.

'Then he tried to get Tom Sorrell,' Mr. Sills said. 'Five hundred dollars.'

'Mr. Sorrell said he didn't know at first what the fellow was driving at,' Professor Ball put in.

Mr. Munn looked at Professor Ball. Professor Ball did not seem to be aware of the heat, not even with that long black coat buttoned up over him and the heavy white bandages on his hands. The skin of his face was perfectly dry. It was yellowish in color and delicately creased like well-worked leather. He was staring out of the alley window at the blank brick wall, and watching him, Mr. Munn remembered how in this room that day of the rally a year before — almost exactly a year but seemingly so much longer — Senator Tolliver had raised his eyes to that wall as into a distance. Professor Ball was doing that, looking beyond them.

'Mr. Sorrell didn't know what he was driving at,' Professor Ball repeated. 'And that is, I take it, understandable. An honest man — and Mr. Sorrell is an honest and worthy man — wouldn't readily grasp such perfidy.'

'My God!' Mr. Munn said, 'I oughter have let them hang the bastard.' He drained his glass, looked into it as though to verify the fact that it was empty, and then struck it twice sharply on the table. A negro man entered from the hall, and Mr. Munn pointed at the glass. 'Won't you take one this time, Professor?' he asked Mr. Ball.

'I have never found the indulgence necessary,' Professor Ball answered, 'but thank you.'

Mr. Munn looked inquiringly at Mr. Sills.

'Not another one,' Mr. Sills said, shaking his head, 'not in this heat. I don't see how you do it. And it this hot.'

'There's worse things than being hot, I guess,' Mr. Munn rejoined.

'But Trevelyan,' Professor Ball said — 'to return, gentlemen, to the matter of Trevelyan.'

'I oughter have let them hang him,' Mr. Munn repeated meditatively.

The negro came back with the drink.

'It would've been convenient, all right,' Mr. Sills said.

'No,' Professor Ball replied; 'it would have been convenient, as matters have developed, but it wouldn't have been right. Mr. Munn was serving the cause of justice. And not for hire. For the love of justice, than which there is no nobler sentiment in the human breast.'

'I was a sucker,' Mr. Munn said, with a trace of bitterness, 'and this is what we get.'

'No,' Professor Ball rejoined; 'justice is justice. You should have no regret.'

'As a matter of fact——' Mr. Sills remarked, then coughed dryly, deprecatorily, while both of the other men looked at him.

'Yes?' Mr. Munn said.

'As a matter of fact, I've wondered about that fellow Trevelyan. Before this came up. Maybe he was guilty.'

'We found the knife,' Mr. Munn said aggressively, 'and the watch. What do you want for evidence?'

'Well——'

'Well——' Mr. Munn repeated. 'And God knows you couldn't ever expect a jury to believe that story about the frog finding the knife. Now, could you?'

'Well, I didn't say you could. All I said was, maybe he was guilty. A feller who could do what he's just done, could do——'

'If you don't mind, Mr. Sills, I'd prefer not to discuss the case.'

'Suit yourself,' Mr. Sills answered. 'The nigger is dead that had the knife, and you can't unhang him. All I was saying was——'

'If you'll excuse me, Mr. Sills, I don't want to discuss it.'

'Suit yourself,' Mr. Sills said again, and shrugged slightly. Mr. Munn thought for an instant that he detected a flicker of amusement, or triumph, in Mr. Sills' eyes, and anger gripped him. Then, scrutinizing Mr. Sills' face, he wasn't sure, it was so colorless, so unmoving. He took a quick gulp of his drink.

'But this, gentlemen, now this,' Professor Ball was saying — 'this is more immediate. The other is past. And this, now, is serious.'

'Serious enough,' Mr. Sills agreed; then added, 'But what to do, that's the question.'

'He took an oath,' Professor Ball reminded them.

Mr. Sills turned to Mr. Munn, saying: 'Sorrell said he'd

just about as soon pay the five hundred, even if it would sure pinch him a right smart, if he thought that'd settle anything. But he said it'd all happen again, sooner or later.'

'He took an oath,' Professor Ball said. 'It was a sacred oath, before God, and we all took it.'

Mr. Sills went on: 'Mr. Sorrell said he was for running him out of the country. Even if that wouldn't do any good, he said it would give him a lot of satisfaction.'

'It was an oath,' Professor Ball repeated once more.

'Well?' Mr. Sills demanded, almost peevishly, turning toward the old man.

'Well ——' Professor Ball was looking out the window at the blank brick wall beyond and the glaring light.

'We can't decide anything,' Mr. Munn said. 'It's for the council to decide.'

'And soon,' Professor Ball added.

Mr. Sills nodded his head, and repeated, 'Soon.'

'We can't decide anything,' Professor Ball continued. 'We have no authority as individuals. But we just wanted to let you know, my boy, valuing your opinion the way we do.'

'Thank you, sir.'

'We just found out. We just happened to run into Mr. Sorrell, and he told us. He was upset, and he'd just come in to town ——' Professor Ball rose from his chair, and stretched forth his right hand, with its club-like bandage, toward Mr. Munn. 'I must go now. Doctor MacDonald ought to be informed, and others. There should be a meeting of the council immediately.'

'Good-bye, sir,' Mr. Munn said, shaking hands.

Professor Ball shook hands with Mr. Sills, picked up his hat from the table, and left the room.

The two men remaining looked at each other for a second, but neither made a move to sit down.

'Well ——' Mr. Sills began.

'It's a God-damned mess,' Mr. Munn declared. He looked nervously about the room, with the glance of a man who thinks he may have left something behind. Then he turned abruptly to Mr. Sills. 'I'm sorry, but I've got to go,' he said. 'I've got an appointment.' He took out his watch. 'I'm late for it now.' He said good-bye and hurried out into the alley and up a side street toward the hotel.

He waited for his mare, striding back and forth in the hallway of the livery stable, driving his heels into the soft, ripe-feeling substance underfoot, inhaling the ammoniac odor of the manure and the sweetness of the hay, while the negro man did the sad-dling and brought her out. His stomach felt cold and clotted, and at the same time the solid mass of the heat bore down on his body like the weight of water on a diver at great depth, a weight pressing surely and relentlessly at every point. He thought that he should not have taken that last drink.

The negro brought out the mare.

'Gitten tow'ds home early, ain't you, Mister Perse?'

'Hell, no,' he said, hearing his own sharp, irritable tone, like the tone of a stranger, and experiencing an access of shame that, perversely, fanned the irritation so that he snapped his jaws shut and dug his heels into the mare's flanks. She plunged as if stung by a fly, and then he found himself out of the shadow of the stable and in the sudden, vibrating glare of the afternoon.

He rode straight out of town, out the Murray Mill Pike.

He crossed the little wooden bridge over the branch, which was stagnant now and edged with a greenish, copperish scum, and drew rein even with the clump of cedar. There the buck-berry bushes were, and some elder and sumac. The white dust from the road powdered the leaves of the bushes. It was this time of year, and this kind of season, dry like this with the dust accumulating undisturbed on the motionless leaves by the road-side, when Duffy had been killed. When the body fell, the white dust would have received it like a cushion, breaking the weight of the fall, and puffing out in a small, white cloud from the impact. The dust would have sucked up, instantly, whatever blood drained from the wounds. Then the body had been dragged off the road into the buckberry bushes. The murderer would have scraped his foot over the spot where the blood had drained from the wound into the dust. He would have looked up and down the road, quickly, and then he would have scraped his foot, almost automatically, over the spot. He would have done that.

Standing beside the mare at the edge of the road, Mr. Munn stared down at the ground, as though some trace might remain. There was nothing, only the white dust. He mounted, and rode on.

Trevelyan's shack was precisely as he had remembered it, box-like, built of vertical boards from which the whitewash had scaled off a long time back, set flat on the bare, trodden ground. A large gum tree stood near the house, the earth seeming to recede from around its roots. Under the gum tree a hen was fluffing and wallowing in the dust. When Mr. Munn rode up to the gate, it left off, and went under the house.

From the doorway, Trevelyan's wife watched him as he approached and dismounted. He dropped the bridle over the sagging gatepost, and strode toward her over the turfless ground. She had her hands clasped together at the level of her waist. She was barefooted, and he noticed how her feet, which were streaked with dust, looked small and bony, like a child's feet, even though she was not a small woman.

'Good afternoon,' he said, and watched her face as she prepared to speak. In it there was a kind of preliminary gathering, an effort, that would come to focus in the word she would speak.

'Howdy-do,' she answered.

'Is your husband here?' he demanded.

'He's here,' she said, nodding slowly.

'Can I see him?'

'If'n you'll just step in, and set down,' she replied, 'I'll git him. He's a-choppen some stovewood, and if'n you'll ——' She let one of her hands move in a gesture of invitation that seemed to fail before it had well begun.

He shook his head. 'No, thanks,' he said. 'I'll just go back and talk to him, if you'll tell me where he is.'

'He's in the back, a-choppen,' she said. 'But if'n you'll step in ——' She made a weak gesture.

'No, thanks,' he said, and moved quickly away. He did not want to be with the woman any longer.

He turned the corner of the house, and passed under the boughs of the gum tree. He heard the sound of an axe stroke on wood, a sound thin but satisfying and clean in the emptiness of the afternoon. Then he saw Trevelyan. The man was some fifty yards back of the shack. Mr. Munn saw him swing up the axe, and caught the flash of the sun on the blade.

When he was within some twenty feet, he called sharply, 'Trevelyan!' and then approached the man, who leaned lightly on his axe, waiting.

'Howdy-do,' Trevelyan said.

'Trevelyan,' Mr. Munn began, and stepped to a position directly in front of him, 'I understand you tried to blackmail Mr. Tom Sorrell. For five hundred dollars.'

Trevelyan's impassive face did not change, or changed only by a slight narrowing of the eyes, as though the light were, for the moment, too great. He said nothing.

'I want to know. Now.'

'I ain't a-messen in yore bizness,' Trevelyan said, measuring his words out, not looking at Mr. Munn now, but off at the horizon, his eyes squinting, 'an' I don't aim to have no man messen in mine.'

'I want to know. And no lie.'

'Lie! Ain't air man ——' Trevelyan's hand tightened on the

axe handle, and over the big knuckle bones the red, too-thin skin whitened.

'You fool,' Mr. Munn said evenly, 'you've got a place here, and, by God, now ——'

'Fifteen acres,' Trevelyan answered, and spat into the dust, 'and ever God's foot mortgaged.'

'— and, by God, now you go and fix it so you'll have to leave the country. You do that, and those men the only friends you had ——'

'Naw, naw,' Trevelyan interrupted, and he turned his eyes, still squinting, upon Mr. Munn; 'naw, they ain't no friends of mine. They ain't done nuthen fer me. I ain't beholden to 'em. To no man.'

'Well, they might do something for you now, something you won't like, Trevelyan. I'm not saying, but I'm saying this: you better clear out. And now. Now. Today, not tomorrow. Here ——' Mr. Munn pulled a wallet from his pocket and took two bills, a ten and a five. 'Here,' he said, 'here, you take this and clear out. Now.'

Trevelyan only looked at the money, his face unchanging.

'You clear out. Far as it'll take you. You write me where you are. I'll let you know when to come back.' Mr. Munn's voice sank lower, hurrying, while he thrust the money toward the big man, almost touching the sweat-stained blue cloth of his shirt. 'I'll see your crop's cut and fired. Like I did before. I'll ——'

'Hit ain't worth a toot,' Trevelyan said.

'I'll see it taken care of.' He thrust the money forward.

Trevelyan was shaking his head, slowly. 'Naw, hit ain't worth a toot. Let hit rot in the field, fer all of me. But I ain't a-leave-en. Ain't no man gonna run me outer no country.'

'You fool!' Mr. Munn crumpled the money in his hand. His voice rose. 'You fool, you clear out. Now. You don't know.'

Trevelyan unhurriedly spat, then looked away. 'I was aimen

to git out,' he said. 'I was aimen to git me that money from that bastud and git out. Oklahoma, and git me a start. They say a man kin git a start.' He finished, pausing almost as though in reminiscence.

'Now!' Mr. Munn insisted.

'Naw, not now. Ain't no man a-tellen me to git out. No man. Not even you, nor no mortal man.'

'It's no favor to me,' Mr. Munn said bitterly, 'your going. I ought to let come what will come. I haven't got any claim on you. It's you got a claim on me. Because I was fool enough to pull your neck out of the rope once.'

'I never ast you,' Trevelyan retorted.

'Your wife did.'

'I never ast you and I never knowed when she done hit. You done hit because you wanted to. I never ast no man fer nuthen. Not since I was born. You done hit because you wanted.'

'I damn well wish I hadn't,' Mr. Munn declared.

'I'd a-got off,' Trevelyan said.

'They'd hanged you, Trevelyan. You know it, they'd hanged you. They'd put a rope round your neck, Trevelyan——' Mr. Munn made a circle, like a noose, with forefingers and thumbs, and held it to the man's gaze and shook his hands back and forth. The two bills had fluttered to the ground between them.

'I'd a-got off,' Trevelyan said.

'But that don't matter now. Not now,' Mr. Munn went on, jerking his hands apart. With the extended forefinger of his right hand he stabbed once at the sweat-soaked blue cloth which covered the man's chest. 'Now it matters for you to go. I'm telling you because I got you off the other time. That's why I'm telling you, and I mean it.' He leaned closer to Trevelyan, not eight inches between their bodies, and stared upward at his face. 'Now go!' he commanded.

'No,' Trevelyan answered.

Mr. Munn stepped backward a long, quick pace, as though he had been slapped in the face. 'All right,' he said, his voice suddenly quiet, 'all right, you poor, God-damned fool.'

'Ain't no man e'er put a skeer on me,' Trevelyan said.

Mr. Munn stared at Trevelyan for a moment. Then he struck his palms together, once. The impact made a dry, flat sound. Somewhere, off in the bushes, an insect made a rasping note, twice repeated.

Mr. Munn swung round, grinding his heel on the sun-baked earth. He took three strides toward the house, without looking back.

'Hey!' Trevelyan called.

Mr. Munn looked back.

'You're leave-en yore money,' Trevelyan said. He glanced dispassionately at the ground before his feet where the bills lay.

'You'll need it,' Mr. Munn told him, and turned away.

'Hit kin lay and rot,' Trevelyan answered.

After he had passed the corner of the house, he heard the axe stroke on the wood. He hurried across the yard, and mounted his horse. The woman was standing in the doorway of the house. He averted his eyes from her, and she said nothing. As he wheeled his horse, he caught, out of the tail of his eye, the flash of sun on the swift arc of the descending axe.

He rode down the short, brush-bordered lane leading to the big road. On the right-hand side was a field of tobacco. It was Trevelyan's tobacco. The stalks were spindly and drooping, and the leaves, dry-looking, hung from the stalks. They did not loop strongly away from the base, but sagged as though their fibers had long lost strength and resilience. Between the tobacco hills, even on the hills, the ground was dry, packed, cracked-looking. It had a grayish cast.

'Crawfish ground,' Mr. Munn said aloud; 'crawfish ground.'

Looking at that field, the miserable, drouth-bitten plants and the badly cultivated earth, and the blaze of sunlight over it, he felt a surge of hatred, or of something near hatred, for Trevelyan. He had not had such a feeling earlier.

He rode on, to the pike. He passed the spot where the cedar grove and the buckberry bushes were. He knew, even as he fought against the knowledge, the remembrance, that he had ridden toward Trevelyan's house with the full intention of asking him if he had killed Duffy. He had been going to say, 'Trevelyan, you killed that man. Answer me.' He had not said it. He had said something else. He had been afraid. But not of Trevelyan.

Except for the temperature — and even the night tonight was coolish, too, for it was getting on in August — it might have been that other night when he had ridden out this road, with the two deputies, almost a year ago now. It is the same road, he thought, and I am the same man and I am doing the same thing, but it is a different time and it is a different thing, or is it a different thing, only a different time? — for then I rode here to find the knife and my riding here now is part of that same act, completing itself, fulfilling a single thought, the same gesture or an act of the will.

The men rode, single file, behind him. Except for the soft soughing of hoofs in the dust, or the infrequent, padded chink of a horseshoe on a stone, there had been no sound for a long way. The men had not spoken a word.

Or is it a different thing, he thought, part of the same motion fulfilling a single act of will? But not his own will, it occurred to him. Not entirely his own. In this, now, there is no will, not mine nor anybody's, for there is no will in the act in memory, for it is complete and is in one time out of time, he thought; for as he moved down the road, thinking of that other night, he felt removed, even now, from the present experience, as though it were in memory.

He had felt that way when he reached into the hat and picked up one of the acorns and drew it out and opened his hand and saw that it was the yellow one. Mr. Burden had said, 'Well, if we're gonna do it, we might get it over with,' and had gone outside the schoolhouse and fumbled about by the light of matches under the oak tree in the yard. He had come back into the silent group, and had asserted, extending his hand: 'There's a yellow one here. Might as well let it be the one.'

'Let everybody look at them good,' Mr. Sills had said. 'We don't want any argument later.'

'Not much,' Doctor MacDonald had agreed, smiling.

Mr. Munn had found the yellow acorn in his hand. 'Well,' he remarked, looking at it, 'that's it.' He had lifted his glance from the object to find the eyes of all the men fixed upon him, detaching him from them.

Doctor MacDonald had come to stand in front of Mr. Munn. 'I'll go with you all,' he had offered.

'It won't be necessary,' Mr. Munn had said.

'Not necessary,' Doctor MacDonald had answered, 'but I don't want to pass any responsibility.'

'No,' Mr. Munn had said. He had twisted the yellow acorn slowly in his fingers.

Doctor MacDonald had seemed about to speak again; then had turned away.

Mr. Munn had dropped the acorn into his pocket.

The acorn was in his pocket now. Tonight he again wore the old black coat which he had worn the night before, at the schoolhouse at Grayson's Crossing. He reached into his pocket and felt in his fingers the small, slick, ovoidal form.

When they turned off the pike into the lane, one of the men inquired, 'Hadn't we better leave the horses here?'

'No,' Mr. Munn said in an ordinary tone.

Up the lane a dog barked, and then again, closer. Then it dashed into the open, stopped, and barked again. Its shape was vague in the darkness.

'The bastard!' one of the men exclaimed.

Three of the men slipped off their horses, and passed their bridles to be held by others still mounted. They began to fumble on the ground beside the lane. The dog continued to bark. One of them struck a match.

'Put that light out,' Mr. Munn ordered.

The flame went out.

One of the men straightened up, and stepped slowly toward the dog. The other man waited. The first man held at his side a short, club-like stick which he had found. The dog barked twice, circling the man, and then ran in close and veered off. The man made no motion. He let the club hang loosely by his side. The dog again rushed in. The man took one long stride toward the dog, the club whipped over, and for an instant, the instant before the sodden crack of the impact of wood on flesh, the forms seemed to be almost merged in the darkness. Then the man swung back, and the dog, with a kind of contorted jerking of all four legs, tried to shove itself along. It tried to stand, but could not. It had not yelped, not even at the instant of the blow. The moaning sound that it now made was very similar to the moan of a human being.

The man lifted the club and again struck. The wood cracked, breaking in half. 'Damn!' the man cried, 'God damn!' He flung the piece of broken club into the dark mass of weeds by the lane.

The dog moaned again, and again tried to shove itself along the ground.

'Can't somebody find something?' the man demanded fretfully.

The other two men stirred about, feeling along the ground with their feet or bending over.

'A chunk of rock, or something,' the man said.

'God damn it, it's too dark,' somebody exclaimed.

The dog kept on moaning. The horses were moving restively.

'We can't stand around all night,' another man complained.

'Aw, hell!' one of the men on the ground said in a tone of fatalistic disgust, and moved toward the dog. He withdrew his hand from his pocket. There was a faint click. The man was opening a knife. He leaned forward, over the dog, pushed the head back with one foot, thrust the blade downward and then jerked it sidewise. He straightened up, peering at the mass on the ground before him. He had cut the dog's throat. He stepped to the side of the lane, and bent over to drive the blade of the frog-sticker into the earth, time after time, to clean off the blood. Then he shut the knife, and dropped it into his pocket.

Somebody else had taken the dog by the hind legs and had dragged it into the weeds. The men moved up the lane, single file. The paleness of the dust of the lane was visible before them. They walked their horses on the side of the lane away from the field of tobacco. On the side by the field there were no trees or brush. On the side where they moved, a scraggly row of trees made a deeper darkness. Mr. Munn stared across at the tobacco field. It was too dark now to make out anything over there, but he thought how the spindly, miserable plants had looked and how he had felt when he saw them. Now he felt nothing.

As they neared the end of the lane, one of the men asked in a harsh whisper, 'Reckon has he got another dog?'

'No,' Mr. Munn said.

'Reckon did anybody hear that barking?' another man queried.

'It's a right smart piece up here,' somebody said, whispering.

'Better leave the horses here,' Mr. Munn directed. And: 'Mr. Sass, will you and Mr. Mock take charge of them?'

The horses were led into the shadow of the thicket. The men paused, and drew together into a compact group.

'Maybe we better wait and see if anybody heard that dog,' a man whispered.

'No,' Mr. Munn said, 'we won't wait.'

The men adjusted the cloths on their faces. Without further talk, two of them separated from the group, and moved off toward the rear of the house, skirting the brush along the fence. They were quickly out of sight. 'All right,' Mr. Munn said.

Still in a compact group, the rest of the men moved to the gate. Mr. Munn cautiously pushed it open. The men moved across the yard toward the house, soundlessly. They pressed themselves against the walls of the house on each side of the door. A man who wore no cloth over his face but who had his hat pulled down stood directly in front of the door. He reached his hand out and struck the boards of the door. At first there was no sound from within. Then there seemed to be a stirring inside, at the window. The men pressed themselves more tightly against the wall. The position of the single man who was facing the door was in the line of vision from the window. There was a sharp movement from within. 'Wait a minute,' a voice said.

The door swung slowly inward, and there the vague form of a man stood blocking the opening.

'Hello,' the unmasked man in the yard said. And at the word the man who had been crouching nearest the door thrust his foot into the aperture, jammed a pistol at arm's length against Trevelyan's body, and commanded, 'Come on out!'

Another man, pistol in hand, flung himself against the door, driving it violently from Trevelyan's grasp.

Trevelyan stepped slowly forward. His hands rose with a retarded, groping motion above his head.

The woman's voice called sharply from the interior dark, 'Harris! Harris!'

'What do you want?' Trevelyan asked.

'Come on out,' one of the men ordered.

The woman's voice called, more shrilly, 'Harris!'

'Shet up!' Trevelyan called back over his shoulder. Then,

turning his head slowly toward the men, 'What you aimen to do?' No one answered him. He stood there, naked except for a pair of overalls hitched over one shoulder, and peered at the men. 'What you aimen to do?' he repeated.

'Start moving,' Mr. Munn said.

'Kin I git my shoes?' Trevelyan said.

'Start moving,' Mr. Munn ordered.

They walked rapidly toward the gate, Trevelyan in front and the two men with pistols holding the muzzles against the flesh of his back. They had reached the gate when the woman called again, from the doorway now. In the darkness of the doorway, she was visible only as a blurred and unformed patch of lighter color. 'Harris!' she called. 'Where you going, Harris?'

'You git back,' he told her, not turning his head.

She came out into the yard, hesitating about halfway to the gate, and calling, 'Harris! Harris!'

The two men who had gone to the rear of the house came running across the yard to join the group. They passed within fifteen feet of the woman.

'Tie him,' Mr. Munn said.

They tied Trevelyan's hands behind him, pushed him into a saddle, and mounted. The man on whose horse Trevelyan sat got up behind another man.

Before the last man was up, the woman ran across the yard, not toward the gate but toward the corner nearest the group, not twenty feet away. 'Harris!' she screamed. 'You listen, Harris! Don't you go, Harris!' She was gripping the palings of the fence, leaning against them.

Trevelyan twisted around toward her. 'I reckin I kin take a whuppen good as the next man,' he said.

The last man mounted. He held the bridle of Trevelyan's horse for a lead.

'Harris!' the woman screamed.

'Shet up!' Trevelyan said.

The group moved down the lane at a trot. The woman ran back toward the gate as though to come out of the yard and pursue them. But she stopped at the gate. They heard her call once more.

Some half a mile up the main pike, the horsemen took a side road. When they turned into it, Trevelyan asked. 'Where you goen?'

No one answered him.

'What you aimen to do?' he said. 'Whup me?' He looked from side to side at the cloth-covered faces of the men who rode stirrup to stirrup with him. They rode looking straight ahead, as if he had never spoken. 'You kin whup me,' he said, 'but ain't no man kin skeer me.'

The road gradually gave way to an untraveled track over which the grass and weeds had run, covering old ruts. The horses now went forward at a walk. On each side of the track the trees grew thick and tall, so that the darkness was close between the trees like the interior darkness of a hall or corridor. But the sky was lighter now, for the clouds that had earlier concealed the stars were breaking up and drifting off toward the northern horizon. But along the lane there was no breath of wind. The leaves hung soundless and motionless.

The lane gave abruptly upon a clearing some forty yards in diameter. In contrast with the close shadows of the lane the area seemed light and the sky very open and wide and of immeasurable depth in those spaces where no clouds were. To the left of the area and directly ahead, the woods looked black and solid. To the right the ground broke precipitously away into an abandoned quarry working. Here the track doubled back to take a shelving descent on the shallower side. It disappeared into the water that now, some fifteen yards below, filled the great cavity. The horsemen left the track and moved across the weed-grown ground toward the lip of the quarry.

There they dismounted and tethered the horses to a fallen

tree. Trevelyan stood in the middle of the group and looked from one man to another. No one looked at him. Nor did they look at each other, but off at the woods, or back at the darkness of the lane through which they had come, or across the lip of the quarry. For a moment they stood apathetically, like strangers who have waited a long time in a railway station at night or in an anteroom at a hospital.

Then Mr. Munn commanded, 'Cut the rope.'

The man who had killed the dog drew the knife from his pocket and snapped open the blade. The long blade concentrated a little light to gleam dully. While the man fumbled with the rope, Trevelyan stood stock-still. Although he wore nothing but the overalls, and his bare feet were tangled in the dew-drenched grass, he did not appear to be cold. Once he shook his head and winced when the man, trying to insert the blade in the knot, twisted the rope on his wrists. Then the man made a quick, jerking motion with the knife, the same motion he had made when he killed the dog, and the rope fell to the ground.

Trevelyan brought his hands slowly and crampedly forward. He inspected them, working the fingers and flexing the wrists. Then he let his arms fall to his sides.

'Trevelyan,' Mr. Munn said, and pointed toward the quarry, 'you get over there.'

Trevelyan hesitated.

Several of the men held pistols in their hands, but loosely, pointed at the ground.

Trevelyan moved toward the brink of the quarry. The ten men approached him in a ragged half-circle. They hesitated some twelve or fifteen feet away from him. Trevelyan glanced from man to man around him. He put his tongue out and ran it over his lips. 'Well,' he said, 'if'n you gonna whup me, why don't you do hit?'

'Trevelyan,' Mr. Munn went on through the cloth of his

mask, 'it's not a whipping.' He went closer. 'It's not a whipping,' he repeated. 'You tried to blackmail Sorrell. You tried twice. Do you deny it?'

'I ain't sayen I did, and I ain't sayen I didn't,' Trevelyan answered slowly, almost meditatively.

Mr. Munn went closer. His head was thrust forward a little as he stared at the man who formed the center of the tightening half-circle. 'You did,' Mr. Munn said. 'You took an oath and then you broke it. You were going to sell out, Trevelyan. Weren't you, Trevelyan?'

The man made no reply. He seemed, for the moment, to be looking across the open space toward the black woods. Mr. Munn took another step forward. He held the pistol in his hand now. In his hand it felt cold and foreign. 'You did, Trevelyan. You went to see Sorrell again yesterday afternoon. You threatened him. He ordered you off his place, and you knocked him down. Then you telephoned that deputy and saw him and tried to make a deal with him about turning Sorrell in, but not having to testify——' Mr. Munn took another step. 'Didn't you, Trevelyan?'

Trevelyan replied: 'You ain't skeeren me. Not none of you. Nor air man.'

'Didn't you, Trevelyan——'

'Go on and whup me,' Trevelyan said.

'Didn't you, Trevelyan?' Mr. Munn thought: I am talking to him and as long as I talk to him we will not do it, I will not do it, that's why I'm talking to him, why don't we go on and do it?

He looked about him at the other men. They held pistols in their hands, but their faces were covered. It seemed to him that only the hands holding the pistols, not those blank, cloth-shrouded faces that could not be seen, were alive and real. At that moment the mask was suffocating to him. Its privacy was hideous, cutting him off from everything, from everyone. From all the world. He lifted his left hand, slowly; then, as though stifling, he tore the mask from his face, and took a long stride toward Trevelyan, and thrust out his head and called, 'Trevelyan!'

The man's mouth moved without sound, then said, 'I knowed hit was you.'

'Trevelyan!' Mr. Munn thought how sick, how afraid, how stifled, those men were under their masks. He gulped a full, deep, exquisite breath, like a man who rises from a long dive, and with burning lungs and bursting heart plunges, chest-high, into air.

'And you, Trevelyan' — and he took another stride — 'you killed that man, you did; answer me!'

He was almost upon him. Trevelyan moved, lifted his arm. The pistol exploded in Mr. Munn's grasp. He swung back from Trevelyan, seeing, even in that light, the man's narrow eyes go suddenly wide.

Like a belated echo, another shot was fired. Who fired it, Mr. Munn did not know. Trevelyan staggered, and crossed his hands on his chest with a movement that was sad, almost womanly, humble.

Then, there came the volley.

Trevelyan sagged, then fell backward over the lip of the quarry.

There was not a sound. There was nothing there in the little space before the men. Even the grass did not look trodden. It was as though nothing had been there.

The smell of gun smoke hung on the air, sharp and cleanly like the smell of a disinfectant.

The men let their arms, which had been outstretched, sink to their sides.

'He fell over,' somebody said in a hushed tone. It was as though he had just witnessed an accident.

Nobody moved.

'Somebody oughter look,' a man hazarded.

Mr. Munn tried to say, 'I'll do it.' But he could not.

One of the men approached the rim, somehow as with an air of stealth, and peered down. He returned to the group. Then he said, 'He's in the water.'

Somebody remarked: 'It's deep there. On this side.'

Another man walked to the rim and looked over. When he came back, he said nothing. The men got on their horses and rode slowly across the open space. The sky was lighter now, the clouds almost gone. The legs of the horses made a swishing, silken sound in the dew-damp weeds and grass; the saddles creaked a little; insects gave their small night noises, familiarly.

My shot, Mr. Munn thought, my shot, did it hit him?

One of the men removed the cloth that had masked his face, and stuck it into a side pocket with the easy gesture of a man who crams his handkerchief into his pocket. Mr. Munn looked at the man's face. The other men took off their masks. Mr. Munn looked at them. Their shadowy faces were remarkable to him, the same faces, but remarkable. They were like faces a man finds on returning to the scenes of his youth, the same faces, recognizable still, but only in their astounding and reproachful difference.

Along the overgrown track the riders strung out in single file, Mr. Munn in front. He seemed to feel the eyes of all of them fixed upon his back, pressing, grinding, boring in as with a physical pressure. He had the impulse to plunge his heels into the mare's flanks and break into a gallop up the long dark corridor between the trees, to leave them all behind, staring; but he mastered it. Then he tried, as with the discovery of caution and cunning, not to hear the subdued sounds of their motion. He fixed his own gaze on the point, far ahead, where the dark forms of the two rows of trees converged against the sky, trying to draw the awareness of the men out of himself and delude his senses into the absolute emptiness, the loneliness, which he thought he must have.

My shot, he thought, did it hit him? But the thought only flickered at the edge of his consciousness, like something caught out of the tail of the eye, and he put it from him, discovering, complacently and craftily, how easy, how unexpectedly easy, it was to do so if he focused all his powers upon that spot where the dark trees converged. The thought was not important, not really. He experienced a sense of release, of pleasure, at the discovery of its unimportance. The only thing important now was to fix his eyes upon that point, yonder, far up the track, and keep them fixed there. That was important.

A short distance before the pike, after the weed-grown track had given way to the road, Mr. Munn pulled his mare to the side, and let the men come even with him. 'Good night,' he said, his voice having, to his own ears, a barren and croaking sound as though made by some artificial contrivance.

'I thought you might spend the night at my place,' Mr. Wyngard suggested.

'No,' Mr. Munn answered shortly. 'I can cut through here to my road.'

The men moved off and away from him. He watched them move away, their definite forms disintegrating into the uncertain shadows; and though solitude had, the minute before, seemed so beckoning, so desirable, he was now filled with a perverse and sudden despair, now that those forms were moving away from him.

He rode at a trot, giving himself as completely as possible to the rhythm of the motion, the easy, lulling sounds of hoofs and leather, the anonymous, familiar closeness of the shadowed landscape. Those items belonged wholly to the moment in which he existed, a moment without affiliations with the past or the future. He tried to sink into that moment, trying to escape from time by surrendering most completely to time. He felt like a man who, in the ease of a dream, walks a wire across space, surprised that what had in waking reality seemed so impossible is so easy, but at the same time still aware that with a single misstep, a single failure in balance, he will go hurtling down to one side or the other. The immediate, ignorant moment was like that wire to him.

But while he moved forward, surrendering himself to the moment, complacent and surprised that it was so easy, after all, to live by that definition of life, he grew increasingly aware of what was, apparently, a purely physical discomfort. He felt like a man who thinks himself recovered from an illness, and goes about his normal affairs to find, unexpectedly, that the sickness is still there in his bones and vitals. It is not because of *it*, he thought, because of what happened. His mind automatically refused the statement of what had happened; the fact itself was denied in namelessness. But the discomfort increased. The knowledge which his mind denied rose in his bowels. I'm sick, he thought, it's just that I'm a little sick. The nausea rose in him like sediment in a disturbed vessel.

Finally, he slipped from the saddle and vomited on the grass by the road.

He clung to the stirrup leather, supporting himself, until his strength returned. When he came to the branch that ran across the road, under a little plank bridge, he again dismounted. Trees grew thickly there, along the water, but where he knelt the grass was soft under his knees. He sank his hands and wrists into the cool water, wetting his sleeves. From his cupped hands he supped up the water and rinsed his mouth, and then drank. Then, leaning over the surface and holding his face close, he bathed his face in the water and pressed the coldness of his hands against his eyes. Feeling the water on his face, he thought suddenly of Trevelyan's face in the water. In the water of the quarry. The man had said, in the water. He rose quickly, clumsy with haste, and stared at the water before him. It was black under the trees. A man would lie in the water and the water would be over him and inside of him and he would become a part of the water. The water which he had just drunk so avidly felt cold and inimical within him. Again he had the impulse to vomit, but controlled himself.

He struck his hands together violently, the fist of one into the palm of the other. 'The fool!' he exclaimed, 'the God-damned fool; the poor God-damned fool!'

He felt better then, and rode on. The whole matter almost seemed then, on the moment, like something known for a long time. He would fix his gaze, as before, upon some distant point and bend every energy upon it, so that he seemed to be drawn out of himself. And so powerfully could he distract himself in this exercise that, as he rode up the drive toward his own house and saw a faint light in one of the windows downstairs, no question crossed his mind. He saw the light, and accepted it; that was all.

He went directly to the stable, and unsaddled the mare. Then, having the key to the front and not to the side door, he returned across the yard, under the maples. A few prematurely fallen leaves rustled beneath his tread.

Not until he had pushed open the door and stood on the threshold, the key still in his hand, did the significance of the light, which he now saw falling faintly into the hall from the half-open door of the room at the left, really take hold upon him. He had told May that he might not come back until very late, or perhaps not at all, and that she should get Rosie to sleep up at the house. He drew the door softly shut behind him.

'Perse,' he heard his own name pronounced. It was May's voice.

He stood stock-still, with his hand still on the knob of the door behind him. Then she came into the hall. Her small figure was outlined against that dim light from the room behind her.

'Perse,' she repeated.

He tried to speak to her, but the words would not come, his throat was so dry and constricted.

'Perse, what's the matter?' she demanded, her voice rising and her gaze unwaveringly fixed upon him.

'Nothing,' he managed to say, and took a step toward her.

'But Perse ——'

Staring at her, he could think of nothing in the world to say to her.

'But Perse, there is.' She retreated before him, her eyes still fixed on his face. She pushed the door fully open behind her, not turning to look, and stepped back across the threshold into the room. He came close to her, and she took another step back, pronouncing his name and lifting one hand a little in an indeterminate gesture.

The lamp on the table in the middle of the room was turned down so low that the flame flickered weakly along the wick and the shadows swam unsteadily, encroachingly, in the corners and over the floor. What little light there was, the woman's blonde hair caught. It was loose over her shoulders. She was wearing a blue kimono. It seemed too large for her. When she lifted her arm, the looped and flowing sleeve emphasized its fragility and the aimlessness of the gesture.

'Oh, Perse!' she exclaimed. 'I can't stand it. What's the matter, Perse?'

'Nothing,' he answered, as she stared at him.

'You never tell me,' she said weakly and lamentingly, her arm rising in that gesture and then subsiding. 'Not anything.'

He reached out as if to pluck at the flowing garment. But she stood too far away from him.

'It's so late; you stayed out so late.' And then: 'You've been drinking, Perse. You've had whisky.'

'No,' he denied.

'What's the matter? Oh, Perse!'

'God damn it!' he uttered, and stepped quickly to her and seized her by the shoulders.

'You're hurting ——'

'Well,' he said. He drew her to him, more tightly. Then he began to kiss her on the face.

'Don't, Perse, don't! Don't; I want to talk to you.'

He continued to hold her. Then he began to force her back, beyond the table.

'No, no!' she exclaimed, and a tone of desperation came into her voice.

'Yes,' he said.

'No. No. Not now.'

He paid no attention to her.

'No. Later, maybe later——' She tried to thrust him back, and mixed with the tone of desperation there was a hint of wheedling, guileful but hopeless.

After he had forced her past the table to the divan, she struggled with him with a strength which he had never suspected. Then, suddenly, she was as passive as a dead body, although her hands remained crushed against his chest as in resistance and revulsion.

Chapter nine

THE first fields were cut. Men moved slowly, stoopingly, across the wide fields. They bent between the heavy plants, and lifted the heavy blade of the cutting knife and slashed off the stalk at the base, to leave the stob protruding from the hill. In the open places, where the tobacco had been cut, the wagons waited, and the mules drooped their long, bony, spatulate, patient heads.

The fall sharpened early. The first curing fires in the loaded barns had been lighted, and the blue smoke began to settle out like haze over the bare fields in the late, level light. Everywhere there was the thin and pervasive odor of burning, which, mingled with the other, more natural odors of the season, the dry, pungent, leathery odors of earth and withering vegetation, fed the sense of recession and finality. In the afternoons great flocks of grackles, gathering in their autumnal multitudes, would wheel over the fields. When they flew low enough, their burnished blackness would glisten in the light, and the air would be full of the vigorous whisper of their wing-beats. When they settled in the trees along a lane, or in the woods bordering the fields, or in the groves about the houses, their cries would be incessant.

Mr. Munn, ever since he had grown up, would see the great flocks of grackles, on bright days in the fall, sweeping across the blue sky, from horizon to horizon, or fountaining upward and outward from a tree or a grove where they had been disturbed, or splaying from the air wantonly over the wide expanse of a field, like bright, black seeds flung from a sower's liberal hand; and almost always, if the press of his immediate occupation was not too strong, he would let his gaze follow their flight. He would observe the sweep of the flock on the sky, the swaying but sure convolutions of the wide-flung mass like the curved and reaching and self-fulfilling forward thrust of a breaker, or the movement of a field of grain in the wind. That spectacle always spoke to him of an inevitability, a surety, a completeness beyond his grasp or, even, definition. That perfection, that victorious indifference, filled him with a loneliness which mingled insidiously with the minute tightening of his muscles and the new tingling of the blood, like a start of hope, which the sight had provoked.

During those years spent in Philadelphia, when he was studying law, that feeling had come to him merely as a momentary touch of homesickness. One clear afternoon, as he walked down a quiet street between the rows of dull-colored brick houses, the grackles came sweeping over the roofs, not flying very high, and settled in the trees of a little park just ahead. He stopped stock-still, one hand on the iron fence in front of a narrow dooryard. Then, slowly, he walked on down the street, toward the little park where the grackles were. In the overmastering loneliness of that moment, his whole life seemed to him nothing but vanity. His past seemed as valueless and as unstable as a puff of smoke, and his future meaningless, unless — and the thought was a flash, quickly dissipated — he might by some unnamable, single, heroic stroke discover the unifying fulfillment.

He was on his way, that afternoon, to see a relative, a distant cousin who had once known his mother and with whom his mother had maintained for years a desultory and unreasonable correspondence. Miss Sprague — 'your cousin Ianthe,' his mother called her — and his mother had met only once, at a small summer resort in south-central Kentucky, Thermopolis Springs. His mother had spent several weeks there one summer when she was a young girl, and Miss Ianthe Sprague, some ten or twelve years her senior, almost old enough at that time to be considered an old maid, had come with an aunt to stay at the Thermopolis Hotel. They had spent several weeks together at Thermopolis Springs, and though they never saw each other again, they wrote letters. Mr. Munn had wondered before he went to Philadelphia, and wondered even more after he went, what events of that summer at Thermopolis Springs could have fixed the two women together in their meaningless, but apparently stable, bond. He could imagine, well enough, how their time had been spent, sipping the water from the spring, sitting together and talking on the long, shady veranda of some white, wooden hotel, watching the men play bowls, or dancing in the pavilion. But his mother had once remarked that Ianthe Sprague had always been in bad health, no better than an invalid, and had practically been confined to a chair. She must have sat in her chair to watch the dancers for a while before being carried up to bed.

He had seen some of the letters which the two women exchanged. The letters exhibited no trace of intimacy. In their letters the women never referred to that little fragment of the past which they had shared, except, perhaps, by way of giving an account of some person whom both had known. The letters were brief and bare recitals of commonplace facts. Miss Sprague would write of the weather in Philadelphia, of the price of coal, of the repairing of a house in her block; never of anything different from those topics. But in his childhood and early adolescence, Percy Munn, even though he was well acquainted with the letters, found that the name 'Ianthe' raised in his mind an image of great delicacy and beauty. In one of his father's books he read a poem with the title 'Ianthe':

> From you, Ianthe, little troubles pass
> Like little ripples down a sunny river;
> Your pleasures spring like daisies in the grass,
> Cut down, and up again as blithe as ever.

It seemed to verify his imaginings.

In Philadelphia he found Miss Sprague, now almost totally blind, sitting in a high-ceilinged, dingy, overheated room, in which the unmoving air held the odor of camphor. On the walls and on the tables and on the what-not, dozens of photographs hung askew or were propped at slovenly angles. The woman, who actually could not have been much more than fifty years old, looked seventy. She was lean to emaciation, and the skin hung in dry, gray folds and pouches from her neck and jawbone. Her hands shook as with perpetual cold. She leaned peeringly forward when she spoke in her outworn voice. About her shoulders a black shawl was wrapped, and on the front of her lusterless, black-silk dress there were spots which had been left, apparently, by spilled food.

Miss Sprague lived in her own house, but on the upper floor. There, on the second floor, she would be. When the slatternly little Irish maid let him in, he could see Miss Sprague turn her head, with a careful and creaking motion, and peer toward him.

'How are you feeling, Cousin Ianthe?' he would say.

'Not much worse,' she would answer, 'except for the weather.' Or: 'Maybe a little better, thank you, but I don't know. Is it getting any colder, outside?'

When he first began to come to see her, he tried to lead her into talking of his mother, and of herself. The sight of her, at first, stirred to a kind of painful and reproachful life those boyhood notions that had clustered about her name. He had completely forgotten those notions. Now, the sight of her revived them, and shocked them. He was like a man who puts his leg down unexpectedly and feels the twinge of an old wound, or fracture. As in a last, desperate or thrifty, automatic effort to salvage something of his own past being which was inherent in those notions, he tried to make her picture for him the self she had been, that summer a long time back, before his birth, when his mother had been a young girl. But it was no use. She could not do it. She could not, it seemed, because she had really always been as she was now. There was not even any pathos in her present condition, her increasing blindness, her increasing poverty, her illness, her loneliness; there was none of that pathos of the falling off from youth and beauty and vitality. Rather, her present being was a sort of goal toward which, confidently, she had always been moving. This present being had always been, he was sure, her real being, and now she was merely achieving it in its perfection of negativity and rejection.

But once she did say, 'Your mother was a beautiful young girl.' When she said that, Percy Munn, who had never before realized, actually, that his mother once had been young, was moved so that tears came to his eyes. His mother now was not old, but she was ageless, it seemed. A widow, she ran the farm competently, and prayed much. She was taciturn and cold, except for those rare moments when, with a kind of shameless unveiling of the spirit, she tried devouringly and terrifyingly to seize upon her son's love, or at least to establish some communication with him. At those moments, embarrassed, he could never respond, and so she would turn coldly again upon herself; and when he, in turn, would try to penetrate to her, her withdrawal would be complete. When Miss Sprague spoke, he saw his mother as she was now, and, on the instant, as she had been, surely, that summer, young and expectant, poised at the edge of the long hotel veranda, listening to music or watching the men at bowls. He felt that he, almost, could look into her eyes as she stood.

In the thought of his mother, there was pathos; but in Miss Sprague, none. She lived, in this overheated, motionless air that reeked of camphor, as in her true medium. This was her triumph.

After the second visit, during which the conversation waned to a slow repetition of the details of his train trip, the weather in southern Kentucky, and the furnishings of the room which he had rented, he proposed that he should bring something to read aloud to her. She said that she would be grateful. When he asked her what he should bring, she replied, 'Anything.' He bought a sentimental novel, feeling certain of his choice. But he had not been reading for ten minutes before he knew that her attention was wandering. She peered at this object in the room, and then at that, and breathed unevenly. He continued to read for an hour or so, and when he left she thanked him. The next week he resumed the novel. But he never finished it. She finally said that what she would like to hear was the newspaper. But when he read the newspaper to her, he discovered that her attention flagged at the long, important, consecutive pieces. What she liked was the short, flat statement that had no possible reference to her life, advertisements of merchandise which she could neither buy nor use, the notice of the death of an obscure citizen in a distant part of the city, or of the birth of a child to a couple of whom she had never heard, or of the construction of a building which she would never enter. The novel had a direction, it described lives that were moving toward fulfillments, it pretended to a meaning. Therefore she could not listen to it. She could not listen to the long, consecutive articles in the newspaper. But the fragmentary, the irrelevant, the meaningless, such things she could receive and draw her special nourishment from. Automatically, she rejected everything else; for, fixed now in her room and failing in vision, she was like some species of marine life that, lodged on the floor or on some rocky shelf, sustains itself on what the random currents bring, absorbing the appropriate matter and ejecting all else, with a delicate and punctilious, but unconscious, discrimination.

And she did not like to talk of the past, and avoided his questions. Indeed, she had little memory of the past. That, too, she had rejected, for out of memory rises the notion of a positive and purposive future, the revision of the past. The photographs which cluttered her room and which she never looked at seemed to be, paradoxically, the very symbol of her discipline; they were the trophies of temptations overcome. But Percy Munn persisted for a while, vainly, in his questions and suggestions, even after he had begun to sense the logic of her refusal, and the magnitude of her achievement.

All the time he was in Philadelphia he went to see her regularly. He had nothing in common with her, and he was, he knew, nothing more than a meaningless shape to her. There was no charity in his visits, for he knew that she did not desire his company. He was lonely in Philadelphia, but he did not make his visits because of that fact; he knew that she had nothing to say to him and that he had nothing to say to her. Or rather, he did not go to see her because he expected any direct alleviation of his loneliness. His communion with her was like the communion which a worshiper may hold with the cold, unhuman, blank, and unbending stone of the carved image. She, too, represented something as cold and unrelenting as fate, for she and he had, in however small a proportion, the same blood in their veins. They had a common ancestor, a man whose full name Percy Munn did not know, or had forgotten, and whose bones had lain for a long time now in an obscure crossroads graveyard somewhere in Virginia.

Once he told May about his weekly visits to Miss Sprague. He described the house and the neighborhood, the way the Germans had stared at him in the hall, the very details of Miss Sprague's room and the life lived there, and, tentatively, how he had felt when he sat there and read the newspaper to her.

'That was certainly nice of you, Perse,' May said, patting his arm in approbation, 'reading to her and all. I'm sure she appreciated it.'

'She didn't appreciate it a damned bit,' he asserted.

'Why, that's terrible, Perse. She should have, and you doing all that for her.'

'I didn't do it for her,' he said shortly. 'I reckon I did it for myself.' That was it, for a fact, he thought; he had done it for himself. He saw that clearly now, so many years later.

'For yourself?' May asked, her tone puzzled.

'Yes,' he replied, 'for myself.'

She did not say anything else.

During the weeks when the summer slanted off into fall, he thought rather often about Miss Sprague. She had, for a time, while he built up his law practice and wrapped up his life in May, dwindled into a rarely remembered episode of his past. But now that May was gone and he was alone in the house, and in fact so often stayed away from town for days at a time, the recollection of Miss Sprague, and speculations about her, began to occupy a place similar to the place which she had occupied during those years in Philadelphia. The fact, he decided, was not strange, for in those occupationless days and nights, the items of the past which, in the forward drive of his hopes and activities, had seemed to be flashing from him into distance, like objects seen from a moving train, now appeared with an importance and simultaneity that surprised him. And he scanned those items for some explanation, some hint of interpretation, for the present. Then, baffled, he would try to thrust them from his mind completely.

He did not know whether Miss Sprague was alive or dead. Since his mother's death, he had had but one letter from Miss Sprague. He had written to her to tell her of the death of his mother. After some weeks he had received a letter from her saying that she was very sorry that Mrs. Munn was dead and sympathized with him in his bereavement. The letter was curt and detached, almost anonymous.

Now, a good many years after the event, he had the impulse to write to Miss Sprague. But he decided against it, for, even as the impulse came, there came the conviction that the letter would not be answered. To answer his letter would be a concession, a weakness, for her. Now she would be, whether alive or dead, beyond such concessions; that letter to him on the occasion of his mother's death had, he was sure, been the grudging last.

Alone much of the time now, standing in the yard or walking across the fields, or sitting on the porch in the evening aware of the new edge to the air, or staring up at the dark above his bed, he occasionally wondered about the nature of Miss Sprague's loneliness. He tried to feel himself back across time and across the bounds of personality into her special loneliness. He recalled how, during those periods of loneliness and homesickness in Philadelphia — and he had been lonely during all those years — he had wondered how anybody could be so alone, so cut off, so withdrawn, as Miss Sprague, and still live.

He himself was much alone now, and by choice. Even though he knew that work waited for him at his office, that obligations were, one after another, slipping past the promised date of fulfillment, he could not bring himself to go to town, to meet the men whom he had seen commonly and pleasantly, to say the things which he had so often said before, to sit at the desk where he had sat. He only went in when the pressure of business was so great that it could not be ignored, or when the girl who worked for him telephoned to remind him of an appointment of special importance.

The strange thing — and the strangeness of it grew upon him day after day — was that he was almost glad for May's absence. He had been almost glad that morning after the death of Trevelyan, when he woke up, in the full light of day, to find the house empty except for the negro cook, who silently set the food before him and watched him with a furtive and insolent curiosity. He had waked on the couch in the living-room and had stared at the ceiling while the feelings of unease, loss, and isolation that filled him, achieved in memory, as a saturated solution settles out its characteristic crystals, the precise structure of fact and chronology.

He was stiff and cramped from lying on the couch, and his mouth dry as though from drinking. He rose slowly from the couch and walked, with an almost experimental motion, across the carpet to the front windows. There, he flung back the curtains and let the full brilliance of the sunlight strike into the room. That light, falling across the window-sill and spreading over the carpet at his feet to illuminate the marks worn by long and familiar use, seemed almost to deny his recollections. The carpet was prevailingly blue, a dull blue, with a large design of flowers, blue too. But it was so worn and faded that for large tracts the design was lost. At his feet Mr. Munn could see the coarse, brownish cords of the foundation fabric, for the nap at that spot had been trodden almost entirely away. Morning and evening, people had stood here to adjust the curtains, or alone in the room, to stare for a moment out across the yard and beyond the maple trees to the pasture. Fleetingly, Mr. Munn thought of those people, his mother, his father, relatives, servants whose names and faces he had forgotten, people dead before he was born; and thought, I am not like any of them. He turned abruptly from the window. He saw, on the marble-topped table, the lamp. The bowl was dry, the wick charred down, and the chimney streaked with smoke. He had fallen asleep without blowing it out; it had burned out during the night or, perhaps, even after dawn.

May, he learned, had left very early. She had sent the cook down to tell Old Mac to hitch up the buggy and bring it round. Then she had gone away in the buggy, with the old negro man driving. About ten-thirty Mr. Munn, walking in the front yard, had seen the buggy slowly approaching up the drive. He had waited at the gate, but the old negro man, hunched forward over the reins and apparently not seeing him, had gone on past. Mr. Munn had walked back to the stable. Upon his approach, the negro seemed to be entirely engaged in fumbling with a stubborn piece of harness.

'Where did you go?' Mr. Munn had demanded.

The negro had kept on fumbling with the harness strap.

'Well,' Mr. Munn had insisted, 'answer me.'

'I'se gonna answer you, Misser Perse,' the old man had said, 'soon ez I kin git shet of this-here. Hit looks lak my jints is gitten so bad I caint do nuthen. Now looks lak you'd say hot weather better'n cold weather. But naw. Here 'tis, hot weather——'

'Where did you go?' Mr. Munn had asked.

Without raising his eyes from the harness strap, the negro man had answered, 'Over to her folks' place.'

'Her aunt's place, Miss Burnham's?'

The negro man had nodded, still fumbling with the strap. Mr. Munn had turned on his heel and gone back to the house.

Two days later, the man from the Burnham place had come, driving Miss Burnham's surrey, to ask for May's clothes and things. Mr. Munn had been there at the time. He had stood in the middle of the floor of the big room upstairs while the cook put May's things into suitcases and boxes. He had thought that that was the time for him to go down and get on his mare and ride over to the Burnham place and talk to May. He had felt sure, standing there in the middle of the floor and watching the pieces of clothes being dropped limply into the boxes, that if he went over there and talked to her she would come back. He had not thought of what words he could say, or of what thoughts and feelings, even, would seek expression in words. Merely, it had occurred to him, if I go talk to her . . . But he had not gone. He had stood in the middle of the floor, as though rooted to the spot, and then the negro man, with a humble and apologetic stoop, had begun to carry the boxes and bags down.

Mr. Munn had stood at the window of the bedroom and watched the negro drive off, with the surrey piled high with May's suitcases and boxes. Then he had looked about the room, moving here and there as though hunting for a mislaid object.

By evening, however, he felt more composed. His composure had been mysterious to him, as on the night of Trevelyan's death. It had been, to his mind, a composure weighty and profound, but dangerous, like a great boulder balanced on the lip of a ravine, but balanced so precariously that, in the end, a breath of wind or the ignorant scurrying of some small ground creature may send it crashing.

One night, as he walked in the yard under the maples, three or four negroes passed the yard on the way back to visit one of the cabins. They were laughing and talking as they passed, and he leaned on the top board of the fence and listened to them until they were out of hearing. Then, a little later, he heard singing. They had, apparently, gone to Old Mac's cabin, and were singing there. He could not make out the words. Suddenly, he visualized them all, sitting in Old Mac's cabin, where a little fire would be smouldering, although the night was warm enough for the door to be open, sitting there around a smoky lamp, or standing loose-jointedly in the shadows, and singing together, with their heads thrown back and their eyes half-closed.

'God damn! God damn! God damn!' he repeated, aloud and measuredly in the darkness, and his hands gripped the dry, alien boards of the fence. The whitewash powdered, furrily, against the flesh of his hands. He swung on his heel and strode away across the yard.

During that period he avoided his accustomed activities around the place. Once or twice, as he went incautiously about some ordinary occupation, the currying of his mare or the inspection of the wood that had been cut for the tobacco-firing, some motion of his own or the sight of some familiar object shook, insidiously and suddenly, his massive composure. Warned, like some convalescent sufferer by the flare-up of an old symptom, he withheld himself, husbanded himself, that nothing should strike him suddenly beyond his strength. So he sank when possible into a blank absorption with the fact of the moment, a leaf on the ground at his feet, a white, unmoving spot of cloud on the blue fall sky, the faded pattern on a dish, the hum of the flame of a lamp. As he felt the need to protect himself from the disturbing contact of other persons, so more and more he felt the need to protect himself by denying memory, as it were, from the contact of the self he had been. And his mind closed like a valve against all thoughts of the future.

Late one afternoon, however, he took down his shotgun and walked across the barn lot and down across the fields back of the house toward the fringe of woods along the creek that watered the farm. When he had reached the brush along the creek and had slipped from sight, he felt relieved and safe. He pushed through the brush, the reddening sumac and buckberry and brittle elder, and entered the open space under the tall shagbark hickories. Their trunks were straight as columns, and unbranching for a long way up. The light filtered goldenly through their unstirring leaves. Yellowish leaves fallen from the hickory boughs lay on the level ground. He paused for a moment and looked high overhead and all around him at the walls of leaves that cut him off so privately from the entire world. Then, slowly, he moved across the open space, toward the creek.

The ground broke sharply downward toward the creek bank. Here a few sycamores grew, with enormous, white boles from which the umber bark crisped back, and beyond them, willows. The water of the creek had shrunk to leave a gravelly strip shelving off below the level where the willow roots clove to the earth of the bank. Mr. Munn, clutching the willows for support, let himself down off the bank to the little strip of beach. With his gun in readiness, he began to move down the creek. There would be a wider place farther down, he remembered; there the visible stretch of sky would be wider, and the water would spread out, without current apparently and as smooth as a pond, reflecting the sky and the overhanging trees. In a little while now, the doves would begin coming over, toward the water. They would head for that place, as they always, year after year, had done. They would come over, their sharp, nervous wings beating and their too-small heads outthrust. Their swift forms would look black against the paling, peach-colored sky. They would utter their sweet, breathless, complaining cries.

He reached the wider space and stood in an embrasure of the willows. He fixed his eyes on the sky, waiting. A little way upstream the water made a soft, riffling murmur as it slid over stones into the stillness of the wider basin. That was the only sound he could distinguish.

The first dove came over, high, from the west, and dipped and swung back. It sank, flutteringly, at the edge of the water, downstream. He had had two chances for a shot, when it first swung back and then when it started to flutter down. The gun had been raised, and his finger on the trigger, but he had not fired. Now he watched the bird that, too far away for a good shot, was prinking at the edge of the water. Then the bird rose, and flew off downstream. He was a little ashamed and irritated that he had passed up the shot, but, unreasoningly, he had not been able to bring himself to press the trigger.

When the next dove came over, he shot it. It came over the trees straight and rather low, and so swiftly that he had opportunity for scarcely more than a snap shot. Even as the explosion first rang in his ears, he saw the dove veer sharply, as though it had struck an invisible wire, and saw three bits of feather floating from the spot where the dove had been, and saw the dove skid sideways in the air, and then, with two or three wild wingbeats, plunge straight down. With the old exaltation big within him, he glanced quickly upward to see if another dove was coming over, and then ran toward the spot where it had fallen.

It was stone dead. It lay on the gravel, one wing in the clear water and a small bead of blood on its head and another at the neck. The beak was slightly parted, as when a bird lifts its head after taking a sup of water. Mr. Munn, bending to pick it up, was suddenly seized with revulsion. He straightened up, almost retching. He averted his eyes from the dead bird, and leaning on his gun, as from weakness, stared at the sky.

How empty and deep and steadily clear it was! he thought, and gazed upward. He left the bird where it lay, one wing in the water. Some animal, he thought, would find and devour it. He clambered up the bank, which was steeper here, and moved hurriedly across the strip of woods toward the fields. The sheltered, cut-off chamber of the woods was now, if anything, oppressive and inimical to him. He pushed his way through the fringe of brush and undergrowth, and found himself, with relief, on the edge of the open fields. He began to walk rapidly up the gradual rise toward the house, which was concealed in its grove. 'Something's the matter with me,' he said, hurrying. Then: 'Something's the matter, I've got to stop this.'

Two days later he went to the Burnham place to see May.

Miss Lucy Burnham, one of the two children of General Sam Burnham, devoted herself to him as long as he lived, and then, after his death, to his memory. Her mother died shortly after the return of the General after the war, leaving the two daughters, according to her last injunction, to look after their father. At the funeral he stood between the two girls, with a hand on the shoulder of each, and the tears streamed from his blue eyes and down into his thick, golden mustaches. The older of the two girls, Lucy, remained his prop and slave, as her mother had been.

Sam Burnham, commissioned a brigadier late in the war, was a vain, windy, amiable, aimless, and handsome man. He had entered the war as a politically appointed major, ignorant of even the first principles of his new occupation, but very large and military-looking in his uniform. Though he never distinguished himself, he was not a coward and not entirely a fool, and his good humor gave him with his brother officers a certain not quite contemptuous popularity which made his promotions possible. Late in the war there were few enough men who could even dress a company, and so, after Atlanta, he became a brigadier. But after the war he was lost. He had never made decisions for himself; his father, his wife, his superior officers or some able adjutant had always managed his life. Now, his father was senile and bankrupt, the war was over, and his wife was dead.

After the life of the state began to settle into order, and he began to recover from his personal confusion, he drifted into politics. Before the war he had had some political experience, and now it seemed the only occupation in which his love of talk, his amiability, his large-molded good looks, and his military record would receive their proper reward. He was, within limits, successful. But he became steadily poorer, and steadily more contemptible in the eyes of his colleagues. There was money to be made in politics, even in obscure offices, but he was honest. While other men demanded money, or information by which money could be made, he demanded only flattery. His vote or influence could be had for that, and men knew it.

Once his wife, willingly and capably, had managed his affairs. Then his daughter Lucy assumed the obligation. She was a poor manager, stubborn and pliable by turns, suspicious and trustful. In his many absences she tried to hold the farm together, but when he was at home she devoted all her energies to pleasing him. After her sister, Ruth, whom she considered a mere child, had eloped with an unknown and penniless young man from Arkansas, she increased the rigor of her devotions to her father. And when, shortly after her sister's marriage, General Burnham was defeated for re-election and began to fail in health, her abnegation became almost complete. She rarely left his side. She read to him much, novels for the most part, but tried to keep the newspapers away from him for fear that they would upset him. She would bring flowers to him from the un-worked garden by the house, and say, in the coaxing voice of one speaking to a child, 'See, papa, see, aren't they pretty this year?' Or she would comb and brush his luxuriant long hair, and stroke his fair, almost unseamed forehead, and pat his still-yellow mustaches. Then, sometimes, he would take her hands and, while she knelt beside him, hold them gently, and say in his vibrant, melancholy voice: 'I've seen a great deal of the world, my chick. I'm an old man, and I've seen a great deal, pomp and circumstance and wealth and honor and valorous deeds, but — and what I say I know to be true — a kind and loving heart is the greatest thing in the world. And you have a loving heart, my Lucy.' At such a moment, so great was her joy, she felt repaid for everything.

Her own youth was passing. Young men from the section had courted her, but one after another she had dismissed them. Their attentions had, at first, been pleasant and flattering to her, but she would say to herself, and to them, 'I must take care of papa; not everyone has a papa like mine.' But the feeling grew in her — and more rapidly and firmly after the ill-advised marriage of her sister — that all the young men were beneath her. Or, more accurately, that not one was worthy to be brought to papa as his son-in-law. After her sister died, down in Mississippi, and some church ladies down there wrote and inquired if they should send the little child, she dismissed the last of the young men. She absorbed the child, May, into the life she had created about the easy-chair and the footstool of her father. The child was taught to tiptoe to the General and curtsy, and say in a small voice, 'I hope you are feeling better, Grandfather,' and, 'I love you, Grandfather,' and, 'Here is a rose I plucked for you, Grandfather.'

General Burnham was killed in an election-day quarrel on the streets of Bardsville. Although he had almost ceased to have any meaning for the community, the dramatic circumstances of his death revived for a moment his vanished importance. His funeral was a public occasion. The pallbearers were, like the deceased, veterans of the war, and a Confederate flag covered the coffin. A volley was fired over the grave. While the echoes yet rang in the frosty air, Lucy Burnham, in a frenzy of grief, tore herself from the supporting arms of her friends, and was scarcely prevented from flinging herself into the grave. Percy Munn, then a boy just entering adolescence, heard the wild, pure cry wrung from her heart and saw her drunken lurching toward the open grave. He was to remember the moment, and much later was to try, puzzledly, to correlate its passion with the cold, trivial, foolish, and futile woman whom he grew to know. That day he also saw a motionless, thin little girl, some six or seven years old, whose face appeared to be molded of a scarcely tinted wax, and who stood near the grave but seemed to be aware of nothing around her. That was his first sight of May.

When Miss Burnham recovered from the stupefying effects of her grief, she turned herself, grudgingly and almost resentfully at first, to the care of her little niece. But the child was so gentle and tractable and affectionate that, more and more, she gave herself without reservations to her. One bright morning in early spring, a clear day that seemed in its softness of air and penetrating brilliance to promise, almost prematurely, the new season, she sat by an open window and brushed the child's yellow hair. Even though a fire smouldered in the grate, the window was up, for the first time that year, and the fresh odor of the earth came into the room. Miss Burnham looked perturbedly out over the tumbled garden, where great brown spikes of weed stalk thrust up among the rosebushes and the knotted, leafless wistaria clutched and dragged down the rotted trellises, and out over the brown fields beyond, and then returned her attention to the child's head, over which the sunlight spilled. Under that light the child's long hair was a clear, luminous gold. Suddenly Miss Burnham dropped the brush, and plunged her fingers into the hair, as into a healing stream, and with tears on her cheeks, cried out: 'Oh, sweetheart, sweetheart, I'll be so good to you. Make me be good to you, always!' Then she pressed the child to her bosom, and holding her with one arm, stroked again and again the golden hair, murmuring, 'Your hair, it's just the color of his, his own little granddaughter; it's gold like his.'

The child became her whole life. Gradually, she paid less and less attention to the operation of the place. The negro hands and croppers would come up to the house to get directions or to ask a question, but she would let them stand around an hour, or two hours, while she bathed the child, or pressed a ribbon for her, or put ribbons on her hair. The men would lounge on the back porch, looking off across the yard or talking in low voices. 'Miss Lucy, she shore doan mind burnen the good Lawd's daylight, she doan, now,' they would say, laughing. After a while she would come out to them, with an artificial air of briskness and business, and with a temper that was ready, at the slightest provocation, to break into a flood of recriminations which they could not understand.

She lost over half of the property. The house, a six-room, weatherboarded, one-story structure built around an original dog-run cabin, fell into serious disrepair. Some of the weatherboarding sagged loose to expose the old logs and chinking beneath; some of the boards of the front steps rotted out; in the front rooms, where the roof leaked worst, the plaster fell off in patches from the ceiling; the last vestiges of paint disappeared from the exterior. But Miss Burnham, even though each year left her more threadbare and rusty in her black dresses, always found, somehow, the money to buy new clothes and ribbons for the child. And, as her house decayed and her own clothes grew more shabby, she became more vain and overbearing in her relations with her neighbors. She began to invent achievements and honors for her father, but at first with such cunning, such casual references, and such diffident parryings of curiosity that they were accepted by all but the most wary. Then, as though emboldened by success, she enlarged the scope of her inventions and began to push back into an ever and ever more magnificent and fantastic history.

Miss Burnham hated all the young men, whose sharp eyes, even as she talked, always seemed to fix upon a cracked pane or threadbare patch of carpet or, even, upon her red, chapped hands. She hated them and was contemptuous of them, but she hated Percy Munn most of all. With her he was more polite and attentive than any of the others were, but he was also the most silent and watchful; and, from the very first, she seemed to know that he was the one most to be feared, that he was the one who would take May from her.

He married May after a courtship of two years. He could have married her earlier, but he wanted to establish his practice and to have a little money ahead. Almost as soon as he had returned from the honeymoon in Louisville, he sent men over to put a new roof on Miss Burnham's house, and to paint it. He ordered them simply to go and begin work and to say, if questioned by her, that the matter had been entirely arranged. But while the men worked, she seemed oblivious to them; and she never mentioned the matter to Mr. Munn or, as far as he knew, to May. The roof and paint might, for all she showed, have come like a natural event, a rainstorm or the change of seasons.

'It's sweet of you, Perse,' May said, 'to be doing all that for Aunt Lucy.'

'I hate to see property going to pieces,' he answered. 'And anyway, the place'll be yours some day, I reckon.'

'It'll make her so happy, having it fixed up,' she declared.

He did not tell May, however, that he had mortgaged some of his own land to buy the mortgage on Miss Burnham's place. Nor did he ever discuss the matter with Miss Burnham. He rarely saw her. May visited her often, but only occasionally could she be persuaded to come to the Munn place. Mr. Munn knew that she hated him, and that she would never forgive him, not for taking May, or painting her house, or saving her from eviction. And as he drove his buggy, that September morning, toward her place to talk to May and persuade her, if possible, to come back to him, he knew that Miss Burnham, no matter how the event turned out, would find in it a cause for new, and a fulfillment of old, hatred.

He hitched his mare to a paling of the fence, tried the paling to discover that it had rotted loose, swore, and transferred the loop to another and more substantial paling. Then he walked toward the house between the lines of twisted, shaggy cedars. The negro woman who answered to his knock left him standing on the porch until she returned to announce, 'Miz Lucy say you kin go in the parler.'

He followed her into the hall and she pushed open a door to the left and stepped aside.

'It was Miss May I wanted to speak to,' he said.

'Miz Lucy say she be here,' the woman answered, and went away down the hall.

He entered the parlor, which was almost dark. The air in the room was cold and still, with a dusty odor. Without thinking, he moved toward the nearest window and stretched out his hand to part the curtains; then he decided that it would be impertinent. He returned to the open space in the middle of the floor. The room was not very large. The two ponderous, glass-fronted bookcases, which rose to the ceiling, the chairs and the love-seats, the what-nots and the embroidered screens, the great cracked vases — these objects crowded around him in the gloom, weightily and oppressively. He stood in the midst of them, aware of the excited beating of his own heart, and breathed the odor of dust and horsehair.

Miss Burnham was a long time in coming. She came at last,

moving toward him with a skirring sound of her black-silk skirts and with her head bobbing nervously forward on her long neck as though in a scarcely restrained and irritable asseveration. He waited, holding his hat in his hands before him, and she moved directly at him, as though she did not see him, or as though he were not there at all, and then stopped in front of him with the air of one who is startled at an obstruction. She said, 'Good morning, Mr. Munn.' Her head continued to jerk slightly back and forth with a painful, mechanical motion, like a metronome asserting a rhythm that had nothing to do with the events about her.

'Good morning,' Mr. Munn responded.

She did not ask him to sit down, and made no motion toward a chair. She continued to stand directly in front of him.

'I'm sorry to have troubled you,' he apologized, after waiting. 'I reckon the girl didn't understand me. I asked if I could see May.'

'She did not misunderstand you,' Miss Burnham said.

'Well,' Mr. Munn began, and hesitated. 'I don't want to trouble you. I just wanted to speak to May.' Under the necessity of her gaze, and the small regular jerking of her head, he continued: 'You know, we had a — a misunderstanding, and I wanted to talk to her. It's not serious. That is, it shouldn't be——'

That abstracted gaze and that movement of her head were unchanged. His voice trailed off.

'You may not see my niece,' she affirmed.

'Isn't she here? I thought——'

'She is here,' Miss Burnham said.

'She is here?'

'But it is not possible for you to see her.'

'It's important,' Mr. Munn asserted, his tone rising. 'I have to see her.'

'No,' she answered.

'I beg your pardon.' He took a step toward her, and she gave ground. 'I've a right to see her. Every right.'

'You have forfeited any right,' she announced.

'I've every right,' he said. 'I want to see her.'

'I should think shame would forbid,' she retorted, her high-pitched voice breaking a little. She brought her hands together in front of her and clenched them.

'Shame——' he began.

'Shame,' she repeated. 'After what you did. To come here, after what you did, whatever it was. She won't tell me. Not a word. But she sat in a chair and cried, hour after hour, Mr. Percy Munn, that's what she did, and that's what you made her do, Mr. Percy Munn, and now you want to see her, you——'

'Is she sick?' he asked.

'It's not your affair, but she lies there in bed, with her beautiful golden hair out over the pillow, and the tears run down her cheeks. I'd think you would sink through the floor with shame, Mr. Percy Munn, or put a bullet through your head. If I were a man I'd do it for you. Like my father, the General.'

'I want to see her,' he said, somewhat abstractedly.

'No,' she rejoined.

He advanced toward the door, but she blocked him, their bodies nearly touching.

'No!' she repeated, with a ring, almost of long-deferred joy, in her voice.

'I'm going to see her,' he insisted, and she put out her arms to bar the doorway.

He seized her by the wrist. Even at the moment, he knew how ice-cold the flesh of her wrist was. Her whole body shook. 'Remember!' she exclaimed. 'Remember you're a gentleman — if you are one!'

He did not release her.

'Take your filthy hands off me,' she said.

Still, he did not release her. Instead, he looked into her face, almost with curiosity. He stared into her red-rimmed eyes and observed the feeble, frightening twitching of her head, and in a flash thought how easy it would be to knock that rotten old head in with one blow of his fist. One blow, like a rain-rotten melon. His grip tightened on her wrist.

'All right,' he replied, and dropped his hand from her wrist.

'I'll tell May,' she said gaspingly, triumphantly, 'everything.'

'All right.'

'Everything,' she reiterated, 'and you'll never lay eyes on her again.'

He stood stock-still, looking at her. 'All right,' he said.

She stepped out into the hall, and pointed, quiveringly, toward the front door. 'Now get out!' she almost screamed.

When he got home, he changed clothes, ate some cold food in the kitchen, went to the toolshed and got a cutting knife, and hurried down to the field. They were cutting the last field of tobacco now, not a field he had out on shares but part of his own crop. He approached the men, said, 'Hello,' and began to work down a row. The men, Mr. Grimes and two negroes, looked up to greet him soberly, then returned to their occupations.

Mr. Munn felt the knife sink into the stalk, splitting it almost to the ground, almost as though by its own weight. Then he swung the blade and lopped off the heavy plant, just below. The blade of the knife was clean-looking and flashed in the sunlight. Now and then he paused to hold up a plant in both hands and feel its weight and look at it closely. It was going to be a fair crop, he thought again; good considering the season, anyway. Then he would lay the plant by, to wilt out before it could be racked on its stick.

'Hit oughter weigh out pretty good,' Mr. Grimes remarked, watching him inspect a plant.

'Looks like it,' Mr. Munn answered, almost grudgingly.

'I'm a-gitten on,' Mr. Grimes said, straightening up. He was a spare-made man, and the faded blue shirt hung loosely about his shoulders. His eyes were a pure, used-up blue, faded like the color of the shirt. He had long, ragged, reddish mustaches which wagged extravagantly when he spoke. 'A-gitten on,' he repeated, 'nigh onto sixty, and I seen a lot of terbacker. Hit's a-bout all I know, I reckin. And I seen a lot pore-er terbacker'n this-here in my time.'

'Yes,' Mr. Munn said.

'This patch of ground here' — and he moved his slow gaze up the slight rise, across the earth where nothing now showed but the blunt stobs — 'I alluz say, if'n they ain't but one hand of terbacker growed, hit'll be growed here. I seen a lot of diff'rent places in my time, and I put a plow-point in a lot of diff'rent pieces of ground, but I say, let a man break ground along this-here crick. Give God's will and weather, and hit'll git him a little somethen fer his sweat.'

'It's good enough ground,' Mr. Munn agreed. He looked down at it, at his feet, as though discovering it. He laid the plant he held on the ground, with the other plants that were wilting there. One of the negroes passed down the next row with an armful of tobacco sticks. With a clatter he dropped the staves there between the rows, and began to rack up the plants already cut there. Mr. Munn bent to his task. He felt the sun on his back, even through his shirt, and on the back of his neck. He thought of the season's changing, how it would be not so long, and took a relish in this last heat on his flesh.

'Yeah,' Mr. Grimes said, 'goen on thirty-six years ago, I set a stand of terbacker in this selfsame field. Fer yore pappy. And hit made out a good crop. But I moved on. But I come back here twicet afore this-here present time. Hit looks lak a young feller gits restless and moves on. No matter what kinder ground he's got to work. Hit looks lak.'

'I reckon so,' Mr. Munn remarked, scarcely hearing, bending with the knife.

'Good ground,' Mr. Grimes said. 'Hit gives a man fer his sweat.'

Mr. Munn's knife fell, and he seized the plant.

'Fer his sweat,' Mr. Grimes repeated, 'if'n a man kin git a piece of money fer what hit makes.'

Mr. Munn straightened slowly up, holding the plant. 'By God,' he declared deliberately, weighing the plant in his hands, 'by God, and this year we'll get something.'

'I done heared hit said afore,' Mr. Grimes said.

They finished the field, except for a few plants at the low end. One of the negroes was there, still cutting and laying the plants to wilt. They stood for a moment, Mr. Munn and Mr. Grimes and the other negro, looking back over the bare earth. The earth was reddish in color, and the stobs stuck up out of it, row after row. They racked up the last plants that were ready, and the negro climbed onto the wagon. The wagon moved slowly off across the field toward the barn, which stood at the head of the rise, a tall, blank, gray, box-like form against the distant clarity of the horizon. Mr. Munn and Mr. Grimes began to walk after the wagon.

'Hit's nigh all in now,' Mr. Grimes remarked, looking over the empty field.

'Yes,' Mr. Munn said, somewhat shortly.

'A powerful sight of terbacker,' Mr. Grimes went on, 'done come off that-air ground, one time and anuther. I set terbacker on that-air ground afore you was born. Hit growed thar afore yore time, and afore mine.'

Mr. Munn did not answer. The two men walked along the edge of the field together until they came to a path that branched off across the pasture. Mr. Grimes hesitated. 'And hit'll be a-growen thar when you and me is dead and gone to a better land,' he declared.

'Good-bye,' Mr. Munn said.

'Good-bye,' Mr. Grimes replied, and started down the path

across the pasture. He walked with a high-shouldered, hunching movement, with his small head outthrust. Mr. Munn, when he got to the edge of the barn lot, looked back, and saw that Mr. Grimes was gone. He had reached his shack, which stood by a single big tree on the other side of the pasture, and had gone in.

When he turned around and started across the barn lot, he saw a negro man approaching him. It was Old Mac. 'They's somebody at the house fer you,' Old Mac announced.

'Who is it?'

'Mr. Bill Christian,' Old Mac told him, 'and anuther gemmun.'

Mr. Munn quickened his pace. 'You don't know who?'

'Hit's a red-headed gemmun,' Old Mac said. 'His head, you mought say hit incline to red.'

Mr. Munn, almost running, went toward the house. He slammed the back door, went through the kitchen, and down the hall, calling out.

Mr. Christian and Doctor MacDonald stood in the yard under the maple trees. Mr. Munn ran out to them, with his hand stretched out. At the sight of them, as they smiled and advanced toward him, he felt a sudden and unexpected surge of pleasure, of relief, as at hard-won safety.

'By God!' Mr. Christian shouted, 'where you been keeping yourself?'

Mr. Munn hesitated, as though embarrassed. 'Hanging round the place,' he answered.

'By God,' Mr. Christian said, 'I just figgered I'd come over and see how you was making it. Cap'n Todd's boy, he's over courting Sukie so much I just couldn't stand to watch it. He's a good boy, but God-a-mighty, the calf eyes he makes, it makes a man want to puke. I just said, hell, I'll go over and see Perse——'

'That's fine,' Mr. Munn declared, 'that's fine!'

Mr. Christian gestured toward Doctor MacDonald: 'And I just run into the doc, here, in town — didn't I, doc? — and I just thought I'd bring him along.'

'That's fine,' Mr. Munn responded. He's lying, he thought; they planned to come. But he was glad.

'Sure,' Doctor MacDonald said.

'You'll stay to supper,' Mr. Munn invited, then urgingly, 'sure, you'll stay. I'll tell them to put plates on. May' — he paused, then gathered himself and continued quickly — 'she's not here right now, but you'll stay.'

The two men looked at each other, then back at Mr. Munn. 'Fine,' Mr. Christian said, and Doctor MacDonald grinned and nodded.

'Finished your cutting?' Mr. Christian asked, as they walked toward the house.

Mr. Munn said that he had finished, or just about.

'I've finished and started firing,' Mr. Christian said, 'and it looks pretty good, for the most part. By God, I'm just gonna set back for a spell now. That's a fact. I'm gonna do me some hunting this fall if it's the last thing I do. I durned near missed out last fall. But this fall I ain't. I seen a passel of birds over on my place, a passel of 'em. You, Perse, you'll have to come over and hunt some with me. We ain't done any hunting in a long time. And I got me a couple as good coon dogs as you ever laid eyes on. You just come on over and fix to stay a while ——'

'That's fine,' Mr. Munn said, and Mr. Christian laid his heavy hand on his shoulder.

They sat around the table in the shadowy dining-room and ate the steaming food. They ate fried ham and chicken and mashed potatoes and late snaps and squash, and hot bread, and then pie and coffee. Mr. Christian leaned over his food and his bald head gleamed subduedly in the lamplight. His big jaws worked smoothly and powerfully. He said, 'Now, Perse, I'm a man as shore-God likes good vittles.'

After they had finished eating they sat around the table and talked and smoked. 'Well,' Doctor MacDonald remarked after a little lull in the conversation, his tone controlled and easy, 'I saw by the paper this morning they found that fellow Trevelyan.'

Mr. Munn made a sharp intake of breath. 'Yes?' he said.

'Yes,' Doctor MacDonald answered, and paused to inspect the tamping of tobacco in his pipe. Then he raised his eyes suddenly to gaze straight across at Mr. Munn. 'Yes,' he repeated, 'they found him. Some kids out prowling round with their .22's looked down in the old quarry. They saw him caught in the cat-tails.'

Mr. Munn's hands were gripping the edge of the table.

'They ran all the way to town,' Doctor MacDonald went on.

No one spoke for a minute. Doctor MacDonald continued to gaze straight across the lighted area of white tablecloth at Mr. Munn's face.

Mr. Christian scraped his chair back a little. 'Perse,' he demanded, 'you got any more coffee?'

Mr. Munn went to the door to the pantry and called for another cup of coffee. He returned to the table and resumed his seat. The negro woman brought the coffee and, at a gesture from Mr. Munn, set it before Mr. Christian. Mr. Christian took a long draught of it, then set the cup down clatteringly.

He said: 'Perse, when you gonna come out and hunt birds with me, huh? You're coming soon, ain't you? When the season opens up?'

'Yes,' Mr. Munn answered.

'You better come soon, now. Yeah, you come out, and we'll crack down on them birds, now.'

'Yes.'

'And that Miss Sukie Perkins I got, she's shore as smart a coon dog as you ever laid eyes on.'

Chapter ten

HE WOULD lie in the big bed in the dark and listen to the obscure night noises or to the distant howling of a hound, or for the creak of one of the old boards under the pressure of a foot, and wait for her to come. The latch on the door would lift slowly, the iron making a small, clean clicking sound when the bar was finally released from its bracket, and the door, white in the shadowy room, would begin to swing stealthily inward. The heavy door moved softly and evenly now, but the first time she came to the room, he had been wakened from a half drowse by the squeal of the hinges as the door swung inward. He had risen up in bed, ready, before seeing the uplifted hand, to call out in his surprise.

Later, she had oiled the hinges.

'The door didn't screak tonight, did it?' she had demanded, putting her head down on his shoulder so that the breath of her whispered utterance was against his ear.

'No, it didn't,' he had said, and then remembered that it had made no noise. At the time he had not noticed, being so engrossed with his eagerness, waiting to see if she would appear.

'I fixed it,' she had told him.

'Don't blow in my ear, it tickles.'

'I oiled the hinges,' she had whispered. 'I put some of papa's gun oil on them. When you all were out hunting this afternoon. Don't you think I'm smart?'

'Yes.'

'Well, why don't you thank me? Maybe I saved your life. Maybe papa won't hear that door now, and shoot you.'

'He probably would,' he had said.

'Aren't you going to thank me,' she had demanded, 'for fixing it?'

'I'm going to fix you if you don't stop tickling my ear,' he had answered. Then she had set her teeth, not gently, in the lobe of his ear. 'Damn it, Sukie,' he had said, and holding her hair twisted in his hand so that she could not lift her head from the pillow, had kissed her on the mouth.

But the hinges worked silently now, not like that first time. The door would swing gently, carefully, open, and she would slip into the room, and stand with one finger to her lips in mock warning while she pushed the door shut and lowered the latch into place. Sometimes, when there was no moon, it would be so dark that he could scarcely make out her shadowy form there against the white blur of the door, but he would know exactly how she would be, standing there, and would smile answeringly as though she could see his face. When the door was latched, she would move quickly across the room toward him, her kimono fluttering with her motion. She would shiver with the chill, for there was rarely a fire in the room, or would pretend to shiver, and standing by the bed to pull off the kimono, would say, 'Get over, I want the warm place, I'm freezing to death.' Then she would pull the covers about her, and shiver, and pretend that her teeth were chattering, and thrust her cold feet against his.

'Take them off,' he would whisper.

'I will not' — and her teeth would chatter. 'I freeze to death coming inch by inch down that hall — I almost catch pneumonia — all on account of your baser nature — and you won't even warm my feet — you dog ——'

'You've got a baser nature, yourself.'

'No — no' — chatteringly — 'not — right — now.'

Now she would shut the door and run quickly to the bed, her kimono fluttering, but the first time, having forestalled his half-awake exclamation by her lifted hand and having closed the door upon its creaking hinges, she had moved, almost with an air of deliberation, toward him, and had leaned over and taken his head between her hands and had kissed him. That had been the first time they had ever kissed. Then, standing there by the bed, in the frosty air, she had drawn his head against her, and he had heard her heart knocking strongly and surely under the curved ribs.

After the first shock of surprise, when he saw her standing inside the door with one hand raised warningly, there was no surprise. But they had never talked about themselves, or their feelings. They had not been together very often. Now and then they had sat before the fire in the living-room, in the evening, with Mr. Christian, and perhaps Benton Todd, engaged in a comfortable, desultory conversation until the time when Benton Todd, looking at his watch, would remark, 'It's getting on, I better be going,' and Mr. Christian, getting to his feet and stretching his big arms upward, would say: 'Well, boy, I guess I'll be turning in. You folks, too, I reckon?' And once she had gone out with them to hunt quail. She had worn a red sweater and an old coat of her father's, and he had watched her moving slowly through the tall, sun-goldened sage grass behind the careful, eager setters. They had scarcely ever been alone together.

But that particular afternoon she had brought him out from town in her buggy. Waiting at the corner for Mr. Christian, who was to come back to town the next morning and so could bring him in, he had been surprised to see Lucille Christian drive up. 'Papa had some things to see about,' she had explained, 'and he had to stay out at the place. So I came in to do the errands.' Then she had added, 'And get you.'

'That's fine,' he had said, climbing into the buggy.

They had talked briskly and aimlessly while the buggy moved down the streets of Bardsville. After the downtown streets where the stores were, where people walked about, quickly now, for the day was cold, there were the streets with white, wooden houses set well back on lawns now brown, behind the bare, black-trunked maples. Those streets were deserted, except for a few children, well muffled in coats and stocking caps, who ran across the lawns and kicked the brown fallen leaves and uttered shrill cries that had no meaning. Otherwise, life seemed to have withdrawn deeply and secretly within the houses. The window-panes gleamed dully like ice on a pond. They passed the last houses, and were between the open fields.

Mr. Munn raised his head to scan the sky. 'It's funny,' he said, 'but in town, you know, you don't notice much what the weather's like.'

'There're a lot of things you don't notice in town,' she returned.

He continued to look at the sky, which showed no sun, and at the lead-colored horizon. 'What?' he asked.

'Oh,' she answered, 'yourself, for instance.'

'Yourself?' He looked directly at her, but she did not meet his gaze.

'Yes, yourself.' She looked up the road, over the horse's head. Then she continued: 'Yes, when I was in St. Louis, all that time, I didn't know a bit what I was like, really. I never noticed myself. I did things, and I never knew why.'

'Not often, any place, a man's too sure why he's doing something,' Mr. Munn said. Then: 'Not often, but sometimes, by God.'

'I never was,' she told him, 'before.'

'Are you now?'

'Surer,' she replied. 'Now.'

They fell silent for a few minutes, looking at the fields and the distant woods. Then she asked, 'Are you?'

'Am I what?' He knew what she meant, but like a man who plays for time, he parried the question.

'Sure,' she said.

'Not always.'

'I thought you were, always.'

'Why?' he demanded.

She paused, then went on: 'Because you look that way. The way you move. The way you say something. You say it like you were sure. And what you've done.'

'What have I done?'

She continued to look up the road. 'Oh, nothing, that is, not any one thing,' she replied, 'not any one thing. Just everything sort of taken together, you know.'

'Well, I don't know,' he said.

'Oh, just everything. And I'm not the only person feels that. Other people do, too. They have the same impression.'

'I reckon nobody's sure most of the time,' he rejoined.

The landscape about them was very empty, and the sky. The bare fields, corn stubble, tobacco stobs, or brown pasture, lay along the road; along the fencerows the trees were leafless now; the woods along the horizon looked blue and smoky. The horse's hoofs made a hard, chipping sound on the pike. Once or twice they heard a crow cawing from somewhere back in the fencerows. They met no one on the road.

After a long silence, she said, 'If you're chilly, you'll find a laprobe in the back.'

'Are you?'

'Not really,' she answered.

'I'm not, either,' he asserted, 'or not very.' But he reached back to get the robe. She lifted the reins, and he spread the robe across her knees and drew it up to her waist. At that moment, she turned her head and looked him directly in the eyes. 'Thank you,' she said.

That night she had come to his room, for the first time.

She was, it seemed to him, two persons. There was the person who came to his room, and stood with one finger to her lips while she gently pushed the shadowy white door shut behind her; and there was the person whom he saw moving about the house in the daytime, talking casually and easily to him or to her father or to Benton Todd, or humming a tune under her breath. The two persons seemed quite distinct to him. With the first were associated all the small night noises, melancholy, exciting, and insidious, which worked upon his consciousness while he lay waiting for her, sometimes in vain, and staring at the door, or while she lay beside him — the sound of a mouse gnawing dryly and minutely in the wall, the hoot of an owl in the woods or the distant barking of a dog, very faint and hollow, the unnamable, hushed creakings of old joists and beams. With that person he talked only in whispers, for if his voice rose she would reach to lay a finger on his lips and say, 'Shh!' Once he said to her, 'You know, you're almost like two people to me.'

'Yes,' she replied.

'The one who's here right now, and that other one I just see around but never really talk to.'

'It's hard to just be one person,' she observed. They fell silent for a while, then later, as though there had been no interrupting silence, she said: 'I love papa, and if he knew about this it would almost kill him, I know. And I love you. You see how it is.'

He said nothing, listening to her breathing in the stillness and waiting for her to resume. She went on, 'If everything, everything you were and wanted and owed to people — everything — matched up just once, even for just a minute so you were really one person, completely, then you would be almost too happy to live.'

'I reckon so,' he said.

'It would be like when you love somebody, and are in their arms, like that very instant, only more.' Then, after a moment: 'But, you don't know you are you then. You just know you are.'

He said, 'If everything matched up, completely, maybe it would be the same way, maybe you wouldn't know you are you, the way it is now.'

'No,' she replied, 'I'm sure you wouldn't know.'

She seemed to him to be two persons, but sometimes, about the place in the daytime, or when all of them were together, some gesture or inflection or passing expression of her face would suddenly blur the two identities in his mind, and he would look sharply at her. Then, in an instant, the two identities would again be distinct, and there before him would be the girl who was cool and friendly with him and made jokes with her father and moved so casually and competently about the place, running the house, leaning with flushed cheeks over a boiling pot, carrying out a basin of feed for the chickens and calling, 'Chick! chee — che-che-chick, chick!' That was the person who belonged to the daytime, to the cheerful, common sound of pans and pots rattling, to the clack of Mr. Christian's boot heels on the doorsill and to his amiable, demanding bellow, 'Hey, Sukie, where are you?' and to Benton Todd.

Benton Todd was in love with her, very obviously, Mr. Munn could see. Mr. Christian, that day when he had come to the Munn place with Doctor MacDonald, had said he couldn't stand to hang around and watch Benton Todd's calf eyes. He had said it made him want to puke. Benton Todd, when he came to the Christian place, would follow Lucille Christian around the house while she was occupied, or pretended to be occupied, with her tasks. She would go out to see that the evening's milk was properly put away, or that a basket of eggs was ready to be carried in to town early the next morning, or to help with cooking the supper. 'You can come on,' she would say to Benton Todd, 'if you want to,' and he would follow her. She would give him things to hold, pans or baskets or dish towels, thrusting them suddenly at him and saying cheerfully, 'Here, Bent, just hold this a minute, will you, please?' Then, as likely as not, she would go off and leave him standing with the basket of eggs or the damp towel; or he might follow her about, still faithfully carrying the object.

If he could not be with Lucille Christian he would seek out Mr. Munn and ask him question after question. He would want to know what Mr. Munn thought about some case he remembered from his law reading at school, or about some detail of the management of the Tobacco Association, or about some matter of politics, the chances of Senator Tolliver's election.

'If he's elected,' Mr. Christian had once said, overhearing Benton Todd's question to Mr. Munn, and raising his head from his newspaper, 'if he's elected, by God, he'll never sit in the Senate. I'll twist his durn head off his neck——' And there had been the ripping sound of the newspaper being pulled apart in his hands. Then he had added, 'With my own hands.'

More and more the very sight of Benton Todd grew to irritate Mr. Munn. He was a nice boy, Mr. Munn was sure of that, and smart enough, but Mr. Munn blamed his youth, his innocence, and his apparent conviction that you could just go out and set everything right because you were right. His constant questions, and his very air of respect when he asked them, worked upon Mr. Munn's feelings like a reproach, like an unjust accusation from a trusted friend. But when he saw the boy following Lucille Christian about the house, trying to talk to her as she whisked busily and, Mr. Munn was sure, unnecessarily from room to room, or saw him standing alone, trustingly and somewhat ridiculously, in the middle of the floor where she had left him, with a basket or a pan dangling in his large grasp, he was tempted to stamp out of the house or to protest, to demand why in the world she treated the boy that way, why didn't she send him about his business if she didn't love him.

'What do you let him hang round for?' Mr. Munn demanded of her one night, when she lay beside him in the dark. They had been silent for a long time, staring up at the ceiling.

'Shh!' she said, and laid a finger on his lips. 'Don't yell. You'll wake up papa, and then where'll you be?'

'What do you let him hang round for?' Mr. Munn whispered.

'Who?' she asked, still keeping her finger lying lightly on his lips and with it tracing their contours.

'You know who,' he said — 'Benton Todd.'

'I told him to go away,' she whispered.

'Well, he hasn't gone.'

'You're jealous,' she murmured, and patted his lips with her finger.

'God, no, I'm not jealous,' he said.

'Yes, jealous. You're jealous, and he's just a kid. And your greatest admirer, too. Why, mention your name and he's ready to get on his knees; he thinks you hung the moon.'

'I'm not jealous,' Mr. Munn said deliberately, 'but it's not fair to him. I don't like to see him standing round holding some damned thing in his hand and looking like he didn't know how it got there.'

'You ought to be glad he's around to hold things,' she retorted. 'If he weren't around I might get you to hold things for me.'

'That's not very probable.'

'I'll bet it's not very probable,' she said, 'but it's not very sweet and polite of you to say so.'

They were silent for a time. Her finger remained on his lips. Now and then she moved it a little, parting his lips very lightly.

'It's not fair to him,' Mr. Munn whispered.

'Shh,' she urged, and pressed his lips, although he had only whispered.

'It's not,' Mr. Munn repeated. He hesitated: 'Unless, of course, you do intend to marry him.'

She giggled softly. Then she said, 'My, my, Mr. Munn, what high ground you take!' And she giggled again. Then she stopped suddenly, withdrew her finger from his lips, and remarked, 'What a pretty picture you paint of everything.'

'Everything ——'

'My being in here, and everything.'

'I didn't mean that,' he whispered, 'you know——'

'A really good woman,' she said, 'would be so insulted she'd jump right out of this bed and go in the other room.' She stopped for a moment. 'But I'm not going to,' she added. 'It's too cold.'

Certainly, Benton Todd was decent enough, and Mr. Munn liked him. Only when Mr. Munn was out at the Christian place did that irritation overpower his ordinary feeling for the boy. Mixed with his liking for Benton Todd there was a certain sense of guilt. The boy had no business mixed up with the Brotherhood for Protection and Control, Mr. Munn was sure, and he felt, obscurely, a responsibility for the boy's joining. It was that damned simple-minded, hero-worshiping streak in him, Mr. Munn thought, and was uncomfortable that he himself was the object of Benton Todd's admiration. Now the boy was riding around the country at night, likely to get shot or jailed, because he figured he was saving the nation.

But Lucille Christian would have to take some of the responsibility, too, he felt. He had felt that for a long time before he was able to see the whole picture. At first he had thought that Benton Todd joined just because he guessed the girl's sympathies to lie that way, or because he wanted to swagger a little before her and drop dark hints. Then Mr. Munn had decided that Lucille Christian had let slip, somehow, the information that he and Mr. Christian were in the thing. Or perhaps she had come right out with it, either because she was worried about it or because she wanted the boy to get in. But Mr. Munn didn't know positively how much she knew.

He discovered that she knew everything, and had known everything for a long time.

One evening when Mr. Munn was there for supper, Mr. Christian looked up from his plate and remarked: 'Well, Sukie, you better get Aunt Cassie to sleep up here tomorrow night. I'm going possum-hunting over on Rose Creek, and I won't get in till mighty late. Like as not I won't get in till day.'

'All right,' she said.

Mr. Christian turned to Mr. Munn. 'Say, Perse, don't you want to come? Tom Abernathy's got two new dogs he claims are mighty good, and we're gonna try 'em out.'

'I've got some things to see to out at the place,' Mr. Munn answered. 'I'm sorry.'

'Tomorrow night's Saturday night, you can catch up on your sleep Sunday morning. Why don't you come, huh?'

Lucille Christian, Mr. Munn noticed, was looking half-amusedly from one to the other.

'Can't do it,' Mr. Munn said.

'Why don't you all stop pretending?' Lucille Christian asked, so casually that at first Mr. Munn did not grasp the full significance.

'Huh?' Mr. Christian demanded.

'You're not fooling anybody,' she said. 'Why don't you stop?'

'Huh!'

'Don't *huh* me,' she told her father, and laughed. 'You're not any more going possum-hunting than you're going to fly to the moon.'

Mr. Christian held his fork in mid-air, a slice of ham impaled upon it, and stared at his daughter. She was smiling at him. 'You're both dirty, low-down, plant-bed-scraping, barn-burning night riders. And then you lie to me about it. That' — and she took a sip of coffee and with a judicial air set the cup down — 'makes it worse.'

'Now see here, Sukie ——' Mr. Christian began.

'Yes, papa?' she inquired smilingly, as though nothing had happened.

'Now see here. You don't know a thing. Not a thing. You ——'

'I'd be silly if I didn't,' she said. 'Everybody else does. I bet half the people in the county could just offhand name you twenty-five apiece of the members of whatever high-falutin thing it is you call yourselves. And half of those would name both you all, you, papa, and you, Perse.'

'Yeah, yeah,' Mr. Christian returned, 'and if all that's true, how come the sheriff hasn't been out here long ago to get me? And get Perse, huh?'

'Scared,' she said, and took another sip of coffee. 'Plain scared.' She set the cup down, smiled brightly at them both. 'He knows that just as soon as you all got put in his jail, a lot of your little playmates would come and take his pleasant little jail apart.' Then she added, 'And take him apart, too, maybe.'

'You don't know a thing,' Mr. Christian said sourly.

'I know they couldn't get those men over in Hunter County convicted this fall. After they arrested them. Everybody said the jury was full of night riders.'

'Talk,' Mr. Christian declared, 'just talk.'

She addressed herself to Mr. Munn: 'Won't you have some pickled peaches?' And she held the dish toward him. Then to her father she said: 'Why don't you admit it, papa? I know all about it, anyway.'

'You don't understand. Not a thing.'

'It's plain, anyway,' she retorted, and laughed. 'I don't mind. I really don't. That is, if it's what you've got to do.' She turned serious, and looked directly at her father, whose heavy fist lay on the table with the fork it clutched pointing upward.

'It's not a thing for womenfolks to be messing in,' he told her.

'I don't mind about you,' she said. 'If I were a man, I'd probably be in myself.'

Mr. Munn looked soberly across the table at her. The lamp-light falling on her face made the flesh take a golden tinge. He knew that her eyes were blue, but in that light he could not really make out their color, they appeared so dark and deep. 'If you were in,' he said slowly, 'you might not find it very pretty.'

'I wouldn't expect to,' she returned. 'I'm not a child.'

'Pretty!' Mr. Christian exclaimed, and the haft of the fork he clutched struck hard on the table. 'Well, it ain't very pretty either that it's been ten years since tobacco got a fair price, and the land in this section's all mortgaged, and half the folks nigh starving. I'd do anything I could lay my hand to. Before God I would, and I don't care who knows it!' He scraped his chair back, and rose abruptly to his feet. He said, 'There comes a time.'

'Sit down, papa,' Lucille Christian commanded in a different, and quiet, voice. 'Sit down, and finish your coffee. I know.'

He sank slowly back into his chair. During the rest of the meal he did not speak another word. Then, afterward, he said that if he was going to be up late the next night he'd better be getting to bed, and clumped upstairs. Mr. Munn and his daughter had followed him into the hall, where he picked up the lamp he would carry up with him. As he mounted the stairs, his posture seemed a little like that of an ageing man. Or perhaps, Mr. Munn thought, it was a trick of the light. He watched Mr. Christian all the way up and out of sight. The shadow cast by the lamp Mr. Christian held moved up the wall beside him, enormous, swaying and bouncing with a soundless and free elasticity as though by its efforts it dragged the man upward, like a dead weight.

When Mr. Christian had disappeared beyond the head of the stairs, Mr. Munn turned to the girl. 'Did you get Benton Todd into the night riders?' he demanded.

'No,' she answered thoughtfully, studying his face.

'You didn't tell him about your father being in? Or me?'

'He's not a fool,' she said. 'Everybody else knows, and knew a long time back. And why shouldn't he? He was around here a lot. And was here nights when you all were off riding.'

'Did he ask you about it?'

'Yes, but I lied to him. I told him I didn't know anything.'

'You didn't get him into the night riders? You didn't encourage him?' Mr. Munn demanded, leaning toward her.

'No,' she said. 'I tried to keep him out.'

'Why?'

'His father,' she replied. 'On account of his father. He's a nice old man, and papa likes him so much, you know, and he'd resigned from the board, and all. If he ever found out Benton was in the night riders, you know how it would be.'

'Is that all?'

'Well ——' and she hesitated. Then: 'He's not much better than a boy.'

'He's old as you are,' Mr. Munn said.

'I'm a year older.'

'That doesn't make any difference,' he insisted.

'People are different,' she said. 'You know that.'

'That was the reason?'

'Yes,' she answered.

He leaned over, slowly, and kissed her. That was one of the moments when the two persons she seemed to him, bafflingly, to be were merged into a single identity. He put his arm around her shoulders, and standing in the unsure light which the lamp gave, with the table cluttered with the dirty dishes behind him, beyond the open door of the dining-room, and with his gaze fixed on the blank wall, he was filled with a joy and certainty which seemed to him, at the moment, final.

'Good Lord!' she said suddenly, and stepped back from his embrace. 'Suppose Martha'd come in to get the dishes and see us.'

'Suppose,' he repeated, with an inflection that made her look questioningly at him.

'Well, it would be a pickle,' she observed matter-of-factly.

'Sure,' he agreed. 'Sure.'

'Sure,' she said, 'but you don't *have* to have that expression on your face,' and laughed. 'Besides' — and she paused, and re-

garded him amusedly — 'if you'll get it off, I might come down
to see you tonight. Even if I do freeze to death getting there.'

'That's not the point,' he replied.

'Gratitude' — she gave a mock sigh and shook her head
deprecatorily at an imaginary audience — 'gratitude and
chivalry for you.'

'That's not what I meant,' he said.

He did not know exactly what he had meant. Those two
identities which had seemed to merge at the moment when he
leaned toward her and kissed her were now quite separate.
Again, as before, there were the two people, the one who made
jokes with her father and hummed aimless snatches of songs
and moved about the household occupations with heels tapping
briskly and cheerfully on the expanses of bare board, and the
other one who, tonight, would stand just inside the shadowy
white door, with her finger to her lips, and then approach his
bed. He shook his head.

'What's the matter?' she demanded.

'Nothing,' he said.

'But there is.'

'Do you love me?' he asked.

The negro woman entered the dining-room and began,
clatteringly, to stack up the dishes.

'Yes,' she answered.

'Will you marry me?' he said.

'Shh,' she cautioned, her fingers to her lips warningly, and
motioned with her head toward the negro woman in the dining-
room.

'Will you marry me?' he repeated, his voice the same as before.

'Maybe,' she said, 'but not if you bellow. You're worse than
papa.'

He had asked her that question before, and every time she
had answered it evasively. But he had not mentioned the
matter to her for some weeks now. He had begun to learn to

accept the situation as it was, as she apparently accepted it, without torturing himself for a final definition of it. But he had only begun to learn, for sometimes, still, when she was lying beside him, or when she was with other people and he caught a sudden inflection of her voice or gesture, or even when he was alone and remembered, as with a stab of surprise, how different his life was from what it had been not long before or from what he had ever guessed it would be, he experienced that appetite for definition, for certainty, that would seize on her promise as on a symbol for everything it demanded. Or rather, in trying to extract her promise, he was like a man who tries to find in the flux and confusion of data some point of reference, no matter how arbitrary, some hypothesis, on which he can base his calculations. But she would promise nothing. Now he had not tried to make her promise for a long time, not since the night when they had stood shivering, side by side, before the window of his room to watch the patch of flame on the dark horizon.

That night, before they had noticed the fire, he had asked her to marry him, and she had said, 'Maybe, when the time comes.'

'Don't you love me?' he had demanded.

'Yes,' she had told him.

'Why won't you promise me, then?'

'No,' she had said. 'That's like making a dare. It would be like daring life.'

'That's nonsense.'

'It would just be a dare, and I haven't got the nerve. I just haven't.'

'That's nonsense,' he repeated. Then he had become aware that she was weeping. She had wept almost silently, but he had felt the bed quivering with the force of her suppressed sobbing. 'What's the matter, what's the matter?' he had demanded.

'Nothing,' she had said.

He had put his hand on her face to find it wet with tears.

'Darling, darling, stop it, you must stop it. I didn't think you were the kind would ever cry about anything. Darling, you mustn't,' he had insisted, holding his hand on her face.

'I haven't cried in years, not years,' she had managed to say, still sobbing, 'but I just can't help it. I can't.'

'I love you, I love you,' he had declared. 'I promise I'll love you always.'

'Don't promise' — and the sobbing had choked her — 'anything, ever. Promising means time and I don't want to think about time; I don't ——'

'Hush, hush,' he had said.

Later, moving from the bed toward the door to return to her room, she had hesitated with her face in the direction of the window. 'Look,' she had whispered, pointing. He had slipped out of the bed and gone to the window. The night had been unusually dark, the dark mass of the earth scarcely darker than the sky. But a patch of flame had been on the horizon, a single center of rich, cherry-colored glow fading outward and upward into the enormous hollow of darkness. A dog had barked very faintly, very far off.

Lucille Christian had come to stand beside him. 'What is it?' she had whispered.

He had told her that he did not know, and had drawn her to him. She had shivered as she stood there against him, watching the distant point of light in the darkness.

He had told her he did not know what the patch of flame on the horizon was; but he did know. He knew that it was a burning tobacco barn. It was a barn belonging to some man who, after receiving warnings, had not listed his crop with the Association. He knew that a band of men from some other locality, Band Number Six, he remembered, Mr. Burden's band from over in Hunter County, had picked up its guide, a mounted man waiting in the shadows by the roadside at an appointed place, and had been led to that spot where the flames now made that little center of rosy light against the black sky. And he knew that some other night, soon, he himself would stand and watch men apply the match and then would mount and ride away, the hoofs of the horses drumming the frosty earth and the flames climbing the sky behind him. He knew, because that was the way it had already been.

There were burnings all fall. As soon as the tobacco in the barns began to cure, the fires began. At first there were only a few, then there were the letters. Then there were many fires. Some men who received letters listed their crops immediately with the Association. Others sat up night after night, alone or with their sons or hands or tenants, guns ready. They waited, lying behind piles of brush or in the protection of a fencerow or behind a stone fence, while the cold stiffened their fingers on the metal of a rifle or shotgun, and their eyes blurred with sleep, and high in the empty, black, metallic sky the steady stars seemed to be withdrawing into a more and more incalculable distance. Sooner or later for some of those who guarded their barns, there came the night when out of confidence or weariness they relaxed their vigilance and stayed in their beds. And once or twice the night riders came just at dusk when men were at supper and expected no danger.

Some of the larger growers sold their crops, half cured and hanging in the barns, to the companies, and the companies undertook to guard the barns. One gang of hired guards was surprised, half drunk at its post, and the men were whipped, dragged through a creek, and left lying, bound and gagged, by the roadside. The barns which they had been supposed to guard were burned. The night riders exchanged shots with another gang, and two men, under cover of the firing that drove the guards back to the protection of a cedar fencerow, galloped by the barn and flung two charges of dynamite against the wall. Galloping past the barn, they had lighted the fuses from cigars which they held clamped in their teeth. The charges blew in one wall of the barn, and the curing fires in the barn ignited the tobacco.

It was reported that one man, a Mr. Sanderson of the New Bethany community, had been burned to death in his barn, or had been shot and flung into the flames. He had, his wife said, left the house with his shotgun to guard his barn, as he had been accustomed to do for some time. But after the burning of the barn he had not appeared. His wife had run to the spot where the flames still rose, calling his name, and then, when there was no answer, she had run frantically and stumblingly across the fields to the nearest house, where there was a telephone. Men had come back with her to stand aimlessly before the glowing mass where the barn had been or to wander about the fields calling the man's name. The next day, when the ashes had cooled enough, they began the process of sifting to find what might remain of the body. They found nothing but the twisted metal which had apparently been the barrel of the shotgun. The body, it was assumed, had been completely destroyed.

But Mr. Sanderson was not dead. He was found two weeks later, seventy-five miles away, over toward the central part of the state. Some boys out possum-hunting found him cowering in a thicket. His clothes were in tatters and he was almost barefoot. His beard was matted with mud and small fragments of dry leaf. He was nearly starving. He remembered nothing. When the boys questioned him, he put the knuckle of his right forefinger into his mouth, like a confused and frightened child, and peered from face to face. When they built a bonfire and tried to warm him, he was so terrified that they had to hold him. After a little while he became quiet in their grasp, but he kept shaking his head like a sick man who is too weak to protest otherwise against an injustice, and the tears flowed silently and resignedly out of his red-rimmed eyes.

Later, he was identified and sent to his home. His health

gradually improved, and by spring he was able to go about his ordinary occupations. But he could never remember what had happened that night when his barn was burned, nor in the two weeks when he wandered over the countryside hiding in the woods and ditches.

Toward the end of the curing period the numbers of burnings over the section increased. Just before the elections violent encounters were frequent between peaceful and respectable men. Prayers were offered from the pulpits that order might be restored, and sometimes that the injustice that had caused the disorder and the lifting of the hand of brother against brother might be corrected. 'Hit's a curse,' Mr. Grimes said to Mr. Munn, 'laid onto the land, hit looks lak.'

Mr. Munn stood in front of the stable door and tightened the girth on his mare. Mr. Grimes had climbed the fence to the lot, getting stiffly and awkwardly over the whitewashed boards, and had slowly approached Mr. Munn.

'Howdy-do,' he had greeted him, and then, after Mr. Munn's reply, had stood and studied the light that faintly tinted the edges of the slate-colored clouds on the western horizon. The sun was already out of sight. Then, at last, he said, 'I'm a-leave-en.' He did not take his gaze off the western sky. 'Come January,' he added. 'I thought I'd be a-tellen you.'

'I'm sorry,' Mr. Munn replied. He raised his head from his task and looked at the man.

'I'm sorry to be a-tellen you,' the man said. In the fading light Mr. Munn tried to read the man's face, but it showed nothing.

'I wanted to be a-tellen you early,' the man continued, 'so you could be looken round and make a trade.' He hesitated, then resumed in an apologetic tone: 'Not you'd have no trouble, not with a good place and give-en good furnishen and all. You got a name fer hit.'

'You made a good crop this season,' Mr. Munn said, 'drouth and all. You'll get some money out of it.'

'Hit's a good crop.'

'Aren't you satisfied here? You've been here before. You came back.'

'I'm satisfied,' Mr. Grimes admitted, 'but that ain't all.'

'What is it?'

Mr. Grimes returned his gaze to the west. The color was fading now from the edges of the low clouds, and as their own slate color darkened they seemed to gain in weight and solidity. 'This carryen on round the country,' he said. 'Men carries on and revels round the country at night. Burnen and sich. I ain't a-sayen who's right and who's wrong. Hit ain't fer me to say. The Book says, jedge not. Hit's fer God A-mighty to say. But I ain't easy in my mind. And I'm a-leave-en.'

'You mean you're leaving this section?' Mr. Munn asked.

'I'm gitten old,' Mr. Grimes answered, 'and I reckin I don't know nuthen but terbacker, come right down to hit. But I alluz say, a man kin put his hand to hit when the time comes. I'm a-leave-en.'

The mare stirred restively, and Mr. Munn patted her on the neck, murmuring to her. Then he said: 'If you don't want your crop in the Association next year, you can hold it out. If that's it. I prefer for you to have it in, but I wouldn't want you to go on that account. There's plenty men who raise on shares have held their crops out.'

'I ain't easy in my mind,' he declared. 'They's some as won't tech terbacker, snuff, smoke, ner chew, ner lay a hand to hit fer a liven. They say hit's a God's curse.'

'A man living round here hasn't much choice,' Mr. Munn remarked.

'Hit's come to my mind hit's a curse,' Mr. Grimes said, 'like they says, and hit a curse all these years and me too blind to see.'

Mr. Munn leaned over and tightened the girth on his mare. 'I don't reckon it's that bad,' he returned.

'Hit's a curse,' Mr. Grimes insisted, 'laid onto the land, hit looks lak.'

Mr. Munn swung up to the saddle. From his height he looked out over Mr. Grimes' head and over the fields, where darkness was gathering. It seemed to gather and rise from the fields, rising to extinguish whatever little light yet showed in the upper air. 'Well,' he concluded, 'I'm sorry you're going.'

'Hit ain't yore doen,' Mr. Grimes said.

Chapter eleven

WHEN Mr. Munn rode out of the shadowed lane toward the white picket fence, that was dimly visible, a figure rose from beside the carriage block at the gate and waited for him. Closer, he saw that it was a negro man. Then he saw a few horses hitched to the palings of the fence, for the hitching-rack would not accommodate them all. The negro said, 'Howdy-do, boss, kin I hitch yore hoss?' and reached for the bridle.

Mr. Munn swung out of the saddle and dropped the rein. 'Thanks,' he replied.

'Is you one of the gemmun gonna spend the night?' the negro asked.

'Yes,' Mr. Munn said. He fumbled in the saddlebags and pulled out a small packet, tied up in newspaper.

'I jes' wanted to know, boss, so I'd know to put her in the stable. All the hosses fer the gemmun whut spends the night I puts in the stable.' Then, when Mr. Munn seemed to hesitate, the negro added, 'Misser Ball, he say jes' come right on in, jes' go over to the 'cademy house, over yander, and jes' push, he say jes' open the big dohr, and dar 'tis.'

'Thanks,' Mr. Munn said, and entered the white gate, which sagged under his touch and with its motion set up a loud clanking of plowshares that hung on a wire for weights. A dog growled suddenly, a deep-throated, powerful growl near at hand, and another dog, a little farther off, barked.

'Ain't nuthen to worry 'bout,' the negro man assured him, 'ain't nuthen. Dey's all tied up tonight. Ain't tied up, dey eat a man, ha'r and hide, liver and lights. Yassuh. Pow'ful mean. Yassuh——' As he moved away, he heard the negro still talking, saying, 'Yassuh.'

The dogs continued to bark while Mr. Munn walked over the brittle leaves toward the dark, formless bulk that was the building. He could see cracks of light where the windows were. Up the hill he could see, vaguely, the mass of another building, and a little light. That, he decided, must be the dwelling-house. He reached the academy building and fumbled for the door. His hand came into contact with the rough surface of a log, and then chinking. He found the latch, lifted it, and entered.

When he entered the long room, he was aware, even as his eyes adjusted themselves to the sudden light, of a tenseness, a hush. The backs of all the men were toward him. He quietly closed the door, took off his gloves and coat, and moved toward the nearer of the two big fireplaces that heated the room.

'That's the size of it,' a man at the other end of the room was saying. Then there was silence again, except for the nervous shuffling of some man's boots on the board floor. The men were scattered in several groups about the room, sitting on top of desks or lounging against the walls. Doctor MacDonald stood in front of the other hearth, his head bent over a piece of paper. He raised his head, straightened to his height, and passed his gaze deliberately over the men assembled. Then he said, 'For the benefit of Mr. Munn, who has just come in, I'll read this communication again.'

'I'm sorry to have inconvenienced the meeting,' Mr. Munn apologized. 'I miscalculated the distance, I reckon.'

'This is a letter received by Mr. Murdock, here,' and Doctor MacDonald inclined his long head toward a heavy-featured, dark man who lounged against the wall, near one of the lamp brackets. Then he added, 'Unsigned.' Having pronounced the word, he smiled confidentially at the men, with the air of one who feels it unnecessary to point the humor of a situation, and then began to read.

Dear Mr. Murdock,

If you knows what is good fer you, you will git rid of them niggers on yore place and git you some white croppers like a white man ought. When January gits here you better hunt you up some good hard-workin white men and make you a trade and git rid of them black bastards.

He folded the piece of paper. 'I needn't tell you what Mr. Murdock's reactions are,' he said.

'They ain't no secret,' Mr. Murdock remarked glumly. He walked across to the fireplace before which Doctor MacDonald stood, spat upon the burning logs, and addressed himself to the company. 'Ain't no man gonna tell me who's gonna crop on my place. That is, till the bank takes it over.' He spat again, and walked back to resume his place against the wall. He added, 'Which ain't gonna be long, I'm free to tell you, unless something happens.'

'A lot of folks been saying ain't no man gonna tell 'em when they could sell their tobacco,' Mr. Burden said. 'It's all whose shoes it is pinches.'

Doctor MacDonald grinned. 'That's a way of putting it,' he admitted, 'but there's a difference. Now——'

'Durn it,' Mr. Christian said. Mr. Munn had not seen him before. He was sitting humped over in one of the desks, concealed by a group of men. 'Durn it,' he said, 'say it's whose shoes pinches. Say it, and I say, well, by God, I've just decided it ain't gonna be mine, it's gonna be somebody else's for a pissing-spell.'

'I don't mean to say I'm backing down,' Mr. Burden explained, shaking his mass of dark, unkempt hair so that the forelock fell over his brow. 'It ain't a secret I've done things of late I never thought I'd set my hand to, but I reckon there's been many a man could say that before he turned his eyes to the wall. But I ain't backing down. I was just remarking. All I said it was, was whose shoe it is pinches.'

'There's a difference, now, you'll grant,' Doctor MacDonald said. He smiled and wagged his pipe at Mr. Burden. 'The fellow who wrote this note to Mr. Murdock is some poor God-forsaken, belly-dragging blackguard that blames his bad luck on a nigger. Any white man that's honest and got jaybird sense and wants to crop can get a place round here. The niggers aren't crowding him any. It's a little different down in Louisiana, where I come from, maybe, but not here. You'll grant now, Mr. Burden' — he addressed Mr. Burden pleasantly and patiently, as though explaining something, the course of a disease, perhaps, or the meaning of a symptom, as though making an effort for the simple and non-technical description — 'you'll grant there's a difference between this sort of thing' — and he tapped the paper, which he held in one hand, with the stem of his pipe — 'and the meaning of our' — he paused slightly, grinning again — 'endeavors. There's ——'

Professor Ball, who had been standing by the wall, a little aloof, leaned his tall, emaciated body forward, and thrust out a bandaged forefinger. 'A difference,' he said croakingly — 'the difference between justice and injustice, darkness and the holy light.'

'That's telling 'em, Professor,' Mr. Christian exclaimed. 'I just had it on the tip of my tongue.'

Doctor MacDonald was waiting for them to finish. He was standing very straight, but casually, for his erectness always had about it a certain impression of repose, and confidence, as well. His long arms hung loosely, the wrists showing out of the too-short sleeves. He looked from Professor Ball to Mr. Christian and back again, with a bearing of courtesy and toler-ance, and waited to be sure that they had finished speaking. Mr. Christian again sank back upon himself, paying no at-tention, apparently, to what was going on around him. Then

Doctor MacDonald said, speaking very deliberately: 'You all know I said when you elected me that I'd try not to get you into any more trouble than necessary. Well, we've been in plenty of trouble. Over half a year now. We all got into it together, and we don't know how much good it's done.' His voice moved along casually and conversationally, but it was distinct even at the other end of the room. He paused. Then he continued, his voice gaining a certain sharpness: 'But it hasn't done enough good. I know that. You know it. This fall the companies have managed to buy tobacco. They've paid high for it, but they've managed to get it. Enough to tide them over. That tobacco is in their warehouses. In Bardsville, in Millville, in Alltown, in Morganstown.'

He paused again. He let his gaze wander from the group before him, as though for the moment he had forgotten them, and seemed to find his interest at the far end of the raftered ceiling. Then he fixed his eyes upon them, and leaned toward them, confidentially, thrusting out his long, bony face. 'It's in their warehouses,' he repeated. 'Millions of pounds. It's lying there, in those warehouses. In Bardsville, in Millville, in Alltown, in Morganstown. Just lying there. Well' — he grinned at them, amusedly, almost apologetically, confidentially, drawing his lips back so that the long dog-teeth were exposed, and leaned closer — 'I'm proposing a little trouble, boys.'

There was silence in the room for a moment, except for the comfortable, domestic drone and hiss of the logs being consumed in the big fireplace behind him. Then, in a flat, uncommunicative tone, some man said, 'Well, I'm durned.'

'Well?' Doctor MacDonald asked, leaning.

Nobody said anything.

'Well?' Doctor MacDonald asked again, with a suggestion of mockery in the word.

Then a dozen voices broke out at once. Boot heels scraped on the boards as men moved restlessly about. Doctor Mac-

Donald, grinning, lifted his hands for silence, and held them up while the noise subsided. 'It's the last card,' he said.

'The truth,' some man agreed.

'The last,' Doctor MacDonald repeated. 'There won't be any more.'

The voices broke out again, and subsided beneath his lifted hands.

'The last card,' Mr. Munn said, very loud. Some of the men turned to look at him, then others. 'The last card,' Mr. Munn reiterated. 'It's take it or leave it. And I say, take it——'

'Take it!' a voice called.

'Take it,' Mr. Munn said again, 'for it's the last chance. But there's another reason. Mr. Burden, yonder' — he pointed at the man, who from under his dark, shaggy forelock stared stolidly at him, shaking his head — 'he said tonight he's done things this year he never thought he'd set his hand to. So've you. So've I, and, by God, I say so. And so've you. There's no use to name them. You know. Everybody——'

'It had to be,' Mr. Murdock said.

'By God——' Mr. Christian exclaimed, starting up from his seat and looking savagely about him; but he sank back without finishing his sentence.

'It was a mistake,' Mr. Munn said. 'But it's done. It was a mistake, because when we tried to fight against the companies we had to fight against some of our own people too. People who couldn't see and understand, but our own people. But this'll be different. This'll be clear. Clear as day. Them or us. When we march in——'

'March!' a voice exclaimed.

'March in,' Mr. Munn said slowly. 'When we march in, it'll be clear. Not a half-dozen men with a handful of matches and a can of coal oil. No. A thousand. Two thousand. As many as we need. All of us. And in column. Then' — and he was filled with certainty, a deep, sure, clean conviction that engulfed him like a flood, and he scarcely heard his own words — 'it will all be different. It will all be clear as day.'

Slowly, he sat down. He sat on one of the benches against the wall and leaned back against the uneven surface of the logs. The voices went on, and he heard them. The men would go. They were voting, and they would vote to go. He felt a tightening of his muscles and a prickling of the skin across his back and shoulders. Through the heavy cloth of his coat he felt the roughness and solidity of the logs against which he leaned. Gradually he relaxed, listening to the voices.

The men would go. They had decided on Bardsville first. Which was good. The biggest warehouses were there. That was right. Get the biggest ones first. It ought to be before the New Year, some man had said. Or sooner, another had added. Sooner. 'We need time,' Doctor MacDonald had pointed out, 'nothing too hasty. Maybe we've been too hasty in the past, but not now. Now we'll be sure.'

'Time? How much time?' someone had demanded.

'By New Year's, we ought to be able by New Year's,' Doctor MacDonald had answered. 'But we have to drill the men. That takes time. We couldn't get all of them ready by that time. But we don't need all. Say, about a thousand.'

Some man had said: 'You get more'n a thousand and a lot will have to come a long way. They'll be half a day coming. Some, more.'

'We won't need more'n a thousand,' Doctor MacDonald had told him. 'That'll make a show, I reckon. Later ——' And Mr. Munn, not looking up, had known how at the moment of the pause he must have been grinning easily and confidently at the men around him, shaking his unlit pipe at them probably. And he had heard the voice go on: '— maybe we'll need more.'

'Yeah, yeah' — it had been a voice which Mr. Munn could not recognize. 'There's the other towns, there's the other warehouses. And big ones.'

And Doctor MacDonald had said, never fear, they wouldn't wait too long, not long enough for the companies to take any steps. They wouldn't discriminate too much in favor of Bardsville.

Then Mr. Munn walked over to join the group. They were talking about preparing the men, how to drill them. And how many would go into Bardsville on foot. And whether to burn or dynamite the warehouses. Then one of the men asked if they reckoned there'd be any fighting.

'We'll have the drop,' a man said, 'anyway.'

'Maybe there will be some, sooner or later,' Doctor MacDonald conceded, 'but we'll try to keep the drop.' Then he added, 'Did any of you boys ever hear a bullet go by right close to your head?'

'I ain't honing to, neither,' Mr. Murdock said.

'I reckon I have,' another man asserted. He was a small, knotty-looking man, with a compact, dark, round, almost featureless head. He reminded Mr. Munn of a pig-nut, little, brown, and hard-shelled. The knotty-looking little man said that he had been in Cuba. 'For the duration,' he said, 'and I reckon I heard a few go past.' He slipped one arm out of its coat sleeve, and began to fumble at the buttons of his shirt. 'But there was one I didn't hear.' He pushed back the shirt and the thick layer of wool underwear to expose in the lamplight the flesh of his shoulder. 'Yeah, there was one didn't go past.' He thrust his bare shoulder forward, exhibiting it. In the firm, tightly muscled flesh there was a star-shaped depression large enough to accommodate a thumb-tip, puckered and white against the brownness of the surrounding surface. · He looked anxiously, with a kind of poorly concealed pride, from face to face of the peering men.

'Now, I be dog-gone,' one of the men exclaimed slowly, and reached out to lay a finger in the old wound.

'A Mauser ball,' the small, knotty-looking man said; 'it was a Mauser done it. That was a kind of rifle them bastards used down there.' He glanced down at the mark as though to verify its presence, and observed: 'One thing funny, now, you know it never hurt none to speak of, that is, right at first. Not a mite. But it shore-God knocked me down when it hit.' He paused, then added, 'It was outside Santiago.'

'I see it cracked up the clavicle some,' Doctor MacDonald said.

The small man looked up at Doctor MacDonald soberly. 'I don't know what name it goes by,' he answered, 'but it cracked a right smart.' Then he grinned, for the moment, with his small, brown, unformed face looking like a boy's.

'Well,' Doctor MacDonald said, 'if you never heard one sing by your head, there's one thing you can lay to. That's that it'll sound a lot worse when it happens than you ever reckoned it would.'

'Now that's a mouthful,' the small man agreed.

'I ain't honing to hear one,' Mr. Murdock said again.

The small man looked up inquiringly at Doctor MacDonald. 'Was you down there,' he asked, 'in Cuba?'

'No,' Doctor MacDonald answered.

The men began to turn away from the small man, to each other and to the fire. Some of them were putting on their overcoats and mackinaws. The small man stood by himself now, his shirt and underwear still pulled back to expose the scar of the old wound. He himself looked down at the scar. Then, tentatively, as though there might yet be pain in it, he prodded it. He looked around, secretively, at the other men, but they were shaking hands and saying good night to each other. He fastened his clothing, pulled on a worn mackinaw and a black fur cap with ear-flaps, and moved toward the edge of the largest group.

The men began to leave, going out the door by twos and threes. Professor Ball stood at the door, very erect, saying good-bye to each man as he went out. Finally, all of them had gone, except Mr. Munn, Mr. Christian, and three other men from over beyond Bardsville. They stood in front of one of the fireplaces with Doctor MacDonald. Professor Ball approached them, and said, 'Well, gentlemen, I feel we have had a very successful meeting.'

'It had better be,' one of the men observed, a thin-nosed, dry-skinned fellow with drooping, sandy-colored mustaches. His name was Peebles, and he came from over near Monclair. He spoke, and then, with deliberation, spat upon the declining embers.

'How do you reckon your people are gonna take to this?' Doctor MacDonald asked.

'They ain't gonna complain none,' the man said, 'not much, no-way. They been on short rations so long they're nigh ready fer anything you name. Take me,' he added, and tapped his chest. 'I ain't no diff'rent from ordinary, but what I been through, eight children and them about to be wrapping their feet in tow-sack to go out in the weather, and I'm durn nigh ready fer anything. I ain't no diff'rent from ordinary.'

'Well, anyway, your distinguished neighbor isn't going to the Senate,' Doctor MacDonald remarked. 'That's something. Even if he did win his suit against us, and get his God-damned tobacco back. What Dismukes paid him for that oughter keep his feet off the wet ground for a spell.'

'He got paid, all right,' Mr. Peebles said, 'I'll lay to that. But he spent a sight of money trying to be elected.'

'Elected or not,' Mr. Christian put in, half as though to himself, 'he'd never got there, not if I had to wring the bastard's neck with my own hands.'

The man named Peebles looked at Mr. Christian, and glumly nodded. 'You ain't the only one felt that way,' he said.

Doctor MacDonald started to bank the fires, but Professor Ball reminded him that it wouldn't be necessary, that tomorrow was Saturday and no school. Professor Ball began to blow out the lights, and the men gathered their coats. Mr. Peebles asked if they were sure his staying wouldn't put them out, and Doctor MacDonald said no, that a few of the boys boarded there during the week, but they went home over Friday night till Sunday night, and there was plenty of room. The last lamp was blown out, and the long room had only the fading firelight. Doctor MacDonald pulled open the heavy door.

The cold of the air struck like a blow. Mr. Munn walked slightly behind the other men. He lifted his eyes to the deep, vaulted darkness above the trees, and filled his lungs with the probing coldness of the air. He felt very tired, but light and relieved and cleansed, like a man who, convalescing from a long sickness, goes out into the open air for the first time. That night he slept more soundly than for many months. Sunk in the big feather bed, he seemed, as he closed his eyes, to be flowing and falling, effortlessly, deeply, deliciously, and forever.

By eleven o'clock on the night of December 30, most of the people of Bardsville were at home and in bed. Some men still hung about in the saloons, hunched over the bar to look at their reflections in the mirror, or standing back from the bar with a glass in one hand and the other raised to affirm some disputed point; the barmen, however, were already beginning to glance at the clocks and to execute their movements with a greater and greater, and a more impersonal, deliberation. Small groups still sat about in the lobbies of the two hotels, but the conversation was waning. A few bands of boys and young men roamed up and down the streets of the business section, flinging firecrackers that exploded with a hollow, echoing sound between the rows of buildings, and then laughing suddenly and prolongedly. Or they stood on the corners, under the arc-lamps, with their hands thrust into their pockets and their shoulders drawn against the briskness of the air. But away from the business section the streets were deserted, except for a few isolated figures that would hurry along under the bare boughs of the maples, their heels making on the brick pavements a small, clicking sound as regular and empty as the ticking of a clock. The houses between which they passed were darkened, with only, perhaps, a little light showing through the glass above a front door or under the drawn shade of an upper room.

At fifteen minutes after eleven a locomotive whistled for a crossing to the south of town, and then, soon after, slid heavily alongside the deserted depot. The night man at the station came out, and with a greeting muffled by weariness and disinterest, handed up a paper to the engineer. The fireman clambered up over the tender and fumbled clankingly at the spout of the water tower. Rushingly, the black water, streaked with a feeble and fluctuating silver in the light of the station lamps, poured into the reservoir. The few passengers who had descended at the platform disappeared up the street. The station man went back into the office, where now he could stoke up the fire in the round-bellied iron stove, set his alarm clock, and doze on a sagging cot until four o'clock. A voice called, 'All er-board,' without emphasis. From the lighted interiors of the coaches a few faces pressed against the glass of the windows to peer out at the deserted platform. The steam feathered whitely from the cylinders and the train began to pull away. North of town it whistled again, and the sound prolonged itself wailingly over the fields and the woods, and was heard by wakeful persons in the bedrooms of houses on that side of town.

Standing at the edge of a dry elder thicket that bordered the lane just before it crossed the tracks, Doctor MacDonald heard the approaching blast of the whistle. The long, glaring beam of the headlight knifed through the dark, lighting unreally the hanging leaves of bushes and the grass along the tracks. Then the locomotive plunged over the crossing with a multiple thunder of wheels, and as it passed, the figure of the fireman was for a moment visible, bent to heave a shovelful of coal into the firebox door. Then the last coaches whipped past, the dry leaves along the track sank in the failing gust of the passage, and the train fled away down the tubular corridor of light before it. 'On time,' Doctor MacDonald said, extinguished the match by which he had read his watch, and clicked shut, with a gesture of finality, the watchcase.

'She was on time,' Doctor MacDonald repeated.

'The engineer,' the man said, and nodded toward the woods across the lane, 'now I wonder could he see all them fellers over there.'

'If he did,' Doctor MacDonald replied, 'he'll have something to tell his kids when he gets to Chicago tomorrow.' His eyes were fixed after the disappearing train. A pale, flame-colored reflection from the open firebox lightened the billowy under-side of the otherwise invisible plume of smoke that trailed over the locomotive. The fireman would be stoking for the cut northward.

'Naw,' another voice said from the shadow of the thicket, 'the engineer sets on the other side, he couldn't see nothing over here.'

The train was out of sight now.

No one spoke for a minute or two. There was no sound except a faintly rasping, dry, restless sound from the dark woods across the lane, a sound like a breeze in dead leaves before they fall. But there was no wind. Doctor MacDonald began to sing under his breath, almost wordlessly: 'The old gray mare come trotten through the wilderness, trotten through the wilderness, trotten through the wilderness. The old gray mare come ——'

'It's cold,' one of the voices said subduedly.

'It's this standing around,' the other voice rejoined.

'Well,' the first man said, 'I hope we don't find it no hotter before day, huh?'

Under his breath Doctor MacDonald kept on singing: 'We come to a creek but we couldn't git acrost, we couldn't git acrost, we couldn't git acrost ——'

'Do you reckon there's any chance it's true about word getting out?'

Doctor MacDonald sang softly, '— but we couldn't git acrost ——'

'It came pretty straight,' the other man answered, 'from a man drives a team for the Alta.'

Doctor MacDonald stopped singing. 'If there is a home guard, or whatever that fellow said it was,' he said, 'it'll be a passel of warehouse hands and clerks and young bucks with nothing better to do. Unless they brought in some other men on the train. And we'll know that in a minute. Soon as he gets here.' He began to sing, so softly that the words were indistinguishable now. The other men were silent.

Mr. Munn said, 'I hear him now.' Doctor MacDonald stopped humming.

There was the sound of a horse galloping up the lane from the pike, an increasing sound of hoofs on the soft earth of the lane like a roll on a damp and sagging drumhead. The bulk of the horse and rider loomed suddenly out of the dark, almost upon the group, and the rider slid out of his saddle.

'Well?' Doctor MacDonald demanded.

'Not a thing,' the rider reported, 'not a thing stirring. We walked round uptown and down by the warehouses, and watched the train come in. Not a thing stirring.'

'Ah,' Doctor MacDonald said, with a gentle and sibilant exhalation of his breath. Then he took his watch from his pocket, and struck a match against his trousers. Shielding the flame with his cupped hand, he peered at the watch, and, briefly, his long, bony face was illuminated. 'Eight minutes to twelve,' he asserted matter-of-factly, and extinguished the match. Then: 'Mr. Murphy, Mr. Sykes, we're ready.' Two of the men who had been standing beside him at the edge of the lane turned abruptly into the darkness of the thicket, and with a crackling and trampling of leaves and dry elder stalks, led out their horses.

'Tell Mr. Sills to move in,' Doctor MacDonald ordered. 'Tell him to hit the bottom of Jefferson Street as near to twelve-thirty as he can. He knows what to do from that point. And' — he turned to the other man, who had already mounted — 'Mr. Sykes, you tell Mr. Murdock to hit the Cherry Creek bridge at the same time. He knows, then. But tell them not to touch a wire till five minutes before they move in. That's all.'

The two men wheeled, lifted their horses into a gallop, and almost immediately, long before the sound of hoofs had faded out, were lost in the darkness. Doctor MacDonald peered after them, then directed: 'All right, Mr. Mosely, tell Mr. Hamer to start. And to make them keep formation all the way.'

The figure of a man moved from the edge of the elder thicket, crossed the lane, and entered the grove on the other side.

Doctor MacDonald began to sing again, very softly, almost tunelessly: 'Rock of ages, cleft for me, let me hide myself in Thee, let the water ——'

Mr. Munn tried to make out his face, but could not. There was only the paler blur in the darkness. Then he looked up at the sky. Only a few stars were visible. There'll be, he thought, more than six hours till light.

'It's shore-God now cold,' a voice said.

No one replied.

Mr. Munn tried to move his toes inside his boots, but they were stiff and cramped. He had not realized how cold he was. Now, up to the knees, his legs were almost as stiff and dead as posts. He could not detect the words of Doctor MacDonald's

singing any more, they had sunk so low. He tried to remember
how the words of the hymn went.

A voice called out, subduedly and indistinguishably, from
the woods across the lane. The gentle, dry, rustling sound like
a breeze increased in the woods, then, suddenly, was a peremp-
tory shuffling and crackling. A single figure appeared in the
lane.

'They're coming,' Doctor MacDonald said.

Then there were the others. They came out of the woods,
shuffling the dead leaves, to hesitate raggedly in the open lane
and then form four abreast and move toward the railroad
tracks. They carried guns on their shoulders, and strips of
white cloth were across their faces. A few other men, masked
too and with white bands on their left arms, stood in the lane,
and kept saying, in harsh, suppressed voices: 'Move up, there!
Move up, four abreast! Make it four abreast, and hold it.'
The head of the column moved up the lane, and turned down
the railroad track toward town. But in the lane it was constantly replenished, the men there filtering from the strip of
woodland, hesitating, then forming and moving away after
the others. The last men came from the woods.

They all passed, and the lane was empty. The sound of their
crunching tread died away. There was silence except for the
stamping of a horse beyond the elder thicket.

Doctor MacDonald looked at his watch. 'Mr. Burrus,' he
said, 'it's time for you all to be getting on to the telephone office.
You'll make it about right if you start now.'

'Sure,' a voice responded drawlingly. The man walked off
down the lane. In a minute there was a crackling of brush
down the lane, and then the sound of hoofs.

Mr. Munn wondered, idly, why Doctor MacDonald did not
start. He wondered what time it must be by now. It could
not be long, now. In a minute, in two minutes, they would
mount, and move in. The cold had climbed past his knees,

but somehow he was not really uncomfortable, and did not feel disposed to stamp his feet and swing his arms, as some of the other men had done. He felt very calm, now, very detached.

Doctor MacDonald was speaking. 'Get the telegraph wires at exactly twelve-twenty-five,' he said. 'And you, Mr. Murray, you and your boys get the telephone wires on the pike at the same time. Then come in by Jefferson to Fifth. Pick up anybody loose on upper Jefferson.'

The two men moved off.

'We're ready,' Doctor MacDonald announced, and turned back into the elder thicket. Mr. Munn and the three other men remaining followed him. They led their horses out into the lane, and mounted. Twenty yards or so down the lane toward the pike, they stopped, and two of the men rode into the grove, which was more open here.

'Well, we might as well put on our fancy-dress,' Doctor MacDonald said. He drew from his pocket a strip of white cloth and adjusted it over the lower part of his face. He pinned a white band around his left arm. Mr. Munn and the other man put on their masks.

Horsemen began to file out of the grove and proceed at a walk toward the pike. Doctor MacDonald, accompanied by Mr. Munn and the other man, trotted to the head of the uneven line. At the junction of the lane and the pike they stopped, then moved out into the pike. 'Form them here,' Doctor MacDonald ordered, and Mr. Munn and the other man moved back along the line, passing the word.

Four abreast the long column moved forward at a trot. The pike stretched out straight before them, its paleness distinguishable in the darkness. Down the slight slope ahead, the few lights of the town were visible. They are lights in the streets, Mr. Munn thought, and in houses; and in other houses, the houses that are dark, people are sleeping. Behind him the metal of horseshoes chinked and rang on the gravel of the pike with a steady sound.

The head of the column reached the end of the slope. There the first houses were, jumbled shacks set back in treeless yards, their gray masses undefined in the darkness. This was nigger town. In one shack a lamp was burning. Mr. Munn saw it as he rode past, and could catch a glimpse of the board table on which it sat and of the bare interior of the room, and he remembered how the wavering lamps had lighted those other cabins that night when he had hunted the knife.

'Twelve-thirty,' Doctor MacDonald said. 'Burrus ought to be in the telephone office by now.'

'Yes,' Mr. Munn replied.

'And the wires down,' Doctor MacDonald added.

The column swept into a regular street. The houses, beyond the bare trees, were darkened. The street lights were out. They passed a fork in the street, where another street joined at an angle, and Mr. Munn, turning in his saddle, could dimly see that the last section of the column was diverging into the other street. It would cover, he knew, that entrance to the town.

Far away, almost lost in the sound of hoofs, there was the report of a gun. Then, immediately, a volley, followed by a few spattering explosions, all innocent and unimpressive from distance. For an instant, Mr. Munn scarcely grasped the meaning of the sound; then he knew that it was Mr. Murdock's men. They had hit the Cherry Creek bridge and were over.

'West,' the man on the other side of Doctor MacDonald said, and cocked his head. 'It's west, and it's Murdock.'

'Here goes,' Doctor MacDonald announced in a conversational tone, but as though he had not heard the other man. Mr. Munn saw that he held in his right hand a revolver. He raised the revolver slowly, muzzle upward, and Mr. Munn, with the inheld breath, waited for the explosion. It came, sudden and blasting, just by his head. A long moment, and there was the roar of the volley behind him. His own revolver leaped in his hand at the recoil, but the individual explosion was swallowed up and lost.

Lights appeared in a few houses along the street. Somewhere farther down the street, a woman screamed, one scream painful and sustained, then two short, gasping cries that concluded on a complaining note. The lights in the houses began to go out. After the head of the column had passed, the woman began to scream again.

'They ought to slap her and put her in a cold bath,' Doctor MacDonald pronounced dispassionately. 'That brings 'em out of it.'

At a trot the column climbed the rise toward the corner of Jefferson and Main. It had reached the business section, now, and moved between the stores where the cold-looking, shadowy glass of the display windows gave blankly on the street. Just before they reached the corner, Doctor MacDonald commanded: 'Hold your boys along here, Perse, at the corner, you can see four ways there. They'll come up the hill here, and go out Jefferson when they go.'

'Yes,' Mr. Munn said. He pulled his mare over toward the curb. The column moved past him, and he watched it, the uneven lines, the white, anonymous masks under the flopping hat-brims. A good many of the mounts, he could tell even in such a light, were jaded and work-worn. They thrust their long necks out, and their bony, hammer-shaped heads jerked mechanically with the motion of their bodies. Some of them had been ridden pretty far already; and it would be farther before morning.

His own band, and the band that would act with his, were at the end of the column. Just before they came up even with him, he lifted his hand, and raggedly they drew to a halt. 'Mr. Allen, Mr. Todd,' he ordered, 'you all go down Main, west, to the next corner so you can keep an eye out up and down that cross-street. Anything stirring, and one of you come back up here.'

'All right,' the man named Allen said. Benton Todd, sitting his horse very straight, said nothing. The two men detached themselves from the main body, turned the corner, and trotted off down the hill to the west.

'The rest of you just form four abreast,' Mr. Munn directed, 'at the corner there' — and he pointed to the corner — 'and wait till it's over.' Then he added, 'We'll be the last out, on this side of town anyway.'

The men moved into position at the corner, juggling their mounts into a crude order.

'God-a-mighty, hit's a-gonna be cold here,' one man said, 'wind outer the north rising now like hit is and come-en down Jefferson. Us standing here, and ain't nuthen to break hit.'

'It won't be long,' Mr. Munn said. 'Besides, we're supposed to stay here.'

'I ain't complainen,' the man replied.

The rest of the column of mounted men was far down Main Street, to the east, now. Down there, along the tracks, were the warehouses, all of them strung out along Front Street. Mr. Munn wondered if they were putting the dynamite to them yet. He guessed that the men on foot had already passed down at the foot of the slope. He pulled off his right glove and held his hand to the wind. It was coming from the north, all right, as far as he could tell with the buildings and all, and it was freshening. He hoped it wouldn't get much stiffer. A high wind, and there'd be a good chance of burning up the town when the warehouses went. But an east wind would be the most dangerous. An east wind would bring the fire right up the rise, this way, through the middle of town.

The lights were on in the lobby of the hotel, a few doors down the street. But the lights that had at first come on in the rooms upstairs were out now, all but one, one on the top floor. It

made a streak of yellow light under a lowered window-shade.
Down Jefferson, southward, there was a single shot, and Mr.
Munn turned toward it. Two blocks away a body of horsemen
were wheeling off of Jefferson into a cross-street. Then, as they
wheeled, they fired a volley into the air. Mr. Sills, Mr. Munn
thought, and his men. Mr. Sills, he thought. He tried to imagine Mr. Sills, his small, thin, gray face set and expressionless
beneath the white cloth, riding along the dark streets, prefacing
his dry-voiced orders to his men with a cough, lifting a revolver
as he rode, and firing, suddenly, into the darkness. It was
absurd. But Mr. Sills was down there, with a hundred men,
and they would go back down the next street, to the edge of
town, and wheel, and fire a volley, and again come back up
Jefferson, and fire. And the people would stay indoors, lying
in their beds, propped upon one elbow with their ears straining
and their hearts knocking, and their wives would clutch them
by the arm until the nails cut the flesh, or the bolder men would
peer secretively out of darkened windows at the horsemen, Mr.
Sills and his men, as they rode past. They were all afraid of
Mr. Sills, tonight.

'Look,' one of the men said, and Mr. Munn followed his
pointing finger. 'Look, there's a fellow coming out the
hotel.'

A man came unsteadily from the hotel doorway, and stood
for a moment motionless on the pavement.

'I believe ——' one of the men began. Then another cried:
'Watch out! he's got a gun.' But before the words were out of
his mouth, the man had fired.

'The bastard,' the first man uttered, and fumbled for his own
revolver.

The man on the pavement fired again, but the report of his
shot almost merged with the boom of the heavy-caliber revolver
of the horseman. The big pane of glass in the main hotel window collapsed with a shattering sound just behind the man on

the pavement. The man on the pavement wavered, and fell forward.

'By God,' somebody said, 'you got him!'

'The fool!' Mr. Munn exclaimed, 'the poor God-damned fool.' Then: 'See about him.' And he rode toward the spot. Two men, the one who had fired the shot and another, slipped out of their saddles, and ran to the fallen man.

Mr. Munn, from his saddle, looked down at them as they turned the body over, and fumbled at the buttons of the coat.

'He's alive,' one of the men said excitedly. 'His heart, I can feel it!'

'Where's he hit?' Mr. Munn demanded.

'Hit!' The other man, the man who had fired the shot, stood up. 'Hit! the bastard's drunk.' He looked down at him disgustedly. 'He's puked all over hisself.'

'You might-er killed him,' the other man said.

'He might-er killed me.'

'Listen,' Mr. Munn said, 'you're supposed to fire when you're ordered. You understand?'

'Ain't no bastard gonna shoot at me,' the man retorted.

Mr. Munn looked down at him for a moment. 'Fire,' he repeated, 'when you're ordered, I said. Do you understand?'

'All right,' the man said grudgingly.

'Now drop that fellow in the lobby of the hotel,' Mr. Munn ordered, 'and get back in line.'

He watched them drag the fallen man toward the doorway, kicking aside the shattered glass on the pavement as they did so; then he returned to his position at the intersection of the streets. All the men there were staring down the slope of Main Street, eastward. There at the foot of the slope, under the distant arc-light, he could see the column of men on foot passing toward the warehouses. Mr. Munn took out his watch. 'It won't be very long now,' he remarked.

'Wonder what took 'em so long,' one of the men said.

'I don't know,' Mr. Munn answered, 'unless we just miscalculated. I've heard it said it takes a lot of men marching together a lot longer to get somewhere than it does one man. I don't know, but that's what I've heard said.'

The last men passed at the foot of the slope. There was nothing but the empty street, on which the store windows looked, and the thin string of arc-lights reaching one block beyond Front Street, down there. He heard the sound of a volley somewhere to the south — Mr. Sills again, he decided — and an answering volley behind him to the west, much nearer. That would be Mr. Murdock coming up.

'I bet a lotta folks does sumthen tonight they ain't done in a long time,' one of the men said, and snickered.

'What's that?' another voice demanded.

'Pee in the bed.'

There was laughter.

Then another voice: 'Them puny little old six-guns ain't nuthen. Just wait till they hear them warehouses go, and then what!'

There was more laughter.

Then there was silence, the silence, all at once, of a sleeping town. One of the horses pawed at the pavement, then stopped. The arc-lamp above made a small, humming, empty sound. The shadows of the horses and riders spread out blackly around them on the pavement. The men were silent, as though straining to listen.

A group of riders, a buggy, and several men on foot came down Jefferson Street, from the north, and approached the corner where Mr. Munn was. It was Mr. Murray's band, which had waited to cut the wires, and the men they had picked up as they came in. When Mr. Munn questioned the men who had been picked up, they all, except the old man in the buggy, seemed frightened, and protested that they had been out so late just because they had to and that it had nothing to do with what was going on, and they gave their names in uncertain voices. But the old man was different. He was furious and fearless. He was Doctor Potter, he shouted, and he had already been up half the night with a patient, and he'd be damned if any gang of blackguards was going to keep him from getting to bed.

Mr. Munn ordered two men to go with him and see him home. 'I don't want them!' he shouted. 'I don't need protection. Not from a gang of cowardly ruffians. You'll all be in the penitentiary. You ought to be. You haven't any right, you blackguards!'

'It's not for you to say, Doctor Potter,' Mr. Munn finally said, and motioned to the men to move on.

Doctor Potter shouted back something unintelligible as he drove away, slowly, down Jefferson.

The other men, three of them, who had been picked up were ordered to stand back in a deep doorway of the store at the corner. Two of the men from Mr. Murray's band dismounted, and stood in the street, just in front of the doorway. 'You won't be hurt,' Mr. Munn told them, 'if you stay right there till it's over.'

One of the men began snuffling. His wife was sick, he said, and she would be worried; he had to get home to her.

'You're lying,' Mr. Munn said. 'You just thought of that. Now get back in there and shut up.' He had scarcely listened to what the man said; he was straining his ears, waiting. There were two more volleys; then, again, the silence.

The arc-lamp over his head hummed. He fixed his eyes eastward, down Main Street. A cat came out of an alley there, some thirty-odd feet away, and began to pick its way, fastidiously, across the street. It stopped to nose something in the gutter, then proceeded. A piece of newspaper slid over the pavement before the wind. It made a rustling, rasping sound.

The cat was halfway across the street.

The sound, when it came, was at the first split instant more like an undefined bodily impact, a pressure on the head, than like a sound. The sound filled the air, and would not go away. It filled the air to bursting. It hung like a great grape, swollen and clustered in its reverberations. Then it was gone. The cat was frozen there in the middle of the empty street. The sound had passed. In the painful, empty silence that ensued, Mr. Munn heard the tinkling, brittle sound of glass striking the pavement. A piece of glass that had still clung to the shattered window of the hotel lobby had been dislodged.

Under the pressure of the bit, his mare ceased her plunging.

Down the hill, there was a volley, then a burst of shouting. The second explosion struck, less powerful than the first. Before its reverberations had fulfilled themselves, there was the third, still farther off. There'll be one more, Mr. Munn thought, the Alta warehouse, the last one. He clamped his knees and his knuckles tightened on the rein. A single tongue of flame, curved like a whiplash in the fresh wind, towered beyond the roofs at the foot of the slope.

The last blast came, and its echoes died off.

'A million dollars,' a man remarked, loud but prayerfully — 'a million dollars, and gone just like that.'

Now the sky was reddening with the flames.

'Gone,' another voice rejoined flatly, 'like them salts through the widder-woman.'

Down Jefferson, Mr. Sills' men swung the corner again. Again there was their volley. Then there was silence; and then, from an indeterminate direction, a sound like the sound of a horn, low-pitched, pervasive, penetrating. It came three times.

'They're blowing now,' somebody said.

'They're gitten ready to go, blowen on that shotgun barr'l.'

'They'll be coming soon,' Mr. Munn said. 'Right up by this corner.'

'There they come now,' a man called, 'some of 'em.'

A group of men were turning into Main Street, two blocks down. Just around the corner they stopped, and clustered together on the pavement. Mr. Munn strained his eyes toward them. He could not tell what they were doing. No more men came from around the corner. The group was still clustered there, milling about. Then two figures detached themselves from it. One figure seemed to stagger toward the middle of the street, then it fell. The other disappeared around the corner.

Some of the men in the group down there were, apparently, entering a building. No one paid any attention to the figure that lay in the street.

'Mr. Simmons,' Mr. Munn directed, 'you ride down there and see what's going on.' He pointed down the slope of Main Street.

'Yes, sir,' the man said, but before he had touched heel to his horse, more men were running into Main Street from around the corner, below. They ran directly toward the first group, struck it, and merged with it. Then more men appeared. They picked up the figure which lay in the middle of the street. A single horseman, down there in the middle of the street, gesticulated toward the crowd. The man named Simmons was now approaching that other horseman.

More men, a solid column of men, swung into Main Street, and moved up the slope toward the intersection of Main and Jefferson. The man named Simmons passed them as he galloped back. Beyond the approaching column, over the roofs, the sky was marked with a line of flames.

Simmons drew up beside Mr. Munn. 'Cassidy's saloon,' he said, breathing heavily, 'some of 'em tried to bust into it. Their captain and another fellow, they tried to stop it, and they knocked out the captain. That was him laying in the street. The others, they come then and stopped 'em. My God, the doc, he's down there raising hell, he's ——'

'Doctor MacDonald?' Mr. Munn demanded.

'Yeah, Doctor MacDonald, that's him on the horse, and, by
God, what he's telling 'em! He's calling 'em names I didn't know.'

Mr. Munn looked off down the slope. The head of the marching column was very near now, the men swinging along irregu-
larly four abreast, laughing and shouting. Just then, a few
random shots were fired from the column.

'Did Doctor MacDonald send any word?' he demanded.

'Yeah, yeah,' the man said, his eyes fixed on the approaching
column. 'He said if you caught anybody trying to bust in a
saloon or anything, just pick 'em up, no matter even if they're
our fellows or not. He said beat hell outer 'em if you had to.
He said shoot 'em in the leg.'

'He said that?' Mr. Munn asked.

'That's what he said,' the man answered, 'and he's sending
word off to Mr. Sills and Mr. Murdock, too.'

'Thanks,' Mr. Munn said. And then: 'Just drop back into
line, will you please, Mr. Simmons?'

'Excuse me,' Mr. Simmons replied, and pulled his mount
back into the formation.

The column was rounding the corner, the nearest men little
more than an arm's length from the head of Mr. Munn's mare.
The men were laughing and shouting. Somebody fired a double-
barreled shotgun into the air, the two barrels in such quick
succession that the reports almost blended.

Mr. Munn studied the flames above the roofs.

'By God!' a voice shouted from the column — 'By God, we
done it!'

Another shot was fired, close at hand. The glass clattered
from the show window of a store beyond the column.

Another shout: 'We done it!'

The men kept swinging past, shouting and laughing. The
cloths had slipped down, carelessly, on their faces, or had been
removed now. Mr. Munn looked at his watch. Another half-
hour, he thought — no, three quarters.

Three horsemen were riding alongside the column, approaching. One of them, Mr. Munn could see even before they reached the corner, was Doctor MacDonald. He wore no mask, now. He rode up, smiling, his lips drawn back and his pipe stuck between his teeth. 'Hello,' he said, almost casually. He had not removed the pipe.

When he drew up, Mr. Munn said in a low voice, 'I hear you had some trouble down the hill?'

'Yes,' Doctor MacDonald answered, 'but I gave somebody some trouble, too.' Then he looked sharply at Mr. Munn's face. 'Listen,' he said, 'don't let it prey on your mind. If a man's in a fight, he don't look to see whether or not his gun's got a pearl handle and a monogram.'

'It's too bad,' Mr. Munn remarked soberly.

'Son, the good Lord never got any thousand or so men together for any purpose without a liberal assortment of sons-of-bitches thrown in.' He grinned and looked at Mr. Munn sidewise. 'Not even for the purpose of burning tobacco warehouses, which is a thing to make the heavenly choir tune up. But' — he hesitated, his eyes following the marching men appraisingly — 'the next fellow up and does a trick like that, busting in that saloon, and it's gonna be me or him. Next Wednesday when we hit Morganstown, it'll be different, or I'll know why.'

'Well,' Mr. Munn rejoined, 'otherwise I guess we've had plenty of luck. So far.'

'Boy, we had plenty,' Doctor MacDonald declared. 'Not a word getting out, nothing.'

Mr. Munn watched the flames. They rose straight upward now. 'One piece,' he said, 'was the wind dying down. We didn't burn up the town.'

'For a minute there,' Doctor MacDonald said, 'it looked like we might have to untie the boys down at the fire department. Just after we'd got 'em all nice and quiet and resigned to their condition.' He looked at his watch. The last column was approaching. Then, with a different voice, he commanded: 'Give 'em half an hour, or better. In fifteen minutes my boys will start out; we're going out and hit Jefferson on the edge of town. The same time you start out north on Jefferson, Sills will be going out south.'

'I don't reckon on any trouble,' Mr. Munn said.

'No, it looks now like all that home guard stuff was hot air.' Doctor MacDonald lifted his reins. 'So long,' he said, nodded to the two masked men who accompanied him, and touched his mount's flank. He and the two men moved briskly off, southward down Jefferson. Mr. Munn decided that he must be going to give Sills his last directions.

The head of the column was well up Jefferson Street now, to the north. The men were singing. They sang, 'The old gray mare . . . ' and the reports of guns punctuated their voices. Some of the men straggling at the end of the column were firing at the glass of show windows of the stores.

'The God-damn fools,' Mr. Munn exclaimed.

'What's that?' the next man demanded.

'Those fools,' Mr. Munn said somberly. 'Shooting that glass out'll hurt us. It'll hurt us bad.'

The sound of the singing came back down the street:

> '. . . came trotten through the wilderness,
> Trotten through the wilderness.'

'Yeah,' the man rejoined, 'but did you ever feed a dog you'd kept chained up and hungry and not hear him growl when he got his teeth in the meat?'

Mr. Munn made no reply.

'That's all it is; they don't mean no harm,' the man continued. 'They're just showing they got their teeth in.'

To the east the flames were lower now, but still strong. There was no more sound of gunfire. The last sporadic shots, faint to the north and south, had ceased. The arc-lamp hummed. Down the street a small group of men came out of a doorway.

With surprise Mr. Munn saw the three women with them. The men held the women by the arm, whether to assist them or to keep them from running away he could not tell.

'It's Burrus,' a man said. 'He's taking the ladies back to the telephone office.'

The women had entered a building down the street, the building with the telephone office in it, Mr. Munn figured. That means it's about time, he thought, for us to be pulling out. The men who had escorted the women disappeared into an alley. Mr. Munn looked at his watch. It would be about another five minutes, he decided.

Burrus and his men came out of the alley, on horseback now, and moved toward the corner. Mr. Burrus lifted his hand in salute as he passed. 'We're pulling out,' he announced.

'Good night,' Mr. Munn said.

Mr. Burrus and his men cantered off up the street. The sound of the hoofs died away, and they were lost to view.

Mr. Munn turned in his saddle. The men regarded him, their faces with the white cloths shadowed by their hat-brims. 'All right,' he said. He lifted his revolver and fired into the air, once.

Benton Todd and the man named Allen were coming toward the corner.

Mr. Munn motioned to the two men guarding the prisoners in the doorway. They approached, and mounted their horses. The three men whom they had been guarding remained, half-hidden in the shadow. Mr. Munn walked his horse to the spot, and looked down at them. The man who had snuffled and had said that his wife was sick stood behind the other two. 'Come on out,' Mr. Munn ordered. 'You all can go now.' They came out, the last man somewhat hesitantly. 'You can get on home now to that sick wife you haven't got,' Mr. Munn said.

The man raised his face, mottled and empty in the uncertain light, and ran his tongue over his lips. Suddenly, looking at him, Mr. Munn hated him. He felt the blind impulse to cause him pain, to show his hatred, to torture him. Leaning from his saddle, he exclaimed, 'Get away from here! Go on! Quick!'

The man backed away a couple of steps, his face still raised emptily, then turned and fled. The other two men were already gone.

Mr. Munn lifted his arm. 'Let's go,' he said loudly, and lifted his mare to a gallop. The men swung in behind him.

As they went out of town, all of the houses were dark. But inside of them, he knew, there were the people. They lay in their beds, listening, staring up into the dark. Or they peered from the darkened windows.

At the top of the slope outside of town, he looked back. The glow of the fires still lingered. But the flames were down.

It was some fifteen minutes later, a couple of hundred yards beyond the place where four of the men had turned off into a side lane to go home, that he first thought he heard the sound of hoofs behind him. But he dismissed the matter from his mind for the moment. Then, not much later, he was sure, or almost sure. He could hear, he thought, the hollow tattoo on a wooden bridge which they had crossed just a little earlier.

'Do you hear anything?' he demanded.

'I don't reckon I do,' Mr. Simmons replied; 'nothing special.'

Cantering along, Mr. Munn strained his ears. He tried to sort out the sounds. There was the sound of the horses in his own band, and that other sound, if there was another sound. He was sure, then he was not sure. It was not reasonable, he thought. He knew that he was the last out of town. Then he said loudly, 'Stop!'

The horsemen grouped compactly in the middle of the pike.

'Can you hear anything?' he asked. 'Anything coming?'

For a moment, no one answered, then a man said, 'Maybe. I ain't sure.' He slipped from his saddle, and, crouching at the edge of the pike, put his ear to the earth. The other men peered down at him. He rose quickly, and said, 'Yeah, yeah, some-body's coming.'

'Yes?' Mr. Munn demanded.

'Horses,' the man declared, 'and a lot of 'em.'

Mr. Munn scanned the sky. It was a little lighter now. It was not dawn, but the clouds were thinning.

'Some of our boys going home,' a man suggested.

'No,' Mr. Munn said, 'we're the last out. Out this way, anyhow.'

'We could bushwhack 'em,' a man proposed, 'get behind that fence and let 'em ride past and bushwhack 'em.'

'No,' Mr. Munn decided. 'A fight won't do us any good. Come on!' He leaned forward and the mare responded beneath him. Beside him and behind him the hoofs pounded the hard pike. The wind flapped his hat-brim. The fields and woods were black on each side, but between them, ahead, lay the paleness of the pike. If they could make it to the New Bethany crossroads with a decent lead, they could, Mr. Munn was sure, throw off the pursuers. They'd have a chance, a good chance in that tangle of lanes there in that locality and in the woods. If they had a decent lead. But they had to have a lead, because there, toward the crossroads, the pike ran straight and the patch of country was open, and now, momently it seemed to Mr. Munn as he raised his face in the wind and looked fleetingly at the sky, the dim light that seeped through the breaking clouds was increasing. But it was not yet dawn. There ought to be more than two hours till dawn, he figured.

Out of the tail of his eye he noticed that Mr. Simmons, who rode beside him, was looking back. He looked back over his shoulder. His men were no longer compactly together. They were stringing out down the pike behind as the horses failed the pace. 'God damn it!' Mr. Munn said aloud, 'some of those plugs won't last to Bethany.' No better than plow horses, he thought disgustedly, irritably.

'This keeps up,' Mr. Simmons was shouting at him, 'and they'll be taking some of the boys.'

Mr. Munn shook his head. 'No,' he denied, 'not that.'

'Better bushwhack 'em while we got a chance,' the other called. 'We still got some cover here.'

Mr. Munn glanced to one side of the pike. It was winding here. Through brush and the black cedar thickets. That paleness against the darkness of the thicket would be stone wall. Limestone. Here was cover. Good cover, if they were going to bushwhack. He shook his head. 'No,' he repeated, not looking toward Mr. Simmons, but forward strainingly toward the next turn in the pike as though his own intensity might draw all the mass behind him, and himself, more swiftly toward the security of that next bend, and the bend beyond.

Beyond the turn, he again looked back. The men were stringing out behind. Worse than before, he thought. And in his mind he cursed the fools who were pursuing, fools who had no part, no real interest, no concern, with the whole business, idle, swaggering smart alecks, or fellows with some miserable little job with the companies, hangers-on at the depot, at the hotel, fools who stood on the street corners and felt big. 'The bastards, the bastards,' he whispered over and over, cursing them, feeling trapped and betrayed. And they were gaining, he knew they were gaining. They would have fresher horses. Better horses.

'The last chance,' Mr. Simmons shouted, against the wind of their passage, 'if we're gonna bushwhack 'em.'

Mr. Munn shook his head. He did not look back. He did not dare, thinking how the last men would be leaning forward, with their eyes glued on the vague figures fleeing ahead, how they would be flogging their horses, desperately, while the pursuers clawed at their backs.

He took the last bend. There was the straight stretch to New Bethany Church. Beyond the church the roads divided, the lanes dropped off into the creek bottom, and into the woods. If they could make it there, they could go back along those lanes, into the woods, in the darkness where on the padded earth a hoof would make no sound, and they could separate, and the pursuers would waver and hesitate and would not know what to do, for no man among them would want to be apart from the others. But before that, there was the straight stretch. It seemed more open than he had remembered, and longer. And a luminousness seemed to come from the ground there, to make everything plain there, the pike, the bare fields, the rail fences. The rail fences. Like the tumbled rail fence, he thought in a flash, in that open spot at Murray Mill that night, that open spot that had seemed, as he hesitated before advancing across it, so innocently, dangerously empty and so light.

He did not hear the first shot. Mr. Simmons shouted at him, 'They're shooting now!'

'I didn't hear them.'

'Durn, I didn't neither,' Mr. Simmons answered; 'I heard the bullet go past me.'

Then Mr. Munn did hear a report. One of the men was firing in answer.

'No good,' Mr. Simmons called, 'them durn little six-guns; they got rifles.'

Mr. Munn thought that he heard a bullet pass his head. But he wasn't sure. He heard the reports of the revolvers.

'Oughter bushwhacked 'em!' Mr. Simmons was yelling.

It looked so far to the church. You could scarcely see it ahead. And all the pike and the fields and the fences were so plain in that light that seemed to come upward out of the earth.

Mr. Simmons was shouting, 'Them bastards kill me, Munn, and 'fore God, I'll hant you!'

The church, a blur of whiteness against dark trees, crawled toward them. It crawled, painfully. Behind, the revolvers popped irrelevantly, flatly. The hoofs drummed the hard pike.

Then, as though with surprise, he observed that they were even with the church. There were the crossroads, the forked lanes toward the fords at the creek, the woods and the dense darkness.

They were past the church. He swung down the nearest lanes, blindly, hoping that the mare would manage her footing. They plunged across the shallow waters of the ford, and the splashing from the horse next to him drenched him to the thigh.

But he felt nothing. Ten yards beyond the ford he pulled into the protection of the trees. 'Hurry!' he called sharply, 'hurry!' and was not sure that his own voice was speaking, for it seemed calm, not the voice that should belong to him at the moment. 'Hurry! Get off! You Simmons, Allen, Snyder, get the horses back a little way. If they come across that ford, cut down on them.' He stared toward the ford. The water glinted dimly there. He felt the heaving of the mare's breath between his knees. 'But they won't,' he said. 'They're afraid. They won't come down there, and come across.'

He slid from the saddle, staggering almost when his feet touched the earth.

They did not come to the ford. He kept his eyes fixed on the spot. Twice there was an uneven volley from the direction of the pike. He could hear some of the bullets, very high, whipping through the twigs and the cedar fronds. 'Don't shoot,' he told the men. 'Don't shoot unless they try the ford.'

Then, after a little while, after he was sure that the men at the pike had gone, he heard a voice say, soberly, 'I got hit.'

'What?' Mr. Munn demanded. 'Where are you?' He had not recognized the voice; a dull, flat, aimless voice, it had been, saying, 'I got hit.'

'Here,' the voice answered. 'Here I am.'

Mr. Munn moved gropingly in the darkness of the cedars.

'Strike a match, somebody,' another voice said.

A match flared, then another. A man holding a match was kneeling beside a shape on the ground. Mr. Munn saw that.

The match flickered quickly out. He moved toward the spot where it had been. They struck more matches, the other men, and leaned over the shape on the ground. Then they managed to make a torch.

The man on the ground, Mr. Munn saw, was Benton Todd. 'Where's he hit?' Mr. Munn demanded.

'Up in the leg,' a man said, 'just in the leg.' He held a clasp knife and was trying to slit the trousers off Benton Todd's leg. The trousers were sodden with blood. Another man was fumbling at the boot, and muttering irritably, 'God damn it, God damn it, can't you get that light closer?' But the man with the torch did not hear, apparently, for he was leaning forward with his gaze fixed on Benton Todd's face.

'It didn't hurt much,' Benton Todd said detachedly. Mr. Munn did not recognize the voice. 'But I didn't know it was going to bleed so much.'

'Don't you worry, boy, don't you worry,' the man cutting off the trousers uttered, 'we'll get it off, we'll get you fixed up in no time. No time a-tall.'

Benton Todd seemed to be paying no attention, now, to the men about him. He was looking upward, beyond the torch and the clustered faces enclosed in that fading bulb of light of which the torch was the center, and beyond the cedar boughs. The torch flame was reflected tinnily in his eyes.

'Gimmie a knife, I can't get it off,' the man at the boot complained peevishly; 'it's all stuck up and I can't get it off.' Another man pushed him aside, and began cutting at the leather. The man who had been working at the boot raised his own hands into the torchlight, covered with blood and muck, and with an expression of distrust and solicitude inspected them, as though they, too, were wounded.

'I think——' Benton Todd said, somewhat tiredly, not looking at the men, 'you better try to stop it.'

They were putting a belt around the wounded thigh, which

was now naked. The blood welled out of the small puncture there, and flowed darkly, but glintingly, over the white flesh. They drew the belt as tight as possible, and they packed handkerchiefs on top, and under the wound beneath, where the bullet had entered. Two of the men had taken off their shirts and were tearing them into strips. The handkerchiefs soaked up the blood, soggily.

'Bent, Bent,' Mr. Munn called, leaning. 'Hey, Bent! Listen here——'

Laboriously, Benton Todd directed his gaze upon Mr. Munn. Then Benton Todd moved his lips, dully. 'That blood,' he said, 'it came out of me.'

Mr. Munn could not remember what he had intended to say. Benton Todd's remote, incurious, gnomic gaze withdrew, left him, sought again the darkness of the cedar boughs above.

Benton Todd bled to death while they leaned over him and watched him. They could not stop the blood, which seemed to well prodigally and inexhaustibly from that small aperture.

One of the men held his hand to Benton Todd's chest. He straightened up, and said, 'He's a goner.' He looked at Mr. Munn.

'All right, all right,' Mr. Munn rejoined, as though irritably.

'It'll be tough tiddy for the Captain,' one of the men remarked.

The men crowded around the body, and leaned over it, and peered down at it. The torch was guttering out. For a moment or two no one spoke.

'Tough tiddy,' another man said, then 'and no denying.'

Mr. Munn shook himself as though rousing from a sleep. 'Listen,' he directed, 'some of you all get a buggy. Get the first one you can find. It don't matter whose. And start on toward Captain Todd's place. That left road down at the church will take you across to his pike. We'll catch you.'

'Catch us?' somebody echoed, inquiringly.

'I'll be glad to have as many as want to come with me,' Mr.

Munn offered. 'I'm not ordering anybody, understand. I want those who come of their own free will.'

'You aiming to chase 'em?'

'Cut them off,' Mr. Munn said shortly. 'We can cut them off before they hit town. The road this lane here joins, we can take it, and hit the pike before they make town.'

No one answered, for a moment. Then a voice: 'Dammit, you didn't want to bushwhack 'em back there on the pike when it might-er done some good. Now it won't do no good, and you want-er go and fight.'

'I just want those who come of their own free will,' Mr. Munn answered.

'Durn if you don't beat me,' the voice exclaimed.

'Now,' Mr. Munn added.

'All right,' the voice said fatalistically, 'all right, I'll go.'

Just before the first signs of dawn, Mr. Munn and seven other men lay behind a tumbled stone wall beside the pike, considerably less than a mile out of town, and fired carefully into a mass of mounted men on the pike. The men had been riding slowly along, idly lounging in their saddles and laughing and joking with each other. At the first volley, the mounted men, some thirty of them, broke and fled down the pike toward town. Two bodies were left lying in the middle of the pike. Later, when the panic wore off, the men returned from town and got the bodies of the two dead men. Three other men had been wounded, but not so badly they could not sit their horses.

Mr. Munn, alone, for the other men who had lain behind the stone wall with him had now gone home, overtook the party that was escorting the buggy with the corpse of Benton Todd. He overtook them a few hundred yards south of the entrance to the Todd place. They had had a hard time getting a buggy, they told him, and they asked what had happened.

'We had a little brush with them,' he said.

'Did you all hit any of 'em?' Mr. Allen demanded.

'Yes,' Mr. Munn answered abstractedly, riding alongside the buggy and watching the bare foot, which protruded from the blanket-wrapped bundle propped in the seat, jog uneasily with the motion of the vehicle.

When they got to the gate, Mr. Munn said that he would ride on ahead. The men looked at each other relievedly, but answered nothing. He grasped the pull-rope that worked the gate, and the gate swung open, and he urged his tired mare forward up the slight rise toward the house. Just back of the house, over the woodlot, a saffron light streaked the lowest clouds.

Mr. Munn leaned against the doorpost, and knocked. The mare stood in the yard, her forefeet wide apart, and her head drooping. He looked at her, and waited for the sound of steps within. His clothes felt like lead weighing upon his shoulders.

Captain Todd, wearing trousers and a coat, which he held together under his chin with one hand, stood in the open doorway and looked at him.

'Benton,' Mr. Munn managed. Then: 'Benton, he——'

'He isn't staying here,' Captain Todd said. 'He hasn't been staying here for several weeks. I can't precisely say where you'd find him——' His gaze passed beyond Mr. Munn. Then, slowly, he fixed his eyes upon Mr. Munn's face, and as he stared, his head twitched, almost imperceptibly, from side to side. Mr. Munn, with an effort of will, turned, and saw the approaching buggy and the horsemen. He saw them quite clearly in the new light that was rapidly suffusing those pastures and fields and bringing into familiar certainty the features of all the landscape beyond.

Chapter twelve

THE troops came on a special train that reached the Bardsville depot late in the afternoon. For two hours before the arrival, a gradually increasing crowd congested the waiting-rooms and lounged along the platforms of the depot. It was an unusually mild afternoon for even so late in January, and many of the men did not wear overcoats. Those who did wear overcoats let them hang loosely unbuttoned or thrust them jauntily back, and stood on their heels with their hands in the pockets of their trousers. The sun shone brightly, making the double set of tracks along the platform gleam like burnished silver, and flashing on the wings of the white pigeons that wove familiarly back and forth against the blue clarity of the sky or lighted on the gravel beside the platform to peck, with a dignified condescension, at the grains of popcorn which people threw to them. When the children who played along the tracks ran past them, they scarcely noticed, not taking wing, and merely eyed the disturbers.

A child, a little boy of some six or seven, first observed the approaching train. He stood in the middle of the tracks, with his right arm rigidly pointing northward, and screamed, 'The soldiers, the soldiers, the soldiers!' until a woman came and drew him to the platform, and slapped him sharply on both cheeks. She was a pale, thin, poorly dressed woman, and when her son had ceased his screams of excitement and only whimpered, she looked around at the nearest people and said in an explanatory, apologetic tone: 'It looks like he just will get all worked up like that and carry on. It looks like children, the more ——' But her voice trailed off, for no one was listening to her. Everyone was straining to see the train. The other children had congregated on the tracks, staring northward, where the little plume of black smoke hanging above the cut seemed to come no nearer; then, reluctantly, at the sound of the still-distant whistle, they merged into the expectant crowd on the platform.

At last, flecking off steam like spittle, roaring and grinding on the polished steel of the rails, shaking the boards of the platform with the vibrations of its mass, scattering the pigeons in a crazy, tumultuous flock, the locomotive pulled past, and there, drawing to a stop, were the coaches, and within them, pressed to the glass of the windows, those peering, inquisitive faces that seemed, all of them, all alike under the brown, wide-brimmed hats. The train stopped. The conductor descended, somewhat warily, with his eyes fixed on the crowd. Then, as though reassured, he planted his feet firmly, wide apart, on the gravel, and surveyed the faces. But no one was watching him. The people were watching a large, red-faced man, in uniform, who seemed oblivious to them while he descended the steps, as though the descent required infinite care, as though it required all of his energies and attention to trundle down, successfully, that enormous belly, over which the tan cloth was buttoned and buckled to bursting. Just as his foot touched the gravel, and he raised his eyes, blinkingly and unresponsively, toward the people, the small brass band at the far end of the platform drove into the initial strains of 'The Star-Spangled Banner.' Blinkingly, the large man saluted, and the younger man descending behind him paused on the last step and saluted.

As the music exploded on its last note, a man separated himself from the crowd and rushed toward the officer, his hand extended in greeting and his smile exposing the liberal amount of gold among his prominent teeth.

'Major Pottle?' he inquired loudly.

The large man nodded, and said, 'Yes, sir.'

'I'm the mayor,' the other man explained, 'Mayor Alton, to be exact, and I welcome you and your men.' They shook hands, and the mayor, leaning confidentially and insinuatingly toward the large red-faced man, began to talk earnestly into his ear, but in so subdued a tone that the nearest persons in the crowd, no matter how hard they strained, could not understand a word. The major looked straight ahead of him unseeingly, as though he heard nothing and were absorbed in his own inward processes, and slowly blinked his pale blue, protruding eyes.

The men climbed down from the coaches and were formed in company front on the open stretch at the south end of the platform. There were two companies of infantry. The stock cars with the cavalry horses were switched to a siding, and the cavalry men began unloading. All the while the band was playing. The train pulled out; the soldiers remaining on it leaned from the windows and waved back. They were on their way to Morganstown. The next day one of the companies of infantry and a squadron of cavalry from the force at Bardsville were to be marched to French Springs, eleven miles away, where there was no railroad.

Mayor Alton, clutching Major Pottle by the arm, steered him toward a baggage truck at the south end of the platform, the officer's unwieldy bulk moving slowly, but unprotestingly, almost somnambulantly, as though in the grip of a superior will. The mayor, with a kind of creaking and exaggerated nimbleness, clambered onto the baggage truck, and extended a hand to assist Major Pottle. But Major Pottle ignored the hand. He clutched the edge of the truck with both hands, placed one foot on the tongue of the truck, and with his neck reddening above the collar and his pale eyes bulging, heaved himself upward. He rose to his feet asthmatically, and stood beside Mayor Alton, who at that moment extended his arms to still the music, and began to speak.

'Friends and fellow citizens,' he began, 'to say that peace is returned to our distracted community, is today my happiness. If — and I say this with both sadness and pride — my request for military assistance had been granted that sad and fateful morning when we awoke to find in ruins the properties and investments of those great business organizations which, more than any other factor, contribute to the happiness and prosperity of our thriving community; if my judgment had been heeded, if then ——'

'Shut yore mouth 'fore you fall in hit,' a voice called from the crowd.

'If then,' Mr. Alton proceeded, 'my request had been granted, our sister communities, which likewise have suffered from the torch of the accursed vandals ——'

Mr. Christian laid his hand on Mr. Munn's shoulder, and leaned toward his ear. 'By God,' he whispered, 'I do believe that snaggle-toothed bastard is talking about me.'

' — would have been spared the tragic blows that befell them. But now we can see that peace has returned to us. Now the loved ones of those two gallant lads who gave their young lives to avenge the fair name of their city will feel that the sacrifice will not have been offered up in vain. And the man who is bringing us peace now stands beside me. He is Major Pottle. Ladies and gentlemen, I introduce to you Major Pottle, who will say a few words.'

'Old Tub-o'-guts!' a voice yelled from the back of the crowd. 'Let old Tub-o'-guts talk!'

Mr. Alton waved his arms furiously and screamed: 'Get that man, get him! Arrest him!' The two policemen, who had been lounging at the edge of the platform, tried to thrust their way into the crowd, but it was impossible. 'Get him!' Mr. Alton screamed, and waved his arms in the direction of the troops. There the troops stood, motionless, erect, their rifles grounded, the bright sunshine falling upon them. They did not move.

The policemen were swallowed up in the crowd.

All the while Major Pottle gave no sign. He might have been alone, staring owlishly at nothing, puffing his slow breath out between his meaty lips. When the disturbance had subsided, he said that he appreciated the hospitality of Bardsville and he wanted to thank the good people and he was sure he and his men would enjoy their stay in such a fine little city. He stopped speaking suddenly, almost in the middle of a sentence, as though he had merely been thinking aloud and now the thoughts were grinding on, slowly and ponderously, inside his head while he blinked at some object far away beyond the people.

Mr. Alton was gesturing and beckoning to someone in the crowd below him. The crowd wavered and parted there, and Senator Tolliver was assisted to mount the baggage truck. He shook hands with Mr. Alton and with Major Pottle. Mr. Alton thanked Major Pottle for his kind words and said that now he would call for a few appropriate remarks from a distinguished citizen who in the recent distressing situation had, as always, taken a firm stand in favor of law and truth and right.

'The skunk,' Mr. Christian said, scarcely bothering to whisper.

Mr. Alton waved his arm in the direction of the Senator.

'Which one?' Mr. Munn demanded.

'Take your pick,' Mr. Christian replied glumly.

Senator Tolliver was speaking, but Mr. Munn hardly attended to what he was saying. He was, instead, comparing that man who now stood there on the baggage truck, somewhat stooped, sallow, graying splotchily, with the man who had stood on the platform, under the bright bunting and the brilliant sunshine, that day of the first rally. When Senator Tolliver had first got up there on the baggage truck, Mr. Munn had felt, looking at him, the firmness of the hatred within himself. With relish, he had been aware of it, it was still there, strong and solid and sure within, something he could depend on and cling to, something real, the same thing which he had held in his mind, cherishingly, on waking at night, as one fingers a token or a keepsake, which is nothing in itself, but which means the reality of one's past, the truth of one's feelings, the fact of one's identity. The hatred was there now, perfect and safe within, something to hold to.

For a moment or two the Senator's voice would rise, full and sonorous and compelling as it had been that August afternoon; then it would falter. He was afraid. Mr. Munn, looking at him, was sure he was afraid. He could no longer look out over the massed faces and master them. Instead, he cringed before them, fawning for a momentary favor, grateful, and showing that he was grateful, for a respite. Or he was, an instant later, suspicious of them, and almost sullen, anxious to be done and gone. Or he tried to bully them. Or worse — and Mr. Munn was almost embarrassed as he listened — he tried to vindicate himself, saying he had always followed the best interest, or what he took to be the best interest, of his section as his guiding star, that if he had made mistakes, the mistakes had come from loyalty and zeal — that he wished to be understood, and to be clear before all men. Clear in my office, he said.

'You ain't got no office!' somebody yelled.

The crowd was restless. Feet scraped on the boards and on the gravel. My God, Mr. Munn thought, he's not the same man, it's a different man. The crowd was stirring uneasily. And I, Mr. Munn thought suddenly, with a shocking clarity, not hearing that voice nor noticing the people, I'm not the same man.

He hung poised on the brink of that thought, as on the brink of a blackness. It seemed to draw him, intoxicatingly, as with a new surety. But slowly, with an effort of will almost, he recoiled from its fascination. He forced himself to look at the objects about him. At the back of the man's head in front of him, at Mr. Christian's flushed, heavy-jowled face, now sullen and brooding. And to listen to that voice. To its cringing, its fawning, its bullying, its lying, its hopelessness, its fear. All of those things were in the voice, and in the sallow face and stooped shoulders and nervous gestures.

The crowd wavered, while that voice went on. The crowd wavered, and to the man leaning over it, talking to it hurriedly and uncertainly, it must have been like the earth along some precipitous trail, the earth, usually so firm and comfortable, that under the frightened foot stirs treacherously, twitching like the hide of a somnolent beast that may wake to leap. Like the beast or like the landslide. Both were there, Mr. Munn felt, in the crowd.

The Senator was saying: '— and I say this to you, my friends, for you are my friends, and I count no higher privilege than the privilege of saying to this body of people now before me, you are my friends — I say this to you, my friends ——' Mr. Munn thought: He has no friends, not even the people who bought him out, body and soul, lock, stock, and barrel. Nobody up there in that big house now. Not those people from Louisville and Washington, any more. Just a few slimy, lickspittle suck-tails who would hang round saying, yes, Senator — yes, sir, Senator, for a couple of drinks and a ten-cent cigar.

'— there is no finer thing than friendship, friendship and loyalty, loyalty to one's friends, loyalty to one's ideals. When I am dead — but I hope and trust our Almighty Father to grant me further years of service to the people of my section — open my heart, and in the words of the poet, you will find graven upon it ——'

The bastard, Mr. Munn thought. Then, the poor bastard.

That night, the night following the afternoon of the arrival of the troops at Bardsville, the two warehouses at French Springs were dynamited and burned, and the long, old, wooden-covered bridge over the river there was dynamited. Some people said that it had been mined to be blown up when the troops came over the next day from Bardsville, and that the explosion that night was an accident. They said it was God's providence, saving the lives of all those soldiers, and a lot of them not much older than schoolboys, and hog-friendly if you'd let them.

The bridge had not been mined. It was blown up by ten sticks of dynamite, two packages of five sticks each, attached to the lower part of the central stone pier. At the blast the pier had toppled over, the old stonework disintegrating into a heap of rubble, about which the waters, when the last echoes had died away between the high banks, lapped lullingly. The wooden superstructure, as it lay crumpled up on its side, had been fired. It burned slowly, but to the water's edge, like an abandoned hulk, no longer seaworthy. But while the men had been out in a skiff preparing to affix the two charges of dynamite to the pier, Doctor MacDonald, on horseback at a gap in the timber and heavy growth that lined the steep banks, had looked down at the undulating blackness of the water and at the long, poised, undifferentiated mass of the bridge stretching across to be lost in the darkness of the farther bank, and had musingly said, 'It wouldn't be hard, you know, to figure out some way.'

'Some way to do what?' a man had demanded.

'To do it when they were coming over,' Doctor MacDonald had answered, still musingly. 'A man could figure it out, all right.'

No one had answered.

'I wasn't really suggesting anything,' Doctor MacDonald had said, and had laughed once, briefly, in the darkness. 'I was just sorter figuring.'

Looking down the bank, Mr. Munn had thought, yes, and there's good cover along here. It got so a man's mind ran that way.

The roar of the explosion up at the settlement a half-mile away had come. The men from the skiff had clambered up the bank. Doctor MacDonald and the others had lifted their reins. With a boom, and a sound of grinding that filled the air, the bridge had heaved upward, and over. It had not taken more than a couple of minutes to fire the superstructure. Behind them, slowly, the flames had mounted as they galloped up the pike.

That night, also, Monclair, the home of Senator Tolliver, was burned to the ground. The men who fired it were unknown. When Doctor MacDonald heard the news by telephone the next morning, his surprise was complete. Deliberately, he replaced the receiver upon its hook, but as he turned from the instrument, his face was drawn and white with fury, and his hands, hanging from the corded wrists, clenched and unclenched.

Monclair was the first dwelling-house to be burned. The Munn place was the second. Despite the threatening letters which he had received and which Mr. Murdock and Mr. Sills had received, Mr. Munn had not anticipated the act. Others, he guessed, had also received such letters and had said nothing about them. He had never mentioned the letters which he himself had received. Not a week before that night at Professor Ball's academy, the night when Doctor MacDonald read aloud the letter to Mr. Murdock, Mr. Munn had received such a letter. That letter had directed him to take no negro tenants for the coming year. Sitting in his office, at his desk, he had read the scrawled words. The paper was torn and dirty, a scrap of wrapping paper, apparently. The writing was smeared, as though the paper had been carried loose in a pocket. The letter had been mailed, the postmark indicated, from Morganstown. Sitting there, Mr. Munn had, for a moment, tried to visualize the man who might have written the letter: a man gripping the cracked stub of a penny pencil, hunching over a kitchen table under a tin lamp, twisting his face in the painful and awkward concentration. But he had not been able to visualize that face, a face, he had been sure, like so many of those faces which he might see on the street on a Saturday afternoon, long, bony, red like dried clay, or sallow, a face like faces which he had seen staring up at him at the organization meetings of the Association. It had been, in his imagination, like all those faces. But he had not been able to fix it and be sure of it, for the true face would not be like any other face; it would be different from all those other faces, individual, positive, unique, full of its own life, its own cunning, its own hope, bitterness, appetite, and hatred. Slowly, he had torn the sheet of paper into small bits, and had dropped them into the basket beside his desk.

The third and last letter he found in the mailbox at his farm. It read: 'We done told you twict to throw them niggers off yore place and put some white min on like we said and you aint done it. Instid you go and git shet of a white man which is named Grimes and put on a nigger in his place. We give you thre days to git shet of them black bastuds.' Mr. Munn read the letter, straining to make it out in the failing light, and then looked up the long drive across the meadow to the grove where the house was. The grove, except for the dark masses of the cedars, was leafless now, and the upper part of the house was visible.

For five nights he slept with a loaded rifle propped at the head of the bed. At first he considered getting one of the men to come up and stay at the house with him, one of them who had been on the place a long time, one he could depend on, but he dismissed the idea. It wasn't their trouble, he decided; and decided that, after all, nobody would bother him, that the letters were a meaningless threat. He did, however, put one of the dogs in the house each night, giving it the run of the front hall, the back hall, and the kitchen, for if anybody tried to fire the house he would probably begin with the porches, the only wooden parts exposed. The dog inside would certainly notice any prowler who got that close to the house, even if the dog outside were disposed of before giving an alarm.

During those five nights Mr. Munn would wake, thinking that a sound had disturbed him. He would take the rifle and creep to a window to peer out over the dark-dappled yard, where the trees were, toward the open ground of the meadow. There would be nothing, or nothing but those sounds which were so much a part of the night that they were nothing. Then he would go back and climb into the big bed, and try to go to sleep. He could not go back to sleep readily, no matter how tired he had been upon first getting to bed. Things would come to his mind, faces and speculations and events from the past that crowded through his head with a clamorous and independent vigor above his will, crowding devouringly and aimlessly like a mob breaking at last into a locked mansion. Those things, it seemed to him, must go on and on living their independent realities over and over, forever in new combinations and couplings and with new variations. They must go incessantly on like the distracted water of the sea, shifting and retreating and approaching and shattering itself and rejoining, while he slept or while his attention was torn from them by the demands of the day. He would think of May. He rarely thought of her when he was elsewhere, but here in this room, often. She was part of this room, more of a part of it than he was now; for he had grown away from it; he felt like a stranger in it now except at those unstable moments when the past flooded obliteratingly over the present. Once, upon waking and sitting up in bed, he seemed, by some trick of the light or trick of the mind, to see her there sleeping. How small she had been sleeping, with her life withdrawn deeply within her, small and curled up, like a child almost, and with her pale hair out on the pillow.

The sixth and seventh nights after receiving the last letter of warning, he slept in town at the hotel, for court was in session, and he had a case coming to trial. Both mornings, immediately after getting up, he telephoned his place, but nothing had happened. If they had been going to carry out the threat, he began to feel, they would have done it already. He spent the eighth night at the Christian place. That night his house was burned down.

That night the jangling of the telephone bell over and over drew him from the light doze into which he had fallen. As he tried to decipher the sequence of the rings, Lucille Christian suddenly laid her hand on his shoulder and said, 'Two longs and three shorts, that's our ring.' She sat up in bed.

'Wonder what it is?' he said.

'Be quiet,' she ordered. 'Papa's getting up.'

Motionless, they listened to the sounds in the next room, the sudden rasping of a chair on the floor, then steps, and the creaking of a door.

'I better try to get back,' she whispered to Mr. Munn. Her fingers were tight on his shoulder, pressing into the flesh.

'Wait till he gets downstairs,' he said.

'The telephone's just at the foot of the steps,' she answered. 'If he's looking this way he'll see me.'

She slipped out of bed, put on her kimono, and hurriedly tied the big sash. Leaning toward the door, she said, 'He's talking now, I can hear him.'

Mr. Munn got out of bed.

Then, there was the heavy sound of Mr. Christian's feet hurrying up the stairs, and his voice calling, 'Perse! Perse!'

The girl stood rigidly in the middle of the room, then she motioned toward the door. 'Go to the door,' she ordered, 'stop him. I can't get out,' and she darted toward the corner of the room between the door and the windows, and flattened herself there against the wall in the deepest shadow. Mr. Munn, moving toward the door, caught a glimpse of her face, a whiteness there in the corner, but he could not make out its expression.

Mr. Christian was beating on the door and calling, 'Perse! Perse!'

Mr. Munn opened the door.

'The telephone,' Mr. Christian exclaimed, 'they want you on the telephone, your house, they say ——'

Mr. Munn seized Mr. Christian by the arm and drew him into

the hall. 'All right,' he said, and ran down the stairs toward the telephone. Mr. Christian stood at the head of the stairs looking down at him. With his eyes fixed on Mr. Christian's figure there above him, Mr. Munn picked up the dangling receiver, and spoke into the telephone. 'Yes?' he demanded.

It was one of the negroes from his place, breathless and gasping as from running and incoherent with excitement. The house, the negro managed to say, was burning up. It was almost gone now. He had run as hard as he could over to Mr. Goodwood's place to call up. But the house was about gone.

He ran into his room, seized his clothes and boots, and came back to the door to block Mr. Christian just at the sill. Out of the corner of his eye he had caught sight of Lucille Christian still pressed against the wall in her corner. He dressed standing there at the doorway, blocking it, while Mr. Christian waited in the hall.

'My house is burning up,' he told Mr. Christian.

'How was it?' Mr. Christian demanded.

'They tried to make me get rid of the negro croppers on my place,' Mr. Munn said. 'I wouldn't do it, so they burned the house down.'

'You want me to come with you?'

'No,' Mr. Munn replied. 'There's nothing you can do. Or me, either, I reckon. But' — and he looked up an instant from lacing his boot — 'let me find out who it was and ——' His voice trailed off. He tied the laces.

'Let me find out,' Mr. Christian said.

Mr. Christian followed him halfway down the stairs. Very loudly, Mr. Munn called, 'You're going to lock up after me, aren't you?' That, he thought, would give Lucille Christian her chance.

'No,' Mr. Christian answered, 'it don't need it.'

As he rode away, Mr. Munn cursed himself for his stupidity in not letting Mr. Christian come with him. That might have made it easy for Lucille Christian. Or again, it might not. Mr. Christian might have wanted to go to her room to tell her he was leaving. Then he thought he should have asked Mr. Christian to saddle his mare for him. That would have worked it. But Mr. Christian would go on back to bed, now. That would fix everything.

It was near sun when he reached his place. The flames had been down for a considerable time, but the heap of smouldering timbers still winked palely in the gathering dawn. One of the cedars nearest the house had caught fire and had burned to a blackened spike from which rose a thin trail of smoke, straight upward. Over at one side a group of negroes were standing about, looking at the ruins. On the other side, two men held the bridles of some saddled horses, and closer to the ruins a group of men stood. They were cavalrymen. The lieutenant who was in charge introduced himself. He was named Prentiss, he said, and he just wanted to find out if Mr. Munn had any idea about the burning and if he had had any threats or anything like that. Mr. Munn said no, there had been no threats, that the whole matter might be an accident. The lieutenant said that that wasn't likely, that it was night riders all right, because one of the negroes had seen three or four men riding off across the meadow, lickety-split.

Mr. Munn shrugged his shoulders. 'I don't know anything about it,' he said.

After a while some of the negroes began to move off. The children had grown sleepy and querulous after their excitement. One child began to cry. Mr. Munn looked at the stuff the negroes had managed to save, only a few pieces of furniture from the downstairs, the sofa, a couple of chairs, a picture off the wall. When the first man had waked up, at the sound of a dog barking, they said, the fire was already coming out the upstairs windows.

A good part of the walls of the house were still standing. The walls toward the corner where his bedroom had been were almost intact. Looking up at them, he thought, aimlessly, of himself and of other people before him sleeping in that room, protected by those walls, cut off by those walls from the weather and the night outside, and the world. Those walls had made a little world inside. That world was gone now. It was gone, liberated and absorbed into the air outside, dissipated in the flame and smoke. He was not sad at the fact. Now that it was a fact, now that the thing was done, it was like something done a long time before, something he had grown used to. He had not realized before, before he stood there to observe the gray ash flake off the smouldering timbers and a last few wisplike flames flutter outward, and then withdraw, how tenuous had grown the threads that tied him to the life, and the lives, that had been in that house.

The young lieutenant came over to stand beside him. 'Tough luck,' the lieutenant remarked, 'losing your house like that.' He looked meditatively at the ruins. 'And a right nice house too, it looks like.' He paused again, then asked, 'Were you raised here?'

'Yes,' Mr. Munn said.

'The crummy bastards,' the lieutenant exclaimed, 'burning a man's house down.'

'I reckon so,' Mr. Munn remarked.

'I'm sorry we didn't get here in time to do any good.'

'Thanks,' Mr. Munn replied.

'We got to be pulling out,' the lieutenant observed. 'Good-bye,' he said, and offered his hand. Mr. Munn shook hands with him. He hadn't noticed the fellow's face before. It struck him as vaguely familiar. 'Good-bye,' he answered.

'I know how you feel,' the lieutenant said. 'You must feel tough.'

The cavalrymen mounted and rode off across the meadow. Mr. Munn watched them go. No, he decided, the lieutenant was wrong. He didn't feel tough. That was not it. There was no word to name it with, exactly.

He went down to Old Mac's cabin, and sat on the chunk of limestone that was the step, while Mac's wife cooked him some breakfast. After a while she called him in and gave him three eggs fried up with some side meat, and some hoecake and coffee. He ate with a good enough appetite. While he ate he remembered how the young lieutenant had reminded him of somebody. He turned that over in his mind. Then he had the answer. The fellow reminded him a little of the way Benton Todd had looked. That was it.

When he got through eating, he rode on back to town. There was nothing else he could do out at his place, and, besides, he had the case coming up. When he got to his office, the girl there said for him to call the Christian place right away, that they had been calling for him all morning. He reckoned that Mr. Christian wanted to get the news about the burning. He had trouble getting on the line, and when he did get on he had to wait a long time before the negro cook out there called somebody to the telephone. Lucille Christian came. Her father, she said when she finally came to the telephone, had had a stroke, and she was afraid he was going to die. The voice that spoke to him out of the black tube which he pressed coldly against his ear was alien to him.

But Mr. Christian did not die — not soon. He lay beneath the high, carved headboard of his bed, inert as a log almost, and without sound except for the dry rasp of his measured and grudging breath. His face, now splotchy in its color, was frozen in a pained and inquiring grimace, and his glance was fixed.

But Mr. Munn did not see him when he went out to the Christian place. He was never to see him again after that night when he left him standing halfway down the stairs, barefooted, his nightshirt wadded into his trousers.

When he got out to the Christian house that next morning, Lucille Christian met him in the hall. Her face was chalk-white, and her eyes, no longer blue, seemed dark and sunken.

'How is he?' Mr. Munn asked.

Looking at him, with her hair falling half loose about her face, she seemed unable to speak.

'How is he?' he repeated.

'It was terrible,' she uttered hoarsely, in a whisper which was as dry and impersonal and alien as the sounds which had come from the telephone receiver.

'Can I see him?' he asked, looking at her, and took a step toward the staircase.

She did not take her gaze from his face, and her right arm, as though with an independent volition, thrust forward at him. The fingers clutched the fabric of his sleeve, twisting it. 'No,' she said. 'No!'

'No?'

The grip tightened on his sleeve.

'It was terrible,' she whispered retardedly, in that voice.

They had quarreled, she finally managed to tell him. Her father had found her. He had come into the room where she was, there was no telling why, but it had seemed as though to look out the front window at Mr. Munn riding off, and he had seen her standing there. She could not remember what he had said. There had been so little time, before it happened. But she could remember his face. She had screamed at him, and his eyes had suddenly popped out and he had opened his mouth like a man trying to call out, but he hadn't made a sound. She had screamed at him: 'No, I'm not yours! I don't belong to you! Or to anybody!'

When she repeated those words now, in a whisper, the tears rose in her dry, starting eyes. Then, slowly, while her strong fingers twisted the cloth of his coat sleeve, she said: 'I said that

to him. I said that. Oh, Perse, that's the way I am inside.'
Then: 'Oh, Perse, you see how I am.'

He tried to put his hands on her, but she withdrew from him.

That night, sitting in his room at the hotel, under the single, hanging, unshaded electric bulb that lighted indifferently the worn carpet at his feet, the dresser with its cold-looking mirror, and the bed, Mr. Munn wrote a letter to May. He was sure, he wrote, that she would agree with him that a divorce was the best thing for them under the existing conditions.

Chapter thirteen

THE pale sunshine washed over the wide boards of the floor, on which Mr. Munn's eyes were fixed. Professor Ball's voice proceeded: '— will sing unto the Lord, for He hath triumphed gloriously: the horse and his rider hath He thrown into the sea. The Lord is my strength and song, and He is become my salvation: He is my God, and I will prepare Him an habitation; my father's God, and I will exalt Him. The Lord is a man of war: the Lord is his name. Pharaoh's chariots and his host——' He held the book in his left hand and his right forefinger traced each line as he read it, pausing at the end of a verse, then moving forward again. He did not lift his glance from the page as he read on through the chapter, but now and then he would close his eyes behind the spectacles, and the forefinger would move on, line by line keeping pace with the uttered words, and the voice would become more emphatic, more rapt. '— the mighty men of Moab, trembling shall take hold upon them; all the inhabitants of Canaan shall melt away. Fear and dread shall fall upon them; by the greatness of Thine arm they shall be as still as a stone; till Thy people pass over, O Lord, till the people pass over, which Thou hast purchased.'

While he read, the five women, his daughters, who sat in the tall, unvarnished, ladder-backed chairs facing him, never took their eyes off his face. All of them sat with the same posture, erectly and easily, their busts carried high, their hands clasped gently in the lap. The four boys, pupils at the academy, had their heels hooked over the bottom rungs of the chairs, and their heads already bowed, as though in preparation for the prayer that was to come. Cautiously, they glanced up now and then, while Professor Ball's voice went on, at the blue sky beyond the windows or at the open door of the dining-room, where the table was already laid. Behind the boys, with Mr. Munn, sat Doctor MacDonald and another man, Doctor MacDonald cocked lankily back in his chair, his brown hands lying on his knees, his face impassive. From under his slightly lowered eyelids, he was regarding his wife. Her back, as she looked up into her father's face, was not quite turned to Doctor MacDonald. The line of her cheek and the small, sober arch of her brow were visible. A streak of sunlight fell across her chestnut hair, which was drawn smoothly back to a knot on the nape of her neck.

Professor Ball shut the book clumsily with his bandaged hands, pushed his spectacles into a firmer position on his thin nose, and laid the book on the mantelshelf behind him. Creakily, without a word, he sank to his knees, placed the palms of his bandaged hands together before his face, and closed his eyes. The skirt of his long, black coat almost brushed the floor about his knees.

The five women, and the others, got to their knees, and bowed their heads.

'O Lord,' the voice of Professor Ball said. It paused; then resumed. 'O Lord, who art above all things, for all Thy blessings we thank Thee. And ask for Thy blessing, though in our sins we are not worthy. But in our unworthiness, we call out unto Thee. Thou hast shown Thy power and cast the horse and his rider into the sea, O Lord, but desert us not. Thou hast brought us over, O Lord, dryshod, but do not let us linger in the wilderness of Shur. Nor taste the waters of Marah, which are bitter, O Lord, and which now we taste. O Lord, as Thou led out Israel to Elim, lead us now, that we may see the twelve wells of water flowing there, and the three score and ten palm trees. Lead us, O Lord, and smite those who would rise against our face.' His voice stopped, and the slow, brittle sound of his breathing was audible in the room. Then, quietly, he said: 'Lord, we thank Thee. Amen.'

He rose, and standing with his hands propped inertly on the high back of a chair, looked away from the people before him, and out the window, where the morning light fell through the bare branches of trees.

The other people began to move about. All of the women except one went into the dining-room. The little boys talked to each other in low voices. Portia Ball, who had lingered behind her sisters, said: 'Breakfast won't be ready for about five minutes. I'll call you all.' Then she followed the other women into the dining-room, and shut the door.

'Let's go outside and get a breath before we eat,' Doctor MacDonald said to Mr. Munn. Mr. Munn nodded, and followed out into the hall, and to the porch. Doctor MacDonald took out his pipe, packed it, and lighted it. He balanced himself with his toes sticking over the edge of the porch and looked out over the slope toward the academy building. The new smoke, bluish and paling against the sky, was wreathing up from one of the two big chimneys there.

Doctor MacDonald took his pipe out of his mouth. 'A lot of praying goes on round here,' he remarked.

Mr. Munn nodded.

'Yeah,' Doctor MacDonald went on, 'that's a fact. I reckon I've worn out a right smart carpet with my knee-caps since I married Cordelia. And me not a churchy man, so to speak. Come down to it' — he took a drag of the pipe, and slowly, with relish, exhaled the smoke — 'short of being an infidel, and just damning my soul outer pure and unadulterated cantankerousness, you might say I go as far as the next man in wrapping myself in carnal concerns. I'm not proud of it, but you know how it is; a lot of things, good and bad, comes closer to a man's hand than praying and reading in the Book, and a man goes his way. And things I've seen done, seen with my own eyes, mind you, looked like something a little different from the workings of God's grace.'

'I reckon everybody sees something like that,' Mr. Munn observed, 'if he lives half his span.'

'Yeah, yeah,' Doctor MacDonald said abstractedly, a hint of impatience in his tone, 'but the things I've seen done. With my own eyes. Before I hit here, and I reckon I've seen my share here, too. It looks like those things and getting down on your knees don't belong in the same world. But take the old Professor, now, he's been putting me on my knees quite a spell, going on two years now.' He grinned, looking directly at Mr. Munn. 'Not that I'm complaining; I had some time to make up in that position. Besides, he's a man for you now, and I respect his ways.'

'It's a comfort to him, I take it,' Mr. Munn rejoined. 'Things going like they are must be hitting him pretty hard.' He paused, then looking off down the slope added glumly, 'I reckon a man could do with some comfort.'

'Well, lately the old man's been asking the Lord for a pretty special brand of comfort. More my variety than you might take his to be,' Doctor MacDonald said. 'It used to be we got the loving-kindness chapters both morning and evening prayers, but lately he's been asking the Lord to mix in pretty direct and smite the Ammonite. He's been giving us the blood-letting texts, breakfast and supper. Like this morning, about the horse and his rider.'

Mr. Munn spat off the edge of the porch, and stared at the spot beneath where the splotch of saliva darkened a dried oak leaf. 'That'd suit me,' he said, 'but there's so God-damned many horses and riders now over at Bardsville, and Morganstown, and all. I'd wear out some carpet with my knees, if I reckoned it'd do any good.'

'Well, it's been the hip-and-thigh stuff pretty regular with the Professor for some time now,' Doctor MacDonald stated. 'Just the front part of the Book.'

At the sound of the door opening, Mr. Munn turned. Cordelia MacDonald had come out. 'It'll be ready in a minute,' she said, 'if you aren't starved to death already.'

'Starved?' Doctor MacDonald echoed, and laughed with pleasure, looking at her. 'Starved is the word for it.'

She approached her husband, and stood beside him, her hand resting lightly on his arm.

Mr. Munn watched the woman's face as she looked up at her husband, who held his arm about her shoulders and laughed in his pleasure and confidence. That look, surprised on the face of the woman — a woman whom Mr. Munn scarcely knew, whom he had scarcely noticed before, who had always seemed rather plain to him — that look stabbed him now, so that abruptly he turned away.

She was a plain woman, or on the plain side, anyway, he had always thought, when he had noticed her on the streets of Bardsville. Walking down the street there, alone or with one of the sisters, she had never seemed to be the sort of woman people would notice much at all. She and her sisters — they all looked alike in their black or gray dresses buttoned up to the throat with that single row of small, severe buttons — had moved decorously down the street, with their eyes fixed on the pavement a little ahead of them, or into the distance, and people had said, now and then: 'There go the Ball girls. Old Professor Ball.' And they told each other: 'He's got some book learning, now I tell you, the Scriptures and in the original tongues, too; and Shakespeare, you just name it. He knows it by heart. Shakespeare, now, he named all his girls with names out of Shakespeare's plays.'

'Yes, sir,' Professor Ball had said to Mr. Munn after breakfast that first day he had ever been at the Ball place, 'I named them all out of Shakespeare's plays. Every last one of them — Portia, Viola, Cordelia, Perdita, Isabella. Noble names, every last one, names a woman could be proud of. That's what I told my wife when the first one came; there's no nobler name than Portia for any female. She wanted to name her Mary Lee. After her own mother. But I pointed out to her all the advantages a girl would have with a name like Portia. Something to live up to. A help in forming a Christian character. She said her mother was a Christian character, and I said, I'm not denying that, she's as fine a Christian character as has been produced locally in my time, but you can't expect imperfect Nature working in one small county to compete with the masterpieces of the immortal bard. She said she hadn't thought of it exactly that way. So we named the infant Portia. And we never regretted it.

'And all the rest of them, when they came along. Noble names, every last one. The youngest, Isabella, now we almost named her Desdemona, but we decided against it at the last minute. But Desdemona's a fine name, and many a man's given his female children worse. But we decided against it. My wife decided me. She was lying there in bed — she never really got up after she had the last one, she just lingered until the Lord saw fit. She was lying there in bed, and I took down the book and read her what Shakespeare had written, trying to make up our minds. Then she pointed something out to me, and I bowed to her perspicacity. She said, now doesn't the book say that man she ran off and married was colored? I said, yes, in a way, you might say he was, but he was a gentleman with a fine character, even if he did have an overhasty disposition. And he was more sinned against than sinning. But, she said did I think it was right to give our baby the name of a young woman who had been connected with a man who was colored, even if the man wasn't exactly a negro? I agreed with her. I said we ought to spare even the tenderest sensibility. So we named the baby Isabella.'

When people saw the Ball sisters walking down the street, they said that you couldn't tell them apart, unless you looked close. But they were different, Mr. Munn decided, very different, despite their deceptive similarities of dress and posture. Portia, the oldest, was already a widow. Her face added to the quietness and gravity of all their faces a sadness, but a sadness disciplined by the will that had marked the firm lines about the mouth; and this sadness was mixed, at moments when she was unaware of eyes upon her, with a faint, though luminous, expectation. She was the most pious of the sisters. She had occasionally said, Doctor MacDonald reported to Mr. Munn, that at the end of her journey all would be consumed in brightness. Meanwhile, she ran the house, directing her sisters in their tasks. She wore a cord of heavy keys at her waistband, the keys of cupboards and pantries and smokehouses. She often sat alone with her father. Viola, who was childless, read a great deal and wrote voluminous letters. Her husband helped on the farm, and she taught the youngest boys in the academy. They were all different — Perdita, Isabella, Cordelia. But, to Mr. Munn, Cordelia especially.

Sometimes Mr. Munn had wondered how a man like Doctor MacDonald had married a woman like Cordelia. Everything about them seemed different. Ordinarily, you would expect to find Doctor MacDonald's wife a very young, pretty, high-spirited woman, very dark or very blonde, positive anyway, and with a streak of fun. The way Doctor MacDonald cocked a cigar or stuck a pipe between his teeth, the way he sat a horse, the relish he took in things, the dash about him, his grin, all of those things would lead you to expect in his wife something different from Cordelia. She was not very young, thirty, perhaps. She had been getting on toward being an old maid when Doctor MacDonald married her, wrapped up in her household tasks, watching the younger men come to see her sisters Perdita and Isabella, sitting at church with her father and Portia, not with Viola and her husband or with Perdita and Isabella, who would be sitting with a couple of their suitors. And she was quiet and grave, like all the sisters. She was, at first glance certainly, plain, with her dark dresses buttoned up to the neck by that careful and forbidding row of buttons, and her eyes downcast, and her hands folded on her lap. But Doctor MacDonald, whose eyes would wander toward her when she sat apart from him, had married her, and Mr. Munn began, finally, to feel that he understood why. She was precisely the one thing Doctor MacDonald, during those mysterious earlier years — about which he never talked except to give some offhand, isolated anecdote, the years in Mississippi, Louisiana, and Mexico — had not had, and now had easily, complacently, and casually. Her qualities, her gravity, her earnestness, her restraint, her downcast eyes — those were the things best designed to challenge him and, in the end, to engage him. She was somewhat like those small dull, compact apples that in the flush of the harvest are passed over almost with scorn, but late in the winter, when the fine, brightly colored fruit has grown too mealy and insipid, can stir the appetite as though in the darkness of the storage cellar they had managed to keep and augment the ripe, full, winey richness of the last sunshine of the summer.

Doctor MacDonald had married her, and the marriage which had at first seemed to Mr. Munn an incongruity began to seem natural and clear. When Doctor MacDonald would talk, his eyes would wander to fix on Cordelia, or on the door through which she had left the room. And sometimes, though rarely, the coolness of her gravity, her reticences, would fall away, and as she looked at Doctor MacDonald, as that morning on the porch before breakfast, she would, for an instant and in a single glance, be exposed in her secret warmth and fullness and steadfastness. When Mr. Munn detected such a look, he would, as that morning on the porch, feel it as a blow, and would turn away. The impact, the stab, of that look was not the pain of a recollected loss. No, it was pain at something which he had never had. He felt cheated, and impotent, and was filled with envy of the other man, to whom, apparently, it had come so easily.

But though Mr. Munn would turn away from that transitory look on her face, he had quickly learned to search for it, to spy on her and wait for it. It was rare and fleeting, but he knew that it would come, sooner or later. He visited the Ball place when he could get time. The demands on him at his own farm were at their slackest now, and since the house had burned, there was no place for him to sleep there except the gear room, where he had rigged up a cot and an old washstand. Besides, he could no longer put his heart into the work there. It was not the discomfort of the draughty, unceiled gear room and the hard cot, or the sight of the blackened ruins of the brickwork, that distressed him. The very fields, the slow voices of the negroes talking to him about the plant beds or the stock or the fencing, their silences, reproached him and withdrew from him. When he was there he felt that his life had no direction and his efforts no meaning. He began to think that he might sell the place if he could, if a time came when land would be worth anything again. He thought that he might sell the place, and go away. But not until things were over, one way or the other.

He went to the Ball place now, as he had gone to the Christian place before. But there was a difference. At the Christian place he had been caught up into a life there; the small night noises, the distant barking of dogs and the creaking of timbers, the shadowy, white door swinging inward and Lucille Christian standing there, with her finger raised to her lips, her whispered conversation. It had been a restricted, distraught, confused, feverish, and undirected life, but a life which was real, and his own. But at the Ball place, he had no life truly his own; he watched the life of others move soberly, and sympathetically, about him, and beyond him.

But that life at the Christian place was over forever. He knew that. From the moment when he had heard Lucille Christian's voice on the telephone that morning after the burning of his house, he had known, although he had been unwilling to acknowledge, that it was over. A few days after Mr. Christian's stroke, he had gone back to see Lucille Christian. They had sat in the dining-room, with a single lamp burning uncertainly on the big table between them, with their shadows, large and possessive and black, on the walls behind them, and had eaten in silence. Once or twice, as by accident, their eyes had met, but uncommunicatively and shortly. They had sat there, still without speaking, after the cook had carried out the dishes and the sound of her activities in the pantry and kitchen had ceased. Finally, looking down at the tablecloth and then off at the shadowy wall beyond her, he had asked her to marry him. When he was free.

'Oh, Perse, Perse,' she had cried, 'why do you have to talk about that? That isn't important. Now.'

Meeting her eyes fully at last, he had said, 'It is important.'

'No.'

'People have to have something to look forward to,' he had told her, looking across the pool of light, as across a distance, at that almost unfamiliar face, 'something to move toward, to hope for. Some direction.'

She had shaken her head, saying: 'We can't know anything, now. We can't do anything. Not anything.' Then, in the silence, for he had made no reply, still with his eyes fixed on her face across the pool of light, she had said, very quietly and distantly: 'I don't feel anything any more. Not anything.'

That night he had slept at the Christian place. He had expected her to come to him. He had watched the door, waiting for the latch to lift stealthily. But it had not moved. He had stood just inside the door, leaning forward with his brow pressed against the slick, cold surface of the painted wood, filled with his angry and despairing desire. Eventually, standing there, he had become aware of a repeated, almost imperceptible sound, a hoarse, dry susurrus, painful and regular. It had seemed to come from beyond the wall to his right. Then, he had identified the sound: it was the sound Mr. Christian made.

At the end of the next week Mr. Munn again went out to the Christian place. That night Lucille Christian came to his room. At the door she stood in the accustomed posture, closing it, with her finger lifted as before. And even at that instant, the gesture, now so ironical and superfluous in the new context, told him more positively than her words had been able to tell him how empty she was, and how arbitrary and automatic and meaningless her actions. But denying that knowledge, he felt for a moment that she was as she had been. But it was only for a moment. She lay in his arms shuddering as though from cold. It was as though the half-playful shivering of those times when she had said, chatteringly, 'Warm my feet, I'll catch pneumonia all for you,' had been a kind of parody, fatuous and grim, of this, the truth.

He tried to comfort her. He told her that he loved her and would love her always. Finally, she succumbed to him.

Then she told him: 'I tried — I tried, Perse. But it's no use.'

He said nothing.

'We can't be with each other any more. Not for a long time, anyway. Or never.'

'I love you,' he said. He thought: love. The word rattled in his head like a pea in a dried pod.

'It's not you,' she answered. 'It's me, the way I am.'

'I love you.'

'We can't be with each other,' she said; 'it's too awful, I can't stand it.'

'All right,' he replied. He knew a loathing, suddenly, of himself for the emptiness of the act he had performed: a vicious and shameful pantomime, isolated from all his life before it and from any other life, cut off in time, drained of all meaning, even the blind, fitful meaning of pleasure. He was infected by her emptiness. Or her emptiness had discovered to him his own. She had held it up to him like a mirror, and in her emptiness he had seen his own. 'All right,' he said.

The next morning she did not come down to breakfast. He ate scarcely anything, hurried out to the stable and saddled his mare, and rode off.

Three days later he received an answer to the letter which he had written to May. But the answer was not from May. It was from Miss Burnham. It ran:

Percy Munn:

Yours of the 4th inst. received. My niece will not consider giving you a divorce. I do not believe in divorce and neither does my niece and she will not consider giving you one. And I can inform you now that you will not be able to get one yourself, for you have not got any grounds for a divorce because our Heavenly Father knows there was never a purer sweeter more dutiful girl and you have no complaint and you drove her from your house like a dog. Also I can tell you too that my niece is going to have a child. I get on my knees every night and pray our Heavenly Father that this unborn child will never know the kind of creature its father is. I will devote my life to raising this child and nurturing it just as I have devoted my life to raising my niece, and I thank our Heavenly Father that it will have in it some of the blood of General Sam Burnham, for you cannot make a silk purse out of a sow's ear, as the saying goes. And I can tell you Percy Munn that you will never speak to this child, you will never lay eyes on it, if I can prevent, so long as there is a breath in my body. So help me God.

Very r'sp'ly yrs,

L. BURNHAM

More and more the room at the hotel became intolerable to him. He would go to bed and close his eyes, but sleep would not come. The walls, the ceiling above him, the floor beneath, seemed to shut him in upon himself, to leave only himself as real, as only the darkness is real when one shuts his eyes. The thought of the other rooms up and down the hall, like this room, and of persons lying within them, sleeping or sleepless and staring, merely validated his own isolation; and validated the isolation of those other persons. The carpet of the room worn by other feet than his, the stained basin into which other hands had been plunged, the bed that had creaked and sagged beneath other bodies, all of those items, and a dozen more, the cold and rigorous and undifferentiating mirror, defined him as separate from those other persons, as locked within himself. Sometimes he would get out of the bed and go to stand at the window to look down, as he had done that night of the first rally. He would stand at the window and his gaze would follow the progress under the pale street-lamps of some unidentified, late walker. Once or twice he felt the impulse to dress and hurry after that unknown person and walk beside him to his destination. For that person would have a destination.

Even though the room had become almost intolerable for him, his practice compelled him to be often in town, and there was no other place for him to stay. He fell into the habit, however, of taking a bottle of whisky up to his room. It helped him to sleep, he thought.

But at the Ball place it was different. The steadiness of the life there, although it was not his life, steadied him. If that spied-on and awaited and rare expression in the eyes of Cordelia when she looked at her husband stabbed him, or if the calm fulfillment on the face of Portia at the moment after her father's prayer when she rose to her feet disturbed him with its alien secret, those things, nevertheless, sustained him. And there was Professor Ball, who had read, 'The Lord is my strength and song'; and Doctor MacDonald.

In Bardsville, the guardsmen camped in the little park across from the railroad station. Day after day Mr. Munn had seen them there. And he had seen them in the evening, on the roads at the edge of town, silently sitting their mounts. They were guarding the town, and people were grateful to them for it. People would go down to watch them parade, or to watch them lounging on the grass in their idle moments. The soldiers hung round the drugstores and poolrooms and saloons, making jokes, swaggering a little. And some of the hangers-on would fawn on them, and make jokes too; only a few would stare insolently at them, not speaking. In the early evening soldiers would walk slowly down the streets with girls beside them. Some of the officers went to dinner in the big brick houses where the warehouse managers and the most successful buyers lived, and Mr. Gay, who owned the Merchants' Bank, and Mayor Alton and Judge Howe. Or the officers helped to drill the men who formed the Home Guard. The town accepted the soldiers; they fell into the life there, scarcely altering the pattern. They were guarding the town. They were saving the town. Their sentinels paced up and down at night or sat their mounts by the roadside. At night they paced up and down alongside the blackened areas where the warehouses had been. In the day workmen were busy on those locations clearing away the débris and digging for foundations. There would be new warehouses.

On good afternoons men would pause on the pavements opposite those blackened areas, leaning against the barriers and peering, men wearing overalls, men with lean, red, rawboned, weathered faces and long mustaches. Or a single rider, booted and black-coated, would draw rein there and stare at the piles of brick and rubbish, at the workmen bent over their occupations, and at the soldiers. Then, such a rider would lift his rein and move slowly off. But those other men would lean at the barriers, singly or in groups, and peer. Sometimes one of them would call to a guard, 'Sojer, whut you a-doen here?' Or,

'Little sojer-boy, you better git home to yore mammy, er she won't have no little sojer-boy.'

'Get on off, get on off,' the guards would say when the watchers came in past the outer barrier. 'Get on off, you can't stop here.'

Sullenly, the watchers would withdraw.

Mr. Munn saw the soldiers at their camp. Sometimes he would pause, when he had occasion to go to the depot, and watch them about their affairs over in the little park. Watching them, he once thought of a time when he had been camping with some boys, a long time back, when he was ten or twelve years old. One of the boys, little Bill Christian, he remembered — and thought of that little girl, almost a baby, who would not come clearly to his mind, who now was Lucille Christian, Lucille Christian, who had laid her finger on his lips and said, 'Hush, hush,' in the dark, who was out there now, in that house with the sound of that rasping breath in the next room — little Bill Christian had had a tent, and the boys had camped in the tent. Across the park, among their little tents, the soldiers laughed and talked.

Or he saw the soldiers on the street, and looked quickly and curiously at their faces, trying to wrench out a secret, as it were, as he had looked at the faces of those people who had come to his office with their troubles, as he had looked at the face of Bunk Trevelyan's wife that first day. He looked at the faces of the soldiers; but the faces told him nothing. One day on the street, he met the young lieutenant who had been in charge of the cavalry detail the night his house burned. The lieutenant recognized him, and nodded friendlily. And once Mr. Munn had occasion to go down Front Street, where the warehouses had been. He saw the blackened ruins, the workmen, the guards, and the men leaning against the barrier. That night of the raid, at the moment of the first blast, when the air had reeled, sodden and swollen with sound, he had felt a release, a certainty. That was of that time, not this. Now, in the light of full afternoon, he watched the picks of the workmen rise and fall, and the indifferent guards.

'The warehouses,' Doctor MacDonald said, 'that don't mean a thing. We want warehouses, don't we? Don't we want somebody to buy our tobacco?' Then he grinned. 'It's what goes in them counts. And' — pausing — 'what gets paid for what goes in them. I don't see why the warehouses make people downhearted. Or I do see — they're blind as bats.'

'I'm not downhearted,' Mr. Munn told him, 'but people are. You can tell.'

'All we need is to keep up membership in the Association. And in the other. Give them meetings, get 'em together and give 'em something to do, something to think about, nurse 'em along. That's all we need. Keep that up ——'

'And money,' Mr. Munn said gloomily. 'There isn't any more advance money, and we haven't got our price yet, the companies feeling so cocky with their soldiers here, and people need money.'

'Money,' Doctor MacDonald replied. 'Sure. But just enough money to eat. Just that. In a pinch just that, and this is a pinch. A man don't need much in a pinch. It'll surprise you, by God. I lived once, six weeks it was, on just a handful of parched corn a day and a jack rabbit or a prairie chicken when I could get one, and me on the move, too. Moving fast,' he added as though by way of parenthesis, and grinned confidentially. 'That was down in Mexico.'

'It'll take more'n parched corn,' Mr. Munn declared, 'and people in debt already.'

'Yeah, yeah; just let anybody start to crack down on mortgages and throw people off their places. God-a-mighty, when the Professor gets me down on my knee-caps these days all I ask the Lord for is to let those bastards start foreclosing mortgages.' He stabbed the air with the stem of his unlit pipe, and his eyes narrowed. 'God-a-mighty, just let them start foreclosing, that's all we need. That'll heat people up.'

'They cracked down on Senator Tolliver,' Mr. Munn observed. 'He was living in the office there on his place, and they've evicted him. He's still got some influence, I reckon, and if they'd evict him, they'd evict anybody.'

'They used him, and they're through. He's a second-hand corncob now, I tell you. And nobody gives a damn. Do you?'

'Do I give a damn?' Mr. Munn echoed. Then he answered, 'No, I don't.'

'You used to be pretty thick with him, and if you don't give a damn now, who do you think does?'

'I don't,' Mr. Munn answered shortly. He remembered the Senator standing there on the baggage truck at the depot, afraid of the crowd, cringing before it, suspicious of it and desperate, and his face sallow and sunken in the afternoon light. 'And nobody does, I reckon,' he added.

'Well, for one, I don't, God knows. And nobody does. That's why they cracked down on him. But if they turned out some God-forsaken little bastard with forty acres and that not good for sassafras, you'd give a damn, and plenty of people would. If they started that.'

'Yes,' Mr. Munn said slowly.

'But they're too smart,' Doctor MacDonald went on. 'They won't do it, because they're too smart. Not now. But just let the Association crack, and won't anybody be a thing but hired hands for the Merchants' Bank and the Alta Company. What we've got to do is keep the Association together. The companies can't last forever without tobacco. They can't keep those soldiers here forever. If they build warehouses, they've got to put something in them.'

'We don't control near half the crop,' Mr. Munn objected.

'Well, tobacco comes out of plant beds,' Doctor MacDonald retorted, 'don't it?'

Mr. Munn looked at him. 'We did it before,' he said. 'I reckon we can do it again.'

'I reckon we can,' Doctor MacDonald agreed, and grinning, his lips curled back from the long teeth.

Doctor MacDonald was like that. He would give that easy, soft laugh, like a man looking out on things from the confidence of his own inner, secret world. Because he was confident and easy in that inner world, he was easy and confident at whatever he set his hand to in the outer world. He would lift his arm in a slow, half-lazy motion to knock out a pipe or to lay his hand on his wife's shoulder, and you could see, below the too-short sleeve of his coat, the tendons slip slickly and strongly, like a piston in oil, beneath the brown skin of his wrist, the slowness, somehow, suggesting the potentiality of speed. Or he would swing himself lankily to his saddle, and turning to speak, would gather the reins as in idleness; but the restive horse would become still as a post. A handful of parched corn, he had said. That was what he had had, down in Mexico, and moving fast. But it had not been the handful of parched corn that sustained him, Mr. Munn somehow felt; not that, for he had been sustained by something else, a nourishment within himself.

Doctor MacDonald was right, Mr. Munn admitted to himself. With luck it could be done, it was possible. If people were like Doctor MacDonald. He wondered how much he himself was like Doctor MacDonald. He, he himself, could take a lot, he was sure. He had taken a lot already. The Association, that was what was left. If they could win. If they didn't win. He did not think beyond that except to think what could there be, for him, beyond that. The Association, that was what he was now, if he was anything. He thought: if I am anything. But Doctor MacDonald — let the Association go to pot, let everything, and Doctor MacDonald would still be himself. You could guess that.

Doctor MacDonald did not change. At the meetings with the captains and commanders, or meetings held for a few bands of the men, meetings held in empty barns or in farmhouses with the windows shuttered and a single lamp turned down low and the men half-listening for a warning from the watchmen down the road and in the woods, Doctor MacDonald could still lean toward them, casually, as he had at first, and talk easily and confidentially. The way he must talk to a woman whose husband was sick, or whose child, Mr. Munn once thought. And the men would gradually relax, and listen to him, and when they spoke their own voices would sound natural again and their postures would lose that impression of a crouching, anticipatory strain. Even after the night when the troops tried to raid a meeting, and would have succeeded except for the watchmen, Doctor MacDonald did not change. Some of the people, Mr. Sills and Mr. Burden, urged him not to have another meeting after that, not until things quieted down. 'No,' Doctor MacDonald said, 'now's the time,' in the voice of a man saying it's time for dinner, or time to lock up for the night. At the next meeting, he knocked out his pipe, and observed: 'Well, gentlemen, they almost bagged us. And I reckon we all know why.' Half-amusedly, he looked about him, from face to face. Then he added, as though in afterthought: 'Somebody let it slip. Somebody just let it slip. All we've got to do' — and he hesitated, and the men looked at each other, almost furtively — 'is to find out who it was. Because,' he said gently, 'he might just let it slip again.' And he grinned, and stuck his hands into his pockets.

Only once did Mr. Munn see a change in him. It was on a gusty Sunday morning. A man who lived down the pike from the Ball place rode up to the gate, dismounted, and approached the house. Doctor MacDonald, watching him walk up the rise toward the house, said idly, 'There comes Parsons; wonder what he wants.' Parsons had come to deliver a message. Mr. Sills had been trying to get the Ball place on the telephone, he said, but the line was down. Coming up, he had seen an old gum tree fallen across the line down the pike a piece. It was so rotten it was ready to come down if you looked hard at it, anyway. But Mr. Sills thought Doctor MacDonald ought to know that a gang of men had taken out a Mr. Elkins over near Bardsville the night before and whipped him with a whip. The men had beat on the door and told Mr. Elkins to come out or they would put dynamite under the house, and he had come on out because he was afraid for his wife and family. They whipped him, then they got the wife and children out and dynamited the house anyway. They just hurt one wing of the house, though, Mr. Parsons said. Nobody knew exactly why they did it.

'It don't matter why,' Doctor MacDonald interrupted, and rose from his chair and strode to the hearth.

'One of them said it was because Mr. Elkins didn't fire his nigger tenants,' Mr. Parsons said, 'and then again some of them said it was because he wasn't in the Association. But they was all drinking hard, it looks like, saying one thing and another.'

'It don't matter why,' Doctor MacDonald declared. His long face was pale with the fury that was growing in him. 'It just matters who. By God, if I just knew who!'

'Mr. Elkins was an anti-Association man,' Mr. Parsons observed, as though in placation.

Doctor MacDonald wheeled at him. 'I don't care if he was president of the Alta Company; I don't care if he's anti or not. They did it without authority. If they're Association people did it, they did it without authority. If they're not Association——' He paused, his hands clenching and unclenching about the pipe he held.

'They're not Association,' Professor Ball said; 'they're not our people.'

The stem of the pipe in Doctor MacDonald's hands snapped. He flung the thing into the fire, turned on his heel, and went out the door without a word.

Our people, Mr. Munn thought. Then asked, 'Our people, who are they?'

'It was that fellow Lew Smullin phoning saved me,' Doctor MacDonald said. 'But by the barest. Yes, sir, there wasn't a minute to spare. It was getting on toward sundown, but nearer dark than you might expect for the time it was — it'd been raining off and on all day and still overcast, and promising to drizzle — and that was luck, too, I reckon. I'd just got in from making my rounds and was getting dried out in front of the fire, when the telephone rang and Viola answered it and said it was for me. It was that fellow Smullin. He just said, right fast and near a whisper, This is Smullin, Smullin, over at the courthouse, they got a warrant out for you and they're coming, with soldiers; they been gone quite a spell. Then he hung up, quick, before I really caught on what he was saying. By that time Portia and my wife'd come in, and I told them not to get excited, but the soldiers were coming to arrest me, and I was going to get my horse and get out the back way by the old road they used to get timber out by. You'll have to hand it to those girls now; they didn't do any cutting-up. They didn't say a word. Cordelia went sort of white, and took hold of the back of a chair with one hand. Then she said, All right, I'll go down to the stable with you while you saddle up.

'But Portia said no, that wasn't the thing to do. That they'd be watching the back, if they had any sense. And I said, well, the Lord knows they'll be watching the front if they're here, and I'd take my chances. She didn't answer me, just looked out the window. Then she said to Viola, just like she was telling her to do something round the house — Portia, she's boss in the house here — she said, Viola, get me the bandage box. Viola let her jaw drop and looked at Portia for a second, and I guess my jaw dropped some too at her asking for the bandage box. But Portia said, Viola, this is no time to delay. And Viola ran off. Then

Portia said, Cordelia, you go to the stable, quick, and saddle up papa's horse. I said no, I'd saddle up and I didn't want the Professor's horse, I wanted my own. You know that old gray horse the Professor rides round is so fat it can't go better'n a walk. But she grabbed my arm, and said to Cordelia, go on, do it. And said to me, pull off your coat, quick. Look here, I said to her, who's this warrant for, you or me? I'm going to get my horse. Then she said, Take off your coat, Hugh, so we can bandage up your hands. I burst right out laughing. For a fact. Then they just bandaged me up, like the Professor. And they got one of the Professor's old long, black coats and I put it on — both of us being tall and spare-made — and one of his old black hats that flop down. Then we went down to the stable, where Cordelia had his old gray horse saddled up. Soon as I got on, Portia said, Turn your coat collar up, and hang your head down like papa when he's riding along thinking, and they can't see you haven't got a beard.

'Well, I met them down the road a piece. Not a long piece, either. About a half-dozen of soldiers, and two or three deputies, I reckon. I just lifted up my hand the way the Professor does when he meets somebody on the road, and prayed the Old Marster'd make those bastards notice the bandages and all. Well, they did. One of the deputies said, Good evening, Professor Ball, and I rode on with my chin dug down in my breastbone so hard it hurt, just like I was the Professor busy thinking.

'I went on over to the Campbell place and spent the night. They almost busted a hame laughing when they got a good look at me, too. But it was just as well, Portia figured it out. I couldn't got out that old back road if I'd tried. There was soldiers out there, too. Those soldiers I met on the road wasn't but half of them, the others coming round on the old road and scattering out back. They'd a-picked me up, sure. You'll have to hand it to Portia, now. She's a smart one.'

'Yes,' Mr. Munn said, 'a smart one.'

'But I reckon it's going to be laying low a spell for me,' Doctor MacDonald said, 'like I been doing for more'n ten days now. I been spelling round in different people's houses, the Campbells and Donelsons and Nelsons most, but not a night or two at a place in succession. — Night, did I say night? I been doing most of my sleeping in the daytime, and up half the night tending to my patients. Looks like it comes a spell of wet weather and the roads mire up or a fellow gets in a fix like this or one way or another, and everybody in the damned county goes and gets down sick and wants you to doctor them. Cordelia or some of them gets the calls at the house and they pass them on to me——'

'They'll hook you,' Mr. Munn said fatalistically, 'if you aren't careful. They'll hook you on a fake call.'

'Play sick to hook me,' Doctor MacDonald retorted, 'and I'll make somebody sick. I'll take him apart unless God-a-mighty's got a new way patented for putting a man's parts together. I'll take him apart like a clock.' He seemed pleased with himself, smiling. Then, soberly, he added: 'What I can't figure is why they up all at once and try to get me. They been round here quite a spell now, and they just suddenly up and try to get me.'

'I'll tell you,' Mr. Munn said. 'They figure they got some evidence now that'll stand up in a court of law. I don't know what it is, but that's it. They think their evidence'll stand up.'

'They got next to somebody.'

'Sure,' Mr. Munn agreed. 'Somebody.'

'They never would've known to lay for the boys at Fulton's plant bed if they hadn't got next to somebody. And get Turpin and Mosely.' He shrugged. 'Anyway, I'm glad it's Turpin and Mosely sitting over there in the jail-house, and not me.'

'They won't give them bail,' Mr. Munn said.

'Well, you can be durned sure, then, they wouldn't give me bail if they got me. But they won't get me. I don't like to be indoors so much. Just let me sit round the house a couple of days and I need calomel, damned if I don't. I'll just stay outer their way till they get tired and call off the dogs.'

'If they've got evidence, they won't get tired soon.'

'Neither will I,' Doctor MacDonald said cheerfully, 'long as folks'll put up with all the visiting round I been doing lately.'

'They won't get tired,' Mr. Munn replied slowly, 'unless——'

'Unless what?'

'Unless the Association'll play ball. Make a deal.'

'Which it won't do,' Doctor MacDonald said.

'Unless,' Mr. Munn remarked quietly, 'they catch you. Then they'll try to force a deal by putting the pressure on you. On whoever else they can get. Me, for instance.'

'They won't catch me,' Doctor MacDonald announced. 'It ain't in them.' He lay back at ease, propped on his elbow on the bed, and the smoke curled comfortably up from his pipe. His boots, damp and stained with half-dried mud, stood by the bed. He wriggled his toes in his heavy wool socks, and complacently studied their motion. 'Another thing I can't figure,' he said, 'is Smullin calling me up and telling me about the warrant. Never saw the man half a dozen times in my life. Never said more'n howdy-do then.'

'I've seen him a lot, being round the courthouse the way I am,' Mr. Munn said, 'but I can't say I know him, exactly. Nobody does. He never says a thing. Just hangs round a bunch of men, on the edge; one of those fellows — you know the kind — they hang round on the edge and never say a thing.'

'He's sure a God-forsaken, broken-down-looking old bastard.'

'He's that,' Mr. Munn agreed.

'Well, I can't figure out him calling up. You'd figure him sucking along with the gang at the courthouse. And all they want is to keep on warming chairs with their fat asses.'

'Maybe,' Mr. Munn said meditatively — 'maybe he just didn't want to see you get caught.'

'Hell,' Doctor MacDonald exclaimed, 'he ain't a farmer, what does he care?'

'Maybe he just cared,' Mr. Munn answered. 'Maybe he's a damned fool.'

'Damned fool is right.' Doctor MacDonald laughed. He flexed his long legs, rumpling the patchwork quilt on which he lay. 'I reckon he was taking a chance on his job, calling me.'

'Yes,' Mr. Munn said, 'he was.' Yes, he thought. All those years dragging his club foot round town, trying to sell a little life insurance or hail insurance or fire insurance to people. Hanging round groups of men at the post office or the depot or on the street corner, trying to get up nerve to say to somebody, 'I wonder if you'd be interested in some insurance, now I was just wondering——' And then stopping, waiting for the man to answer, 'No.' And going home at night to the little house at the edge of town. Nobody else had been in that house, not for years, not since his old mother, Mrs. Smullin, died, people said. Going home, and lighting a lamp and pulling down all the shades, and eating something off the kitchen table. Something he'd bought and taken home in a paper sack. All that before getting the job, God knew how, at the courthouse. Now he could sit round there in the afternoons and evenings, listening to the men talk. He didn't have to try to work himself up to say, 'I wonder if you'd be interested, I was just wondering——' He could just hang round and listen, and not worry. Except for being a damned fool, and making that telephone call.

'He came mighty near waiting too long; another five minutes and they'd have had me,' Doctor MacDonald was saying.

'Yes,' Mr. Munn rejoined.

'A miss is as good as a mile, though,' Doctor MacDonald said. 'Yes.'

'I hope he don't lose his job,' Doctor MacDonald remarked. Then: 'He sure didn't stand to gain anything. The poor old fool.'

Mr. Munn studied him. 'There're a lot of fools,' he observed. 'You,' he said slowly, 'for instance. You're a fool. What did you stand to gain? All you stood to gain was to have to hide out to keep from jail.'

'Or the rope,' Doctor MacDonald answered, 'if the bastards can play it their way.'

'We're all damned fools. A lot of us, anyway.'

'People are damned fools in different ways. They got different stuff in them.'

'You can't figure out Smullin,' Mr. Munn told him. 'Well, I can't figure you out.'

'Neither can I,' Doctor MacDonald returned amiably. 'Been trying for years. But I can't do it.' He leaned back comfortably, shoving the pillow.

'I can't figure myself out,' Mr. Munn said, 'sometimes.'

Doctor MacDonald let the smoke drift easily from his nostrils. He glanced up at the low ceiling, as though in reflection; then about the room, letting his eyes rest upon the steady flame of the lamp on the dresser, and then, casually, upon Mr. Munn's face. 'I reckon a man goes his gait,' he said, and yawned.

They said nothing for a time. Then Doctor MacDonald swung his legs off the bed and rose. He said that he had to go out and see one of his patients, and that he'd be back some before day. Sitting on the edge of the bed, he pulled on his boots. Then he went across to the dresser and peered at himself in the mirror. He ran a comb through his bushy hair, yawned once, and stretched his arms above his head, almost touching the low ceiling, filling the room, making his shadow on the wall behind him look like a big, awkward bird. Then he said, 'So long,' and went out the door.

Mr. Munn slept there at the Campbells'. He scarcely woke up when Doctor MacDonald came in. In the morning, Mr. Munn dressed as quietly as possible in order not to wake him. He was sprawled out on his side of the bed, snoring gently, with his long, bony head thrust into the pillow and one big hand grasping the bedpost, as though sleep itself were not a passivity, but was at its secret core, when all the accidents of softness and ease had been stripped away, an act of will and tension.

Mr. Munn managed to get out without waking him. He did not see him again until the night the troops came again to the Ball place for him.

They tried to circle the house and to close in, slowly, on foot; but the dogs scented them. The dogs barked wildly and throatily, rushing away from the house, filling the woods to the west of the house with a distant, hollow clamor, vibrant as in a cave.

'It don't sound very encouraging,' Doctor MacDonald remarked. He leaned forward in his chair, drawing his legs under him, easily but as though in readiness to rise.

Mr. Munn said nothing. He was listening to the dogs. One of them was circling, swinging back.

'Durn it,' Doctor MacDonald exclaimed, almost peevishly, 'can't they leave a man alone? And this the second night I been home in three weeks.'

The door to the next room swung softly open. Cordelia stood there. Her hand was on the knob, and she did not move. She said nothing. Behind her, seated around a lamp, were the others, with their heads lifted to listen.

'Maybe it's not that,' Mr. Munn suggested. But the barking was closer, and circling.

'Durn,' Doctor MacDonald said, and stood upright from the chair in a sudden motion.

The dogs were retreating toward the house. Their barking was furious, deep-throated, incessant.

Professor Ball stood behind Cordelia at the door.

'Come here,' Doctor MacDonald commanded, and Cordelia came to him. She laid her hand on his arm.

'Don't get excited,' he told her.

The others crowded into the room.

'Do those kids know I'm here?' Doctor MacDonald demanded.

'No,' Portia said, 'they don't know.'

The dogs were near now.

'If it is anything, I can't get out now,' Doctor MacDonald asserted. 'They're all round.'

The others looked at each other, not speaking; except Cordelia, whose eyes were on Doctor MacDonald's face.

'I'll try the loft,' Doctor MacDonald said.

Professor Ball moved toward the hall door, Portia by his side.

'No,' Doctor MacDonald ordered. 'Sit down. Go sit down like you were.' They stood and looked at him. 'Like you were,' he said sharply. 'Be talking, or something. I'll get in the loft and pull the ladder up after me.' Almost casually, he removed Cordelia's hand from his sleeve, then turned and was at the hall door in three abrupt, plunging strides.

They heard his feet heavy on the bare boards of the stairs.

'Where's Isabella?' Portia suddenly demanded.

No one answered, each looking questioningly at the others.

Portia started toward the hall door. 'I'll get her,' she said.

'Sit down,' Professor Ball directed. 'It's too late. Sit down, like he said.' He laid an arm around Cordelia's shoulders, then withdrew it. 'Go sit down,' he repeated, 'in yonder.' He raised his right hand and, clumsily because of the knobby bandages, plucked at his beard.

On the porch, one of the dogs barked frenziedly. There was a pounding at the door.

The women had gone into the next room.

'Sit down,' Professor Ball ordered Mr. Munn, and moved toward the hall, slowly.

Mr. Munn let himself down, almost warily, into his chair.

He heard the voices in the hall, Professor Ball saying: 'Good evening. What can I do for you?' and another voice: 'We've come for Doctor MacDonald. Where is he?'

He heard Professor Ball's voice answer: 'Come in, gentlemen, but I can't oblige you. He is not here.'

'That won't do any good,' the other voice answered. 'We had word. He's here.'

'He's not here,' Professor Ball's voice repeated.

By an effort of will, painfully, Mr. Munn conquered his impulse to rise from the chair.

'He can't get out,' the voice said. 'There's men all round.'

The door from the hall swung fully open and a man in uniform stood there. Other men were behind him.

Looking at the man, Mr. Munn thought: I can stand up now, I can stand up, it's the natural thing to do now. He stood up and looked at the man.

'All right,' the man at the door said back over his shoulder, to Professor Ball, 'we'll search the house. If you want it that way, you can have it.' He stepped into the room. 'Who are you?' he demanded of Mr. Munn.

'My name's Munn,' Mr. Munn said, and heard his voice natural and even.

'What are you doing here?'

'Do you have a warrant for me?'

'No,' the man replied.

'All right, then, it's none of your concern.'

'Well, we will have 'fore long' — a chunky man with a pock-marked face stepped up even with the officer, and nodded toward Mr. Munn. 'You're Percy Munn, I know you. You're one of 'em, too. They'll be gitten a warrant for you, all right.'

'I reckon you're a deputy,' Mr. Munn said, and looked at the man.

'Yeah,' the man admitted.

'Well,' Mr. Munn declared judicially, 'I'm glad to see the deputies they got over here in Hunter County are as big sons-of-bitches as the deputies we got over at Bardsville.'

'I'll ——' The chunky man raised his clenched fist, as though for a blow, and took a step toward Mr. Munn.

'You better be trying to get what you came for,' the lieutenant said shortly.

The chunky man lowered his fist. 'What's in there?' he demanded, and nodded toward the closed door across the room.

Mr. Munn did not answer.

'My daughters are in there,' Professor Ball, standing at the hall door, told him.

'Well, I reckon they ain't turned in yet,' the deputy said, and crossed to jerk open the door.

The women there, faces raised as though in surprise, were sitting about the lamp, their sewing on their knees.

'I suppose,' Mr. Munn remarked to the officer, 'they have to pay you good money to make you get caught out with that' — and with a nod he indicated the chunky man. 'Or,' Mr. Munn added, 'do you like it?'

The officer opened his lips as though to speak. Then, after an instant, he asked, 'What's out that way?' And he pointed beyond the room where the women still sat, with their faces raised in question.

'Bedrooms,' Professor Ball replied, 'where some boys sleep. Pupils of mine,' he added.

The chunky man looked back over his shoulder. 'Yeah, yeah,' he said, almost jeeringly, 'he's a schoolteacher.'

'Why don't you start there?' the officer demanded. Then to the soldiers in the hall: 'Allen, Forbes, go with him.'

Two of the soldiers entered the room, lifting their feet in a cautious tread as though on treacherous ice, or as though afraid of smearing the floor with the red mud that was thick on their shoes. One of them, as he passed, glanced apologetically at Mr. Munn.

The officer stood in the middle of the room, waiting. No

one spoke. The dogs on the front porch were now barking intermittently.

The deputy and the soldiers came back. Then they searched the back of the house and the rooms across the hall. All the while the officer, saying nothing, stood there with Professor Ball and Mr. Munn.

The deputy returned and stood in the hall door.

'All right,' the officer said. 'Let's look upstairs.' He went toward the hall, saying to Professor Ball, 'You better come, too.' Then to one of the soldiers, 'You keep an eye on him.' With a jerk of his thumb, he indicated Mr. Munn.

The women had entered from the next room. They stood grouped closely together, and looked, as from a painful inquiring distance, at the men.

'Just a minute,' Mr. Munn said abruptly.

The officer turned, and looked at him.

Maybe, Mr. Munn thought, maybe. He was conscious of the eyes of the women upon him. He could not see them, but he was aware of them looking, leaning. He thought, If I make a row, maybe they won't go up, maybe they'll just take me and go, and they can't do anything to me, not to me, they haven't got anything on me.

'What do you want?' the officer demanded impatiently.

To Mr. Munn it seemed as though he had just rediscovered the officer standing there, as though he himself had been lost in some great lag of time, and now, suddenly, had risen again into time, like a diver bursting to the surface.

'Nothing,' Mr. Munn answered.

The officer went out, and there was a tramping of feet on the stairs.

No, Mr. Munn thought, it wouldn't have worked, it wouldn't have done any good. He did not look at the women. The feet moved overhead, scrapingly on the bare floors. He heard the sound of doors being opened, then closed. He wondered if he hadn't made the row with the officer because he was afraid. A coward. Then he thought, No, it wouldn't have done any good.

He heard the voices upstairs, suddenly sharp and demanding. Someone was pounding on a door. It was the officer's voice that was commanding, very loud, 'Open that door!'

Mr. Munn moved toward the hall, and the soldier blocked his way.

'It's Isabella,' Portia said. 'It's Isabella; she won't let them in.'

'Get away,' Mr. Munn ordered the soldier, who held his carbine at the port to block the door. He laid his hand on the carbine.

The soldier's face, he noticed flickeringly, irrelevantly, was round and unformed, childish. 'Listen, boy,' Mr. Munn said, speaking quickly, 'lay a hand on me and get in trouble. Real trouble. They haven't got a warrant for me. It'll be trouble for you. Listen, I'm a lawyer, I know.'

Mr. Munn did not take his hand from the carbine. The boy gave a little ground.

'Get away,' Mr. Munn said. 'All he said was keep an eye on me. Get away.'

He pushed past the soldier and ran up the steps, the soldier following.

The officer stood in front of the locked door of the bedroom at the head of the stairs, the deputy on one side and the two soldiers on the other. One of the soldiers held a lamp, the chimney smutted now because the flame had flared and jerked with the motion of being carried about. The light was wavering and uncertain. Professor Ball stood behind the soldiers.

Mr. Munn stood beside the soldier with the lamp.

'Open that door,' the officer ordered, loud. Even in the unsure light Mr. Munn could see that his face was flushing with irritation. As he spoke he truculently thrust his head forward.

'No,' the voice from beyond the door said faintly, 'you can't come in. Not in my room. You haven't any right.'

The deputy grinned. Nodding confidentially at the soldier who had come up with Mr. Munn, he remarked: 'She said no man wasn't come-en her room, didn't have the right. I just reckon you ain't the right man, lieutenant.'

The soldier with the lamp grinned too.

'Oh, she's a lady, she is,' the deputy said mincingly.

'Shut up,' the officer commanded. Then, turning to the door: 'Miss, you oughter let us in. It's the law. We won't bother you. Not a bit.' His voice was wheedling, cajoling, now. 'We'll catch him sooner or later. If he's hiding in there, you won't do him any good acting this way——'

Covertly, Mr. Munn glanced down the hall. It was shadowy there, almost dark, but the loft ladder, it was not there. Doctor MacDonald was in the loft. He had taken the ladder up. He was not in the room there, with the girl.

'——not a bit of good, Miss. Now, Miss, open up, please.'

'No,' the girl's voice replied.

'All right, all right.' The officer's voice was loud again, and harsh. 'All right, Miss, we're gonna knock the door down.'

'I told you I had a shotgun,' the girl's voice said.

'I don't believe it,' the officer answered. 'We're gonna knock it down.'

'She's got a gun all right,' Mr. Munn said.

'How do you know?'

'There was a gun sitting in the corner. I saw it. Right there' — and Mr. Munn pointed toward the corner beyond the door. 'It's gone now.'

'Listen,' Professor Ball told the officer, 'she might shoot somebody. And you'd be responsible. She might do it. She's the youngest, and headstrong and spoiled, spoiled when she was a child, being the youngest——'

'Hell,' the deputy exclaimed, 'she ain't got no gun. She's

bluffen. They're all bluffen.' But he sidled away from the door a little.

Bluffing, Mr. Munn thought. She had the gun, all right. But Doctor MacDonald wasn't in there with her, he was sure of that. Bluffing, yes, she was bluffing. She was trying to bluff them into believing he was in there. She wasn't thinking beyond that, she was just doing that. What she could.

With his fist, the officer struck the heavy panel of the door.

'No gentleman,' Professor Ball complained querulously — 'no gentleman would go and make a young girl like her shoot somebody.'

'Listen,' the officer said, addressing the door, 'we don't think you've got a gun. You're bluffing. We're coming in.'

There was no answer. Then with a small, grating sound, the door swung inward about eight inches. Mr. Munn peered at the aperture.

'I have, you can see it — but don't come close.' Her voice was broken, as though she was crying, or trying to keep from crying.

It was there. Mr. Munn could see in the shadow, not protruding from the room, the muzzle of the shotgun like a small figure eight laid on its side. It was wavering there in the shadow.

'Now, Miss,' the officer was saying, 'just gimme that gun. Just pass it out to me, we aren't gonna bother you.' He did not reach out for the gun, his arms hanging loosely at his sides. 'Come on, Miss, you don't want to make trouble; come on ——'

The soldier standing closest to the wall, out of range of vision from the interior, leaned slowly toward the door-jamb. The officer drew his feet closer together, the knees flexing a little. 'Come on, lady, come on, now,' he kept saying coaxingly.

Mr. Munn saw the soldier lean toward the door-jamb. He saw his hand stealthily rise. 'Isabella!' he shouted warningly, 'watch ——' But the soldier behind him chunked him heavily in the ribs with the carbine butt so that he fell to one knee, gasping. And at the instant he fell, the hand reached round the door-jamb and swept down to seize the barrel of the shotgun, and the officer plunged sideways, and the roar of the gun filled the hall.

'I got it,' the soldier at the door shouted. The shotgun dangled loosely from his grasp.

Downstairs, one of the women screamed.

The officer stepped into the room, his pistol drawn. The soldier with the lamp followed, then the deputy.

Mr. Munn rose slowly to his feet. There, before him on the floor, was the mark where the charge of shot had buried itself in the oak planking.

The women, calling, were coming up the stairs.

The girl was sitting on the floor, her head pressed against the door-jamb and her shoulders shaking with sobs. Professor Ball, on his knees beside her, the skirts of his long black coat almost brushing the floor, as when he knelt to pray, was moving his clumsy bandaged hand over her hair with a mechanical gesture of comfort. He was mumbling something, Mr. Munn could not make out what.

Mr. Munn turned to meet the interrogation and distress on the faces of the women. 'It's all right,' he said.

As Portia moved quickly toward the doorway, the officer came out, the soldier with the lamp behind him. He looked down at the huddled girl. Professor Ball rose, his tall, thin figure weaving crankily. He put out his hand to the wall to brace himself. 'You didn't have to do that,' he told the officer, his voice croaking and distant.

The officer did not seem to hear him. 'Miss,' he said, addressing the girl on the floor, 'Miss, I sure ——'

The soldier who still held the shotgun set it against the wall, almost surreptitiously.

'Miss,' the officer repeated, then stopped.

There was a slight scraping noise down the hall. Mr. Munn turned in time to see, indistinct in the shadow, the long form of Doctor MacDonald hang for an instant from the edge of the loft door before he dropped to the floor.

Chapter fourteen

THE trees were getting on toward leaf, now. But you could still see through their branches, across the square to the courthouse, and beyond. When they were in full leaf, you couldn't. Then, above the massy depth of the green, you could only see the roof of the courthouse and the squat, square brick tower with the clock. That happened all at once. For a while after the buds began you could see the individual boughs hung with that uncertain, irregular green that in the fading light, as now, seemed gray, or seemed, on the very highest boughs where the last ray of sun struck, a pale gold. For a while, day after day, there would be the boughs, visible and individual, and through them you could see the courthouse, the benches under the trees, and the buildings on the other side of the square; then suddenly, one morning, you could see nothing, or for the first time you realized that you could see nothing, and you were surprised as though it had all happened, at one stroke, that night. The season had turned.

Mr. Munn kept on looking out of the window of his office at the leafing trees. He was thinking that things were as they were, you thought, and then, even as you looked, were not. There was, for instance, that small pain in the side, a stitch, nothing more, something so familiar that you scarcely noticed it, part of the unvarying, permeating medium in which your being was supported; then it was that no longer, it was cancer, it was death. Death grew in you like the leaves on the trees in spring, gentle and tender and unobtrusive, and then, in the moment of knowledge, was already luxuriant, full-blown, blotting out the familiar objects. If not the small pain in the side, some word you spoke, some careless gesture, some momentary concession to vanity, some burst of pity, or some trivial decision — that was the bud, the leaf swelling toward recognition.

He shrugged his shoulders, and rose from his chair. Doctor MacDonald had said, 'Well, a man goes his own gait.' And that was true.

He walked idly about the office, in which the light was getting dim. His eyes rested upon the familiar objects: the tall walnut bookcases with the glass in the doors cracked, the stacks of books and papers, dust-covered, in chairs against the wall, the other chair, the chair where Mrs. Trevelyan had sat that day, the filing cabinets, the pictures, the rifle and the shotgun propped in a corner with old envelopes drawn over the muzzles to save them from dust. He had brought the shotgun back from the Christian place, he remembered, after his last bird hunt with Mr. Christian. They had had a good afternoon, that last afternoon, no wind, the sky clear and distant with a tinge of frosty gray, like iron, on the northern horizon as the sun got low, the dogs working in the tawny sagegrass beyond a cedar grove. He had brought the gun back here the next morning, had set it in the corner, and had put the envelope over the muzzle. How long ago that seemed! But he had not used the rifle for more than two years. He had not touched it except to oil it, not since the time he went down to Reelfoot Lake deer-hunting. He had not killed a deer with the rifle that trip. The only deer he had killed had been brought down with a charge of buckshot at less than fifteen paces. He had been leaning against an oak near the run, and the deer had appeared, momentarily motionless, with lifted head, an easy shot. At night the men had sat in a cabin around a stove, their belts loosened and a whisky bottle on the table, warm with the fire and the food and the drink and in the surety of comradeship. But now he could not even remember the name of one of the men. That, too, was a long time back.

The things you remembered, they were what you were. But every time you remembered them you were different. For a long time you would not notice any difference, as you noticed no difference in the spring when, day after day in the warm nights, the leaves thickened on the boughs, or in the fall slowly dropped away; until the time came when, all at once, there was the difference. Every object in the room, in its familiarity, proclaimed a difference, the shotgun there in the corner, the books he had read, the dusty papers filled with his writing. He had written on those pages for some purpose; the purpose was gone now, but there the writing still was, yellowing out, going too, but outliving the purpose that had guided the pen across the sheets. Over the sights of the shotgun, in the flicker of an instant, he had seen the last quail rise in the whirr of wings against the lemon-colored sky, and his finger had pressed the trigger, and the bird had stumbled, as it were, on the air and plunged downward like a stone. There the shotgun was, as it had been; but the unnamable impulse that had made him lift it and press the trigger that afternoon was gone, exhausted in its fulfillment. The acts remained, irreversible in their consequences and not to be undone, but the impulse, the desire, the purpose, had gone. It was hard sometimes to guess what they had been.

He stopped moving about the office. To hell with it, he thought. That didn't matter. The only thing that mattered was to see MacDonald out, now. There was, at least, that.

That was the only thing that mattered, now, for it was the only thing left to matter.

Five days earlier the board of the Association had voted to sell. Mr. Sills and Mr. Munn had stood out against it. But it had been no use. Some had been hopeless, some had needed cash too desperately, some had been afraid. Looking about the table, Mr. Munn had wondered how many had the threat of an indictment hanging over their heads to force the vote.

That's what the evidence was being used for, to squeeze. And after that it might be used for something else. More than once Mr. Munn had wondered when they would come for him: on the street in broad daylight, some night at the hotel?

Mr. Sills had stood by him, but it had been no use. After the vote, Mr. Munn had gone down the stairs by himself, ahead of the others. It was over. The other men hadn't been willing to look at each other. They had known it was over.

Mr. Munn had walked down the street and across the court-house square to the jail. They had let him into the cell. He had not known how, exactly, to say it to Doctor MacDonald.

'Durn it,' Doctor MacDonald exclaimed, 'just like I said, sitting round so much makes me bilious. It's not natural to a man to be sitting round. And this time of year your blood needs thinning like as not, anyway. I'm sure glad they'll be starting the trial in a few days.'

Mr. Munn said nothing.

'Of course,' Doctor MacDonald added, almost cheerfully, 'they might decide to keep me indoors for quite a spell afterward. Bilious or not.'

'You ought never given yourself up,' Mr. Munn said bitterly, not looking at him. 'You ought never come down that night. It wasn't necessary. They would have gone away. After what happened.'

'Hell, Perse, you keep saying that. How did I know what was happening downstairs, hearing that shooting and all? Anything might have been going on, and me in the attic, not knowing.'

'You ought never come down,' Mr. Munn repeated.

'Well, I did,' Doctor MacDonald said, 'and here I am. Only hope I don't stay here too long.'

'Listen,' Mr. Munn commanded, leaning toward him, looking at him now, 'I don't know what evidence they got, but I bet they don't nail you. Wilkins is a good man, a damned good lawyer; he's no fool; he'll see to it that jury's not all one way——'

'Sure, Wilkins is all right, I'm not denying that,' Doctor MacDonald said. 'But I still wish you'd taken the case. Like I asked.'

'And have your lawyer get arrested in the middle of it? They may get me any day. Any day they think they've got evidence that'll stick. Wilkins, he'll manage.'

'Maybe,' Doctor MacDonald agreed, in a tone of friendly concession.

'Listen,' Mr. Munn reiterated, leaning, 'let them nail you, and there's men will take this place apart. Plenty of them. Soldiers or no soldiers. No' — and he shook his head — 'they won't nail you. They'll be afraid.'

'Maybe,' Doctor MacDonald repeated cheerfully. He moved the length of the cell, three paces, short paces for him, and lifted his arms, slowly, almost luxuriously, above his head.

Mr. Munn sat down on the edge of the cot. He felt done in. He felt like a man who, new to a high altitude, runs up an easy slope and finds, suddenly, his knees water and his head giddy with the empty air.

'Bilious,' Doctor MacDonald declared; 'that's what it does to me. My teeth feel green. Like moss on a rotten shingle. Damned if they don't.'

Mr. Munn did not answer, looking down at the stained concrete of the floor. He had the impulse to lie back on the cot, to let himself go. If they got him, arrested him and brought him here, he could just lie back and shut his eyes. Then there wouldn't be any reason not to. He could do it.

'Well?' Doctor MacDonald was saying inquiringly. He was standing in the middle of the cell, staring down at him.

Doctor MacDonald stood there, in his shirt-sleeves and with his vest unbuttoned, tall even in his carpet slippers, the light from the window falling directly on his unkempt, strong-boned

head. He stood with his weight off his heels, like a boxer, or
a man ready to go somewhere. The cuffs of the shirt he wore
were fresh and stiff. Mr. Munn looked at them. Cordelia
brought him a clean shirt every morning, he knew. She
wrapped the shirt up in a piece of paper, every morning, and
left the hotel, and walked down the street, not looking at anybody, and crossed the square and came here. She would stand
in the cell and hold one of Doctor MacDonald's hands with
both of hers.

'Well,' Doctor MacDonald demanded, 'what's the matter
with you?'

Mr. Munn leaned back until his shoulders came into contact
with the stone of the wall. 'The board,' he said; 'they sold.'

'Our figure?' Doctor MacDonald asked, almost casually,
after the pause of scarcely an instant.

'No,' Mr. Munn answered. He did not look at Doctor Mac-
Donald.

'Licked,' Doctor MacDonald said.

Mr. Munn slowly raised his gaze. But Doctor MacDonald
was looking away. He was looking out the window, and his
face betrayed nothing. 'That's right,' Mr. Munn said. 'Licked.'

Doctor MacDonald continued to look out the little window.
Mr. Munn followed his gaze. Outside the window, there was
a bough with the leaves putting out, golden-tinged and pu-
bescent.

'I reckon they just didn't have it in them,' Doctor MacDonald
remarked.

'I did what I could,' Mr. Munn told him. Then added, 'And
Sills did.'

'It just wasn't in them,' Doctor MacDonald said. 'One way
or another, that's what a man does. What's in him. A man
goes along, and the time comes, even if he's looking the other
way not noticing, and the thing in him comes out. It wasn't
something happening to him made him do something, the thing

was in him all the time. He just didn't know. Till the time came.'

'No,' Mr. Munn answered, sitting up on the cot, feeling an alarm stir obscurely in him. 'No,' and hesitated; then, less emphatically, repeated, 'No.'

Almost amusedly, Doctor MacDonald looked down at him. 'Don't kid yourself,' he said. 'Take the Professor, now. Him doing nothing but teaching his boys and reading his books, all that old history and stuff. You'd never guessed it, but look what came outer him.'

Mr. Munn stood up.

'Did you ever notice,' Doctor MacDonald asked, 'how what happens to people seems sort of made to order for them? When you think about it.'

'*Why* don't matter!' Mr. Munn exclaimed, and jerked his arm forward in a violent, sweeping gesture of dismissal. 'We're licked. The reason for things is gone. For what we did. Like flood water going down and leaving trash and stuff up in a tree.' He jabbed his forefinger at the other man's breast. 'That's you,' he asserted, 'left high and dry. Stuck up in a tree.' Then, more quietly, he added: 'And me. Both of us.'

Doctor MacDonald laid a hand on his shoulder, and said, 'Take it easy.'

Mr. Munn sat down again. They talked of the trial, which would begin in two more days.

As he started out, behind Mr. Dickey, who had come to let him out of Doctor MacDonald's cell, his glance fell upon the door of the cell where Trevelyan had been. An old man was in there now, lying on the cot, his thin body lax and huddled like a pile of old clothes. He was in for murder. He had gone out to milk one morning, and had brought the milk in and strained it and put it away; then, with an ice-pick, he had killed his wife as she leaned over the stove preparing breakfast, then his pregnant daughter, who was lying in bed, then the young child at her side. He had killed the son-in-law with a rifle when he came back to the house from feeding the stock. He had called the sheriff. Then he had gone to bed and wrapped himself up in the bedclothes. He had been asleep when the sheriff came for him. Now, in his cell, he lay on his cot, only stirring to reply to questions. He answered questions with a dazed and innocent patience, like a man scarcely aroused from sleep.

Mr. Munn could not recall his name.

'Nuts,' Mr. Dickey said, and nodded toward the cell where the man lay on the cot.

Outside, when he stood in the courthouse yard, he saw the sunshine falling over the roofs of the buildings and on the stones and the young grass. People were moving up and down the street. People he knew. He walked soberly across the square toward his office.

He had gone to the jail afraid to tell Doctor MacDonald what the board had done. He had been afraid of the way Doctor MacDonald might take it. He should have known, he thought now, the way it would be: Doctor MacDonald standing there in the middle of the cell floor, his weight forward off his heels, his face showing nothing. It was Doctor MacDonald who had laid a hand on his shoulder, and had said, 'Take it easy.' It had gone past Doctor MacDonald and had never shaken him.

But the next day when he saw Doctor MacDonald he was not so sure. Watching him stand at the cell door, ready to call Mr. Dickey, Doctor MacDonald said suddenly, 'Don't it smell in here to you?'

Mr. Munn turned to look at him.

'Don't it stink?' Doctor MacDonald demanded.

'Yes,' Mr. Munn admitted, aware, anew, of the fetid, almost sweet odor, as of rottenness, 'I reckon it does, a little.'

'It stunk mightily to me, at first,' Doctor MacDonald said,

'but it don't seem like it stinks now. A man gets used to a thing. It gets natural to him.' He stopped moving about, as he had been doing, his carpet slippers making a dry, sliding noise on the concrete. 'That's what I don't like,' he added, 'it getting so natural. It looks like a stink oughter stay a stink to a man.'

Mr. Munn grinned, thinking it a joke. Then he noticed that Doctor MacDonald was not grinning. Mr. Munn let the muscles of his face relax.

Doctor MacDonald lay down on the cot, staring up at the ceiling.

Mr. Munn called for Mr. Dickey.

While Mr. Dickey was coming, Doctor MacDonald said, 'If I get out, I'm figuring on leaving this country.'

'Leaving?' Mr. Munn echoed, surprise in his tone.

Doctor MacDonald nodded. 'Yeah,' he replied, adding, 'but not so quick anybody'd think he was running me out.'

Mr. Munn did not answer for an instant. 'Where you going?' he then asked. He was aware of the unevenness in his own voice. That unevenness, which he noticed, detachedly as in the voice of another person, defined for him the sense of confusion, betrayal, that at Doctor MacDonald's words had moved smally, almost innocently, in him, like the first tremor of a landslip.

'Out West somewhere, I reckon,' Doctor MacDonald was saying matter-of-factly. 'Arizona, New Mexico, I don't know. Somewhere where people haven't caught up with themselves yet.'

Mr. Dickey was coming, his keys jangling as he searched for the right one.

'I'm not staying round here,' Doctor MacDonald added. 'I might get used to the way this country stinks.'

By seven o'clock in the morning on the first day of the trial of Doctor MacDonald on charges of conspiracy and arson, the courthouse square was crowded. The troops kept the courthouse yard clear. When the doors were opened, the troops permitted only five or six men at a time to approach the building, and at the door each man was searched for arms. By half-past eight word came out that the courtroom was full. Although the crowd thinned somewhat, it did not disperse. The people were restless, but unusually silent. When Mr. Munn and Professor Ball and his daughters walked from the hotel to the courthouse, people made way for them, gazing curiously at the faces of the women, and after they had passed talking in low tones, identifying them. Now and then a man would speak to Professor Ball, who would raise the bandaged right hand in a kind of grave salute. Cordelia walked beside him, leaning on his left arm. She was very pale.

A voice from the crowd called out to her, 'Don't you worry, Miz MacDonald, we'll take keer of him.'

She gave no sign of having heard. Professor Ball raised his bandaged hand in decorous salute.

A scuffling began at the point in the crowd where the voice had called. Another voice cried, 'Hit him again!' The soldiers tried to force a way into the crowd toward the spot; but they could not. Then the disturbance was over.

At the courthouse door the soldiers stopped them. While the women waited just inside, one of the soldiers patted the men's pockets and waistbands. Professor Ball, looking straight ahead, seemed unaware of the searching hands on him.

'They ain't got nothing,' the soldier said, stepping back.

'You can go in now,' the lieutenant told them.

It was that way every day for three days, in the morning and in the afternoon when the court resumed, the crowd thinner each time but still there, the soldiers around the courthouse yard, where the grass showed an incongruous fresh green as of some pasture corner, and the soldiers at the door. And with Professor Ball, it was the same every day, and with Cordelia. Professor Ball sat in the courtroom, very erect, with his eyes fixed before him as though he were paying no attention to what was going on, and his bandaged hands lying on his bony knees, as passive as stones. Cordelia walked beside him, leaning on his left arm, or sat beside him in the courtroom, still holding his arm; but her glance rarely wavered from her husband's face. As for Doctor MacDonald, he leaned back in his chair, at ease but alert to what was going on, with his brown hands lying on the table-top before him. Or he inclined his head to hear some remark which his lawyer made in an undertone to him. Once, when almost everybody was watching a witness, Doctor MacDonald — Mr. Munn was almost sure — winked, with an air of sly humor, at Cordelia. Mr. Munn turned, as quickly as he dared, to look at Cordelia. While she watched her husband, her face was pale, but composed. But something else, certainly, some other expression, a smile, perhaps, had been there on her face; and had fled even as he turned to surprise it.

For three days the case moved without taking on definition. Only on the first day, when the jury was being impaneled, had issues taken on any form. But Wilkins, Mr. Munn thought, seemed satisfied enough about the jury. He had not used his last challenge. He acted as if he had put one over. Mr. Munn studied the men in the jury box. He knew some of them. Some of them, he was sure, would like to see Doctor MacDonald catch it, guilty or not as a matter of fact, just because he was in the Association. But Wilkins seemed satisfied. There must be a couple on the jury who, Wilkins thought, could hold out against anything short of an absolute identification. And maybe against that. Mr. Munn tried to figure out who they were, but gave it up. Wilkins was not telling all he knew.

But after the jury was impaneled, things slacked off. Witness followed witness, each one adding some little detail to the picture of the raid on Bardsville. Officials of the Alta Company, and of the other companies, stood in the box, and recited, to the last penny, the costs of the warehouses that had been destroyed, and the quantity and value of the tobacco that those warehouses had contained. That was what it had been, to them, not a picture of men moving in the darkness, and of the flames standing over the roofs, but the sums which each in turn, standing in the box, read from a paper in his hand. A constable told how he had been sitting in the office and how masked men, with drawn pistols, had come in and tied him to a chair. They had brought in two other men, watchmen, and tied them up too. The masked men had stood around, the constable said, making jokes and chewing tobacco. 'They said they just tied us up for our own good,' the constable said, somewhat sullenly, 'so we wouldn't git in no trouble.' The masked men, he added, had had some trouble with their masks when they tried to spit. And the first explosion, because the police office was so near Front Street, nearly threw him out of his chair. 'They must-er used enough that shot to blow up the town,' he said.

Miss Lucy Mayhew, chief operator for the telephone company, lowered her bony, sallow-skinned right hand after taking the oath, and smoothed the black, lusterless silk of her dress. The prosecutor asked her questions, and she answered them in a low but distinct voice, impersonal as though it were coming over a wire; she did not lift her head when she spoke, and her hands, now and then, patted and smoothed the silk. She fixed the very minute when she had first heard a trampling on the stairs up to the telephone office, for she had just looked at her clock. It was twelve-thirty o'clock, she said. Four men came in, bursting in all at once, and they had white cloths on their faces and pistols in their hands. One of the girls screamed, she said, but she herself, she stood right up to them as good as she could. She wanted to know what their business was.

'And what did they say?' the prosecutor demanded.

'They said, ladies, we hate to bother you, but we just got a

little private business in town, and we don't want anybody to
be making it public.' She smoothed the silk, and her brow
wrinkled in thought. 'At least, that's as good as I can remember
what they said. So we got back from the switchboard.'

'Did they offer you any violence?'

'They waved those pistols some,' she said, 'but they didn't
point them at us. One of them — he looked like the captain or
something, because he had a white bandage on his coat sleeve —
he just said for us to come downstairs, and he took me by the
arm. And two of the other men, each one took one of the girls
by the arm, and one of the girls started pulling back, and he
said, lady, you better come on down or you'll miss something
bigger'n Christmas. They took us downstairs, and the man
with me held my arm going down like any gentleman would
a lady's.'

One of the men had stayed upstairs, she said, and he was the
one who had cut all the wires up there. Or at least she reckoned
so, for all the wires were cut up and pretty bad. He was the
meanest-looking one, anyway, she said. Then the men made
them stand back in the doorway of Gordon's store, which had
a deep doorway. At first there wasn't anything, then a few
men riding down the street, men with white masks on. Then
some more men on horseback stopped up at the corner of
Main and Jefferson, under the street light, and stayed there
the whole time. Then there were the explosions, then the fire
over the roofs, and one of the girls began to cry. It looked
like the whole town was going to burn up, she said. But it
didn't, and after a while men with guns began marching past.

'In military formation?' the prosecutor asked.

'I reckon you might call it that,' she answered. 'It was four
abreast, but not in step exactly. And they were singing and
shouting some. One man got on the sidewalk and shot off his
pistol at the street light and yelled' — she hesitated, smoothing
her skirt. 'Well, it was improper language,' she said, 'and then

he yelled out, Boys, they said we couldn't, but we done it! Then he shot off his pistol, and he hit the street light. But one of the men with us, the one that was captain, he said to one of the others, you go tell that man to move on, he's using strong language like that, and there's ladies here. And he went and told him, and he stopped.'

After the others had all left, all except the men on horseback under the street light at the corner, she said, she and the other operators were permitted to go back upstairs. The men had started to go up with them, and the captain was holding her by the arm, but she had said no, thanks, she didn't want any more assistance from people like that who violated the law. Then the captain laughed, and went away.

After Miss Lucy Mayhew there was old Doctor Potter, who had been picked up the night of the raid, going home from a call. Now, in the witness box, he was still furious, still fuming and biting his words off, as though no time had elapsed and the outrage were still at hand. Then there were the other men who had been picked up, and the station agent, and a drummer who had been staying at the hotel and who had watched everything from his window. For a moment Mr. Munn thought that this might be a man the prosecution was counting on. He had seen a tall man on a bay horse, or what looked like a bay horse, he said, for the light wasn't so good. The man seemed to be in charge, or something. And the man was a tall man, and lanky. 'Like him,' he said, and nodded toward Doctor MacDonald.

But there was nothing there, Mr. Munn thought. It was too easy for Wilkins, when he took the witness for cross-examination.

'You say it was a tall man you saw?' Wilkins asked conversationally of the drummer.

'Yes, sir,' the drummer said.

'By the way, Mr. Tupper,' Wilkins asked, still conversationally, 'where did you say you're from?'

'Huntsville, Alabama,' the drummer replied.

'Well, I've never been in Alabama, and I can't say exactly how men grow down there' — and he hesitated, to cast an appraising glance over the witness, who was a shortish man, and thin — 'but round here the country produces a right smart of pretty well-set-up fellows. Like my client, there.' He hesitated again, waiting for the laughter, which came. Suddenly, he flung out an accusing finger at the witness, and his voice mounted: 'Did you positively, beyond shadow and peradventure of a doubt, identify this man?'

'Well——' the man paused.

'Well,' Wilkins snapped; then added casually: 'I just didn't want you, Mr. Tupper, to be making any suggestions to these gentlemen' — he indicated the jury — 'that you wouldn't back up. In here, or,' he added in an ingratiating tone, 'outside.'

'I object, Your Honor' — the prosecutor was on his feet. 'I object; that's intimidation of the witness!'

Blandly, in a pained surprise, Wilkins turned. 'I didn't mean a thing,' he declared.

One after another they mounted the stand, and raised the right hand, and listened while the words were said to them: '— solemnly swear — will be the truth — nothing but the truth. So help you God.'

'I do,' each one said, clearly or mumblingly, in answer to that aimless, dreary intonation.

How many times, Mr. Munn thought, how many times he had heard those words! Day after day, in this room, addressed to all sorts of people, who raised the right hand, swearing. He thought: the truth. Each person there, on the stand, today, was telling the truth. The officials, with their pieces of paper on which the figures were written, down to a last penny, they were telling the truth: their truth. That was what the event was to them. And the constable, the truth to him — what had stuck in his mind and what he would always mention, for years

to come now, when he told anybody about that night, what
would stay in his mind when he was very old and his past had
begun to flow from him and leave only a few little, dead fragments, stranded out of time — the truth to him was the way
the men had had trouble with their masks when they tried to
spit. And Miss Mayhew would always remember the tangle of
cut wires in the office, just that, and the man's hand holding
her arm coming downstairs. That was the truth to her. But
her truth, and the constable's truth, and the truths of the
others, they were not his own, which was, if any one thing
seizable and namable, that reeling moment of certainty and
fulfillment when the air had swollen ripely with the blast.
But that had gone. Like the blink of an eye; and would not
come back. Even that self he had been had slipped from him,
and could only be glimpsed now, paling and reproachful, in
fits as when the breeze worries a rising mist.

The truths of those people were not the truth that had been
his that night; but that truth was his no longer. The truth: it
devoured and blotted out each particular truth, each individual man's truth, it crushed truths as under a blundering
tread, it was blind.

He scarcely listened to the witnesses. He watched Doctor
MacDonald leaning back in his chair, at ease, it seemed, and
attentive only out of courtesy. What was Doctor MacDonald's
truth? He had never asked himself that question before. Or
he watched Cordelia. Her truth, what was it?

The witnesses mounted the stand; and descended. Wilkins
seemed bored, and confident. For witness after witness, he
waived cross-examination, or asked some single perfunctory
question, contemptuous in its perfunctoriness.

Until Mr. Al Turpin came to the stand. But even then, at
first, Wilkins did not change.

Al Turpin was a beefy man, blockishly built, with a swarthy
skin and thinning, greasy-looking hair. On top of his overalls,

he wore a brown wool coat. He would speak heavily and deliberately for a moment or two, then stop in the middle of a sentence, as though he had forgotten what he was there for, as though if he ceased to speak the scene before him might fade into unreality. While the people watched him, he would blink slowly. Then, at a word from the prosecutor, he would shake his head apologetically, humbly, like a man started out of a drowse, and would wet his lips and resume.

A man moved down the aisle, almost on tiptoe, and approached the table where Wilkins and Doctor MacDonald sat. He leaned over the table, talking earnestly to Wilkins. At a gesture from Wilkins, Doctor MacDonald leaned forward, too. Mr. Munn watched them, trying to place the man who had come in. Then he remembered him as a cousin of Wilkins.

Wilkins looked at his watch.

Doctor MacDonald was nodding at something the man was saying, and Wilkins snapped shut his watch. Then the man went out, tiptoeing up the aisle, for the heavy, deliberate voice of Al Turpin was still speaking, giving the testimony. '— I was a member of the Association,' he was saying, 'and I had my crop in the Association. Going on thirty-five thousand pounds, it was, and fair to middling, the season being what it was and ——'

'I object, Your Honor,' Wilkins said, very loud.

Al Turpin turned his slow gaze upon him, with an expression of relief, almost, or of gratitude.

'I object that this testimony is irrelevant to this case. The poundage of Mr. Turpin's crop and his relations with the Association ——'

'Objection overruled.'

Wilkins sat down, but his hands grasped the edge of the table before him.

Al Turpin resumed. What he got for his crop wasn't bad as some years, he said, but the waiting, that was bad, and people said the price would go down, that the Association was losing members.

Wilkins objected, but was overruled.

'Then I heard some talk around,' Al Turpin continued, 'how some men over in Hunter County was getting together to do something about the way things was ——'

'Was this represented to you as a terrorist organization?' the prosecutor demanded.

'I object,' Wilkins said, rising and waving his arm. 'My opponent is leading the witness!'

'Objection overruled.'

'But Your Honor ——' Wilkins did not sit down.

'Objection overruled.'

'Will you please answer the question?' the prosecutor said to Al Turpin.

'I can't say as it was, if I rightly know. They just said it was some folks getting together and gonna do something. That's what ——'

'I object that this is hearsay and should not be admitted as evidence!' Wilkins exclaimed, almost shouting.

'Objection sustained,' the judge said, then added: 'The witness will please confine himself to matters of direct observation.'

Al Turpin looked about him, working his big hands slowly on his knees. 'I been doing the best I know,' he said. He paused, seemed to sink in upon himself, then began: 'One day a fellow come to me, I can't say for sure what day it was, but it was long 'fore setting-out time last spring. He told me his name, but it's done slipped my mind, it looks like. But he was a sorter middle-size man, you might say' — he stopped, broodingly, for a moment — 'and sandy-haired. And he said to me, Mr. Turpin, you don't look like no man would let his-self be knocked down and spit on. I been a peace-abiding man, but I said, Well, ain't no man wiped his foot on me. And he said, Now, over in Hunter County ——'

Wilkins shoved his chair back with a sudden scraping on the dry floor. 'I object! This is hearsay, pure and simple. This middle-size man' — and he pronounced the words with a hint of mimicry of Al Turpin's voice — 'this sandy-haired man whose name the witness can't remember ——'

The judge struck the desk with his gavel.

'Objection sustained,' he ruled. 'But the attorney for the defense will observe the dignity of this court.'

'Did you or did you not, Mr. Turpin,' the prosecutor demanded, 'become a member of any secret society?' He turned away from the witness and looked, with a sudden glint of cunning and satisfaction, at the packed roomful of people, and then at Wilkins.

Al Turpin did not answer. He seemed to be lost, fumblingly, within himself.

Wilkins was looking at his watch.

'Answer yes or no!'

Al Turpin managed to fix his glance, painful and appealing, upon the face of the prosecutor. 'Yes,' he said.

'And was not the purpose of this society to destroy plant beds and barns and to force membership in the Association of Growers of Dark Fired Tobacco?'

'I object!' Wilkins almost shouted. 'He is leading the witness.'

'Objection overruled.'

The prosecutor leaned toward Al Turpin: 'Answer yes or no!'

'Yes,' Al Turpin replied.

'Was the name of this society The Free Farmers' Brotherhood for Protection and Control?'

Al Turpin's painful gaze left the prosecutor's face and slowly moved over the other faces, more distant, there before him. His bulk shifted slightly in the chair, making it creak in the quietness of the room.

'I object! That is irrelevant.'

'Objection overruled.'

The prosecutor looked at Al Turpin demandingly.

'Yes,' Al Turpin said.

Wilkins, Mr. Munn observed, was looking at his watch, covertly, beneath the level of the table.

'Now, Mr. Turpin,' the prosecutor went on, dropping into a tone of familiarity and lounging closer to the witness, 'just describe the circumstances of joining this' — he hesitated, then pronounced the words with almost a grimace, as though they had an evil taste on the tongue — 'this Free Farmers' Brotherhood for Protection and Control. Or whatever it is.'

Wilkins seemed about to rise; then restrained himself.

Turpin moved his tongue over his lips, looked at the prosecutor, and then cast a sudden, wide, wild glance over the fixed faces.

'Mr. Turpin ——'

Al Turpin let his head sink a little, humbly, and said: 'It was one night last spring; I can't say as I recollect the day it was, but it was in May. I went down the dirt road out past my house, like they said for me to, and I seen a man on a horse standing there on one side the road, and he said to me, Fair weather. And I said to him, Fairer tomorrow. Like they told me to. And I went on till I come to that old tumble-down church. A nigger church it used to be till it got too tumbledown. And I went round to the back and I seen some horses ——'

Mr. Munn thought, It's coming. He felt the weight of the silence behind him. He looked at Doctor MacDonald. He had not moved.

'— and hitched my horse to a sapling. Sassafras, I reckon. I stood there and listened. A horse tromped a little over in the bushes. Then I started walking towards the church ——'

A long time back, Mr. Munn thought, how long; but it was as before him now, suddenly, in his mind, that open space before the dark mill, that open, lighter space before which he had paused that night, the road dipping down across it beside the fallen rail fence, and distantly, the sound of water on stones. That momentary prickling of the spine as he moved into that space, alone, that was with him now, the eyes watching from shadow.

'— and after while they took me inside and stood me in front of a light with it in my face so I couldn't see nuthen, and they said the oath for me to say, a little bit at a time. And I said it.' His voice stopped, ponderously, as though of its own dead weight. Then, his bulk shifting, he said: 'I didn't know how it was gonna be, what I was getting into. I never would taken it. Not a oath before God.' His voice stopped, leaving him there, awkward, motionless.

'Mr. Turpin, repeat to the best of your ability the oath.'

'I object!' Wilkins was on his feet. 'He's leading the witness.'

'Objection overruled!'

'Mr. Turpin,' the prosecutor said sharply.

'A thing,' Al Turpin said, 'a thing don't stick in a man's head so good. I can't say the words, like they were. But I'll say what they went on to say. It said ——'

'I object!' Wilkins cried. 'This testimony is not admissible. This oath — the witness admits, here in open court, that he cannot remember it. If the welfare of my client is to depend ——'

The gavel struck the desk. 'Mr. Wilkins!' the judge exclaimed.

'Your Honor?'

'You will observe the proper dignity of this court, Mr. Wilkins.'

'Your Honor,' Mr. Wilkins said, gravely, elaborately, 'I object to the testimony of the witness on the grounds of inadmissibility.'

The judge leaned forward, wearily, and poured himself a glass of water from the china pitcher, which had blue flowers painted upon it. While he drank, the people in the room watched him. He put the glass down, and wiped his lips with a handkerchief. 'The jury will retire,' he said then, and stuffed the handkerchief into his pocket.

His eyes seemed to be closed while the jurymen went out. They moved awkwardly, clumpingly, scraping their shoes on the boards. When the door had closed behind them, the judge roused himself and said, 'Mr. Wilkins, will you present your reasons why the testimony of the witness should not be admitted into the proceedings of this court?'

It was ruled that the testimony concerning the oath was admissible. But when the jury had been summoned, and the men were moving back to their place, looking covertly at the faces of the people before them as though to surprise there the knowledge which had been denied them, the clock in the tower of the courthouse struck. It struck four times, the resonance of each impact dying away, thinning into a drowsy hum like the sound of distant bees. At the motion of Wilkins, over the protest of the prosecutor, the court was adjourned.

The people rose, and began to move sluggishly toward the doors. Wilkins was sitting beside Doctor MacDonald, talking earnestly to him. Doctor MacDonald was shaking his head.

'I'll wait,' Mr. Munn told Professor Ball, and Professor Ball nodded, not saying anything, not even looking at Mr. Munn, and moved away. Cordelia, at his side, clutched his arm. The people thinned out in the courtroom. Doctor MacDonald went away with two deputies, leaving Wilkins there alone at his table, on which the scattered papers lay.

Mr. Munn started to go over and speak to him, then turned away. He left the courtroom, and walked down the dim corridors and across the yet crowded yard to the jail. He sat on the cot, aware of that faint, sweetish stench, and listened while Doctor MacDonald moved slowly back and forth in the cell, talking. The man who had come into the courtroom, that cousin of Wilkins, had come to tell Wilkins that the soldiers had rounded up just that afternoon six men, and every one of them had been in the band Turpin belonged to. That was what had started Wilkins to stalling, Doctor MacDonald said. 'They got Turpin to turn all of them in. This place'll be running over by night. They just brought another fellow in before you came. He was in Turpin's band, too, I reckon.'

'It's easy,' Mr. Munn said. 'They made a deal with Turpin When they gave him bail we could have guessed. They've got that arson indictment on Turpin, and they're making a deal.'

'If you want to see what makes it stink in here worse'n usual,' Doctor MacDonald observed, 'you can go look down at the far end. They just put Turpin in.' He stopped moving about, and reached out to grasp strongly one of the bars of the door. 'But you can bet they put him in one by himself. They want to keep him all in one piece.'

Mr. Munn rose abruptly, and put out his hand. 'I've got to go,' he said. 'I just wanted to find out how bad it was.'

'Morbid, huh?' Doctor MacDonald remarked, and grinned.

Mr. Munn went back to his office. He sat there, without making a motion, at his desk, and stared out at the leafing trees. He thought, those trees changed in the spring and you didn't notice it, really, until the change was complete; and in the fall, when the leaves dropped away, day after day, until, all at once, you saw the final bareness. He saw the shotgun in the corner, and the rifle. He thought of the deer hunt, down near Reelfoot, and the men around the stove, in the cabin, at night. And of that last afternoon hunting birds with Mr. Christian. He stayed in his office, and the light faded over the roofs across the square. He hated to go to the hotel and tell Professor Ball. He hated to look at Cordelia, knowing what he knew.

The next morning Mr. Munn woke up very early. The light was just beginning to come. He lay on his back, looking up at the ceiling, and thought of the cold, anonymous light unfolding, slowly, over the countryside, over the fields and roads and hedges and the woods, that would be dark longest, and over the roofs of the town, and in bedrooms like this where people slept; but he was not asleep. He felt very tired, but wakeful with a detachment and clarity of mind, as when a man comes out of a fever.

At six o'clock Professor Ball came to his door and he got up. Professor Ball said that he hadn't been able to sleep either. They were the first people in the dining-room. They ate without talking. When he had finished, Mr. Munn said that he had to go down to the office a minute to leave a note for his secretary, and would come back in time to go with them to the courthouse. Professor Ball said that he would go up and see if the girls were ready for breakfast.

Mr. Munn started to go out the back way of the hotel, to take the short cut down the alley to his office, then changed his mind. He wanted to get a newspaper. He got the newspaper, glanced quickly at the headlines concerning the trial, and with the paper under his arm, walked down the square and turned to the right toward his office. He met two men whom he knew, and spoke to them. At the drugstore under his office, a clerk was propping the front doors open. 'It's sure beginning to look tough,' the clerk said, 'for that fellow MacDonald. I was saying just yesterday, it looked like ——'

'Do you think so?' Mr. Munn said, and turned up the stairs to his office.

He unlocked the door to the office and entered. He leaned over his desk and scrawled a few lines to the girl. Then he raised the window so that the place could be airing out. Clear sunlight now fell over the western side of the square. People, almost a crowd, were beginning to congregate. He looked at his watch. It was getting on toward time. He left the door unlocked, for the girls should be coming in almost any time now, and went down the back stairs to the alley. He saw no one in the alley.

He went into the stable to look at his mare. He glanced at his watch again, and saw that he had a few minutes to wait. He did not want to see Professor Ball and the others until it was time to go. It wasn't that they would ask him questions; it wasn't that, but he would discover their eyes fixed upon him. He unfolded the paper, and leaning against the stall door, began to read the account of the proceedings of the previous afternoon. He read on, but realized that the words were meaning nothing to him. He stuffed the paper into his pocket, and stood there.

He entered the hotel by the back way and climbed the narrow back stairs. On the second floor, at the head of the stairs, he saw Isabella, waiting. 'Hurry!' she said to him, whispering breathlessly, 'go away. Soldiers, and some other men, they came for you, they're hunting you. Hurry ——'

The whiteness of her face was there before him in the dim hall.

Chapter fifteen

MOST of the time during the day, if the weather was good, he stayed away from the house. That was safest, he thought, and besides, he didn't want to get the Proudfits into any trouble if he could help it. On the hill to one side of the Proudfit house was the place he usually stayed. The limestone humped out of the soil there, not jaggedly, but in gray, somnolent-looking masses rounded by weather and furred with lichen. Cedars grew there, with roots that grappled under the limestone and in the crevices. The crevices were filled with rotted leaves and cedar needles and earth, black with humus, which had sifted down. In the winter the moisture collected in those crevices and the cold made icy wedges to thrust, little by little, year after year, toward the heart of the stone. At the foot of the bluff, in the bed of the creek by the Proudfit house, the round boulders stood here and there above the surface of the water.

High up, on the bluff side of the hill, a spring poured out of an archway of stone. In its basin there, the perfectly clear water eddied ceaselessly, braiding and swelling, swaying the young fronds of fern and the grass which trailed lushly down to the surface, spilling over the lip of stone and plunging down the slope to join the creek below. 'Soon's I laid eyes on hit,' Willie Proudfit had said to Mr. Munn, 'come-en sliden down that rock that-away, I says, thar my house will set. Sometimes a-nights I lays in bed and I kin hear hit. I lays in bed and I kin recollect the times out in the dry country I laid out some-wheres a-nights and studied on water. In this country the Lord's done give a man water whichever way he turns, fer drinken and washen, hit looks lak, and a man don't know how hit is in the dry country, and the thirsten. I been two days without water and my tongue swole in my mouth. I shot me a buffalo, figgeren on the blood, and I seen they was mud caked on her legs — hit was a cow — and new-caked. I cut open her stomach, and thar was the water she'd drunk. And I supped ever drop. And hit give me strength to go on. The way she'd come from, whar the water was. The Canadian River, hit was, and nigh dry. A man don't know how the dry country is. But even here ain't ever man got him a spring come-en nigh outer the top of a hill, lak me, and fall-en so he kin lay and hear hit. Nor ever man got him a cold-air cave to keep his milk sweet to his mouth. Hit's a feature.'

He had built his house right at the creek bank, with the little branch from the falls running into the creek just behind it. And the cave, where the moisture dripped from the green, pelt-thick moss, was at the foot of the bluff just beside the house. Inside the cave, in the chill shadow, the crock jars of milk stood in rows. Willie Proudfit's wife would set her candle on a shelf of stone, for even at noon the candle was needed, and dip the milk with a tin dipper and pour it into her big, blue pitcher. Then, from another crock, she would take a pat of butter. Holding the heavy pitcher in one hand, but out from her body strongly and easily, she would move across the patch of young grass toward the house. She would set it on the table, by her husband's plate, and smile. 'Willie, now he's the beaten-est,' she would say, 'fer milk.'

'Now I thank you,' he might say, and pick up the pitcher; or he might only look up at her, not quite smiling, and say nothing, for he was not a man to talk much except on those infrequent evenings when, lying stretched out like a cat on the boards of the little porch, he would reach back into his mind for some incident out of those years he had spent on the plains. He would tell it, not exactly for them, it seemed, but for the telling, speaking slowly and tentatively. Reaching back into these past times, he was like a man who, in a dark closet, runs his fingers over some once-familiar object and tries, uncertainly, to identify it. 'They's a passel of things,' he would say, 'on God's earth fer a man to study a-bout, and ain't no man e'er seen 'em all. But I seen some. I seen gullies so deep and wide, you could throw that-air hill in hit, lock-stock-and-barr'l, and n'er no diff'rence to a man's sight. And the gully with colors spread out in the light, fer as air eye can see, lak a flag. Colors like the colors in the sky at sun, and layen thar on the ground lak the sky had come fall-en down.' Then he had paused. Mr. Munn and Willie Proudfit's wife, and her niece and nephew, sitting there in chairs, with Willie Proudfit lying there on the floor scarcely visible in the darkness — they had not said anything. Down the creek, in the patch of marshy ground there, the frogs had been piping. 'The Indians taken them colors outer the earth,' Willie Proudfit, resuming as though there had been no silence, had said, 'and paint theirselves.' And he had paused again, and there were only the night sounds. Then, 'When they dance,' he had added.

'Heathen,' the nephew had said, in the darkness.

'Heathen,' Willie Proudfit had repeated, in his soft, slow voice, 'heathen, in a way of speaken.' He had fallen silent, brooding backward into those times. Then he had said, 'But them dancen, hit ain't only frolic and jollification.' Then: 'They's a passel of things, and the Lord God, he made ever one. In his mighty plan, and ain't a sparrow falleth.'

But some evenings he didn't speak a word.

He was a medium-sized man. His face was thinnish, and it had lines in it, tiny lines that meshed multitudinously in the leathery-looking skin, but it was neither an old nor a young face. The skin was brown like an oak leaf, so brown that against it the bluish-green eyes looked pale, and the very blond hair looked silvery like the hair of an old man. He wore his hair longer than any man Mr. Munn ever remembered seeing, down to his neck behind and cut off square. One Sunday morning, just after breakfast, Mr. Munn saw him sitting on the chunk of limestone that formed the back step, with his wife just behind him cutting his hair. When she became aware of Mr. Munn standing there, she lifted away from the task the heavy, clumsy-looking shears, which made a tiny, dry sound when the blades engaged on the thick hair, a sound like a heel on sand, and looked at him. 'Willie Proudfit's hair,' she said, and smiled. 'Willie was a little towhead when he was a young 'un.'

'A towhead,' Willie Proudfit said, 'but my nose n'er drooped and run.'

'Hit do look lak young 'un's noses droop and run more these days,' she conceded.

'The Indians,' Willie Proudfit said, 'they named me a name in their way of talken.'

His wife ran the fingers of her free hand over his hair. 'I'm gonna keep on a-callen you Willie,' she declared.

'Hit means Man-with-hair-white-like-wind-on-water,' he said. 'They give it to me fer a name. Me being a towhead.'

'Towhead,' she repeated, and ran her fingers through his hair, petting him. She treated him like a child, sometimes, Mr. Munn noticed, with a toying and patronizing tenderness. But she was probably twenty-five years younger than he was, or more. She was girlish-looking and slightly made, except for a fullness of her high breasts, over which the calico of her dress stretched almost tightly. Certainly, she was not yet thirty, and seemed younger except at those times when she fell into long silences, her black eyes, even as she moved about her tasks, seeming withdrawn from the objects about her. It was as though she had absorbed something of the gravity and aloofness of her husband, like a precocious child who is usually with adults or is much alone. She was an energetic woman, and competent with her hands, which seemed to know their occupations so well that when she sank into one of her fits of abstraction they could proceed as though they possessed a life and a way of their own. But now and then, when she was working out in her little garden patch, Mr. Munn, from his place up by the spring on the bluffside, had seen her pause and lean on her hoe, not for a minute or two, but for a long time, looking off down the valley. At first he had thought it was because she was tired, but when suppertime came she moved as briskly as in the morning and was as ready with her smile. Once he had come down from the cover on the bluff and had offered to help her in the garden, but she had said no, she was just fooling around anyway, because she didn't want to stay in the house, the weather being so nice, and he ought to keep out of sight.

He had offered to help Willie Proudfit in the field, too. And had had the same answer. He had insisted: 'Nobody'll know me, not with this beard and all. Hell, I don't know myself in the mirror.'

'Naw, naw,' Willie Proudfit had said, 'but hit don't do no good to start folks guessen. If'n they don't see you round much they'll git used to the notion of you being here painless. They'll hold hit in their heads, but they won't be a-thinken a-bout hit. Some folks knows you're stayen here. They'll just git used to hit. I said you was a feller I used to know out in New Mexico, and yore health was porely and you was stayen here till you got on yore feet. I said yore name was Barclay. I knowed a man named Barclay once, he ———'

'I can go somewhere else,' Mr. Munn offered. 'I'll get you all in trouble.'

Willie Proudfit shook his head. 'Naw,' he replied, 'you ain't a-leave-en. Not and a friend of Doctor MacDonald. And that time they had that-air rally in Bardsville, I was a-standen thar, and I listened to what you said, and I says to myself, that 'un's a man fer you. You ain't a-leave-en.'

'It'll get you in trouble. They'll be getting after me, sooner or later.'

'Won't no man be took in my house,' the other man said, and shook his head; 'not and me able.'

But they had not been after him. Not yet, and the weeks had passed, since the morning when he had run down the back stairs of the hotel and had looked wildly up and down the alley, seeing no one, and had run into the stable. The hall had still been empty, as before. That had been his piece of luck. He had climbed to the loft and burrowed into the hay. He had lain there, hour after hour, with a handkerchief over his face to keep off the dust and with the coarse hay turning into a bed of knives and the sweat covering his body with the effort of stillness, and his throat dry and rasping with thirst. Twice during the day, he had been sure, the soldiers had come. He had heard the voices below, numerous and portentous and excited, but muffled by the hay.

Late at night he decided to come down, to take his chance. He guessed that he couldn't hold out another day. And by this time they must have figured that he had managed to get out with the crowd. He would have to gamble that there wouldn't be a guard on the stables, except the old negro watchman. Not moving, he lay in the hay and thought of the watchman, of seeing his eyes open with surprise to show the whites and his lips spread for a cry. It became, on the instant, sharp as reality for him, the brown face, the lips opening to show the old, broken, yellow teeth; and his muscles contracted as for a spring, or a blow, his fingers crooked — they knew, they were doing their thinking, they had their plans — and his heart gave a sudden, cold, almost exultant knock at the ribs.

No, he thought. And no. Not that. With an effort he straightened his fingers. He felt giddy and hollow, like a man recoiling from the unexpected, irrevocable deed, already performed in an instant outside of will. Then he said, no, I won't.

He did not know whether he had said the words out loud.

It's because I haven't eaten all day, he thought; that's why I'm this way.

Then he began, cautiously, to part the weight of hay above him.

He remembered that the old negro man's name was Jim. He said to himself, his name's Jim.

He crept to the head of the ladder above the hall. Below him, he could make out the faint light. After a while it moved. The watchman was going down to the other end of the stable. Now there was only the fainter light that came into the hall from a street light in the alley. He let himself down the ladder, quickly. He did not have time to look into the alley before he stepped out. He scarcely cared what was there. The old negro man with the lantern, that was what he was fleeing from, it seemed.

No one was in the alley. He moved down the alley, away from the light, trying not to run. He put his tongue out on his dry lips, and thought of water.

They would be watching the roads. He couldn't go out any road. He would have to work down the alleys, and try to get out to the fields through back yards and ditches. That was his chance.

It worked. It was not much more than an hour till light when he got out past the last houses. He managed to reach a patch of woods beyond the first field, crawling part of the way in an old ditch, then following an osage hedge for cover. In the woods he ran wildly through the whipping underbrush and the snatching briars. At the edge of the woods he found a stock pond. He lay in the trampled mud of the edge, with the cold mud sliding up between his fingers and covering his hands, and drank. He lay on the mud then, closed his eyes, and felt that he could never get up. But after a while, he opened his eyes. The dark trees were there, and above, the sky, where light now grew. Those things were there in a stark purity, an emptiness, an innocence, a primal namelessness. He lay, feeling the slow, minute suction of the mud beneath his body, and stared at the treetops, the heave of the dark mass on the sky. The light was growing on the sky. His mind named that: light.

He got up and went on.

He found a garden patch near a cabin at the edge of the woods, and stuffed his pockets with lettuce and young onions. He ate some of the onions as he went along. He covered two or three miles down a lane, where he had the cover of a hedge, before it was too near day to be safe. He hid in another patch of woods all day. There was a ditch in the woods, and he drank some water from it. He ate the lettuce and the onions sparingly, to make them last. But by afternoon the onions had given him a sharp, retching cramp. After the pain had worn off, he slept some, lying on the pile of dead leaves in the thicket by the ditch. When he woke up the last time, it was dark. That night he managed to reach the Campbell place.

He was afraid to approach the house, but he lay in the barn, dozing fitfully. In the middle of the morning, he managed to attract Mr. Campbell's attention. He stayed in the barn for three days. Mr. Campbell smuggled food out to him, and after dark the first night, a blanket and a pillow. 'I don't mind having you,' Mr. Campbell said that night, squatting in the loft, in the dark, while Mr. Munn lay stretched out on the blanket. 'It's not that I mind. It's just that this section right round here ain't too safe. Soldiers on the road out by my place not more'n two days ago.'

Mr. Munn scarcely heard, sinking again into a sweet daze of weariness. 'Uh-huh,' he replied. Mr. Campbell's words flowed away from him. He knew that they would have meaning for him later. But not now.

'Now a little north of here, it's safer. Things been right quiet up there. And there's a feller up there thinks a world of Doctor

MacDonald. The doc stayed up there with him off and on, fishing and hunting. I went up once with the doc, just once, not being much of a hand to be hunting and fishing, and spent a night and a day up there in this feller's place. Feller name of Proudfit, a quiet-spoken feller. You heard the doc speak about him?'

'Yes,' Mr. Munn responded, letting Mr. Campbell's words slide and break and re-form meaninglessly in his mind like quicksilver, 'I reckon so.'

'Well, I'll go see him. I'll go tomorrow and fix it up. This Proudfit feller, he'll do anything for the doc, and after all you've done for the doc.'

'I haven't done anything for him,' Mr. Munn said.

'Well' — and Mr. Campbell hesitated — 'I don't know what you'd call anything, then.'

'Not enough, anyway. And they'll nail him. Yes' — he rolled over on his side as though to rise — 'they'll nail him. They made a deal. With Turpin.'

Mr. Campbell did not speak for a moment or two. Then he replied, in a flat tone, 'Turpin's gone.'

'Gone!' Then: 'Gone where?'

'To hell,' Mr. Campbell said, 'if I had my way. I reckon the Lord'll agree with me.'

Mr. Munn pushed himself up on one elbow and reached out to clutch at the other man in the darkness. 'Listen,' he demanded, 'what's become of Turpin?'

'You got him,' Mr. Campbell said.

Mr. Munn clutched his arm. 'Got him?'

'Over the left ear,' Mr. Campbell went on.

Mr. Munn's breath made a sharp sound. He released his grip on the other man's arm. 'You mean,' he said, paused, then proceeded with a steady voice, 'he's dead.'

'As a doornail,' Mr. Campbell told him. 'I reckoned you knew.'

Mr. Munn lay back on the blanket. 'I didn't know,' he said. 'There wasn't any way for me to know. You see' — he paused, like a man searching his mind for certainty — 'you see, I didn't do it.'

The other man did not answer for a moment. 'Well,' he said then, matter-of-factly, 'it don't make any difference to me if you did. It don't ——'

'But I didn't,' Mr. Munn denied quietly.

'Somebody shot him out the window of your office. With your rifle. Forty yards, and nailed him clean. It don't make any difference to me. Or to plenty others round here, I reckon.'

'I went there,' Mr. Munn said. 'I wrote a note to the girl that helps me. Then I left. I left the door open, because she'd be coming soon. Somebody else ——'

'Did you see anybody when you came out?' Mr. Campbell inquired casually.

'I came out the back way. I didn't see anybody in the alley. Nobody. I went to the hotel, up the back stairs, and there was Isabella Ball standing there, and she said they'd come for me. I hid in the livery stable loft.'

'It's nothing to me,' Mr. Campbell said, 'even if you did do it. It's just that it ain't too safe round here now. I wouldn't even stay at Proudfit's too long. You oughter get out the country a spell.'

'But it wasn't me. You see that?'

'Sure,' Mr. Campbell answered, and shifted his weight so that the boards creaked uneasily under him in the darkness. 'Sure.'

Mr. Munn pushed himself up from the blanket, and reached his arm out. But he withdrew it, and sank back down. 'Well,' he remarked, 'I reckon it'll get MacDonald off.'

'That's what folks say,' Mr. Campbell replied.

The next day Mr. Campbell went off to see the Proudfit fellow. When he got back late at night, he went directly to the barn to talk to Mr. Munn. He said that it was all arranged for him to go, that it was all right with Proudfit. He said he would take him up there, and for him to be trying to figure out a way. Mr. Campbell himself proposed that he could hide in a wagonload of something and get up there that way the next day.

'I can make it by myself,' Mr. Munn said. 'I made it here.' But Mr. Campbell wouldn't permit it. The next night he took Mr. Munn to Proudfit's in a buggy. It was a dark night, and they stuck to back roads when they could. Mr. Campbell said he had a cousin up in that section, and if anybody tried to find out what he'd been doing up there, he could say he'd been to see his cousin. He'd tell his cousin something to fix him, he said.

At first Mr. Munn felt that the Proudfits were disturbed to have him, even though Willie Proudfit, standing on his porch just at dawn the morning of his arrival, had taken his hand and said: 'Pleased to know you, Mr. Munn. My house, hit's yore'n to stay in.' Mr. Munn told himself that in a few days he would go on, as soon as he had rested up a little and got on his feet. But he did not say to himself where he would go. His mind did not really confront the idea of the future. He would say to himself, Now I'd better be deciding, I can't stay on here. But that was all. The words were meaningless for him. The hatreds, the rancors, and the despair that had filled him as he lay hidden at the Campbell place were gone now. There was only a kind of paralysis, a numbness, not painful but pervasive, that crept over him when he said to himself, I better be going now, I better decide. The words had no meaning to him because the idea of the future had no meaning for him. When he tried to think of the future he was like some blundering insect that tries, again and again, to climb up the smooth wall of a dish into which it had fallen.

But his feeling about the Proudfits quickly wore away. He discovered the natural aloofness of the man. Something of the first shyness of Adelle Proudfit passed, and then he recognized that her fits of abstraction and her silences were part of her being. Even Adelle Proudfit's niece, a seemingly frail, dark-eyed girl of about fifteen, who looked much as Adelle Proudfit must have looked, ceased to give him the secret, sidewise, almost suspicious glances in which he sometimes surprised her during the early days of his stay. But later, on days when they did any baking, Sissie would bring up the hill to him two rolls folded in a little square of white cloth.

What was with Sissie a shyness, and a quietness, was with her brother almost a surliness. The same quality was there in both, as in the aunt, but only as the characteristic structure of bone and feature which belongs to all the members of a family may produce in one the effect of beauty and in another that of ugliness. He was dark, too, and slenderly, though strongly, built. He was pious, withdrawing from the others to read a chapter in his Bible every night before going to bed; but in his piety there was a certain nervous and demanding and vindictive quality, as though he would wring from it a final meaning and satisfaction, once and for all. He worked hard in the field with his uncle, with that same nervousness and vindictiveness, not as though he occupied himself with tasks that were a part of the tissue of his being, but as though he wrestled to trip and strike an enemy. He would come in at noon drenched with sweat and almost gasping with fatigue. He would eat in silence, chewing his food doggedly and without raising his eyes from his plate, and when he had finished he would fling himself down on the porch, not casually and luxuriously like Willie Proudfit, but as though he would seize and conquer by violence the needed rest. 'You'll wear yoreself out,' Willie Proudfit would say to him. 'I seen men like you, Sylvestus, and maybe they be goen on lak you fer twenty years. And all of a sudden, they seen the world wasn't no diff'rent, and they'd come nigh a-curse-en hit and theirselves.

And from that-air day on, they wouldn't sweat nuthen but bitter sweat. And eat their vittles in bitterness. Or they'd lay down and die.'

'You ain't wore out,' the nephew would say, 'and I reckin you had it hard as the next man.'

'I seen it hard, off and on, I ain't deny-en. A man gits in a tight, and he lays holt on what he kin and the Lord help him. But that's diff'rent, now.'

'Work's work,' the nephew would respond, lying on the boards of the porch, not opening his eyes, the sweat drying stiff on the dull blue cloth of his shirt.

'A man labors,' Willie Proudfit would say, 'and sun to sun. But he oughter know in his mind one day agin the next day, and not lay up bitterness.'

'Hit'll be layen up bitterness, and you lose yore place,' the nephew observed one day. 'We don't make this year, and git a price.' He opened his eyes, and swept his arm upward with a vicious motion of rejection. 'And you a-talken. That a-way.'

Willie Proudfit said nothing.

'Yeah, yeah, you lose yore place' — the nephew spoke with a trace of vindictive pleasure, like a man driving home a long-sought advantage, found suddenly, at last — 'and what'll you do? You and Dellie? And Sissie?'

'What the Lord'll let me,' the other man answered slowly. 'Lak I done a-fore.'

'Yeah, yeah! Go and crop on somebody else's ground. That's what. And how would you like that, Uncle Willie?'

For a little while, Willie Proudfit made no answer, lying there, looking up, almost puzzledly, at the pattern of shingles between the rafters of the porch roof. Then he said: 'I ain't a-sayen I'd find hit in my heart to lak hit. On nobody else's ground.'

'Well, I'll tell you' — and the vicious triumph in the nephew's voice mounted — 'you wouldn't lak hit. No more'n pappy did.

Fifteen years croppen. His place lost, and fifteen years croppen. Till he died. Naw, you wouldn't lak hit, Uncle Willie.'

Mr. Munn already knew the place was mortgaged. Willie Proudfit had told him that he had bought the place when he first came back from the West, some eleven or twelve years before, and had never managed to pay out on it. For several years now he had barely been managing to hang on, he said. 'I oughter put more in the place in the good years, I reckin,' he said, 'but I put hit in me a house, what was extra. We oughter lived in a pole shanty till ever foot was paid. But I wanted Dellie to have her a good house, hit being that a-way with a woman. A woman laks her a parler. And fer young 'uns. We figgered on young 'uns and room fer 'em. But the young 'uns, thar ain't none. Sissie and Sylvestus, but not our own.' Then he added: 'The Lord's give me more, some ways, than a man kin ask, I reckin. But hit looks lak He holds just one thing back from a man, so a man kin know in his heart He's the Lord.'

On another occasion, later, Willie Proudfit had come out of one of his long spells of silence to say: 'One time, a man could go out West. And maybe git him a good piece of ground. Lak my pappy done, leave-en this country in sixty-one, and goen to North Arkansas. Them days, hit was air man's country.'

'Oklahoma,' the nephew had replied, 'they say a man kin still go to Oklahoma.'

'I'll lay the good ground's all took,' Willie Proudfit said.

'Or somewhere,' the nephew said, 'and git me a job. Leave off a-breaken my back in the field.'

'Maybe I'll be goen to Oklahoma.' Then, after a little silence, Willie Proudfit added, 'I ain't a old man yit.'

And Mr. Munn remembered how Doctor MacDonald, standing in his cell that day, had said that he was going to clear out and go West. Where the country didn't stink like the jail did. And when the news came that the trial was over, and that Doctor

MacDonald was acquitted, he remembered it again, exactly how Doctor MacDonald had stood that day in the cell, speaking the words. Suddenly, while Willie Proudfit stood there before him saying, 'The doc, he's a free man,' a sense of desolation and betrayal overwhelmed Mr. Munn. Doctor MacDonald would go away now, he and Cordelia. Out West. And leave him here, lost. He fought the feeling down. 'That's fine, that's fine!' he said to Willie Proudfit, through lips that felt stiff and cold like tallow.

But only for that moment, for when he lay up by the spring that afternoon, he again felt the same resentment and betrayal when he thought that Doctor MacDonald would go away. He seemed to see, as in the clarity of a vision, Doctor MacDonald standing, with Cordelia at his side — with her hand resting lightly on his arm in that way she had — Doctor MacDonald standing there, showing his teeth in that grin that seemed to come from his secret and unsharable knowledge, and behind him, spread out like a picture, a sunlit plain, or the colors of desert and mountains, or — for the picture changed even as Mr. Munn tried to fix it — the blue waters of the Pacific. Then it was gone. He told himself that Doctor MacDonald would stay here until things settled down. Doctor MacDonald wasn't the man to go off when his friend was in trouble. He wouldn't go away as long as there was a chance he could do anything to help. That was something.

But in the end, and there was no denying the fact, Doctor MacDonald would go. Even standing in his cell, saying, 'I might get used to the way this country stinks,' he had been able to seize on and define a future. He carried his future in himself. And Sylvestus, in his bitterness and vindictiveness, could plan a future for himself, away from here, in Oklahoma, or at some job in a city, somewhere. Willie Proudfit, who would probably lose his place and everything he had in it, and who was on past fifty years old, had been able to lie there on the porch that day and say, 'I ain't a old man yit.' But Mr. Munn could not, no matter how hard he tried, think beyond the moment. He did not have the seed of the future in himself, the live germ. It had shriveled up and died, like a sprouting grain of corn that has been washed out of the hill to lie exposed to the sun's heat.

He could not tell exactly when it had died. Perhaps it had been dying for a long time, drying and shriveling slowly, and he had only come to know that fact, and to know his isolation, when he lay by the stock pond at the edge of the woods, with his body pressed against the cold mud, and saw the impersonal light grow on the sky, above the dark trees. Perhaps it had died long before, and he had been living, only, on the hope and the meaning there was in other men. But now it was dead; and because the future was dead and rotten in his breast, the past, too, which once had seemed to him to have its meanings and its patterns, began to fall apart, act by act, incident by incident, thought by thought, each item into brutish separateness. Sometime he would try to build up some old scene of happiness or distress, to try to make the image communicate to him again the verity of his past feelings. But it was no use. He could remember some incident, what had happened, even to the minutest detail — May's face lighted with pleasure as she turned to him; or the face of Bunk Trevelyan's wife when she had come to his office before his body was found and had said, 'They taken him off, in the night, and I ain't seen him, I ain't seen him, and I come to you'; or the sound of Mr. Christian's breathing, its harshness, its inhuman drag and rasp, coming from beyond the wall that night when he had stood staring at the shadowy, white door, and had waited vainly for Lucille Christian to come to him — he could remember the slightest detail of such an incident, but he could not torture himself into the old response that had been the lively truth of that moment. There was only the new numbness, the new isolation.

He was not afraid. He told himself that he was not afraid.

He had no intention of letting them catch him. But he was not afraid of them. If they tried to catch him there would be trouble. He felt, without ever phrasing it to himself, that that much, at least, a man owed to himself. The fact that he was hunted and couldn't show himself to people and had a price on him, that fact was, he was sure, not the fundamental fact for him. Even at the time when Willie Proudfit brought him one of the handbills offering the reward, that fact had not seemed the fundamental thing. His picture was on the handbill. He knew which photograph it had been made from, one he had had taken, a little while before he was married, to give to May. They must have had it from the photographer in Bardsville. Beneath the picture it read: 'Two thousand dollars reward for the capture of Percy Munn, wanted for murder.'

'Hit looks lak they want you bad,' Willie Proudfit had remarked.

'Yes,' Mr. Munn had said, 'it's a lot of money.'

'They got them handbills ever whar. You better keep lay-en low. Over at Thebes they got 'em all over the settlement, on walls and telephone poles, and lay-en in stores.'

'They didn't nail Doctor MacDonald,' Mr. Munn told him. 'So it's me. They're bound to nail somebody.' Then the bitterness came into his tone. 'And I didn't do it. Whatever else I've done, I didn't do that. Somebody else did it ——'

Willie Proudfit nodded.

'— but I can't prove it. That's the trouble. Nobody'll believe it.'

'I believe hit,' Willie Proudfit said, 'but I don't give a durn. If'n you did do hit.'

If he had done it, it might have been different now. If he had gone up to his office that morning, and looked out the window and seen, under the leafing trees, that man Turpin being taken toward the courtroom to sit there in the chair, with that heavy, blank look on his face gradually turning into despair as the words came out that he had bargained to say. If he himself had seen Turpin, and had seen the rifle sitting there and the cartridge box there on the shelf of the bookcase, behind the cracked glass door, he might have done it. Near forty yards away, forty yards Mr. Campbell had said — moving in the speckled sunlight under the leafing trees, but the rifle propped to the window-ledge, or the desk. If he had done it, he might now feel something, some sense and order, not this numbness. He would lie on his back by the spring, while the falling water made its constant sound, and stare at the blueness of the sky, or the patches of whitish clouds that hung idly in the brightness, and would try to think himself into that context. The deed, then, would have been his; he could have lived in it; and in its consequence. Certainly, it would have been different from this.

He would think of that negro man, the one who had had the knife, Trevelyan's knife. The knife which the negro had found under the corncrib. Where Trevelyan had put it, after he killed Duffy. Where the frog found it — 'a great-big ole bull-frog a-hoppen along this side that-air branch whar my shoats does they walleren.' The negro standing there in the pale lamplight, his voice pouring out, saying, '— and he kept on a-hoppen and a-hoppen, and I throwed my hat at him and I tried to ketch him, but he kept on a-hoppen — hit wuz that big ole red shoat got him, I seen him when she done hit. She done taken him ——' The words had poured out, but after they got him on the horse, behind the deputy, he had only mumbled a little and then had said nothing more. They said that he had never said much at his trial, had just sat there. And afterward in the jail, till they hanged him. Mr. Munn tried hard to remember his name. He would lie there, staring at the dazzling depth of the sky, and try to remember the name. It became almost an obsession with him. That man had been born in such a cabin as they found him in that night, dropped unbreathing and foul onto a pallet on the floor, or into a bed that creaked and sagged, with the light coming in at a patched windowpane, gray or bright, or with the light of such a lamp as lighted the cabin the night they took him. He had sucked milk from a breast, and had crawled in the dust before the cabin with the cabin and trees and the fields enormous around him. He had put food into his mouth, and had eaten it, day after day growing stronger. He had worked in the fields, and talked and laughed at night, and lain in the bed there with the woman whose eyes had followed them with that animal questioning about the cabin that night. They had knocked on the door, late at night, and had come in and found the knife, and had taken him away. Mr. Munn tried, day after day, to remember his name. He could see his face, the way it had looked in the lamplight, the gray lips protesting, saying, 'If'n I knowed that knife was yore'n, I shore would a-brung hit back. I'd a-found whar yore place wuz, and brung hit back, and——' But he could not remember the name.

Day after day, he was idle. He lay by the spring, drowsing, sometimes for hours, for at night he slept badly. At night, after lying for a long time in his bed, watching the square of the window of the little lean-to room, he would sit up, as though to leap out and perform some errand of overmastering magnitude. Once, even, he got up and put on his overalls and shoes, and went outdoors. The moon was very low, just at the wooded western rim of the little valley. The contours of objects now familiar to him — the trees, the barn, the fences, the bluffside — lost definition and merged and faltered aqueously in the shadows and in the uncertain striations of mist and dim light. He walked rapidly until he came to the fence that bordered the road. Then he stopped. He laid his hand to the rough rail, and stood and stared down the road, which was pale against the darkness of the brush beside it. Every slight sound of the night — the water falling, the whip-poor-will very far off, the uneasy shifting of the guinea hens in their trees back of the house — these sounds registered upon him, each perfect, isolated, vibrant with the small re-echo deep within his being. For how long a time he could not tell, he stood there in that anticipatory posture, his fingers gripping the rail, while those sounds, each individual in the wide silence, impinged upon him.

Slowly, he relaxed his grip upon the rail. Those sounds, which had come to him individually and complete with a resonance like that of a struck bell, grew blurred, and dulled. He struck his right fist into the palm of his left hand. He said aloud: 'God damn! God damn, I've got to do something.' And again: 'I've got to.'

Then he felt exhausted. He only wanted to get back into the room, into the bed, to close his eyes. He moved toward the house, hunching his bare shoulders against the night chill.

But some nights, when he did sleep, he had the dream. He had first dreamed it shortly after coming to the Proudfit place. At that time he had come to consciousness weak and sweating, filled with an unutterable grief. But now when he dreamed it, the grief was gone. Even in the dream now, he knew that it had been dreamed before.

That first night he had been sitting out on the porch while Adelle Proudfit sang. Toward the end of the evening she sang about Pretty Polly.

> 'Walk with me, Pretty Polly
>   For we go to the church soon.'
> He said, 'Now, Pretty Polly,
>   It's nigh the full of the moon.'

> 'Not now, not now,' said Pretty Polly,
>   'I'll walk some other day.'
> But he took her by her lily-white hand
>   And led her far away.

Absorbed in his own thoughts, he scarcely followed the tune and the story of sadness and hinted violence in the woods. But

Adelle Proudfit's voice was going on, moving in that melancholy rhythm:

> — wanderer be,
> For a ship sat at the seaside,
> And he got in that pretty ship
> To sail to the other side.
>
> He had not sailed not many miles
> When the awful storm came down
> And beat upon the pretty ship,
> Made it under the sea sink down.
>
> There he met his Pretty Polly
> All wrapped in gores of blood,
> And she held out in her lily-white arms,
> An infant was of mine.

He had risen, and had walked away, across the yard.

That night he had dreamed the dream. In the dream he saw May approaching him, slowly, as from a great distance across which he strained. Her pale hair was down, loose, and she held a bundle in her arms. On her face, as she approached him, there was a great sweetness, but a sadness, and she approached slowly, as though her feet were weighted with lead. Closer, she held out the bundle toward him. He saw that it was wrapped in old newspaper, stained and torn. Then, as he strained toward her and reached to take the bundle from her arms, the paper began to flake away from the bundle, as though disintegrating from its own sodden weight, hanging in shreds over May's hands and bare arms. He saw, then, what the paper had concealed. There, on May's outstretched arms, was a body, a foetus like those which he had seen suspended in liquid in great glass jars at the medical school at Philadelphia, ill-formed, inhuman, dripping, gray like the ones in the jars, and with a stench like death. But May's face had retained the expression of sweetness and sadness, and his own arms had remained reaching toward her as though to take the bundle. Then, the last shreds of the sodden paper fell away from what was the face of that object in her arms. It was the face of Bunk Trevelyan, the redness of flesh and hair faded to grayness, but Trevelyan's face, and somehow, he knew that it was alive and strove to speak. But always, at that moment, May began to laugh. He could not hear the sound, but her face was contorted in a paroxysm of laughter that he thought would never end. Then, not in fury but with a coldness of calculation, almost with a slyness, he raised his clenched fist, thinking that he must stop her laughter, that if she continued to laugh like that all would be lost, everything would shrivel and be blotted out and devoured, and there would be nothing but that soundless ferocity of laughter and himself alone in the midst of it. Then he woke up, that first time suspended, as it were, in the perfect, swollen, and untrembling medium of grief, which in itself was a kind of fulfillment, for in its absolute was posited the absolute worth of all lost happinesses. But now, when he woke up in the darkness of that little lean-to room of the Proudfit house, there was not even the grief.

Some nights, when he could not sleep, he would retrace every incident of the morning when Turpin had been shot. He would say to himself, Now, I left the hotel at seven-twenty. The very look of the watch as he had held it in his hand would come back to him. And he would bring up before his mind the faces of the persons whom he had met on the street. He would repeat aloud, lying there in the dark, the very words they had spoken to him in greeting, and his own replies. He would try to re-create every familiar detail of the office, which he had seen when opening the door that morning: the desk, the bookcases, the chairs heaped with old books and papers, the courthouse and the leafing trees. He would grip those items hard in his mind, his very muscles tensing with the effort sometimes, as though by will he might force a reason out of their blank and taciturn irrationality.

It was not to his violence that they surrendered their answer. Rather, the answer he finally had from them came almost unsought, casually, at the moment of his waking one morning, before he had fully defined himself in consciousness. He woke, that morning, and saw the shaft of sunlight striking through the window, the green bluffside beyond, and the rough boards of the wall. And at the instant when he identified those objects, his mind seemed to say to him, You are lying here, looking at those things, because Professor Ball killed that man.

Then it seemed impossible.

Then he was sure of it, as sure as if he had stood to watch Professor Ball, that morning, mount the darkened stairway and push open the unlocked door and, finding the office empty, stand there in the middle of the floor. Across the square, back of the courthouse, the men had been moving, Turpin and the deputies. And there in the corner of the office, the rifle had stood. And there on the shelf of the bookcase, behind the cracked glass, had been the cartridge box. And it had been done, all of it, in an instant. Near forty yards, Mr. Munn thought, near forty yards, and he probably hadn't fired a gun since he was a boy. Out there, in the courthouse yard, Turpin had reeled and fallen on the grass with that hole over his left ear — Mr. Campbell had said that, over the ear — and as though unseeingly, Professor Ball had stood the rifle back in its corner, and had walked out, pulling the door shut behind him, and had gone down the back stairs.

It was perfectly clear to Mr. Munn how it had happened. And how Professor Ball had moved down the alley, erectly, almost somnambulantly, his white, club-like bandages hanging out from under the black sleeves, and all the while the awareness of his act gradually growing within him. When the force of it struck him, and he understood the full context, he must have intended to go to the hotel and see Cordelia and his other daughters — but especially Cordelia — and tell them good-bye and give himself up. Or had anything been so precise and clear to him then, as he moved down that deserted alley and the sounds of the street reached him unheeded? Mr. Munn was not sure. Perhaps, as he moved down the alley, nothing had seemed quite real to him, and everything had hung suspended in the timelessness of a dream. He might have wandered about the streets for half a day, there was no telling, looking at people and not seeing them, scarcely knowing that his feet proceeded in their regular, dignified tread, and that people stared at his pale and stony-looking face.

Then, later, with Cordelia beside him, and with Portia laying the cool cloths to his forehead, he must have thought, I'll do it in a little while, just a little while and I'll tell them, and I'll go. But he had not.

The bitterness rose in Mr. Munn at the thought. He had run through the blind woods; he had lain in the cold mud and filth and had sucked water into his mouth like a beast; he had gone hungry and had hidden from the sight of people, because Professor Ball had not been able to speak, and say that he had done it. Because Professor Ball had thought, I'll do it in a little while, just as soon as the trial is over and my little girl doesn't need me any more, I'll do it then. Then the trial was over, and Doctor MacDonald was free, and he had not done it.

The days had passed, and he had not been able to speak. When he had heard that Mr. Munn was safe, and hiding, he must have told himself that he would wait, just a little longer; that if they caught Mr. Munn, he would speak up and say he had done it. Meanwhile, the movement of ordinary life in his own house, the sight of his daughters doing their tasks quietly and competently about him, the routine of the occupations on the farm, all those things must have lulled him, and drawn him insidiously, hour by hour, day by day, from his purpose. But, at night, in his room, he must have read his Bible, and struck it with his bandaged hands in his agony and confusion, and walked the floor, sweating like a man who wrestles with a too powerful opponent, and prayed for strength. He had found a strength in himself for acts of which he had never dreamed himself capable. 'It's surprising what a man'll find in himself,' he had said that first night, a long time back now, at the Christian house — and Mr. Munn could remember his face and his very voice as he had said it — 'when the time comes.' The time had come. He had stumbled upon it that morning in the deserted office, unexpectedly as on a stone in a familiar path. He had lifted the rifle, clumsily in his bandaged, unaccustomed hands, and over there in the courthouse yard, in the clear daylight, the man had fallen.

He had never guessed that strength in himself. It had lain hidden all the years of his life, until the time came. But now he could not find in himself another strength in which he had lived, so he had thought, always.

Later, thinking back on those things, Mr. Munn discovered that his bitterness was gone. If he should see Professor Ball, he himself, he decided, would be the one to feel guilty and ashamed, as though he had committed the wrong. If he should be taken, or if he should give himself up, then Professor Ball, he was sure, would speak. He had a momentary vision of Professor Ball's face as it would be if they should meet, the face thin and arid and contorted in its pain. Involuntarily, shudderingly, he closed his eyes as against the actual sight, as one does at the obscenity of suffering.

His discovery, he determined, if it was a discovery, had solved nothing for him. He sank back, as before, into the privacy of that world screened from all the world outside by the green leaves of the bluff or the boards of the little lean-to room. Into that privacy the thought of what he had been or what he might become filtered only thinly, sourcelessly, like light into a sub-marine depth.

Day after day, there would be nothing to obtrude upon him

on the bluffside. Only once, late one afternoon, Sylvestus had come up the bluff and had squatted there on his heels in the pressed-down grass. The sweat stained darkly his blue shirt, and the sleeves stuck to his arms. When he took his hat off, the thick hair was matted clammily on his head, with a line pressed into it where the band of the hat had been. 'Hit's cool up here,' he said, 'but today, hit was a scorcher fer fair. The sun a-bearen down in the field.' He took his knife from his pocket, opened the heavy blade, and began, with deliberation, to trim a stick which he found lying there before him. 'In the field,' he repeated, appearing to study the stick. 'But I reckin you didn't know, hit cool up here lak hit is.' He turned his dark, acrimonious glance upon Mr. Munn, then resumed his whittling. Mr. Munn said nothing.

'I ain't a man to shun and shirk,' Sylvestus said. 'No man kin say hit. Anything air man kin do, I kin do. And will do. But a man's got a right to know he don't sweat fer nuthen. Hit'll be a drout, and sweat fer nuthen.' He paused, studying the stick. 'A drout,' he repeated.

'It's too early to tell,' Mr. Munn rejoined.

'I kin tell. Ever time, I kin tell!' He swung toward Mr. Munn resentfully. 'I seen a blade of corn today, yaller, and hit long a-fore tosselen time. Hit's a curse come on the land, the way folks been revelen and carryen on.' He rose abruptly from his squatting position, and flung the stick into the spring. 'Sweat fer nuthen,' he uttered.

He stood there indecisively, the rigidity seeming to go from his body. He clicked the knife blade shut. 'I didn't mean nuthen,' he said sullenly, not looking at Mr. Munn, 'about yore layen up here.' Then he turned, and before Mr. Munn could answer, plunged off down the trail.

That evening at supper Sylvestus had nothing to say to anyone. He ate with his eyes fixed upon his plate, doggedly. He did not join the others on the porch after supper, but stayed in the kitchen. 'A-readen,' Willie Proudfit told them. 'He'll be a-readen past moon-set lak as not, if hit's a spell come on him. Till they ain't no oil to the wick.'

'One mornen I found him,' Adelle Proudfit said, speaking quietly, 'with his head a-layen on the table, in the kitchen. And the oil plumb gone, and the wick burnt out, and him asleep. He lifted up his head, real slow, and said to me: "I slept, and Him in the Garden." Lak a man might say good mornen, and no diff'rence to his voice.'

'I recollect,' her husband responded, 'and that day he worked hard in the field as air man could.'

'I n'er seen one so young study so on salvation. Goen on twenty-four.'

'A ring-tail fer work,' Willie Proudfit said.

Sylvestus never came back up the bluff, but every baking day Sissie brought him a couple of rolls wrapped in a piece of white cloth. She would never sit down and he was never able to engage her in conversation. She would stand, holding her hands clasped together at the level of her waist, as was her habit, and watch him while he ate the bread. She always watched him until he had eaten the last crumb, and then, always, she left him. He would thank her, or sometimes would say, 'Why don't you sit down and talk to me, Sissie?' But it was always the same: one instant she was there, with her dark eyes unwaveringly watching him while he put the last fragment to his lips, and the next instant, suddenly, she was gone.

Only one time, toward the end of his stay at the Proudfit place, did she wait after he had finished eating the bread. He asked her to sit down, but she did not reply, only shaking her head. When he raised his face from the spring, after drinking, she stooped to pick up the little square of white cloth, and smoothing and folding it in her hands, she said, 'Mr. Perse ——'

'Yes, Sissie?'

'Mr. Perse' — and she paused, smoothing the cloth — 'Aunt

Dellie, she said they's word yore wife's had a little baby.'

'That's true,' Mr. Munn replied.

'Hit's a little boy,' she added, 'ain't hit?'

'Yes, Sissie.'

She laid the cloth between the palms of her hands, and held it there. Then she asked, 'What's hit's name?'

'I don't know,' he said.

She looked at him for a moment, and then, without a word, was gone.

He could not see her as she went down the trail. He watched the open space between the bluff and the house, waiting for her to appear. She emerged from the greenery at last, and moved rapidly toward the house. A little smoke was rising from the kitchen chimney, even though it wasn't much past middle of the afternoon. Then he remembered that she had brought him the bread. They were baking.

The smoke stood motionless, in a long, gray-blue streamer that faded out into the clear air, higher than the bluff-top.

After a little while the girl came out of the house. She carried a bucket in her hand, and he caught a glint of sunlight from it as it swayed with her step. Her figure, shrunk to such a smallness in the distance, moved across the yard and over the stile into the field by the creek. He saw her go down the field between the rows of young plants. At the far end of the field the two men were hoeing. She was carrying them some fresh water to drink.

She approached them, and their motions ceased. Then the figures were all together in one place, there at the far end of the field, very small.

They would unhook their hands from the hoe handle, and push their hats back a little off the forehead. Their lips would be dry, and on their teeth would be the slight grittiness of dust raised from the dry ground. In turn, Willie Proudfit first, then Sylvestus, they would lift the bucket to the lips and let the cool water fill the mouth and slip, sweetly and purifyingly, into the throat. Then they would thank the girl, and look inquiringly at the sun, and grip their hoes, and bend again over the hard earth, each in his way; and the hoes would rise and fall, unflaggingly. The drouth might come. The plants which they had placed in the ground might shrivel and wither there. Or next year the two men themselves might not be there. The place might be lost by that time. Willie Proudfit might be in Oklahoma, there was no telling. Sylvestus might be gone somewhere. But now their hoes rose and fell. They were moving down the field, imperceptibly, surely, as into their future. Beyond them, in other fields out of sight, other men were, and women in houses, and men in the streets of the towns.

He stared at the three figures so far below him in the field, suspended there in the wide, bright, brittle fullness of light, and he almost started up to call, to wave his arms, like a traveler lost in some desert country who sees far off, or thinks he sees, other men of his party moving confidently and serenely and unheedingly to disappear beyond some fold or abutment of the landscape, or into distance. But he did not. He lay on the ground, with his head on his arms, shaken, suddenly, by that common scene below him, more than he had been by the hardships of his flight, or the clung-to recollection of happinesses and distresses past, or the news of the birth of his son.

'Oklahoma,' Willie Proudfit said.

'They say a man kin git a start,' Sylvestus said.

'A long time since I seen hit,' Willie Proudfit said. He shifted a little, and the boards of the porch floor creaked in the dark. Then he said: 'Folks was goen in, then. To git a start. And fer one reason or 'nuther. Some just a move-en kind of folks, just move-en on. Lak I was, them days. The buffalo petered out, and they wasn't no more, whar I'd seen 'em black the ground off yander when a man looked. So I moved on, west. But I come back here. But a lot of folks, they ne'er come back, no-whar.'

He waited awhile, then he said: 'I come back, and left the dry country. But a man ne'er knows. Maybe I'll be goen back. To Oklahoma, maybe.'

'Sweat fer nuthen,' the nephew said, 'in this country.'

'Maybe I'll be goen agin,' Willie Proudfit said, 'and the time comes. If they's a place for a man to go nowadays. My pappy up and left here, and he ne'er aimed to, till the time come. Hit was in 'sixty-one and the war a-starten. My pappy wasn't easy in his mind. He never was no Bible-man exactly, but he studied on the shooten and the killen, and he prayed the Lord to show him which side to take. Which was the Lord's side. One mornen he said, "I ain't a-stayen in this country, on-easy in my mind and with my neighbors." He said, "I'm a-leave-en."

'So he got shed of what he had, land and gear, what he couldn't git on a wagon. And he put two span oxen to the wagon, and we all hit out towards north Arkansas. Pappy had a cousin in north Arkansas who wrote him a letter sayen north Arkansas was air man's country, free fer the gitten, a fair land and flowen. We went down west Tennessee, whar hit was cotton, ever whar a man looked. And to Memphis. We got on a steamboat at Memphis and went down the Mississippi and up the Arkansas. Been took a long time. Then we come to Little Rock. We stayed in Little Rock nigh onto three weeks waiten fer pappy's cousin. And me, I got so I knowed my way all over the hull town, you know how a kid is, a-pryen and a-prowlen. We was campen down on a little crick, and pappy was a-fretten and a-fume-en to be gitten on, and the season wearen. He wanted to be gitten some ground broke, even if hit was late, and a house up fore winter. And the drinken water in Little Rock, hit wasn't so good and pappy one to be cantankerous about drinken water. They's water in that country, but hit ain't good water lak the water here. Lots of folks them days had the flux in Little Rock, they said, and hit was the drinken water.

'But me, I was ten-'leven year old, and ever day Sunday. I'd go up and see the men drillen and gitten ready, some of them drillen with sticks, not have-en no guns yit. One day I says, "Pappy, ain't you gonna be a sojer?" "Sojer, sojer," he said, "you stay away from them sojers, or I'll whale the tar." But I'd slip off and go watch them sojers, lak a kid will. I had ne'er seen sich.

'Then pappy's cousin come. "Amon," he said to my pappy, fer Amon was his name, "I been slow a-gitten here, but sumthen crost my path." He taken a piece of paper outer his pocket, and he had drawed a map on hit, with ever thing marked good. My pappy studied on the map, then he said, "Ain't you goen back?" "Naw, Amon, I ain't," pappy's cousin said, "I'm a sojer now."

' "Sojer," my pappy said, and looked at him.

' "Sojer," pappy's cousin said, "but I ain't a family man, lak you."

'Pappy shook his head, slow. "Naw," he said, "hit ain't that. I had me a good place in Kentucky. And my wife, she's a clever woman and foreminded. I'll lay her agin air woman I e'er seen. She and my boys, they could run my place, and I could been a sojer. If I had hit in my mind and heart. But I ain't. I ain't clear and easy in my mind, this rise-en and slayen and a man not knowen."

'So pappy taken the map, and we loaded up the wagon, and put the oxen in, and crost over the river. That same, blessed day. Fer north Arkansas.

'Hit was air man's country, and the Lord's truth. Fair and flowen, lak pappy's cousin done said. Pappy found him a place in a fork of two cricks, bottom ground and high ground layen to a man's use-en, and a spring outer the ground, and timber standen, scalybark and white oak and cedar and yaller poplar and beech. And squirrels so thick they barked to wake you up of a mornen. "Lord God, Lord God," pappy said real soft, just

standen there looken, after he'd done settled his mind on a spot
to set his house. Then he said to ma, right sharp and sudden:
"Henrietta, gimme that axe!" And ma done hit.

'Some of the folks round there went off and went to the war,
like pappy's cousin, but pappy never the hull duration. Folks
would be a-talken, and a man mought name the war, and pappy,
he'd just git up and walk off. Then word come the war was over.
I was a big feller then, goen on sixteen, and handy if I do say so.
Us boys worked with pappy round the place, and we done right
well. Hit was a good country, fer fair.

'Time come I was goen on nineteen, and I said to pappy,
"Pappy, I been studyen about goen up to Kansas."

'And pappy said, "Boy, I been notice-en you sorter raise-en
yore sap."

'So I taken out fer Kansas. Pappy gimme a horse and saddle
and fifty dollars and hit gold. I figgered I'd go to Kansas and
be a buffalo hunter, lak I'd heared tell. I figgered I was handy
with a rifle as the next man. Many's the time, shooten fer a
steer, I'd took hind quarter, hide, and tallow, that being top
man. Fellers would put up fifty cents a-piece and buy a steer
and shoot fer choice, high man hind quarter, hide, and tallow,
next man, hind quarter, and next man, fore quarter and head,
and next man, fore quarter. Shoot at a shingle and a little heart
drawed on hit in white clay, forty paces free style or sixty paces
layen to a chunk.

'Hit was in Hays City I taken up with a feller named Mingo
Smith. He was a Yankee and he fit the war. He got mustered
out and he come to Kansas. He'd been a muleskinner down to
Santa Fe, and a bull-whacker out Colorado way, and a boss
layen the Kansas Pacific railroad, and he'd hunted buffalo fer
the railroad, too, to feed the men, they wasn't nuthen he hadn't
took a turn to, hit looked lak. He was a long skinny feller, didn't
have no meat on his bones to speak of, and his face was all yaller
and he didn't have no hair to his head, and hit yaller, too.

And him not more'n thirty. "Some day, I'll shore be a disappointmint to a Cheyenne," he'd say, and rub his hand over whar his hair oughter be. He figgered he'd take one more turn, the price on hides goen up lak hit was. Men come-en out to Hays City to buy hides, and all. Mingo, he had some money he'd got fer freighten up from Fort Sill, and a old wagon, and he bought and paid fer what all we needed, and said I could pay him my part outer what we took. So I thanked him kindly, and we hit out, him and me.

'Seven-eight year, and durn, we was all over that-air country, one time and ernuther. North of Hays City to the Saline, and up Pawnee Creek and the Arkansas, and down in the Panhandle on the Canadian, and down to Fort Sill. They had been a time a man couldn't git nuthen fer a hide not seasonable, with the fur good, and summer hunten didn't pay a man powder and git. But we come in to Hays City our first trip, loaded down, and figgeren on what to do till the cold come, and a feller what bought hides for Durfee, over to Leavenworth — give us two dollars and a dime fer prime bull, I recollect — he says, "Boys, just belly up quick, and quench yore thirst, and hit out again, I'm buyen now, summer or winter, rain or shine!" "Is that a fact," Mingo says, "summer hide?" "Hit's a fact," that feller says.

'Mingo up and buys ernuther wagon, and hires two feller to skin — Irish, they was, the country was plumb full of Irish — and a feller to cook and stretch, and I says to him, "Lord God, Mingo, you act lak we was rich." And he says, "We ain't, but Lord God, we gonna be. And I'm durn tired of skinnen, durned if I ain't. I don't mind shooten, but I hate to skin. One thing hit was, shooten rebels, a man ne'er had to skin 'em. Hit's gonna be shooten now, like a gentleman, till the barr'l hots."

'And durn if he didn't say the God's truth. The barr'l hot to a man's hand. The day a still day, and the smoke round a man's head like a fog, and yore ears ringen. If'n you got a stand

— the buffalo standen and graze-en — and drapped the lead one, the others mought just sniff and bawl, and not stampede. If you was lucky. Nuthen to hit then, keep on shooten fer the outside ones that looked lak they mought git restless, take hit easy and not git yore gun barr'l too hot. That next year, I mind me we got two good stand, Mingo one and me one. I was come-en up a little rise south of a crick runnen in the Pawnee, and I raised up my head, keerful, and thar they was, a passel of 'em. 'Bout a hundred and fifty paces off yander, and me down wind. I propped my Sharp's to my prongstick, and cracked down. I started to git up — a man would git up and run to git him his next shot — and got on one knee, and I see they wasn't no buffalo down. I figgered I'd missed, and a easy shot, and I laid back down fer a try. Then I seen a buffalo just lay down, and the rest standen thar, not move-en. I shot agin, and a buffalo come down, and the rest a-standen. And agin. I said, "Lord God," I said, "I do believe hit's a stand!"

'A stand hit was. I laid thar, looken down the barr'l of my Sharp's and the buffalo standen. I laid thar, counten out loud betwixt shots not to go too fast and hot the gun. A long time, and I could see 'em come down, slow, to the knees, when the ball found. Then keel over and lay. And the rest standen round, sniffen and bawlen. A man lays thar, the sun a-bearen down, and keeps on a-pullen on the trigger. He ain't lak his-self. Naw, he ain't. Lak he wasn't no man, nor nuthen. Lak hit ain't him has a-holt of the gun, but the gun had a-holt of him. Lak he mought git up and walk off and leave them buffalo down the rise, a-standen, and leave the gun lay, and the gun would be shooten and a-shooten, by hitself, and ne'er no end. And the buffalo, down the rise, standen and bawlen. Hit comes to a man that a-way.

'Seventy-two buffalo I shot that afternoon, layen thar, a-fore they broke and run. Gitten on to sun, they broke. I laid thar, and seen 'em go, what was left, not nigh a score, and the dust a-rise-en behind 'em. They run north, I seen 'em past sight, but I kept on a-layen thar, lak I couldn't uncrook my hand-holt off'n my Sharp's, and the barr'l hot to a man's flesh. I laid thar, lak a man past his short rows.

' "Durn," Mingo said, "them buffalo down thar, and you a-layen here lak hit wasn't nuthen!" I ne'er heared him come-en. "Boy, go git them Irish," he said, "hit's gonna be night work, a-skinnen." I didn't say nuthen, I taken out fer the wagons to git them skinners when they done got done with the ones they was skinnen. We got back hit was night, and Mingo down thar, skinnen and cussen. But the moon come up, red and swole layen thar to the east, bigger'n a barn. Ain't no moons in this country lak them moons in west Kansas. We skinned by the moon. Didn't nobody say nuthen. Nary a sound but a man grunten, or a knife whetten on a stell, maybe, soft and whickeren lak when hit's a good temper to the blade, and the sound hit makes when the hide gives off'n the meat to a good long pull. Then, off a-ways, the coyotes singen, and come-en closter.

'We skinned 'em all, all seventy-two, and taken the tongues. And the mops off'n the bulls. We loaded the wagon, and started up the rise, not have-en et, and plumb tuckered. Nigh half way up the rise, I recollect, I looked back. The moon was ride-en high, and the ground down thar looked white lak water, I recollect, and them carcases sticken up lak black rocks outer water.

'But a man didn't make him a stand ever day. Not by a sight, I kin tell you. He'd try the wind and git down wind, and start move-en in, slow and keerful, crawlen a good piece maybe. They started move-en, and hit was time. Two hundred paces and you was lucky. But a Sharp's will shoot lak a cannon. Hit's a fact. Three quarter mile ain't nuthen fer a Sharp's, not even on a bull buffalo, if'n you kin hit him. Which you caint. But two-fifty, three hundred paces, a man kin. And under the hump. You shoot, and the herd breaks and runs, and stops, and you run to ketch up, and lay and shoot. And they run agin. That a-way, till they done left you.

'But one way and ernuther, by and large we taken our share, Mingo and me. Winter and summer. And not us only. In Charlie Rath's sheds in Dodge City, many's the time with my own eyes I seen fifty-sixty thousand hides baled up and waiten, and his loaden yard so thick with wagons a man could nigh cross hit and ne'er set foot to ground. Wagons standen nigh hub to hub, and loaded, and fellers just in and likkered up and rare-en and cussen, waiten to git shet of their take. A time hit was, with money free lak sweat on a nigger, and men outer the war and from fer countries, and the likker runnen lak water. A power of meanness, and no denyen. But a man could git a-long, and not have him no trouble to speak on. If'n he tended to his business, and was God-fearen, and ne'er taken no back-sass off'n no man.

'We got our'n and didn't reckon on no end, hit looked lak. But a man's that a-way. He sees sumthen, and don't reckon on no end, no way, and don't see hit a-come-en. They's a hoggish-ness in man, and a hog-blindness. Down off'n Medicine Lodge Crick, one time, I was a standen on a little rise, in the spring, and the buffalo was a-move-en. North, lak they done. All the buffalo trails run north-south, and hit was spring. They was move-en north, and fer as a man could see, hit was buffalo. They was that thick. No pore human man could name their number, only the Lord on high. That a-way, and no man to say the end. But I seen 'em lay, skinned and stinken, black-en the ground fer what a man could ride half a day. A man couldn't breathe fresh fer the stinken. And before you knowed hit, they wasn't no buffalo in Kansas. You could go a hull day and see nary a one. "Hit's me fer Oklahoma," Mingo said, "whar thar's buffalo yit. Down Cimarron way, or Beaver Crick."

' "Hit's Indian country," I said. "I ain't a-relishen no Indians."

' "They's fellers been down thar and done right good," Mingo said. "I heared tell of a feller come out with nigh onto a thousand hides, and not down thar no time."

' "And fellers been down thar and ain't come back," I said.

' "Indians," Mingo said, "I fit Indians down in Oklahoma, when I was freighten. Hit ain't nuthen to brag on. They ain't got nuthen lak this-here." And he give his Sharp's a little h'ist. "The guns they got, ain't no white man would have 'em."

' "I ain't skeered," I said, "but hit ain't the law. Hit's Indian country down thar, by law."

' "Indian country," and Mingo give a spit, "hit ain't Indian country fer long. A feller from Dodge City said they's a gang gitten ready to go down fer buffalo, all together. Said Myers was gonna go down and buy hides and set up to do business right thar, down in Oklahoma, or maybe Texas toward the Canadian. Hit's big doens."

' "You figgeren on goen down with 'em?" I ast him.

' "Naw," Mingo said, "folks gits under my feet."

'We went down to Oklahoma, just us and our skinners. New skinners, they was, our old skinners quitten, nor wanten to go to Indian country. We got two new ones, a French feller and a nigger. We had to give 'em eighty dollars a month and found, because hit was Indian country. We went down thar. 'Seventy-four, hit was, and a drout year with the cricks dryen. And they was grasshoppers come that year, I recollect. But we made out, and they was buffalo thar. Hit was lak a-fore, the buffalo move-en and fillen the land. Hit was lak new country. Fer a spell. And we worked fast and fer. But a man had to keep his eyes skinned, looken fer Indians. And somebody watchen all night, turn about. We ne'er seen none till we got our first take out, up to Dodge City, and come back. Then we seen some, one time. The nigger was down a little draw, skinnen some buffalo Mingo shot, and French was at the wagon, stretchen hides, and Mingo and me was move-en out in the open. They come over a rise, between the draw and the wagons and we seen 'em. We high-tailed fer home, and beat 'em to the wagons, and started shooten. "Whar's the nigger?" Mingo said.

' "He ain't here," French said.

' "God dammit," Mingo said, layen thar shooten, "that black bastud lets 'em slip up and git him, and me with a dislak fer skinnen lak I got. Hit's the thanks a man gits fer fighten rebels four years to set a nigger free."

'We laid thar a-shooten at 'em all afternoon. French loaden, and Mingo and me shooten. When they was a-way off, we used our Sharp's, and when they come ride-en in clost, we used our carbeen and Colt guns. A Spencer carbeen shoots twelve times without stoppen, and heavy lead. Hit was that a-way all afternoon, and hit was a clear night and they couldn't git in clost and us not see. They tried hit but we seen 'em ever time. They left a-fore day.

'Hit come day, and they was gone. They was some ponies layen off here and yander, and close in, not more'n fifteen paces, a Indian. I ne'er knowed one got that nigh, but night time'll fool you. If'n we got airy other, they carried him off. But this one was too clost. We walked out to whar he was a-layen. "Tryen to make a *coup*," Mingo said, "come-en in clost, that a-way. Wanted to git to be a chief." He was a young Indian, and he was shot in the guts. "The durn fool," Mingo said. He poked him with his foot. "Kiowa," he said. Then he squatted down and taken out his knife.

' "What you aim to do?" I ast him.

' "Git me a scalp," Mingo said.

' "Hit ain't Christian," I said.

' "Hell," he said, "I knowed Christians as skinned Indians. I knowed a feller made him a baccy sack outer a squaw's bubby. But hit didn't do so good," he said, and started cutten, "hit wore out right off. But a scalp now, hit's diff'rent, hit's a keep-sake."

'He scalped him, then we looked down the draw fer the nigger. Thar he was, but they'd done taken his scalp. "They made a pore trade," Mingo said, "a nigger's scalp ain't no good, hit ain't worth beans. Hit ain't much better'n mine."

'Them was the only Indians we had trouble with that year, but them fellers went down from Dodge City all together, they had plenty trouble over in Texas. They had a big fight down at a place called 'Dobe Walls, and some got killed, and a passel of Indians. But the Indians was still bad on south a-ways. They was fighten at Anadarko with the sojers, and killen and scalpen here and yander. And raiden down to Texas. And the Kiowas caught a supply train — hit was Captain Lyman's wagons, I recollect — and give 'em a big tussle. We was down to Fort Sill the next spring, and we heared tell from the sojers. How they laid out four days in holes they dug, a-thirsten and no water, and the Indians all around, a-ride-en and a-whoopen and a-shooten. They was one Indian tied a white sheet round him and come ride-en through the sojers four times, and back agin, and lead cut that-air sheet off'n him, but ne'er a slug teched him. Doen hit made him a big chief, and they give him a new name fer hit, lak they done. But a scout got through to Camp Supply, and more sojers come.

'Hit was a bad year, and no denyen, and the Gin'al over to Fort Sill — hit was Gin'al Sheridan as fit in the war — a-gitten ready and sot to stomp 'em out. And he done it. They was run here and yander, lak a coyote and the dogs on him. They run 'em and ne'er give no breathen. Some of 'em come in and give up, but some of 'em kept on a-runnen and a-fighten, the wildest what went with the war chiefs Lone Wolf and Maman-ti and sich. But they come in, too, a-fore hit was done. I seen 'em. Hit was at Fort Sill I seen 'em. They was another chief, named Kicken Bird, what got 'em in. He seen how hit would be, and he said to his people, and he made 'em come in. I seen 'em at Fort Sill. They put them Indians in the corrals — they was stone corrals — and the bad chiefs locked up in the jail, and chained, and in the stone ice house they was a-builden. Ever day the wagons with meat come, and they throwed the meat over wall — raw meat and in chunks lak you was feeden a passel of painters. They taken what stock the Indians had and drove 'em outside and shot 'em and let 'em lay, stinken. Hit was lak the stink when they'd been shooten buffalo and skinned 'em. Git a west wind, and couldn't no man in Fort Sill git the stink of them ponies outer his nose, wake-en nor sleepen. And hit ne'er helped no man eat his vittles.

'They was gonna send the bad chiefs off and git shed of 'em. A fer piece, to Florida. Kicken Bird, they was gonna let him pick out the ones to go, the ones he knowed was dead-set agin the white folks. And he done hit. He named Lone Wolf and Maman-ti, and a passel more, and said they would ne'er have hit in their hearts not to scalp a white man. The time come to git shed of 'em, and I seen hit. Them army wagons was standen thar by the ice house, and sojers drawed up with guns, and they taken out the Indians from the ice house. They had chains on 'em. And thar Kicken Bird come ride-en on his big gray stallion — a man he was to look on, tall and limber, and he could ever-more set a hoss, a sight to see. He got off, and come up close to Maman-ti and Lone Wolf and them was standen thar. "Hit's time," he said, "and my heart is full of a big sadness. But it will be. I love you, but you would not take the right road. But I love my people. I send you away because I love my people, and you would make them kill theirselves a-beaten their head agin the stone. Fighten the white man is lak beaten yore head on a stone. When yore hearts is changed, you kin come back to yore people, and you will find love in my heart for you." That's what they said he said, fer I didn't know no Kiowa talk to speak of.

'The chiefs standen thar, the chains a-hangen off'n 'em, didn't say nuthen. They just looked at Kicken Bird. Then Maman-ti, he said: "You think you are a big chief, Kicken Bird. You think you have done a good thing. The white men talk to you and puff you up, Kicken Bird. But you are lak a buffalo cow, dead and layen in the sun and swole with rot-wind. Indians ought to be a-dyen together, but you would not die with us, Kicken Bird. Now you will die by yoreself, Kicken Bird. You are dyen now, Kicken Bird, and the rot-wind is in you." The wagons started rollen, the black-snakes a-cracken, off toward Caddo crossen. Kicken Bird stood thar, and watched 'em go. The sojers marched off, but Kicken Bird kept on a-standen thar, looken whar the wagons done gone.

'They's things in the world fer a man to study on, and hit's one of 'em. What come to Kicken Bird. He stood thar, a-looken, and then he went to his lodge, down on Cache Crick, nigh Sill. They say he just set thar, not give-en nuthen to notice, to speak of. He et a little sumthen, but he didn't relish nuthen. He ne'er taken his eyes off'n the ground. Five days that away, and come the fifth mornen and he keeled over and died. "I done what come to me," he said, layen thar, "and I taken the white man's hand." Then he was dead. Nary a mark on him, and him in the prime.

'But they ain't no tellen. Some said as how Maman-ti, when the wagons camped outer Sill, prayed and put a strong medicine on Kicken Bird to die. Then he died his-self fer putten medicine on another Kiowa. But agin, maybe his heart was broke in two. Maybe Kicken Bird's heart broke in two lak a flint rock when you put hit in the hot fire. They ain't no tellen. But hit's sumthen fer a man to study on.

'Hit was in May they taken them Indians away from Sill, and me and Mingo hit out agin. Buffalo hunten agin. But we didn't do so good that year. They was peteren out. That's what made them Indians so durn bad, some folks said, them buffalo goen. They didn't git no vittles then, but what the gov'-mint give 'em, and hit spiled more'n lak. We taken what we

could find, but the time was goen in Oklahoma. We heared
tell they was buffalo down Brazos, and Charlie Hart's boys
a-gitten 'em, so hit was down Brazos and up Pease River. We
done what we could, but the time was a-goen. Mingo got lak
I'd ne'er seen him git a-fore. We'd sight buffalo, and he'd go
nigh loco. "Durn, God durn," he'd say, his voice lak a man
prayen "God durn the bastuds." And his eyes with a shine in
'em lak a man got the fever. "Durn," he'd say, "what you
a-waiten fer, you Kentuck bastud?" and we'd move out on 'em.
Light or dark, he'd be at hit. Past sun, I seen him, and not light
fer a man to aim by. Him a-waste-en lead, and them Sharp's
evermore et lead lak a hog slop. Two ounce the slug, and powder
to back hit. "Mingo," I says to him, "hit's a willful waste."
"I'll cut yore scaggly thote," he said, and ne'er said one more
word all night.

'We come outer Brazos and up Kansas way. "They's buffalo
north," Mingo'd say. Days, and we'd see a old bull, maybe, and
a couple of cows. And bones layen white on the ground, fer as
a man's sight, white lak a salt flat. The wagon wheel went over
'em, cracken. We come to Dodge City. They was bones piled
and ricked up thar, a sight of bones. Them nesters and 'steaders
done picked up and brung 'em in to sell 'em. They was buyen
'em back east to make fert'lizer to put on the wore-out ground.
Bones ricked up thar along the Santa Fe, a-waiten, you ne'er
seen sich. They was fellers in Dodge City, but not lak a-fore.
Fellers was setten round didn't have a dime, what had been
thrown round the green lak a senator. Bones and broke buffalo
hunters thar, them days. We was in Dodge City, and Mingo
ne'er outer spitten-range of a bottle. "Buffalo gone," he said,
"durn, and hit'll be whisky next, and no country fer a white
man." But they shore-God wasn't no drout in sight yit. Not
with Mingo.

'We was in Dodge City, and word come the Sante Fe was
payen out good money fer men to fight the Denver and Rio

Grande fer putten the track through where the Arkansas comes
outer the mountains, out in Colorado. Mingo come and said
to git ready, we was goen. But I said, naw, I wasn't gonna be a-
shooten and killen no human man, not fer no railroad, no way.
"Me," Mingo said, "I kilt plenty fer the gov'mint goen on four
years, and kill a man fer the gov'mint, I shore-God oughter be
willen to kill me one fer anybody else. Even a railroad." But
naw, I said. But Mingo went on and done hit, and me waiten
in Dodge City. Then he come on back, and money he had.
"Hit'll be Santa Fe line," he said, "and Irish fer cross-ties."

'Then Mingo said: "Yellowstone, up Yellowstone and they's
buffalo lak a-fore. Hit's the word. Git ready." But I ne'er
said nuthen. "What you setten thar fer?" he said. "Git ready."
Then I said I wasn't aimen to go. "What you aimen to do?"
Mingo said. I said I couldn't rightly name hit, but hit would
come to me. I said I might take me out some ground, have-en
a little money left to git me gear and a start. Mingo looked at
me lak he ne'er laid eyes on me a-fore, and he give a spit on the
ground. "A fool hoe-man," he said, "you be a durn fool hoe-
man." "Maybe," I said, "if'n hit comes to me." "A bone-
picker," he said. He give me a look, and that's the last word
I e'er heared him say. "Bone-picker," he said, and give me a
look, and walked off. He was gone, a-fore sun next mornen.
Yellowstone way, they said.

'I taken me a claim, lak I said. Up in Kansas. And I done
well as the next one, I reckin. I ne'er minded putten my back
to hit, and layen a-holt. And I had me money to git a start,
gear and stock and sich. Two year, goen on three, I stayed. I
was a-make-en out, that wasn't hit. Hit was sumthen come over
me. I couldn't name hit. But thar hit was, sleepen and wake-en.

I sold my stock and gear. I said to a man, "What'll you gimme
fer my stock and gear?" And he named hit. Hit wasn't nuthen,
not to what a man could a-got. But I taken hit, and hit was
ample. To git me a outfit. And I started a-move-en. Down

through Oklahoma, and west. West, lak a man done them days when hit come over him to be a-move-en.

'I went down the way I'd been a-fore, and hit was diff'rent a-ready. But not diff'rent lak when I come back in 'ninety-one on my way back here. The Indians was dance-en then, when I come back through, tryen to dance the buffalo back. They'd been gone a long time then, and the bones. Them Indians was a-tryen to dance 'em back. And Indians ever whar, I heared tell, up in Dakota and west. The ghost-dance, they named hit. They was make-en medicine and tryen to dance back the good times, and them long gone. Hit would be a new world, and fer Indians, they claimed. A new earth was a-come-en, all white and clean past a man's thinken, and the buffalo on hit a-move-en and no end. Lak that time I stood on a rise near Medicine Lodge Crick and seen 'em a-move-en, and ne'er reckined on the end, how hit would be. That-air new earth was a-come-en, they figured, a-slide-en over the old earth whar the buffalo was done gone now and the Indians was dirt, a-blotten hit out clean, lak a kid spits on his slate and rubs hit clean. And thar all the Indians would be, all the nations a-standen and callen, all them what had died, on that-air new white earth. The live ones was dance-en to bring hit.

'They was them as had seen hit. They was them as fell down in the dance and had died, lak they named hit, when they was a-dance-en, and laid on the ground stark and stiff lak dead. They was the ones as had seen hit, the new land. They'd come to, lak a man wake-en, and tell as how they had seen hit. They seen the new earth, all white and shine-en, and the dead ones thar, happy, and beckonen with the hand, and they talked to 'em. Squaws what had chil'en what was dead, they'd see 'em.

'They was some folks as was laughen and scornen. Said them Indians was gone plumb crazy. But not me. One time, long a-fore, when I was young and sallet-green, I mighter scorned.

But not then, in 'ninety-one, when I was a-come-en back, after what hit was I'd seen. I'd laid dead lak them Indians, and seen hit come to me. Hit was how I was a-come-en back. In 'ninety-one.

'But them Indians. They come together in a big ring, a dance-en. Round and round, and a-singen. Them songs they made up, how they'd been dead and what they seen in that-air new land a-come-en. And the medicine man, he was in the middle, a-shake-en his eagle feather, and them Indians move-en round, and a-singen. Then somebody starts to feel hit a-come-en and starts a-shake-en and shudderen, lak the chill. And the medicine man, he waves that-air eagle feather a-fore his face what's a-shake-en, and he blows out his breath at him and says, "Hunh, hunh, hunh, hunh!" And that feller comes outer the ring in the middle, lak the blind-staggers, and the medicine man waves the feather a-fore him, and ne'er stops and says, "Hunh, hunh, hunh!" Till that-air feller gits the jerks, lak a man when the gospel hits him. Then the jerks is gone, and him a-standen, stiffer'n a man on the coolen board, and eyes a-stare-en lak a-fore the pennies is put. He stands thar, how long hit ain't no tellen, and them dance-en and singen, and hit come-en on more Indians, too, and them a-fall-en. They lays on the ground thar, lak dead, and broad daylight, maybe. And the singen and dance-en not stoppen.

'But that was in 'ninety-one, when I was come-en back, not when I was a-goen. A-goen, I was headed west, lak I said, lak a man them days when hit come on him to be move-en. I was down in Santa Fe and seen hit. I went to the middle of town, and seen the folks a-move-en and doen, and I figgered I'd lay over and rest up, maybe. Then hit come on me. Naw, I said, I ain't a-stoppen, hit's on me not be be a-stoppen. I didn't tarry none, only to git me grub and sich. A feller said to me, "Whar you goen?" I said I didn't know, and he said, "God-a-mighty, stranger, goen and don't know whar!" And I said,

"Naw, I don't know, but hit'll come to me when I git thar."
And he said, "God-a-mighty!" And I went on.

'I come into the mountains. Them mountains wasn't lak no
mountains you e'er seen. Nor me. Not lak them hills in
Arkansas or in this-here country in Kentucky. That-air country
was open and high, and the mountains rise-en outer hit. Hit
was June when I come in the high country, and they was flowers
ever whar. I ne'er seen sich. Greasewood with blooms plumb
gold, and little flowers on the ground. And the cactus, flowers
a-bloomen fer as a man's sight. But no smell. Put yore nose to
hit, but they ain't no smell, fer all the brightness.

'I went on to the high mountains. Cedars and juniper I come
to, but scrub and not fitten fer nuthen. Then up higher, piñons,
then oak but hit scrub. Then high up in them mountains, the
big pines standen, and no man e'er laid axe. Look down and
the land was all tore up down below, ever which way, tore up
and a-layen on end. And the ground with colors lak the sky at
sun. Look up, and snow was still layen when I come, and the
sun white on hit, lak on cloud-tops in summer. The wind come
down off'n the snow, cold to yore face and the sun shine-en.

'I come in that-air country, and ne'er ast no man the way.
Outer Santa Fe I seen folks a-goen and come-en, then they
wasn't none to speak on. In the high country I seen Indians
sometimes, ride-en along, or standen, and I made 'em signs
and them me, but I ne'er ast 'em the way. A man could be in
a place in that-air country and they'd be Indians live-en thar,
not a pistol-shot, and him ne'er knowen. Not the way they
fixed them houses, dirt piled up round looken lak a hump outer
the ground. Hogans, they named them houses. The cold come
or hit git dry and the grass give out, and they'd up and move
and build 'em a new house. One day, sun to sun, and hit was
built.

'Summer I was in the mountains, high up. The cold come,
and I moved down and built me a house, lak them Indian

houses, only mine set south, back up under a hunk of rock. Them Indian houses sets east, ne'er no other way. Hit's agin their religion. And I fixed me a shed fer my ponies. That winter I laid up thar. I lived off'n the land. A man kin do hit, put to hit, what with a rifle and snare-en. But I traded the Indians fer some corn, now and agin. But two-three months, and I ne'er seen nobody, hair nor hide. I didn't miss hit, some-how. I'd a-come thar, and thar I was. Hit's past name-en, how the Lord God leads a man some time, and sets his foot. Thar I was, and I knowed they was a world of folks off yander, down in the flat country. A-gitten and a-begetten, and not knowen the morrow. I knowed how they'd been war and killen in the country, and folks rise-en in slaughter, brother agin brother. And men was dead and under the earth, as had walked on hit, standen up lak me or airy breathen man. And no man to name the reason. Only the Lord God. I minded me on the power of meanness I'd seen in my time. And done, to speak truth. A man does hit, some more, some less, but he's got hit to think on.

'Hit looked lak my head was full, one thing and ernuther. Sometimes hit was lak I could see, plain as day, ever thing and ever body I'd e'er knowed layen out a-fore me, all at one time. They ain't no tellen how hit was, but hit was that a-way. All together, lak a man lived his life, and the time not a-passen while he lived it. Hit's past sayen, and they ain't no word fer me to say hit, but hit was that a-way. A-fore God. Hit's sum-then to study on. Then a man feels clean, hit's ne'er the same.

'Summer come, and the snow gone, and I started up to the high mountains. I seen Indians a-move-en, too. They made me signs, and I taken up with 'em. They had 'em sheep and ponies, and was goen whar the grass was good. They was two or three of 'em knowed our talk, not good but some. All sum-mer I was with them Indians, off and on. The grass gone and time to be a-move-en, and they ast me to move too, and I done hit. A man could git along with them Indians if'n he had a mind to. I done hit. They ne'er had nuthen agin me, nor me agin them. Hit come cold, and they was a-move-en down low, and I went with 'em. They helped build me a winter hogan, lak their'n, and they rubbed corn meal on the posts, the way they done fer luck, and sprinkled hit on the floor, and said the words they says to make the live-en in the house be good live-en. They throwed a handful on the fire they'd built under the smoke hole, and said the words. They fixed vittles, and we set on the floor, on sheep skins, and taken sop, side by side. They made cigarettes, lak they do, outer corn shucks and terbaccer, and set thar smoke-en and talken. Hit was lak a log-raise-en in this-here country, and folks jollifyen.

'Five year, and hit was that a-way. Hit was a way of live-en, if'n hit's in a man's heart. And I ne'er had no complaint. I was easy in my heart and mind, lak ne'er a-fore in my time of doen and strive-en. I'd a-been thar yit, I reckin, if'n I had'n a-took sick, and hit bad. Hit was in the summer of 'ninety, and we was in the high country, but hit looked lak sumthen went outer me. I wasn't good fer nuthen. Looked lak I couldn't raise my hand, the pith gone out of me. I'd jist set on the ground, and look up at the sky, how thin and blue hit was over them mountains. Then the fever come. Hit taken me, and I said, "Willie Proudfit, you gonna die." That's what I said, and the words was in my head lak a bell. Then hit come to me, how other men was dead, and they taken hit the best they could and the bitterness, and I said, "Willie Proudfit, what air man kin do, you kin do." But the fever come agin, and I said, "You gonna die, and in a fer country."

'The Indians done what they could. They give me stuff to drink, black and bitter hit was, outer yerbs and sich, but hit ne'er done no good. I'd burn up with fever, then I'd lay and look and ever thing in the world was diff'rent to me. Wouldn't nuthen stay on my stomach, looked lak. And then the fever agin. The Indians treated me good. A man couldn't a-ast more. But the Lord had laid a powerful sickness on me, and I said, "Willie Proudfit, you gonna die."

'But no, ain't no man knows what the Lord's done marked out fer him. And many's the pore, weakid man done looked on the face of blessedness, bare-eyed, and ne'er knowed hit by name. Lak a blind man a-liften his face to the sun, and not knowen. Hit was a blessen the Lord laid on me, and I praise hit.

'Them Indians seen I was witheren up, lak a tree in the sun done had the axe at hits root. Because they done called me brother and give me a name, they done ever thing they could. They built the medicine house, made a fire thar, and set me in the medicine house, and tried to take out the evil. Not jist one day, they was tryen to git the evil out. They set in thar and some of 'em had their faces all covered up with masks made outer leather and painted, and they waved eagle feathers on me to bring out the evil, and sometimes they put stuff on my head and my feet and my knees and my chist, stuff they done mixed up, and sometimes corn meal. Sometimes hit was sand on my head. And sometimes they washed me with suds, just lak soap suds, they done made outer yerbs, and done dried me with corn meal. And agin they done put pine branches on me, and put stuff on the fire fer me to breathe and one thing and ernuther, and me too nigh gone to keer. And sometimes they done made pictures outer colored sand on the floor, and feathers and beads and sich, and they was singen and hooten, sometimes. To git out the evil. And they put me in them sweat houses, little houses not much bigger'n fer a man to lay in, and covered with dirt and sand, and pictures in colored sand, and a curtain outer deerskin fer a door. But hit had to be skin off'n a deer they done run down and smother with a man's hand, not shot or cut fer the killen. They put me in hit, and rocks they done got red hot, and sweated me. And one night they was dance-en all night hit looked lak, and singen, naked and painted white, I recollect, and the fires was burnen big.

'But the fever done had me sometimes, and hit was lak a dream. I was a-goen, and nuthen to lay holt on. And I didn't keer. The time comes and a man don't keer. They taken me out and laid me on the ground. Hit was night. I knowed that, then I was a-goen. I might been gone, fer all I know. They ain't no sayen.

'I might been gone, when hit come to me, what I seen. I seen a long road come-en down a hill, and green ever whar. Green grass layen fresh, and trees, maple and elm and sich. And my feet was in the road, and me a-move-en down hit. They was a fire in me, and thirsten. Hit was a green country, and the shade cool, but the fire was in me. I come down the hill, and seen houses setten off down the valley, and roofs, and the green trees standen. I taken a bend in the road, and thar was a little church, a white church with a bell hangen, and the grass green a-fore hit. Thar was a spring thar, by the church, and I seen hit and run to hit. I put my head down to the water, fer the fire in me, lak a dog gitten ready to lap. I didn't take no water in my hand and sup. Naw, I put my face down to the water, and hit was cool on me. The coolness was in me, and I taken my fill.

'No tellen how long, and I lifted up my head. Thar a girl was sitten, over thar nigh the spring, and she was a-looken at me. I opened my mouth but nary a word come out. Hit looked lak the words was big in me to busten, and none come.

'Then hit was finished and done, and I'd ne'er spoke. The dream, if'n hit was a dream. No tellen how long I laid thar, but I come to, hit was mornen light, gray, fer the rain was fall-en. I didn't have no fever. I laid thar, and my head was full of what all I'd been a-dreamen. They taken me in, and a-fore night I et a little sumthen, and hit stayed on my stomach. My strength come back, not fast, but hit come. All the time I was a-thinken what I'd seen, the church and the green trees standen, and the spring. Ever day. I'd seen hit, I knowed I'd seen hit, but I couldn't give hit the name. Then I knowed.

Hit was the road come-en down to Thebes, in Kentucky, when I was a kid thar, and the church setten thar whar hit takes a bend. I ne'er seen hit since pappy done up and taken outer Kentucky fer Arkansas when the war come and he was on-easy in his mind, but hit come to me plain as day, and I said, "I'm a-goen thar."

'My strength come, and I done hit. I told them Indians goodbye, and they taken my hand. I come to Santa Fe, and up Oklahoma, lak I said, and on to Arkansas. I was gonna see my pappy, and my mammy, if'n the Lord had done spared 'em. I come in Arkansas at Fort Smith, and on east, whar my folks had been. My mammy was dead. Been dead a long time, folks said. And my pappy, he was dead too, but not more'n goen on a year. He was kilt, with a knife. A feller from up Missouri kilt him. He was setten down at a store one night, at the settlement, and ever body was talken and goen on. They was a-talken about the war, and how hit come. The feller from up Missouri, he was cussen the rebels, and my pappy said, naw, not to be a-cussen 'em that a-way, they didn't do hit, no more'n no other man. They had a argument, and the feller from up Missouri, he cut my pappy, and him a old man. The feller from up Missouri taken out, and was gone, no man knowed whar. And my pappy died, layen thar on the floor. I seen the place he was buried, and my mammy. Nobody knowed whar my brothers was gone, been gone a long time. Strange folks was a-live-en in the house my pappy'd done built long back, the house I'd seen him start builden that day he'd stood thar and looked whar hit was gonna set, sayen, "Lord God, Lord God," right soft, and then, sudden-lak, to ma, "Henrietta, gimme that-air axe!" I seen hit, the logs notched clean and set tight, and the chimney true, ne'er sunk nor slipped yit.

'I sold the place fer what I could git. I ne'er hemmed and hawed. Then I come on, on here to Kentucky, acrost Tennessee. I come on to Thebes. Hit was a hot day, when I come, but summer not on good yit. I come over the hill, down the road, and thar was the grass and the trees standen green. Lak hit is, and lak hit come to me that time. I taken the turn in the road, and thar was the church. New Bethany church, hit is. And the spring, and I run to hit, on-steady and nigh blind, with what come on me when I seen hit. I put my face down to the water. I taken my fill.

'I lifted up my head, slow. And thar she set.'

His voice stopped. In the silence, in the marshy ground down the creek the frogs were piping. Then he said: 'Hit was Adelle.'

'Yes,' his wife's voice said, quietly, from the shadow where her chair was, 'I was setten thar, in the shade of a sugar-tree, and I seen him come down the hill.'

Chapter sixteen

It was twilight when Mr. Munn, standing in the side yard, where the woodpile and chopping-block were, happened to lift his head and see the buggy coming up the lane by the creek. Without haste, he propped the axe against the chopping-block, and bent over to pick up an armful of stove-lengths from the bed of old chips and rotting bark. Then he went to the kitchen.

Adelle Proudfit was still there, drying dishes. The lighted lamp was on the table by the stacked dishes. Mr. Munn leaned, and let the wood slide off of his arm into the box with a subdued thudding. Then he turned to her. 'There's somebody coming up the road,' he said, 'in a buggy. They're probably pulling up now.'

She looked at him, as though about to speak, but he continued: 'I'm just going to step out back. It's probably somebody to see Willie, but I'll just get out back till they're gone. I'll be in easy calling.'

He moved rapidly from the house toward the fringe of undergrowth at the base of the bluff. He was looking back at the lane, but nothing now was visible there. The buggy was probably standing at the gate, hidden by the bulk of the house. He did not go up the bluff, but stopped in the first depth of shadow. He sat on the ground, his back propped against the trunk of a cedar. The earth, matted with the long accumulation of fallen needles, was resilient beneath him. He fixed his eyes upon the house, and waited.

The light was fast draining out of the sky, now, and the

darkening bulk of the house, against the darkness of the rise at the other side of the creek, was losing its definition. But the windows showed their rectangles of yellow light against that general obscurity. At last, he thought that he could make out the crunching of wheels over gravel, the sound of the buggy moving off down the lane. But he could not be sure, and now it was too dark to see.

Some little time after he had thought he heard the sound of the wheels crunching gravel, he saw a figure emerge from the shadow of the house and move toward him. Even before it approached the edge of the undergrowth, he was sure, from some scarcely discernible trick of posture or a momentary impression of a long, gliding gait, that it was Willie Proudfit. Mr. Munn did not move.

Willie Proudfit stopped at the edge of the undergrowth, and spoke softly: 'Perse, Perse.'

'Yes?' Mr. Munn answered.

'Hit's all right.'

Mr. Munn came from the secure darkness of the cedars, and stood beside the other man.

'Hit's a lady,' Willie Proudfit said.

'A lady?'

'Doc MacDonald sent her.' He paused. 'To see you. That's what she said.'

Mr. Munn turned his eyes from the man beside him to the house, where light showed at the windows. A sluggish resentment stirred in him: like the resentment of a person who in half sleep is disturbed at some aimless, undefined noise. He passed his tongue over his dry lips, then said, 'A lady?'

'Mr. Bill Christian's girl,' the other man answered. 'I ne'er knowed him but by name.'

They moved toward the house. Willie Proudfit was saying: 'A feller brung her in a buggy from Ashby's Crossen over to Thebes, and then brung her out here. But Dellie, she's make-en her stay the night, and that-air feller's done gone. I didn't ketch his name. He ne'er come in. I went out and ast him to git out and come in, but he said, naw, he ——'

She stood in the middle of the floor, quietly, giving him the impression, somehow, that she might have been standing in that position for a long time. He came in through the now darkened kitchen, and as he approached the next room and saw her standing there, framed in the opening of the doorway, he thought how, that first day in the hotel room, while the tumult of the crowds rose from the street, he had suddenly seen her stand in the middle of the floor, like that, and had been struck by her quietness, the sense of an inner steadiness. She stood there now, as he approached, and the lamplight fell across her face, shadowing one half of it, seeming to define and sharpen, as by a hint of the potentiality of time, the structure of the bone beneath the flesh.

He went through the doorway. Her eyes had been fixed on him as he approached — he was sure of that — but she did not move.

'Hello, Lucille,' he said, and went toward her, holding out his hand. He saw Adelle Proudfit standing over near the table where the lamp was.

'Hello,' she said, and gave him her hand. 'How are you?' she asked. She seemed to be studying his face, fleetingly but intently. Seeing that, he was embarrassed, as though she might penetrate to a secret guilt.

'I'm all right,' he said. 'I'm getting along fine.'

She seemed about to speak, but did not. She withdrew her hand from his, startling him, for he had been unaware that he still held it. Then, as though collecting herself, she explained: 'We wanted to know how you were getting along. That's why I came. Doctor MacDonald told me where you were' — she was speaking with a tone of dispassionate precision, as though delivering a memorized and only half-understood message.

'He thought that I'd better come, and not somebody else; if he came somebody might guess.'

'I appreciate it,' he replied, 'you coming. And Doctor MacDonald wanting to know how I was getting along.' His voice sounded stale to his ears.

She turned toward Adelle Proudfit, saying: 'Mrs. Proudfit was so nice to ask me to spend the night. I'm going back tomorrow. We just wanted to know ——'

'Naw, naw,' Willie Proudfit protested. He had entered the room and was leaning against the wall near the kitchen door. 'Not tomorrow, and you come-en all that way to git here. Ain't no sense, not visiten a spell.'

'No,' his wife interrupted, 'we'd be proud to have you visit.'

'I'll have to go,' Lucille Christian said, 'tomorrow, but I appreciate your asking me. A whole lot.'

Her voice stopped, and she stood there, unmoving, but with no air of expectancy. Mr. Munn felt a compulsion to break the ensuing moment of silence, which seemed, suddenly, endless. But he could think of nothing to say. Then, almost with gratitude, he heard Willie Proudfit suggesting, '— but let's set out on the porch, hit's cool out thar.' Then Lucille Christian turned toward Adelle Proudfit, and took a step toward the front door. 'Yes,' she said, 'it's been awfully hot today, worse than usual for this time of year.' They went out on the porch, Willie Proudfit last, carrying a rocking chair. He placed the chair for Lucille Christian.

They sat on the porch, in the darkness, for more than an hour. They talked slowly, with little pauses between the conclusion of one speech and the beginning of the next. In those pauses there was the sound of frogs down in the low ground, and the dry, unwearying insistence of the insects in the trees by the lane. Their voices would rise and fall, slowly but in a living rhythm, one responding to another, fulfilling it; but the meaning in those voices would seem to escape Mr. Munn, unless, by a sudden effort, he forced himself to attend to them, word by word. That dry, rasping sound from the insects in the dark trees yonder, that unpatterned, unrelenting, interminable sound, drew him, and enveloped him. It was as though it was in him, finally, in his head, the essence of his consciousness, reducing whatever word came to him to that undifferentiated and unmeaning insistence.

Lucille Christian and Willie Proudfit did most of the talking. She asked him how his crops were, and he answered her, unhurriedly, in detail, naming the dates of the planting of each field, and recalling what the weather had been like at each stage in the season. And he asked her how Doctor MacDonald and his folks were.

'They're pretty well,' she said, 'except for Professor Ball. He's failing, they say. I haven't seen him in a long time, but that's what they say.'

'And yore pa?' Willie Proudfit asked. 'I hear'd he'd not been so well off, and I was meanen to ast you.'

She did not answer for a moment, then replied slowly: 'He's all right. Thank you.' Then, in a voice that was suddenly brisk, as though she had gathered herself for the special effort, she added: 'But there's been a lot of sickness round Bardsville. You know how it seems, some years.'

Yes, Willie Proudfit agreed, it looked that way some years. And he asked her how other things were down near Bardsville. She answered him, then began to ask him about people whom she had heard about in this section, where their places lay, how much land they had.

Now and then Adelle Proudfit filled out some detail for him, or named a name. But Sissie did not speak the whole time, and Sylvestus only once. When, for the first time, the heat lightning flickered along the horizon, silhouetting the mass of the hillside breaking toward the valley, Lucille Christian said: 'Look, lightning. Maybe we'll get some rain tomorrow.' Then

Sylvestus stirred in his chair at the end of the porch. 'Naw,' he said heavily, 'begging yore pardon, but hit ain't gonna rain. That-air lightnen, hit's the devil's promise.'

'We need it,' Lucille Christian remarked.

'Hit's a drout,' Sylvestus said, 'a-ready, and sweat fer nuthen.'

Shortly afterward he rose from his chair, and without a word moved away into the darkness.

The talk stopped as he walked away. Then Adelle Proudfit declared: 'He oughtn't to be a-goen off lak that. Not and him worken daytime the way he does.'

'Hit comes on him,' Willie Proudfit said, 'to be up and a-walken in darkness. Sometimes.'

Shortly after that Adelle Proudfit said that she reckoned it was time for them to go to bed, she knew Miss Christian must be tired, and all, coming so far. Inside, she turned up the lamp, and got a thin straw ticking and some sheets out of a closet. 'I'm gonna lay down the pallet for Sylvestus. He laks to sleep on the porch, summers.' She went out on the porch, while the others stood, not speaking, in the area of light around the lamp. They heard her calling, outside, once or twice, the name of her nephew. Then she came back into the room. 'He's done gone, looks lak. But sometimes, he don't answer no way, studyen on sumthen.'

They said good night, and separated. Lucille Christian went into the little room where Sissie slept. It was a little lean-to room, like the one where Mr. Munn had been staying.

Mr. Munn lay awake for a time. He felt that he ought to be thinking about himself, about what he was going to do, and where he was going to go. And about Lucille Christian's coming. But he was tired. He had not felt tired when he lay down, but as soon as those questions came into his mind, a lethargy took him, and he could not even frame them for himself. They were things to be accepted, not answered and solved. Those questions had almost ceased to make their demands upon him. Her coming had revived them. The resentment which had surprised him when Willie Proudfit came out to the concealment of the underbrush and told him that she was there, again rose in him. Then it, too, subsided and dissolved in that lethargy. Very faintly, he could hear the sound the insects made in the trees out there along the lane. Then his thoughts, he himself, had been absorbed into that dry, insidious vibration, which was a kind of life, but life reduced to its most sterile and unaimed rhythm, the ticking, as it were, of the leaves drying in the hot air, the ticking of the dry earth. Then he had drowsed off.

He awoke, in the darkness, to the slight sound of the opening door, which, in the cramped room, was less than arm's-length from the head of the bed. He did not stir. Lucille Christian — for he was sure it was she — moved into the room, and cautiously pushed the door shut behind her. 'Perse,' her voice said, in a dry whisper, 'Perse.'

'Yes,' he whispered.

She did not answer for a moment, then said, 'I had to talk to you, Perse.'

He pushed himself up on one arm, and peered toward her in the darkness. As his eyes strained toward her, desire welled up in him, possessing him like an exaltation. He stretched out his hand and took her wrist. The flesh was cool and firm under his fingers. He was aware of the small shafts of bone within it, and tightened his grip, pressing the flesh upon them. With a slow increase of force, he tried to draw her toward him. Her arm stretched out from her shoulder toward him, but lifelessly, limply, and heavily, as though it were the sodden end of a cut cable on which he pulled. She did not actively resist as he tried to draw her, but he sensed in her the recalcitrance of inertia, a sullen weight at which he was surprised, like a man who tries to pick up a familiar body and finds, suddenly, that in its unconsciousness, or death, it seems to have absorbed, already, something of the obstinate massiness of earth. He felt a flicker of fury, and with his free arm braced himself to exert his strength. Then, even in the dimness, he made out how her hand, below the wrist he clutched, hung limply and witheredly; and he felt the relaxed, unresisting tendons of the wrist. That momentary fury had left him, and the desire.

He released his grip, suddenly, in midair, and her arm fell to her side like an inanimate object.

He peered at her, then said, 'You oughtn't to have come in here.'

'That wasn't what you were thinking a minute ago,' she observed.

'You oughtn't to have come,' he replied sullenly.

'I wanted to talk to you.'

'You oughtn't. Sissie will know, and she'll tell them.'

'No,' Lucille Christian said; 'she's asleep, sound as a child. She won't know.' Then she added, without irony: 'I reckon I got a little practice going quietly. Last winter, you know.'

'We could have talked tomorrow.'

'No,' Lucille Christian answered, 'not tomorrow. Not tomorrow, if I was going to say what I had to say. I had to tonight. I had to come in here, and say it, now. I might have gone away tomorrow, and not said it, and then been wondering all my life how things would have been if I had said it.' She stood in the middle of the little room. In the instant after she stopped speaking, he was conscious again of the distant, devouring insistence of the sound the insects were making off yonder, in the dark, in the trees by the lane.

He let himself sink down again, in the bed. He took his eyes away from her, and lay on his back, and stared upward at the indistinguishable ceiling.

Then she said, 'Light the lamp.'

He pushed himself up. 'They'll see,' he remonstrated.

'No,' she answered, 'they won't see.'

He swung himself to a sitting posture on the edge of the bed, and groped for his overalls, which hung over the foot of the bed. He put them on, then sat down again on the bed. 'They'll see,' he repeated.

'No,' she told him, 'you can turn it down low. But I want the light, even a little. To talk by. You know, we've never talked, not really talked, you and me, in the light. It was always when I couldn't really see you. Your face. I've thought of that sometimes, and I've felt all at once like I didn't know you.' She paused. Then: 'Have you?'

He made no answer.

'Light the lamp,' she directed.

He got up, fumbled in the pocket of his overalls for a match, and moved gropingly toward the shelf where the lamp was. His bare feet made no sound on the boards of the floor. He struck the match, shielding the flame with his hand, and his shadow swayed amorphously behind him on the walls and ceiling, while he applied the flame to the wick. It took, flaringly; then he put the chimney on, and turned down the wick until only a little worm of flame clung uncertainly to the exposed edge.

He returned to the bed, and sat upon it, watching her.

'Don't you want to sit down?' he asked.

She sat in the single chair, a cane-bottom chair, which stood against the wall opposite the bed. Under the dark skirt of her dress, he could see her bare feet set side by side, straight, on the floor. He noticed, detachedly, how high and strongly curved the arches were.

She sat very erect in the chair, with her hands folded in her lap.

'You can see me now,' he said.

'Yes,' she replied, looking at him. Then: 'I had to come in here, now, to talk to you. Doctor MacDonald didn't send me, like I said.'

'He didn't,' Mr. Munn said, not so much in question as in echo.

'No, I asked him where you were, and he told me. I wanted to talk to you. I had something to say to you. But when you first came in tonight, and I saw you come through that door, I felt I couldn't say it. I felt I didn't know you. You didn't look the way I remembered.'

Mr. Munn raised his hand, and meditatively fingered his beard. 'I reckon not,' he remarked. 'Not with all this beard.'

'It wasn't that,' she told him. 'It was you. I felt I couldn't tell you what I'd come to say. I'd have gone back right away, tonight, if there'd been a way. Then lying in there, in bed, I couldn't sleep. That child was lying there asleep by me, and every breath she drew, I thought how long it had been since I slept like that.' She stopped, and her gaze withdrew from him and fixed upon the small, crawling flame on the lampwick.

He sat with his elbows on his spread knees, his forearms hanging loose between them, and waited.

As though by an effort, she resumed, still watching the flame: 'I thought if I didn't get up and talk to you now, I might never. I might look at you in the morning, and you'd be the way you were tonight when you came through that door, and I'd go away, and never say it.'

In the pause she looked at him interrogatively, but her folded hands were motionless in her lap, and she was erect. His face showed nothing.

'My father ——' she began, and stopped.

'Yes?' he asked.

'He's dead,' she said.

'Dead?' he repeated. 'You said — out there, tonight ——'

'Yes,' she said. 'I know. I couldn't say it then. Not that way, and you sitting there. He died three days ago. And was buried yesterday.'

He straightened up, slipping his feet on the floor with a faint, dry, rustling sound. 'I'm sorry,' he said.

'I'm not,' she answered. 'Not with him that way. Lying there, that way. Staring, and his breath coming that way, making that noise. All the time, day and night. No' — and she spoke almost with vehemence, and her hands slowly knotted in her lap — 'I'm not sorry.'

'I'm sorry,' he repeated, as though he had not heard.

'I didn't come to tell you that,' she said.

'What?' he demanded, and sank forward again, with his elbows on his knees.

'I'm going away,' she said. Her hands were quiet now, again folded, and her voice was not much more than a whisper. 'I haven't decided where, but I'm going. I can't stay any longer. Not here. There's no reason.'

'Yes.'

'Maybe St. Louis,' she said; then added, 'but God knows there's no reason for me to go back there.'

'Your aunt; she's there, isn't she?'

'I wouldn't see her' — and the vehemence came back to her voice, which was, however, steady — 'not if she was burning in hell. She's — she's a bitch. You don't know.'

'No. I didn't know.'

'A complete bitch. She's papa's sister, a lot younger than he was. She was his sister, but she was ashamed of him. She'd married a man named Allbright, who went up there and made a little money, and all — but maybe you know ——'

'I knew he was rich,' Mr. Munn said. 'Just that.'

'And when my mother died she took me. Just to have something on papa, she was like that. And somebody to boss. And when Allbright died, she took everything out on me. And she fooled around with men, and before he died, too.'

'She sounds pretty,' Mr. Munn said.

'She was a bitch. And I ——' She paused, moodily studying

his face. Then, suddenly, she said: 'I'm not just telling you all this. It's part of what I wanted to tell you. It's the only way I can think of to tell you ——'

'All right,' he answered.

'We never talked any,' she said. 'Not like other people. What we were to each other, it was all closed up, shut in. It was cut off from everything else, everything we had been. From part of what we were, even then.'

'Yes,' he said.

'My aunt was a bitch. And I — I guess I was too. There was a fellow ——'

'There's no reason to tell me,' Mr. Munn said, staring at the ceiling.

'He taught in a riding school. He was wonderful on a horse. He was an Englishman, and he'd been in the English army, he said. He was awful. He thought he was so good-looking, and a lady-killer, and all. He was so awful, I reckon that was why I began to notice him. Just his being so awful. I'd get out and see him now and then. He was afraid of my aunt. He was afraid of everything, I reckon. Except horses. He wasn't afraid of the worst one. Or any kind of jump. For a while I thought I might run off with him, just because it looked like the only thing to do. And I asked him. But he was afraid. So I told him how awful he was. Everything, and how he wasn't fit to wipe your foot on, and how if there hadn't been something wrong with me I'd never have looked at him. Then he cried, not because I was quitting him, but because I knew what he was like inside. I told him some day a horse would guess what he was like inside, and would kill him.'

She stopped and looked across the room at him. He was lying back on the bed, on his back, with his arms under his head. He gave no sign that he had noticed the cessation of her voice.

'A horse killed him,' she said. 'Threw him and killed him.

I read it in the paper, after I came back here. I didn't even recognize his name at first, everything seemed so different then.' She paused, as though searching her mind. 'His name was Emory Chivers,' she said. Then: 'Why I'm telling you ——'

'It doesn't matter,' Mr. Munn said. 'Now.'

'It was different when I got home,' she resumed, ignoring him. 'With papa. It was all right then. I didn't think much about anything. I was just wrapped up in being a sort of way I'd never been, not since I was a little girl. It was even all right when Benton Todd started to come around ——'

'You ought to have married him,' Mr. Munn said, still looking at the shadowy ceiling.

'He was a child,' she returned. 'Nothing but a child.'

'If you'd married him, he'd be here, today,' he declared. Then added, with a distant and judicial tone: 'Alive.'

'You've got no right to say that.'

'Yes,' he said. 'Alive.'

'Nobody can say; there's nothing to say about a thing like that,' she rejoined. Her hands moved again in her lap, folding and unfolding, then stopped. 'He's dead,' she said.

'So's that English fellow,' he reminded her, 'that Chivers.' She made no answer, and for a little while he seemed sunk in meditation before he said, 'You told him what he was.'

'He was that way, nobody made him that way ——'

'Benton Todd,' Mr. Munn interrupted, still meditatively, 'he did what he thought you wanted him to do.'

'And you,' she retorted. 'He thought you were wonderful, he wanted to be like you.'

He lay there, ignoring her words. 'He was a fool,' he said then.

Suddenly she leaned forward in her chair, and thrust her arms out at him, the hands lifted and bent upward at the wrists, in a gesture of protest, saying: 'It doesn't matter. It's over. I came here to tell you something ——'

'What?' he asked.

'I'm going away,' she replied, speaking hurriedly, and her hands subsided to her lap, delayedly as though sinking through a depth of water. 'Somewhere away from here. I oughtn't ever have come here. Ever. But I'm going away. You said you wanted to marry me. You can go away. You ought to. I can marry you now; we'll go away, and get married sometime and be together.' Her gaze left him, returning to the insufficient flame of the lamp. 'That was what I came here to say,' she concluded.

After her voice stopped, the night sounds seemed to creep back into the room, gradually and as though timidly returning, the sound of the insects and the scarcely discernible sound of the leaves moving in the bushes near the house, for a little wind had begun.

'There was a time,' Mr. Munn said, 'when I could have done it. A long time back.'

'I knew you would say that,' she answered, her voice a whisper.

'I didn't know it,' he admitted, 'until I said it.'

'I knew it when I saw you tonight. When you came through that door. But I had to tell you what I'd come to tell you. I owed it to myself. I had to.'

'I owe it to myself,' he told her, 'to stay here.'

'No,' she said, and leaned toward him again, 'you don't. It's not that we' — and she hesitated, still leaning and looking at him as though to draw his averted face toward her before she said — 'that we love each other. Whatever it is, that's not the word.'

'Love, it's not anything,' he replied; 'not when it's not a part of something else.'

'I couldn't say I love anything. Not now. I'm just cold inside.' Then she sat up straight, and exclaimed suddenly: 'Cold. I've always been cold. That's it, cold. That's why I did what I did, came to you. I was cold; I thought you'd warm me. That's the way about those others. There was something made me think they weren't cold inside; they were warm, I thought. Even Chivers, what he could do with horses. And you ——'

'And me ——' he repeated, not questioningly, but in a slow dubiety.

'You, you, I thought — I must have felt' — her words came rushingly, no longer in whisper — 'I thought you must be warm, after what you'd done, after that.' Her voice sank, all at once, to a whisper. 'To do that you'd have to be warm, have to feel about something. To kill a man.'

'You knew' — he said distantly — 'about Trevelyan?'

'Benton told me. I got it out of him. That's why I came to you, to warm me. But you ——'

'Yes?' he asked.

'You are cold, too. Whatever you did, you were cold. Like me, inside. Whatever you did, even this man at the trial, this Turpin ——'

'Turpin!' he exclaimed, stiffening, almost rising. 'Turpin! I didn't ——'

But her voice was going on: 'Whatever you did, you did because you were cold, because you wanted to be warm.'

He sank back, slowly relaxing again.

'Because you wanted to be warm,' she said, 'because you wanted to get through to something to make you warm. Because you were cold ——'

'I did what I did,' he returned.

'You wanted to be warm. Like some other people. Like my father was. He was, he had it inside himself. That's why he could live by himself all those years, and a big, strong man like that. Why he could be the way he was. Why, you don't know — why, he had a picture of my mother on a table in his room, and he'd look at it every night — I've seen him, when he didn't know — and talk to it sometimes, just say a little something that didn't mean anything, like to somebody around the house. You'd never guess that, would you?' She paused, regarding him. Then she demanded, 'Now, would you?'

'No,' he replied.

'Nobody would,' she said. 'But that's why, and I'd see him and hear him, and lie awake and want to be like that. And then ——'

'Then what?'

'Then you,' she finished. She rose from the chair, but did not move away from it. The faint light struck at an angle upward across her face. 'But it wasn't any use,' she said then. 'I thought it was, at first. But it wasn't.'

'It's too bad,' he rejoined.

'You needn't feel sorry for me,' she told him; then added bitterly: 'I don't for you. There's others worse. Tolliver ——'

'Tolliver,' he repeated, 'Tolliver; I hadn't thought of him in a long time.'

'Tolliver, talking to people all his life, crowds, never being anything except when his voice was talking to crowds; if he had anything in him, any life, sucking it out of crowds, talking. Crowds and women. Never being anything except when he thought somebody else thought he was something. Just that ——'

'The bastard,' Mr. Munn declared, without warmth.

'— like sucking blood, living off something else. That's why he was always after women, not even because he wanted them.'

'The bastard,' Mr. Munn said again. He rose to a sitting position on the bed, and swung his legs over the side to the floor.

'That's why he was after me. I know; I could tell.'

Mr. Munn shifted himself, and looked up at her. 'You?' he asked.

'All the time he was coming out to see papa. Before the bust-up. He was after me. He'd put his hands on me every chance he got. He'd say, "My dear girl, my dear Lucille ——"'

She spoke mincingly, twisting her mouth in mimicry. 'That's what he'd say, "My dear girl, my dear girl ——" '

'I hadn't thought of him in a long time,' Mr. Munn remarked, almost reflectively, 'not really.' Then he exclaimed suddenly, with cold ferocity, 'The bastard!'

'No,' she said, 'no, I feel sorry for him. I did even then, when he was after me, and I was sick at my stomach.'

' "My dear girl, my dear girl ——" ' he repeated mincingly. He got to his feet, and thrust his head out toward her, and glared at her as though in hatred. 'I'd like to cut his God-damned heart out,' he cried.

'He's nothing,' she said, and repeated the words, shaking her head, slowly, from side to side, and moving her hands in a slight gesture of dismissal, like a sick person whose strength is failing.

'I could,' he insisted.

'He's nothing,' she repeated, and she shook her head, slowly, rebukingly. 'Even Chivers,' she added; 'he was something.'

He let himself sink again to the edge of the bed, and sat there, looking at her.

'It's late,' she said at last.

'Yes,' he agreed.

'Maybe I oughtn't to have come,' she suggested expressionlessly.

'Maybe,' he answered.

'I thought I had to,' she said.

At the door, pausing with her hand on the wooden latch, she turned to look again at him, as though about to speak. He was sitting, as before, with his elbows propped on his parted knees, his forearms hanging loosely between them, and his eyes were fixed on the chair, across the room, where she had been sitting. She opened the door, cautiously, a little way, and slipped through the aperture. The door drew to behind her, and the bar of the latch, with a slight, woody scraping, sank into its socket.

After a while he got up from the bed, and moved to the lamp, and leaned toward it, and blew out the flame. No light showed yet at the window. The breeze had died down long before, and an uncertain drizzle had now begun. Its freshness penetrated into the dull air of the room. While outside, on the leaves and the grass, the tentative susurrus of the rain proceeded, he stood there in the dark room.

When Mr. Munn first came out to the back porch, Willie Proudfit was coming up the path with a bucket of milk in each hand. He waited until he had come within a few paces, and then said, 'Good morning.' Willie Proudfit answered him gravely and went on into the kitchen. Mr. Munn stood there for a moment, hearing the slosh of the milk being poured, and then moved off the porch into the yard. The hard-packed earth of the path looked scarcely damp. The leaves and the grass, however, were wet, and beads of water hung here and there, glistening in the clear light.

Willie Proudfit came out of the kitchen door, and approached him. Without speaking, he stood for a moment beside Mr. Munn, casting his glance slowly about him over the yard and the bluffside, and then at the sky, as though he were making his first appraisal of the new morning. Finally he began, 'Perse——' and then hesitated, still not turning toward Mr. Munn.

'Yes?' Mr. Munn asked.

'Perse——' and he hesitated again. Then he swung round toward Mr. Munn. 'I ain't one to beat round the bush,' he said. 'Sumthen gits in my head, and I says hit. Hit ain't in me to do no other way. You know they ain't nuthen right and proper I wouldn't do fer you. You know my house is yore'n fer you to stay in, and me proud to say hit. But they's sumthen fer me to tell.'

'All right,' Mr. Munn replied.

'Last night Miss Christian come in yore room, and you was thar. She come——'

'That's not——' Mr. Munn began, but the other man had raised his hand, almost as in command, and continued:

'She come in thar. Sylvestus seen her a-goen. He was come-en up on the porch to lay down on his pallet, and he seen her. And this mornen he come to me and told me. He done accorden to his lights, tellen me. Hit ain't right, Perse. I was ne'er one to be tellen other folks their doens. A man's got a time keepen clear and easy in his own mind, but hit ain't right, Perse. Not in Dellie's house. Hit ain't acten right to Dellie. Hit's kicken up dirt in Dellie's face.' He looked at Mr. Munn's face, which was as expressionless as wood. Mr. Munn was not even looking at him. Then he reached out to touch Mr. Munn on the arm, and concluded: 'Hit was in me to be a-sayen hit. And I done said hit.'

Mr. Munn still did not look at him, saying: 'Lucille Christian came to my room. She had something to tell me. Something to tell me, she couldn't wait to tell me, she thought. She told me that, and we talked about it. And she left.' He turned his eyes upon him, and added, 'That was all.'

'I'm glad to hear you sayen hit,' Willie Proudfit said. He took his hand from Mr. Munn's arm.

'That was all,' Mr. Munn repeated slowly.

'I ain't a-doubten,' Willie Proudfit told him. 'I know you ain't one to let air man be a-doubten yore word. When you done said hit.'

'It happens to be true.'

'I ain't a-doubten,' Willie Proudfit said again.

'She's going away this morning. Like she planned. So Sylvestus needn't worry.' He stopped, appeared to be reflecting, then amended: 'I'm sorry I said that. That last. I didn't mean anything by it.'

They began to move back toward the house.

Just before they reached the porch, Mr. Munn stopped. 'Bill Christian is dead,' he said quietly. 'He died four days ago.'

'Last night,' Willie Proudfit exclaimed, 'last night she said he was gitten on!'

'He is dead. That was one of the things she came to tell me.'

'Dead,' Willie Proudfit repeated, as though bringing the thought to slow realization, 'and me sayen what I said.' Then he added: 'Hit makes a man feel lak dirt, inside. Sayen them things. Thinken 'em.'

'It's all right,' Mr. Munn said.

They went on, into the kitchen.

At breakfast nobody talked much. Adelle Proudfit talked some, and Lucille Christian, but the others were silent. Toward the end of the meal, they, too, became silent. Lucille Christian's face was very pale, and the skin seemed to be drawn painfully tight across the bone.

After breakfast Sylvestus, who was to take Lucille Christian to the railroad at Ashby's Crossing, went to the stable to harness the horse. The others remained seated at the table for a little while longer, and then went out to the front porch to wait for him. He drove the buggy to the gate, got out and hitched the horse, and approached the porch, where the others were standing in silence. When he came up, Lucille Christian, looking over the fields that lay along the creek, said almost casually, 'Well, we did get a little rain, after all.'

Standing on the ground just at the edge of the porch before her, Sylvestus abruptly struck the toe of his shoe into the earth, and stared down at the scar he had made. 'Hit ain't nuthen,' he returned. 'Hit ain't more'n laid the dust. Hit ain't cleaned air leaf in the field.'

'I thought it might help a little,' she replied.

He dragged his foot across the mark it had made. 'Hit ain't nuthen,' he repeated, as though not to her.

She told them good-bye, shaking hands with each one, Mr.

Munn last. 'I want to thank you for all the trouble you've taken,' she said to Adelle Proudfit. 'I'm grateful and I won't forget.'

'We taken none,' the other woman responded. 'And we want you to come a-visiten. When you kin.'

'Real visiten,' Willie Proudfit added.

'Thank you,' she said. She took one step, to the edge of the porch, as though about to go. She stopped, hesitated an instant, then turned, and quickly leaning over, kissed Sissie on the cheek. 'Good-bye,' she said, speaking quickly, embarrassedly, and went down the path. She moved rapidly, and did not look back until the buggy had drawn a little way down the lane. Then her hand waved once to them.

They stood on the porch, watching the buggy recede, slowly, down the valley. Already the sun bore down brilliantly on the length of the field by the lane, and the earth steamed in the light.

Adelle Proudfit and the girl went into the house before the buggy was out of sight, but the men waited. When it was gone, Willie Proudfit remarked meditatively: 'Hit makes a man feel lak dirt, sayen them things. Her pappy dead, and her lak she is.'

Mr. Munn made no answer.

Without speaking again, Willie Proudfit stepped off the porch and walked toward the stables.

Mr. Munn leaned against the corner post of the porch. The buggy was gone now, hidden by the foliage at the last visible turn of the lane. Willie Proudfit had gone into the stables. He would be sitting there, on a chunk in the musty shadow of the hall, with a piece of broken gear across his knees, mending it. The brown skin of his brow would be wrinkled in attention under the pale hair. Or he might be sharpening a blade, for hay was to cut soon. Such as it was. The sound of the file on steel — small, stern, measured — would be the only sound.

For some time Mr. Munn remained there, looking down the lane, then off across the fields. From the house behind him there came, now and then, the muffled clatter and chink of dishes and pans, or the low murmur of the voices of the women as they moved about their occupations. Some jays wrangled distantly on the bluffside. Then they catapulted brilliantly, glitteringly, across the empty sky, to hide themselves in the mass of the white oak by the gate. Mr. Munn straightened himself, stepped off the porch, and walked toward the bluff.

He stayed on the bluff all day, except for a little time when he went down to eat a silent meal with the others. He lay on his back and looked up at the sky, absorbed in that emptiness, that perfection. There were no clouds, not even a little white boll stabilized singly and gleamingly in the upper distance. Once, toward the middle of the afternoon, he noticed the steady, black fleck of a buzzard which spiraled up, southward, into the area of his vision. He watched it for a while, then grew tired, and turned away. When he looked again, it had been lost in the central reaches of the throbbing brightness. Willie Proudfit, he thought, had once lain on those high mountains, far away. He had stared into the thin blueness of that strange sky. What had he found there? What, Mr. Munn demanded. He could not say. He closed his eyes.

When the sun, reddening and heavy, was almost touching the ridge to the west, he went down the path from the bluff.

After supper, when they had all gone out to the porch, Mr. Munn did not sit down. He leaned against a post of the porch, his back toward the others. The fireflies glowed and dimmed, minutely, rising from the ground in the open space of the yard and pasture. Sylvestus coughed, and scraped his shoes on the boards.

'Ain't you gonna set?' Willie Proudfit asked him.

'No, thanks,' Mr. Munn said, not turning.

'Maybe, he ain't tahrd,' Sylvestus remarked distinctly, but almost as though to himself.

'No, Sylvestus,' Mr. Munn told him, not turning, 'I'm not, as a matter of fact.'

'Sing a little sumthen, Dellie,' Willie Proudfit urged. 'I feel lak hit.'

She began almost wordlessly, stopped, and began again. She sang:

> Thar's a land that is fairer than day
> And by faith I seen hit afar,
> And our Father ——

She broke off. 'I ain't right fer hit,' she explained. 'Tonight.'

'Set down, Perse,' Willie Proudfit said, a hint of fretfulness in his tone.

Mr. Munn did not answer. Then he asked: 'Willie, is Senator Tolliver still staying where he was? In that place over near Monclair?'

'Tolliver,' Willie Proudfit said meditatively, and paused. 'Yes.'

'The last I hear'd he was thar,' Willie Proudfit answered. And added: 'A man plumb ruint tonight. And him what he was.'

'He was a bad man,' Adelle Proudfit's voice declared.

'Set down,' Willie Proudfit invited.

Mr. Munn turned and looked at their forms in the shadow. 'Willie,' he said. 'Willie, I'm leaving.'

After a moment Willie Proudfit answered, 'Naw, naw, Perse' — his voice quiet — 'you ain't a-leave-en.'

'Yes, I'm leaving,' Mr. Munn insisted, 'tonight.'

'They ain't no use to be leave-en.'

'There's a use,' Mr. Munn said slowly, 'I think.'

The other man got up from the floor, where he had been lying. 'Naw ——' he began, 'naw ——'

'Yes,' Mr. Munn replied.

No one spoke for a moment. The insects made their dry, rasping, continuous sound off in the trees by the lane.

'If Dellie will give me those pones left over from supper. And maybe a little bacon.' He stopped, then went on: 'I'm going now.'

'I'll fix you sumthen, I'll cook you some ——' She rose from her chair, and stood there uncertainly, not finishing her sentence. 'You're not a-leaven-en,' she said, then.

'Thank you,' Mr. Munn answered. 'I'll just take those corn pones, and be going.'

'Is hit in you?' Willie Proudfit demanded. 'Set in yore mind?'

'It's set in my mind,' Mr. Munn replied.

'You shore?'

'I decided this morning. I was waiting,' Mr. Munn said, 'till dark.' He moved past them into the house, and started groping his way across the room. Willie Proudfit followed him blunderingly. Then a match spurted, and the dark leaped back, shriveling suddenly back from the flame in Willie Proudfit's fingers. He lighted the lamp.

He followed Mr. Munn on back into the little lean-to room, and stood there, holding the lamp.

'I just wanted to get a few things,' Mr. Munn explained, almost apologetically; 'those handkerchiefs you got for me over at Thebes, and a few things.'

'Hit ain't ——' Willie Proudfit started. He was studying the flame of the lamp in his hand, watching its small waverings. 'Hit ain't what I said this mornen?'

'That? I'd forgotten that.'

'My house is yore'n to rest in, Perse.'

'I know it,' Mr. Munn said. 'It wasn't that.'

The other man seemed unable to withdraw his gaze from the flame behind the smudged and smoky glass. He said, watching the flame, 'You come-en back?'

'I'll be back,' Mr. Munn assured him.

Willie Proudfit raised his eyes and looked at him. 'If'n hit's sumthen laid on a man,' he observed, 'I ain't sayen air nuther word.'

Mr. Munn lighted the other lamp. 'I'll get my things, now,' he said.

There was the sound of the woman moving about in the kitchen.

'I'll go help Dellie,' Willie Proudfit said.

'I don't need anything but the pones,' Mr. Munn told him. But before he had finished speaking, the other man was gone.

When he left, they stood on the porch to say good-bye. He shook hands with them. 'Be come-en back,' Adelle Proudfit said thinly.

'He'll be come-en back,' her husband interrupted, his voice almost harsh.

'Yes,' Mr. Munn said.

Willie Proudfit offered him the horse, but he said no, it was safer without it. Then Willie Proudfit said he could take him a piece in the buggy. He said no, and thanked him, and began to walk toward the gate. He was almost halfway when Willie Proudfit caught up with him. He stood, and laid his hand on Mr. Munn's arm. 'Hit wasn't this mornen?' he demanded.

'No,' Mr. Munn replied.

Adelle Proudfit came after them, and they went as far as the gate together.

It took two nights to reach the neighborhood of Monclair. He had spent the first day in an abandoned cabin which he found in the woods. He came upon it just after dawn when he struck off to the right from the road, hunting water. He had crossed a bridge over a little branch some three miles up the road. It was flowing southward, and since the valley was relatively narrow, he expected to hit it within half a mile or so off the road.

He saw the wide space of sky that opened, milky blue and pale and opalescent, above the spot where the big trees stopped. That, he guessed immediately, was the place where an old clearing had been. But it was now overgrown with brush, with sassafras, elder, second-growth gum, and sumac. A few birds were stirring in the tangle, uttering their first, tentative calls. The dew was heavy on the still leaves. He stood at the edge for a moment. Then he saw the chimney of the cabin.

He pushed his way into the clearing, toward the cabin. There would be water there, he guessed. He came to the remains of a rail fence, rotting now, and so tumbled-down that he could step over it. He passed close to the cabin. The windows were empty. There had never been glass in them, just board shutters which now, with one exception, had fallen from their hinges. The door was broken off. It lay on the ground, and between the cracks in its boards, the grass had thrust. When he got to the corner of the cabin, he heard the sound of water riffling. He found the branch at the back edge of the clearing.

He came back, after drinking and bathing his face, and went to the cabin. When he stepped on the fallen door, one board gave rottenly beneath his weight, so that he almost stumbled. With his arms he struck down the cobwebs, now sagging with dew, that barred the entrance, and went in. There were only two rooms, both very small, and a loft. He walked softly about, almost cautiously, and the old puncheons twisted a little at his tread. At the chimney, patches of sky were visible, for the logs had sagged, pulling away. He looked at a corner. The logs had been badly notched, with weak, slovenly strokes. Most of the chinking was gone. In the first room, there was no object except a hewn bench, from which two legs were missing, and the ladder to the loft. In the other room he saw a glass jar, unbroken, sitting on the ledge of a window. In the bottom was a little accumulation of unidentifiable filth, and above, the glass was bone dry. The light struck dully through the stained transparency. Against the wall, he made out a small huddle of clothing, lying as dropped there. He stepped to it, and on a momentary impulse leaned to pick it up, gingerly, between his thumb and forefinger. A flat, black beetle, polished clean like a button, moved unhurriedly from the spot where it had been concealed, and disappeared beneath the bottom log. Mr. Munn held up the object. It was a man's jacket, once blue, now faded splotchily to dun. The fabric was unyielding and wooden in his hand. It had long since lost the shape of the figure it had clothed, and had stiffened earthily, once and for all, to the contour of the surface on which it had lain. When he dropped it, it struck dryly on the puncheon.

He went back into the other room, and tried the ladder. It was heavily built, and seemed firm. Cautiously, he climbed up. He stretched himself out on the rough floor. The beams were solid. After a little while, he fell asleep. He roused in the early afternoon, ate almost all of the food he had left, and went to the branch for a drink. Then he came back, and lay down until almost dusk.

Just after full dark, he came to a crossroads store. He looked in, and saw that it was empty, except for an old man sitting in a chair propped against the wall. A lamp in a bracket with a tin reflector burned above him. Mr. Munn went in, and bought a package of crackers and a piece of cheese. He put these objects into the pockets of his coat, and went on.

The next morning, looking southward from the brow of a little rise, he saw familiar country. A railroad track bisected the wide, shallow valley, the rails glittering in the light. On each side of the track the clean fields of corn and tobacco lay, the plants standing in long rows of geometrical precision. Cattle were motionless in the distant pastures. The barns and houses, and the groves around them, looked fresh and washed in the limpidity of early morning. He knew that a few miles up the track, east, was Monclair. He left the lane down which he had been traveling, and hid himself in the woods. Twice during the course of the morning he heard trains whistle, and looking down, saw them drawing easily down across the valley, flecking the air only with a little steam and wisping smoke.

In the evening he came down, and began to walk eastward along the tracks.

The house stood back from a rutty dirt road. He knew it was the place, because leaning over close to the mailbox he had been able to make out the name, 'Edmund Tolliver.' It was a new mailbox. The metal was clean and slick to the touch of his fingers, and the black lettering distinct upon it. A stone wall separated the yard from the road, where a fringe of leafy brush ran. The gate was gone, and stones had fallen from the wall beside a broken post. There were no trees in the yard, but the black bulk of woods showed on the rise beyond the house.

At first he thought the house was deserted; then, upon nearer approach, he saw that a very dim light showed around a curtain at one window, or a cloth which had been hung there. His knees tense and crooking beneath him, he stepped upon the loose boards of the porch floor, and laid his hand to the latch. The door gave easily, with only a slight sound.

At the instant of his entering, he made out, by the unsure light of the turned-down lamp, the figure on the bed, covered only by a sheet, the face averted. He closed the door behind him, as with the scrupulous care of someone entering a sick-room. He stood there watching, leaning forward a little, solicitously; and very slowly, almost weakly, while he stood there, the figure moved on the bed and the face turned toward him. He saw the eyes, faintly shining in the light, widen, and saw the lips twitch, preparatory to speech.

'What do you want?' the man on the bed said.

Not answering, he took two long, bent-kneed strides toward

the bed. He laid his left hand on the footboard, and inclined his body a little forward, staring.

'What do you want here?' the man on the bed said.

He leaned, and looked searchingly, peeringly, at that long, sunken face above the crumpled sheet.

'Why,' the man on the bed exclaimed — 'why, you are Percy Munn!'

But for a moment he made no response, leaning there over the footboard. 'I hadn't thought of you in a long time,' he said then, almost whispering, still staring. He added, 'I'd almost forgot what you looked like.'

The man on the bed raised himself a little, as though painfully, and propped himself on one elbow. 'What do you want?' he asked.

'I'd almost forgot what you looked like. You'd gone out of my mind' — the words came slowly, meditatively. 'Then something happened and brought you back to my mind, Tolliver.'

'What do you want?' the man on the bed demanded, almost mechanically now.

'To kill you,' he said, not moving. Then he added, 'I'm going to kill you, Tolliver.' He stopped, as though searching within himself. 'In a minute,' he said, 'when I've looked at you.'

The long, bony fingers of the free hand of the man on the bed shifted aimlessly, closed and unclosed. 'You might kill me,' he said softly. 'You might be the man to do it, Perse.'

'I am,' Mr. Munn answered. 'You know, I killed a man once. At least, I think I did. I was one of them did it. I shot first, I guess. I pulled the trigger, and then, there was blood on him. You know,' he continued, leaning, his voice sinking as in a confidence, 'you pull the trigger. You pull the trigger, and there it is.'

The fingers stopped moving on the sheet.

'You don't notice the noise,' Mr. Munn said; 'not then.' Then he added, 'That comes after.'

'I'm not afraid,' the man on the bed replied.

'The noise,' he repeated, 'that comes after. You, you probably won't notice it at all.'

'I'm not afraid,' the man on the bed said again, as though to himself.

'No' — and Mr. Munn shook his head slightly, like a man trying, puzzledly, to recall something — 'you're not afraid. I thought you'd be afraid.'

'I was almost afraid when I knew you, standing there. But I'm not — not now. A time back, a month ago, maybe, I'd have been afraid. But not now, Perse. Things change, Perse. You don't know how it is, Perse.' He studied the face of the man leaning there toward him. 'Why don't you go on and do it, Perse? Perse, why don't you? You came here to do it, Perse?' And the voice went on softly, almost cajolingly, pronouncing the name.

He took the revolver from his pocket and looked at it.

'I'm going to kill you,' he declared. 'It'll be a favor to kill you. A favor to you. If I didn't kill you, you'd lie here, in this house, and be nothing. Nothing; and you thought you were something. You still think so. You've got a new mailbox, out there on the road, but' — and he leaned closer, shaking his head as in pity — 'but there won't be anything in it. Ever. You'd be nothing. But you know' — and he leaned again, shaking his head — 'you were always nothing. Nothing. Nothing.'

'Nothing,' the voice echoed questioningly. 'A man never knows what he is, Perse. You don't know what you are, Perse. You thought you knew, one time, Perse. When we were friends, Perse.' He lay back, not closing his eyes, but letting the lids droop a little so that no gleam showed. He said, tiredly: 'I liked you, Perse. I like you now. I don't know what you are, but I like you. And you don't know.'

'I do know. I'm nothing,' he uttered distantly, and cocked

the revolver, but did not point it. 'But when I do it, I won't be nothing. It came to me, Do it, do it, and you'll not be nothing. Like that, like words, it came into my head, and I came here. To kill you.' He pointed the revolver. He remained motionless for a moment, then said, 'Not because you are filthy, but for myself.'

Tolliver shut his eyes. The hand on the sheet clenched. The skin over the knuckles was white, like the sheet, which sagged to show the outline of the body. Leaning over the footboard, Mr. Munn held the revolver at arm's length, pointed at the body, high up. The faint rays of the lamp fell palely across the man's face, shadowing the sunken sockets of the closed eyes. The wrinkles and tiny veining on the eyelids showed a little, like the veining of leaves. The man's lips were slightly parted, as though in thirst.

'I'm going to,' Mr. Munn said.

Somewhere in the room a clock was ticking with an unhurried, metallic sound.

'I'm going to,' he repeated, 'in a minute. When I've looked at you.'

He waited, the revolver unwavering.

Then he commanded suddenly, 'Open your eyes.'

The man on the bed gave no sign.

'Open your eyes.'

'Why don't you, Perse?' the voice whispered dryly. But the man's eyes were closed.

The revolver sank a few inches, uncertainly.

'I thought,' Mr. Munn murmured, as in reverie, 'I could do it.'

The man on the bed opened his eyes. 'You couldn't do it,' the voice said croakingly.

The hand holding the revolver sank until it rested against the footboard of the bed. The contact of the metal on wood made a single, small sound. Then Tolliver shifted his head on the pillow, weakly, like a sick man. 'Give me a little water,' he said.

Mr. Munn looked toward the bureau, where a pitcher and glass stood near the lamp. He transferred the revolver to his left hand and took a step toward the bureau. At a slight creaking sound behind him, he wheeled abruptly.

The door from the next room had opened. There, in the opening, one hand still resting on the latch and the other suspended in the air before her breast, Matilda Tolliver stood. 'Ah,' she said, as in a retarded, weary exhalation. Her eyes, gleaming under the brows of her rough-cut, ravaged face, fixed upon him.

He retreated one step, letting his lifted hands subside.

'Matilda,' the man on the bed called, but she apparently did not hear him.

'Matilda,' he repeated.

She stirred, shifting her gaze to him.

'This is Percy Munn,' he said. 'You remember Percy Munn?'

'Yes,' she answered.

'He's come to see me,' Tolliver explained. 'He was just getting ready to give me a glass of water.'

'How do you do?' she asked.

Mr. Munn, wetting his lips, managed to speak, saying, 'I just came in.' He turned, and while he lifted the pitcher with his right hand, with the other dropped the revolver into his pocket. She watched him the whole time. The water made a muted, gurgling noise, spilling into the glass.

He handed the glass to the man on the bed, who accepted it and drank while the others watched him. 'Thank you,' he said, and when Mr. Munn took the glass, he let his head sink back upon the pillow. 'Matilda,' he added, 'why don't you fix Perse something to eat? He must be hungry by now, coming a long way.'

'I was thinking that,' she replied.

'No,' Mr. Munn said, almost violently, 'no. I'm going. I just wanted to see the Senator. I've seen him now. I'm going.'

She crossed the room toward him, and laid her hand upon his arm. 'Sit down, Mr. Munn,' she urged. 'Sit down and rest, and I'll fix you something.'

'I'm going,' he replied, seeming to shiver under her touch.

'Sit down,' she said again.

He jerked from her, taking a full pace backward. The empty glass fell from his hand, splintering on the floor. 'I'm going,' he cried, and flung a sudden, wide gaze about the room, like an animal.

'No ——' she began, and stopped. Her hand, which was in the act of reaching again toward him, paused in the air. 'Listen,' she ordered. 'I heard something.'

They waited, then Tolliver said, 'It's nothing, Matilda.'

'It was,' she insisted. 'Listen.' She went to the outside door, and stood against it, with her hand on the latch, listening. 'It is,' she said. She opened the door a little, and leaned, staring out.

Mr. Munn moved quickly to the other side of the room.

'It is,' she repeated, turning again. 'On the road, horses.'

'The soldiers,' Mr. Munn said steadily. He opened the door behind him, gathering himself.

'A door' — Matilda was saying — 'to the side, the side porch ——'

He found the door in the dark, and opened it. He heard a movement down toward the road. He could make out nothing at the moment, except the lighter space of the open fields beyond the yard, and high, to his left, the darker mass of the woods. Half-crouching, he ran across the yard, stumbling. He ran into the wall, and fell, and got over. Sylvestus, he thought; Sylvestus, he told them. Then: He waited till today, he didn't have nerve till today, all this time, weeks, and didn't have the nerve till today. He ran on across the rough ground, and fell, and ran. 'The bastard, the bastard,' he breathed aloud.

Ahead of him, across the field, were the woods. Down the slope, there were the voices calling, sharply, hollowly, like the voices of boys. At that sound, so empty in the darkness, an astonishing delight sprang up in him, a wild and intoxicating contempt. He scarcely felt the ground beneath him, under his plunging stride.

He fell again, and, rising, saw to one side and above him on the slope, vaguely against the field and paler sky, the standing form of a man. But there — there, beyond that form — would be the woods, the absorbing darkness, the safety, the swift and secret foot. As he lifted the revolver, he was certain. He was certain. But without thought — he did not know why — at the long instant before his finger drew the trigger to the guard and the blunt, frayed flame leaped from the muzzle, he had lifted his arm a little toward the paleness of the sky. He saw the answering bursts ahead of him, and reeled with the impact. Lying on the ground, he fired once more, almost spasmodically, without concern for direction. He tried to pull the trigger again, but could not. Lying there, while the solid ground lurched and heaved beneath him in a long swell, he drowsily heard the voices down the slope calling emptily, like the voices of boys at a game in the dark.

THE END

ROBERT PENN WARREN (1905–1989) was born in Guthrie, Kentucky. After graduation from Vanderbilt University and graduate study at the University of California and at Yale, he attended Oxford University as a Rhodes scholar. He pursued an academic career, teaching at Southwestern College, Vanderbilt, Louisiana State University, where he was a founder and editor of *The Southern Review*, Minnesota and Yale. *Night Rider*, his first novel (1939), was followed by *At Heaven's Gate* (1948) and *All the King's Men* (1946), which won the Pulitzer Prize. Other novels include *World Enough and Time* (1950), *Band of Angels* (1955) and *A Place to Come To* (1977). He also published a collection of short stories, *Circus in the Attic*, and many critical studies and textbooks. A winner of numerous distinguished literary awards, he published several collections of his poetry, and was named the first Poet Laureate of the United States.

GEORGE CORE, who grew up in Lexington, Kentucky, has edited *The Sewanee Review* (which is now celebrating its centennial) since 1973. He has edited several books about American literature, and co-edited *Writing from the Inside* (1983) and the *Selected Letters of John Crowe Ransom* (1985). He contributes regularly to the periodical press.